DEADLY CURE

"What are you planning to do, Creek?" Beth Lowell asked. The old Indian looked up at the young woman from where he stood, over the wounded Joe Porter, and noticed that her pretty face was frozen in fear.

"There is only one thing I can do, Señora," he said, "since our Pai Pai magic has had no effect and we have no Americano medicine."

Beth stood in silence, wondering what herbs the Indian would use on the suppurating, gaping bullet wound in Joe's leg.

"Please, Señora," Creek said, "stand at the foot of the bed and hold his ankles with all your strength."

Bewildered, Beth did as she was asked.

"You must not let loose if he struggles," the Indian said. "And while you are holding him, you must picture in your mind's eye a cross."

"What does it mean?" Beth asked apprehensively.

"It is not for us to understand," Creek said, drawing a long hunting knife from his belt, "only to accept." He held the blade over Joe Porter, its blade glittering in the candlelight.

Standing frozen and impotent, Beth gasped in horrified fear as the ancient Indian brought the long blade down, sinking it into Joe Porter's helpless flesh . . .

THE
BAJA
PEOPLE

Lee Davis Willoughby

A DELL/JAMES A. BRYANS BOOK

Published by
Dell Publishing Co., Inc.
1 Dag Hammarskjold Plaza
New York, New York 10027

Dell ® TM 681510, Dell Publishing Co., Inc.

ISBN: 0-440-00374-1

Printed in the United States of America

First printing—January 1983

PROLOGUE
1767

THE first Catholic priest to come to Baja California, then known simply as California, was Father Juan Maria Salvatierra, a missionary whose obsession was to redeem the pagan souls of the Stone Age Indians and send them happily off to Heaven with the proper credits.

During the Jesuit reign, thirty missions of rudimentary design were established, and several thousand souls officially offered up to God. The task was a grinding one, for the Indians gravitated to spokesmen of the church more for food, medical care and kind treatment than they did for words of religious enlightenment. Ultimately the religious conversion of the Indians was a meager success in its initial years. Not only were the Jesuits in conflict with a harsh and forbidding landscape on the Baja California peninsula that yielded to no man, but they were up against the insatiable greed and corrupt ambitions of the regime in New Spain, later to become Mexico, and of Spain itself, thinking only in terms of sacking the West for its potential treasure. The natives were of little concern to the lay invaders, as were the priests. Many attempts were made from the time of Cortés until Salvatierra to exploit the area of California. These were based on the widespread rumors of easy gold, silver and pearls. And certainly gold did exist in the earth, to be sure, along with silver ore. There were pearls in the sea near La Paz, mostly black and of inferior quality. But nowhere was there to be found the sophisticated civilization, the daz-

5

zling opulence of the Aztecs or the Incas. Instead the Spaniards found only a sorry lot of primitive Indian tribes with no written language, no formal agriculture, nothing at all to compare with the refinements in South America or in New Spain, which was Mexico. The Indians were no more aware of themselves as human entities than were the wild animals they hunted. Finally, the Spaniards pronounced California barren and unconquerable, the legends about the homeland of Amazons ridiculous, a land without promise. This meant that no further permission would be granted by the Spanish crown operating out of New Spain to settle the nearly 800-mile-long peninsula, originally thought to be an island in the time of Cortés.

Father Salvatierra, however, was of another mind from his civilian peers. He was a stubborn, optimistic visionary who believed that it was his divine destiny to go to California and spread the Word of God among the pagans. It took the good priest enormous effort and anguish to obtain the proper permission to make a preliminary attempt at missionizing the area. At last he was granted a license by the Viceroy of Mexico to proselytize, providing that he pay all his own expenses and while in residence not ask for a single peso from the Royal Treasury. These were harsh restrictions, but the dauntless Father Salvatierra possessed enough ardor for a hundred ordinary men. He set about soliciting patronage among the wealthy, convincing them through his eloquence that by supporting his noble enterprise they would be automatically assuring themselves a favored place beside the Throne of Heaven. Thus, Salvatierra was able to commandeer for his use two small ships, a fair supply of stores, a few loyal assistants. He sailed from the mainland of New Spain across the Sea of Cortés, landing at San Dionisio Bay in the month of October, 1767, a Saturday. The very next day he was able to conduct Holy Mass ashore in a new country. The sacred signs were with his venture, he believed, for he had been sent by God to inform a rough and hostile land with the

Holy Word, and to illuminate the souls of its inhabitants with an awareness of life eternal.

The first mission building that Father Salvatierra built was a crude affair made of animal skins thonged together. Left alone on a bleak and arid shore, he immediately set about learning the language of the Indians. The Indians soon learned that this dedicated priest was a different breed entirely from the Spanish soldiers and sailors with whom they had already made brief but bloody contact. From this strange man they received nothing but goodness, kindness, care when sick, and religious parables. So, eventually, the first of Baja's Christian missions, Our Lady of Loreto, was established.

After that, the Jesuit cause began to proliferate slowly in California. One could hardly say that it flourished heartily, but it did manage to survive and broaden its influence. But its growth, ironically, was also to contribute to its demise.

Important men in New Spain and back in Europe eventually decided that the industrious Jesuits were secretly in league with the Indians and were mining great riches from the harsh land and concealing their treasures in unlikely places. They also concluded that the Jesuits were interfering with the country's proper civil development, since they had gained control over who could or could not enter California.

Propaganda had it that the country was actually a paradise of luscious fruits and magnificent stands of timber, that it produced fabulously rich crops, that precious metals and jewels were everywhere abundant, readily available for the taking. Such lies were spread abroad, and they were believed by the greedy. At last even the King of Spain himself believed the stories, and he caused an investigation to be made. False reports of the Jesuit treasure were taken as truth. His Majesty then issued an order for the Jesuits' expulsion. All were given the ultimatum to evacuate, to desert their meager mission establishments that they had labored so long and hard to develop, and to bid farewell to the sorrowing Indians, who had come to depend on them.

Once the Jesuits were expelled, their missionary work was taken over by the Franciscans, who were soon sent on to Alta California. The Spanish government discovered that no Jesuit treasure had ever existed, that the land was as poor as it looked, and that the Jesuits had found their only reward in the conversion of a few thousand Indian souls to Christianity.

California was now open to general exploitation by settlers and traders. No longer could the priesthood deny admission to the peninsula nor expel undesirables. The land lay open to general use. Throughout the New World's Spanish-held territory, Jesuits were rounded up by the soldiery as if they were desperate enemies and held prisoner until they could be shipped back to Spain. The ordeals caused by the priesthood's expulsion were cruel and unwarranted hardships. Many Jesuits perished before they could reach the port of Cadiz and step on home soil.

Don Gaspar de Portolá was the Spanish officer appointed by the Viceroy of New Spain as governor of California, and it was his task to round up the peninsula Jesuits. He landed on the southernmost tip of the peninsula in October, 1767. His subalterns expected to be sweeping up pearls with brooms from the streets of El Dorado, land of gold, the very minute they rushed off their ships. Instead they found only the desolation with which the Jesuits had so courageously dealt: apathy, disease, poverty, and near-famine conditions.

Don Gaspar was profoundly disappointed. Like his men he had believed the tales of ready riches; he expected not only great treasure but fabulous gold and silver mines. The only silver Portolá found was contained in a few modest framed altar pieces that the Jesuits had left behind them in various missions. As for the exotic fruits of California, he was given a few *pitahayas* by the Indians, the fruit of a common cactus, and the best indigenous product the country had to offer.

The Spanish found the absence of treasure a deep frustration. They were ready to torture the priests in order to get at the riches they still believed existed somewhere on the peninsula. Word went out that the Jesuit wealth was being hoarded in one secret mission in a small, hidden valley of the high country mountains in the north. But their persistent, careful scouting could not produce so much as a clue to the whereabouts of any treasure. The fictitious mission in which all this wealth—supposedly equal to the Aztec and Inca booty—was thought to be stored had been named Santa Isabella by the soldiers. The mission, they claimed, was filled to the wooden rafters with gold and silver and precious jewels. When all the treasure in California had been gathered there, the entrance to the valley was sealed off by boulders rolled down from the surrounding cliffs, and no access to the valley was visible.

For the next two hundred years men would be obsessed by the idea of discovering Santa Isabella, the fabled "lost" mission of Baja California, the supreme souvenir left behind by the acquisitive Jesuits. In fact, the only traces left behind were the Indian souls the Jesuits had saved and returned to their Creator, and the seventeen dead priests who had been buried at the various mission sites where they had lived, worked and expired. Seventeen priests stayed behind, and seventeen left for Cadiz via New Spain at Portolá's order.

No priest among the seventeen who were soon to depart was more saddened by the imminent arrival of Don Gaspar de Portolá than Father Miguel Moreno.

The year was fast approaching the season of Christmas, 1767. Father Miguel planned a fiesta at the Mission of Santo Tomas, which lay several miles inland on a low ridge of hills looking toward the sea. East of the mission site rose the formidable Sierra de Juarez, a range of mountains that ascended rapidly to rugged mile-high peaks along the central backbone of the peninsula. Thirty-

five-year-old Father Miguel believed that a lively fiesta—
a time of happy, simple games and serious exposure to
the Christian principles of the Church—would consecrate
rather than desecrate the holy season of the Nativity. He
was going into the high country behind Santo Tomas for
the first time to spread word of the impending fiesta in
person.

Father Miguel and his associate, Father Jaime, knew
well that there was little time for proselytizing. But the
most would be made of it. Taking along as his guide and
assistant a bright lad named Mateo, who had learned
Spanish, as well as several mission Indian bearers, Father
Miguel's small party set off for the high country on foot,
a journey of some forty-five miles into the rugged interior.
The padre was aiming for a certain high-meadowed valley
where Mateo said some of his people lived and where they
would be graciously received as friends. This would be
Mateo's only visit in four years, and his first since becoming a Christian.

Spreading the Gospel was, at least, the ostensible reason for Father Miguel's journey. But strapped to one of
the pack mules that accompanied the small expedition
was a long and narrow chest. It contained a roll of religious oil paintings that Father Miguel had brought with
him from Spain years earlier. The paintings were a legacy
from the padre's family estate, not worth a great deal in
money but priceless to him, and donated to his Order.
Knowing that the Portolá expedition might confiscate or
destroy them in their wrath at not finding the gold and
other treasures they would anticipate, Father Miguel's
other expeditionary aim was to find a secure hiding place
for the paintings. Surely the expulsion would be only temporary; sooner or later the Order would be able to retrieve
the canvases and restore them to their rightful places at
the mission, and he and Father Jaime would be able to
return to their beloved post.

It was a shameful thing to have to hide tributes to the
glory of God, Father Miguel believed, but better to have

the paintings in the hands of a loyal convert than left to Don Gaspar's greedy minions who would probably be no better than the peninsula savages, ready to sack and plunder at a moment's notice. Father Miguel thought that perhaps moving the paintings was a foolish gesture, but Mateo assured him that it wasn't.

"My people are peaceful and serious, Father," Mateo declared on their first day's march from Santo Tomas. "They will welcome you with open arms, poor though they are. They will love you."

"I would far rather have them come to love God," Father Miguel replied. "And afterwards we will pray to find a suitable hiding place for the altar pictures."

"We will, we will," Mateo promised. "There are many sheltered caves in our rocky valley, places that even my people have never explored. They worry about the taboos. I will take you to a secret spot I knew as a boy, a place where I went to be alone, to sleep under the summer stars. You will see. . . ."

Mateo led the march, and Father Miguel was secretly relieved to discover that the eighteen-year-old knew his way. He was an excellent guide, finding water where the padre would have thought none could exist, and snaring game when food was most in need.

Each day the party proceeded approximately ten miles on its arduous trek up through the precipitous mountains, following some invisible trail apparently known only to Mateo. They passed from the arid lowlands to lofty, pine-clad ridges, and finally came into the high plateau country. There, to Father Miguel's surprised delight, were flowered meadows and an alpine landscape he had not believed possible, even though Mateo had assured him in glowing terms of its existence.

On the fifth day the party wound its way through tall monoliths of grey and white granite, emerging from a narrow defile at last into the clear, sparkling air of the summit's highest ridge.

The view was breathtaking. Directly below was the oval

valley, thick with trees and dotted with open pastures, a small lake glistening in the middle distance. To the right, Father Miguel could look down at the far-distant emerald-green fingers of the Colorado River's delta some sixty miles away. To his left he could see the broad sapphire-blue Pacific Ocean. He was almost able to trace the circuitous route they had taken up through the mountain ravines to Antelope Valley, the name Mateo gave to this place he called his home. It was, he explained, the natural grazing ground for the pronghorn antelope.

"The bighorn sheep also live here," Mateo went on. "Mountain lions breed in the the rocky shelters; there are bobcat, coyote, raccoon and skunk." Cottontail and squirrel were everywhere, and in wet winters when the rains were heavy and the snows were light, duck, quail and dove were found in abundance. The Pai Pai could eat their fill. In summer one walked always with wary feet to guard against the bite of the deadly red rattler, called the *zingales*, for it was everywhere.

Mateo settled the party beside a cool spring in the rocks and went off to gather his friends from the other end of the valley. Within half an hour he returned with six fierce-looking Indian youths about his own age, men he had known all his life. They were a long-haired, near-naked bunch, Father Miguel observed, and they smelled rancid. But he did his best to mask his reaction of distaste with a friendly smile. After all, he wasn't here to judge these poor creatures, but to bring them the Word of God, with Mateo's help. This was far more important than cleanliness.

The men hung their heads and grimaced as Mateo led them forward, one by one, to meet his padre. Face to face with Father Miguel, each became suddenly serious, awestruck; they avoided the padre's eyes. None had ever before seen a white man and they were frightened.

Mateo arranged the Pai Pai at Father Miguel's feet and asked the padre to tell the Nativity story.

"My brothers in spirit want to hear," said Mateo, "and I will translate for them."

This seemed hardly the time, Father Miguel thought, and said so; but Mateo insisted.

"Tell them now, Father. My people have great respect for stories. If you wish to bring anyone to baptism and the faith, then you must talk now."

So, then and there, Father Miguel began to speak of the Nativity, borrowing the simplest language he could remember from his long ecclesiastical training. He was unprepared for the response from these simple men. At Santo Tomas the Indians had already been exposed to other white men before he tried to indoctrinate them, so he had their respect and attention. Here he was a totally exotic factor, but their response was electric. He found that he was mesmerizing them; their eyes never left his face. He thought he could have said almost anything to them and they would have listened. But of course he knew that Mateo, his staunchest convert, was paraphrasing his words in terms that the Pai Pai would understand.

It took him about fifteen minutes to conclude his recitation. The Pai Pai youths sat in wondering silence as he made the Sign of the Cross slowly, and said softly that all should pray.

He knelt on the hard earth, bowing his head and closing his eyes, bringing his hands together in devotion to God.

In a sense, Father Miguel considered this the oddest ritual that he could ever remember conducting. However, he knew that he had hit instinctively upon the precisely right dramatic note. Each one of the six half-naked Pai Pai men followed his ritual, kneeling down on the ground before him, bending forward to touch the earth with their foreheads in suppliance. These simple, unenlightened souls had no idea of the potent significance of the Cross. But soon enough he would explain events beyond the story of the Nativity during the week's visit to Antelope Valley. The process would be taken up several

times a day, made into a solemn drama with Mateo's assistance. Nothing hurried, nothing elaborate. These were
people unused to philosophical ideas, so he would have to
proceed carefully. No lengthy, involved sermons; he would
proselytize only with word pictures, keeping them plain
and vivid.

Father Miguel finished his spoken prayer, crossed himself and rose slowly to his feet. Then Mateo was exhorting
his young companions to rise also. The story was over.

Simple gifts were distributed to the six youths from
the mule packs—small strings of glittering, colored beads
and several lengths of bright silk ribbon. To the largest
youth, who turned out to be Mateo's brother, Father Miguel presented a packet of dark mission-ground flour, ex-
plaining that it came from the mission's fields, planted
with seed that grew in another land.

The youths were excited and grateful over their gifts,
babbling like small children in their delight. It was now
time, Mateo told them, to go forward to the Pai Pai village so that Father Miguel could be introduced to everyone.

This was swiftly done, with the six youths and Mateo
leading the way through the stands of pine.

Father Miguel was unprepared for the size of the community they entered. It was composed of some eighty
people—men, women, children and small babies. A stand
of animal-skin tents encircled the stone fire ring in the
center of the large communal village clearing. Beyond the
tents lay the small lake, a marshy pond really, fed through
the summer by subterranean springs. This meadowland
was the Pai Pai's summer home; in severe winters they
moved to nearby caves for protection, Mateo explained. In
summer they enjoyed the crystal air and the constant sunshine.

A few naked children played in the clearing. A dog ran
up and sniffed at Father Miguel's foreign heels, then trot-
ted off. Several old women were grinding cornmeal in
stone vessels by the fire ring and casually chattering away

to one another as Mateo approached with Father Miguel.

At the sight of the padre, one old crone rose to her feet and ran shouting in alarm into the nearest tent. Another averted her face from the padre's gaze; two others jumped up and pointed accusing fingers at him, curses pouring from their mouths. A naked child, terrified by the sight of such a strange man, skittered away behind a tent, shrieking as if in acute pain.

Mateo called out loudly to his people, imploring them to remain calm.

"I have come home with a friend, a man of God who brings gifts and words of peace and wisdom. See," he said, turning to the Pai Pai youths, "he has already shown us his friendliness." Mateo indicated the beads and ribbons, the flour that the youths held out for all to see.

One by one the villagers became calm. They crept out of their tents, moving cautiously into the clearing, eventually moving forward to cluster around Father Miguel, whose smile remained beatific, warm and friendly.

Mateo disappeared for a moment, then returned with the village chief, his uncle. Mateo pushed the dubious elder forward through the crowd of villagers and presented him formally to Father Miguel. The padre spoke to the old man with a soft smile and respect in his eyes. Mateo translated at length, adding persuasions and embellishments in Pai Pai.

Within minutes the elder was relaxed, grinning and laughing; the genial atmosphere of village life was restored. The people drew closer to inspect the padre. Hands reached out to touch his dark, coarse robes, made of material that they had never seen before. Dark eyes stared at the heavy silver cross and chain that hung against the padre's chest.

"We are at home, Father," Mateo said at last when the acceptance ritual was completed. "You are now an honored guest among us. There is no need to fear anything."

"I was not fearful from the very first," Father Miguel

assured Mateo. "God protects those who believe in His Word. I have taught you that."

"Yes, you have," Mateo conceded. "For a moment I forgot. Faith is one lesson, among others, that you must pass on to my people," Mateo added seriously.

The next morning Father Miguel awoke at dawn in the clear, chilly autumn air of the mountain village. The smoke from a pine branch fire in the clearing drifted into the skin tent that had been built for him the previous afternoon. It would have suited the padre to sleep outdoors under the stars, but Mateo and the chief would not hear of it. Occupying the tent was part of his status as a guest, Mateo explained.

"You must let us honor you," said Mateo. "It is soon enough that you will be leaving our land. I want to make you comfortable now, Father, for I will be unable to do so later on." And Father Miguel was obliged to accept the Pai Pais' hospitality.

As soon as the padre had washed, Mateo brought him an earthen jug of hot herbal tea brewed by the old women from local plants. It was strong but not unpleasant, with a sharp, spicy bite to it. This and a crust of unleavened acorn meal bread set him up and he was ready to conduct a brief mass for Mateo and any of the villagers who wished to attend. Almost the entire village turned out, except for a group of young men who had gone hunting, and one elder who was quite ill in his tent. After mass, Father Miguel asked what was wrong with the elder.

"He is soon to die," Mateo told him.

"Then I must see him," Father Miguel insisted.

"He is anxious to see you, Father," Mateo said, and led the padre to a tent among the pines at the village's edge.

"The dying are set apart," Mateo explained as they walked to the tent, "so that their passage from life to death can be made easier. It is our custom."

"Is there no way that the man can be brought into the center of the village," Father Miguel asked, "so that he can see friendly faces? So that his family can be with him?"

Mateo shook his head solemnly.

"No, Father, he is already doomed, a man apart from us."

"This is the time that he most needs friends and those he loves."

"I understand your concern, Father, but it is too late. In your religion, the living must be present to console the dying, and be with them until the end. My people have no such belief. We are obliged to let go of those who are close to death. Their journey must be a solitary one or it will contaminate the living. Even though the old man is the father of my uncle's wife, he can't remain with us."

"But he's here in this tent."

"Only for the time being. Sometime this afternoon he will be moved."

"What will become of him?"

"He will be carried to a cave behind that high ridge across the meadow," Mateo said. "He will be left at the mouth of the cave. My people believe that caves are the entrances to the other world, Father. Not your world of heavenly paradise, but the nether world where all is bleak and hard, where penance is made forever. We have no belief in salvation, only in fear."

Thank God, the padre mused privately, that I have come to release this poor heathen's soul from unbearable bondage. He followed Mateo into the tent.

The old man was stretched out on a pallet, the stench of neglect pervading the air like a disease. His abdomen was grotesquely swollen—from a rotting of the intestines the padre surmised. The odor was nauseating. Gritting his teeth, Father Miguel knelt beside the old man and took his hand, and the elder opened his eyes, muttering in Pai Pai.

"He begs you to help him," said Mateo. "Your God must save him."

"He will," Father Miguel said confidently. "Our God will protect him from eternal torment. All he must do is to accept baptism for the safe passage of his soul into Heaven. Will you tell him this?"

Mateo bent down and whispered into the elder's ear; the old man acknowledged his words feebly.

"He says, Father, that now he'll be able to die in peace. He accepts your word and asks us to wait outside while he dies. We won't have to carry him on a litter to the cave."

"Of course," said Father Miguel. "But I must baptize him first. Bring me some water."

When Mateo had returned, the padre knelt by the old man and performed the ceremony, blessing him at length and finally bringing him into the realm of the faithful.

"Now we must leave him," said Mateo, at a sign from the old man, whose face was calm, his eyes clear and soft. "He believes that your God will care for him," the youth added, "and he will die happy in his new belief."

"It is so. . . ."

"Come, Father, we must leave him to die."

"No," Father Miguel insisted, "I am staying. And we must not move him from the tent."

"But, Father—" Mateo started to protest. The padre held up his hand.

"I will stay with him until the end. You may go if you wish."

Mateo left, and Father Miguel settled down to wait.

Two hours later the elder died peacefully, his gnarled hand clasped between Father Miguel's slender palms as the padre prayed softly and fervently for the eternal repose of the old man's soul.

Father Miguel folded the elder's hands across his chest, made the Sign of the Cross over him, and called out to Mateo, who came into the tent.

"It is all over," the padre declared. "He has gone."

When word of the old man's death in the presence of the padre filtered through the village, all were awed by the simple act of a healthy man witnessing the death of a sick one, and the fact that the elder hadn't died at the cave, nor had any devils appeared to take him away.

"But where did he go?" a village child asked Father Miguel through Mateo. "If he didn't go into the cave, where did he go?"

Father Miguel nodded toward the blue bowl of the sky overhead.

"He is somewhere up there, my child," he explained through Mateo. "It is where we all go eventually, if we are deserving."

During the next few days, without pressuring the villagers, but with the steadfast though unobtrusive support of Mateo, Father Miguel brought many of the Pai Pai into the kingdom of Heaven.

For instance, one of the Pai Pai women was about to have her second child and was already in labor when the elder died in his tent. The woman's first child had been stillborn a year ago, due to a most difficult birth. Hearing about the elder's easy death, she called frantically for Father Miguel, who went immediately to see her, although with some misgivings.

The padre had some rudimentary knowledge of medicine, but he was not a physician; his ancillary fields of interest besides the Church were biology and geology. He despaired that he was unable to perform any physical procedure to reduce the woman's agony and allow a successful birth, especially since local remedies had all proven useless.

If Father Miguel failed to save the child, the whole point of the expedition might fail. Or worse, his life might be taken for upsetting the natural balance of village life, birth and death. The Pai Pai could easily say that he had brought a curse to Antelope Valley, that he was a supernatural being who must be sacrificed at the entrance to some cave. Worse still, to Father Miguel, was the thought that Mateo might be killed as well.

The woman was feverish and nearly hysterical when he

arrived, but his presence was like a balm to her. She was immediately calmed by his gently smiling features. Her normal breathing resumed of its own accord shortly after Father Miguel pressed cool, healing fingers to her forehead and began to pray.

After only a few minutes of ministering to the woman, the child turned in the passage and came into the world, lusty and bawling, a good-sized baby boy. In effect, the woman's faith in the pale-faced Spaniard in dark robes had saved her life, and that of her child.

Father Miguel blessed the newly born boy, baptizing it on the spot. The mother insisted that the child be given the padre's own name, Miguel, along with the Indian name of Autumn, the season in which it was born.

That night the Pai Pai gave a feast in celebration of little Miguel's birth. The feast took place at the fire ring and all males in the village were present. Sheep and quail were roasted; ceremonial bread was baked with imported mission flour.

Usually women and children were forbidden to participate in birth and death ceremonies. Responsible for cooking and serving the food, they would then return to their dwellings until the ceremony was over. But this time Father Miguel suggested that the women be allowed to remain and observe, if only in the background. Mateo was upset by the idea.

"The chief won't even consider it," he told Father Miguel.

The padre smiled tolerantly. "Tell him that all creatures are equal in the eyes of God. Men are the same as women, even if human laws don't always recognize this and treat them as chattel. The women have worked hard to prepare the feast, and the woman I visited carried the child into this world. At least they should be able to watch what goes on." Father Miguel said this as he suppressed a smile, thinking that Father Jaime, his associate at the mission, would purse his lips over such heresy. But nonetheless, it was the way he felt. It couldn't hurt to bring these poor, ignorant people a little closer to common amenities, since they seemed to have few of their own.

"You could be right, Father," Mateo said cautiously, "but it will antagonize the chief. The request is extreme."

"Perhaps, perhaps," Father Miguel allowed. "Ask him the favor anyway. It will make the women very happy, should he agree. If, in the eyes of God, men and women are allowed to attend the Christian Mass communally, why not let them witness a simple feast to celebrate the beginning of a precious new life that they helped to create? They will be one step closer to God because of their participation."

"I will try," said Mateo doubtfully, and went off to see the chief.

The argument worked. Out of deference to the padre, the chief permitted the women to stay for the feast. Squatting silently by their tents, they watched the festivities without joining in, vocally or physically, deeply grateful to Father Miguel for exercising his authority to alter a custom, if only temporarily. It had never happened before and might never happen again. But for the moment it was a happy victory, and they were content to remain in the background and enjoy it.

After three days in Antelope Valley, it became obvious to Father Miguel that Mateo was paying special attention to the chief's daughter. The chief appeared to sanction this, casting a genial eye on the two young people as they sat together in the clearing. Father Miguel wondered if perhaps a union between the two was imminent.

"You told me once that there was no formal marriage in your tribe," the padre said to Mateo one afternoon. "Not like the Christian ceremony that pledges lifelong fidelity and respect."

"We have something that works as well for the Pai Pai, but it is only valid here," Mateo explained. "There is nothing on paper and nothing stated. If the union is approved by both sets of parents, or the elder of the village, then the man must go to the woman's tent and take her. If she refuses to let him, then he has a right to know why, and she will have to remain single for another year before he can ask for his rights again."

"But what if she loves another and is determined to belong to him?" the padre asked.

"Unless she is very lucky, this never happens."

"What about your own case?" the padre asked quickly.

Mateo glanced up, surprised. Father Miguel had a way of leaping through breached openings. Mateo knew exactly what the question meant; his dark face turned a shade darker as he blushed profusely.

"Then you've noticed my interest?"

"How could I not notice it? Will the young maiden Rain accept you?"

"She has already said so."

"Good. I'm happy for you. And does that suggest something else to you?"

"What do you mean, Father?" Mateo asked innocently, knowing full well what the padre meant.

"After your traditional Indian ceremony I must perform the Christian nuptials, making you man and wife. As a Christian, you know you cannot live with the woman of your choice without being sanctified in the relationship through the eyes of God."

"I'd thought of that, and I agree that it's right. But the chief is worried about magic, and doesn't want his daughter to be married by you in the Church. He says it is enough that we follow the Pai Pai custom."

"We must change his mind before there is sin between you and Rain."

Mateo shrugged. "I don't think we can do that. There are other villagers willing to be baptized, Father. Let us content ourselves now with them. Later on you can marry us at the mission."

"No, my son, that is not enough."

"We shall see, Father," Mateo said, and changed the

subject, talking about the possibility of snow coming earlier this year than usual.

There were but two more full days before Father Miguel and Mateo would have to leave for Mission Santo Tomas and still nothing had been resolved about the sacred paintings locked in the wooden chest. Both the question of the Christian marriage and the disposition of the paintings were resolved to Father Miguel's intense satisfaction through an event that he could not have foreseen.

The day after Father Miguel and Mateo discussed the Christian wedding ceremony, the men of the village all gathered at the chief's request in a grove of pines on the far side of the marshy lake, away from the village. This gathering was for the purpose of making a general announcement that Mateo wished the hand of the chief's daughter so that she would be the only one allowed to bear his children. Let any other man who wanted her make known his desire at the meeting, or forever hold his tongue. Infidelity was a crime punishable by death, even if the tribe had no formal marriage ceremony to consecrate the union.

Everyone knew in advance what the chief was going to say, but all treated his words as fresh news. No man protested the proposed alliance. In fact, there was a happy feeling among the men that Mateo had made as good a match as Rain had, and that one day Mateo would return from the mission to become head man in the village.

After the meeting, Mateo went to Rain's tent to announce in a traditional Pai Pai speech that he wanted her to be the mother of his children.

Rain, a petite, full-breasted and rather pretty girl of thirteen listened respectfully. She had a shy, sweet nature and would make a fine mother, Mateo was certain. His heart was bursting with pride that she had told her father she wanted him.

Rain fully expected that Mateo would prove his manhood with her in the tent, and she was prepared to sacrifice her virginity to his demands. But Mateo surprised her by simply gathering her into his arms, kissing her cheek and suggesting that they go out for a walk in the woods close by. He was troubled by Father Miguel's attitude concerning the Christian marriage.

Up until that time, Mateo had told Rain nothing about the Christian wedding ceremony, not wanting to complicate the already important relationship growing between them. He had spoken once again to the chief about Father Miguel's wishes, but the chief had held adamantly to his original position. No Christian marriage would take place at the village. Now, thinking that perhaps Rain would plead his case with her father, Mateo decided to broach the subject to her.

Mateo and Rain wandered out into the cool, sunny autumn day, talking idly of the immediate future. Rain was excited about going with Mateo to the mission.

"It may not be for long," he explained morosely. "The Spanish expedition is due shortly from New Spain. Santo Tomas may be anything but peaceful soon with soldiers arriving. We may have to come back to Antelope Valley. But I want you to see what life is like there while you can."

"I want to see it too," said Rain, excited. "What will happen to the mission when the expedition comes?"

"All the Jesuits will leave this land. Another order of padres will take over."

"Then the work of Father Miguel is for nothing?" Rain observed.

"Oh, no. Many Indians have accepted God and will remain Christian servants," Mateo replied. "But we have no idea how these new padres will worship. They are called San Franciscans, we hear, and may practice a different way of life. We don't know their far-flung plans; it will be a time of fearful change." Mateo sighed. "As I said, many of us will go back to our various villages, all over the land."

"Life isn't simple down there," Rain declared.

"Not like it is here," Mateo agreed. "With you beside me, the years will be good. Especially when we are married in the Church. Then we can consummate our union."

"But my life is yours now," said Rain, playfully brushing her fingers across Mateo's crotch, so suddenly that he stepped back in surprise.

"What's the matter?" Rain asked, laughing. "Don't you want me to touch you?"

"More than anything," Mateo said, forgetting his promise that they must wait until a Christian marriage had been performed, reaching out for her.

But Rain danced away, calling out, "Catch me if you can!" and ran lightly over the soft carpet of pine needles toward a pile of grey boulders.

"Rain," Mateo shouted after her, "wait for me!"

The girl paid no attention, waving to him as she ran. Darting from the shade of the trees she disappeared behind a huge rock.

She wanted to play hide-and-seek, Mateo thought, walking slowly in the direction she had taken. She would tease him for a while, and then, perhaps in the bright sunshine on a high flat rock, she would unfasten her thonged robe, step out of it and invite him to caress her.

Rain skipped around the huge rock, not even looking where she was going, thinking only of Mateo behind her, wondering if he would catch up with her in a moment. She didn't even see the deadly rust-red rattlesnake coiled up in a pool of sunlight on the warm earth until she stepped on it and felt the lightning fangs bury themselves in the calf of her right leg. She screamed and fell backwards, and the rattler slithered away, disappearing into the rocks.

Mateo was dreaming of the consummation of his union with Rain, wondering how he could reconcile his needs with Father Miguel's attitude toward a Church marriage. He knew he couldn't wait long; Rain would make it impossible for him to resist her. In fact, he reflected, it might even happen this afternoon, in a very few minutes. It was inevitable.

At that very moment Mateo heard Rain's shrill cry of terror and ran to find her. When he got to her, she was lying on the ground, clutching her leg and writhing in the dirt. At first he thought she had merely fallen and twisted her ankle, but when he read the expression of abject terror in her dark eyes he knew instinctively what had happened.

"*Zingales*," she whimpered.

Without a word, Mateo scooped Rain up in his powerful arms and carried her, half-running, back to the village. In a few short minutes he placed her on a pallet in her tent where they were to have consummated their union.

Rain's mother, sobbing, brought herbal medicines and molded a mud pack for a poultice. Concerned villagers gathered outside the tent, talking in hushed voices.

Mateo hurried to Father Miguel's tent and woke the padre from his siesta. Hysterical, the usually placid youth told his story, tears streaming down his cheeks.

"Rain was bitten by a rattlesnake, Father."

"When?"

"Not long ago."

Father Miguel grabbed a scarf from his pack and they hurried off to Rain's tent.

"We'll have to work fast," the padre said as they stood looking at the girl, moaning and writhing on her bed. "Was the snake large or small?" He knelt beside Rain.

"A little one, she thinks," Mateo said after questioning the trembling, terrified girl.

Father Miguel did not remove the herb pack from the wound for the time being. Instead he made a tourniquet of his scarf and tightened it just below Rain's kneecap, praying that the snake's venom had not already spread too far into the bloodstream.

The padre looked squarely at Mateo. "I shall have to do

something unpleasant and dramatic. I wonder if your people will allow it."

"What do you mean?"

"I shall have to perform a minor operation," he told Mateo. "Nothing very serious."

Father Miguel extracted his hunting knife from the leather sheath he had taken to wearing at his belt since the expedition began. The knife was whetted daily; the blade could cut a single strand of hemp rope by simply drawing the strand lightly across the cutting edge.

Rain moaned when she saw the glinting steel blade. The chief issued a guttural protest.

Father Miguel continued to hold out the blade toward Mateo.

"Ask if I have permission to cut her flesh slightly in the area of the wound?" he ordered Mateo. The youth turned to the chief and directed the question to him. The chief hesitated only a moment before nodding vigorously in the affirmative.

"If my daughter does not recover," the chief said through Mateo, "her death will be upon your shoulders."

Father Miguel bobbed his head in acknowledgment, clenched his teeth and removed the mud pack from the swollen area of the bite.

"Tell Rain that this will hurt a little," he told Mateo. "Not much, and only for a short time."

Mateo explained to Rain. Then he wedged a thick twig between her teeth, admonishing her to bite down hard on it while he held her two hands.

Quickly and neatly, Father Miguel made two narrow incisions in the wound on Rain's calf, forming a perfect cross. Then he bent down and sucked on the wound, to the shocked gasps of all present, drawing blood and venom and expectorating it. He repeated this procedure several times until he felt certain that the venom remaining near the surface of the wound had been drawn off.

He sat up, wiped his mouth on the back of his hand,

then bent toward Rain and crossed himself. Mateo released Rain's hands and followed suit.

"That should help, God willing," Father Miguel murmured, rising to his feet. "Stay with her, Mateo, and pray for her recovery."

"Will she live?" Mateo asked, near tears.

"If the poison has not spread into her bloodstream, and if she does not surrender to fear, then she will live."

"How long must we wait?"

"I cannot say, Mateo," Father Miguel said. "Rain is young and strong. If she can ward off the paralysis, the bleeding within the body, then she will recover before too long."

The padre bowed briefly to the chief and his woman and went away to his tent. He lay down to continue his interrupted siesta. To worry about the girl would be useless. If his simple procedure worked, the girl would live. If she died, perhaps he would too. And even Mateo. But it was something he refused to brood over.

Later that night the girl reached a crisis. Her fever broke, and she sat up and took liquids. All the next day she grew steadily stronger. In the afternoon she had a long talk with her father, from which Mateo was excluded.

"There is no doubt that you saved Rain's life, Father," Mateo said as they walked together in the afternoon sun. "I owe you mine."

"You owe your life to God," said Father Miguel. "You can pay your debt by bringing the Pai Pai to Christianity."

"I will try, Father."

"You must do better than to try. You must succeed," the padre told him.

"I will succeed," Mateo promised.

That night the chief gathered every male villager around the fire circle, with Father Miguel on his right hand and Mateo on his left.

"I have made two decisions," the chief told the padre through Mateo. "It is my wish, the wish of Rain's mother, and of Rain herself, that the padre will marry my daughter tomorrow morning in a Christian ceremony. He will also baptize the entire village."

Mateo responded emotionally to the chief's edict, but Father Miguel merely smiled and nodded, pleased beyond words.

"The God of the Christians is a powerful deity," said the chief. "I have heard of this, but I have never known it was true until yesterday. If He can find a way to vanquish the deadly sting of a serpent, then we must accept and honor Him. . . ."

At dawn next morning Father Miguel joined the entire village in the clearing. First, he baptized the whole Pai Pai village in a mass ritual, bringing them into God's Kingdom. Christian names could come later. When the mass baptism was over, the padre asked Mateo to bring Rain, now called Maria, forward and he married them, calling upon God's rich, eternal blessing upon the first Christian marriage ever performed in Antelope Valley, and upon their children and their children's children.

With his sparse personal effects packed, Father Miguel sat crosslegged in his tent staring at the narrow wooden chest that contained his paintings. Neither the baptism of the villagers nor the wedding ceremony, although unique in his life and extremely exciting to him, had been the cause of his fitful night. He had dreamt an absurd dream in segments. In it he had built a great cathedral from funds obtained through gold ore. He had discovered a rich lode running through Antelope Valley. The Pai Pai had asked him to turn their wealth into a glorious monument to their new faith, and he had done so gladly, making it a work of art, the paintings altar pieces.

The dream kept recurring in fragments all night, waking him. His intuition told him that the idea of raising a beautiful, ornate symbol to mass conversion was a silly and extravagant one, but he could not somehow shake the reality. He could see the twin spires, lofty and shining, and the great soaring nave with the solid gold altar. It was still vivid in his mind when dawn began to lighten the sky outside his tent. Still, nothing had been done about the disposition of the paintings, nothing since his arrival. He had left this responsibility up to Mateo, thinking that the resourcefulness of the lad would solve the problem. But Mateo had found a million things to do with his people, and now it was almost time to leave for Santo Tomas. The paintings *must* remain in Antelope Valley. But where? They couldn't just be abandoned.

Mateo dealt with the problem as soon as he entered Father Miguel's tent.

"Come," he said briskly, "it's time to go."

"I have been very patient," the padre replied, "but we cannot leave until a certain matter is settled. The chest. . . ."

"Yes, yes, Father. We'll take care of that now."

"What—and carry them back with us? I think not. I must be sure that the Portolá expedition does not get their hands on them."

"Now, now, Father, don't fret," said Mateo, thinking that Father Miguel looked unwell. His features were drawn, there were large circles beneath his eyes, and his voice was faint. He seemed hardly in robust condition, certainly it was questionable if he were strong enough to make the trip down the trail to Santo Tomas. But perhaps the security of his precious paintings would restore the padre to his usual good health.

"Come," said Mateo, "I will lead you to a spot I have chosen. No one in the village is about yet. I have ordered this through my father-in-law, the chief. We two are alone for a while. No one will know where we are going, but even if they do find out, nothing will ever be said to anyone. The Spaniards won't come up to our mountain fortress, and it isn't necessary to kill anyone who knows where the treasure lies, as happened in New Spain a long time ago. For we are not savages, as you have seen. We do not sacrifice human beings to the ancient gods. We will have a new life as Christians. All will be well . . . Come, we must go!"

Mateo picked up the chest and led the way, out across the clearing and into the sheltering pine woods. They passed the spot between the boulders where the red rattler had bitten Rain. They climbed up into the random pattern of jumbled boulders, tossed down in disdain by the giant hand of God, Father Miguel decided. The Holy Spirit must have been angry that particular day of creation, the padre thought, because these were mighty rocks.

After fifteen minutes of strenuous climbing, Mateo reached a wide place in the boulders. He put down the chest and said, "This is it. This is as far as we go."

"I don't understand," Father Miguel said breathlessly. "Why have you brought me here?"

"This is a cave I discovered as a small boy," Mateo said. "No one in the village knows that it is here. That is, no one but the chief. I had to explain it to him before I brought you to my secret place."

"What are you telling me, Mateo? I don't understand."

"Father, this is the resting place for your chest. The altar paintings will be safe here. The air is dry; they can stay here for years, and nothing will happen to them. And if ever you want them, I will come up to the village and get them for you."

Suddenly the whole concept of a secret treasury for the paintings seemed utterly ridiculous to Father Miguel. To leave the paintings here was the same as abandoning them forever. He was tempted to tell Mateo that they would return with the chest to Santo Tomas, the only bonus to their excursion being the mass baptism of the Pai Pai, the recovery of Rain, and the wedding.

"Let me show you," said Mateo, pointing to a narrow cleft in the rocks. "We enter there."

"I see nothing," said the padre.

"Come!" Mateo walked up to the angled slit of rock. He produced tinder, made a flame and lit a votive candle he had brought along.

"We will have God's light with us," he told Father Miguel. "Please, follow me."

Father Miguel watched Mateo slip through the crack in the rock wall sideways, then followed him.

Inside, Mateo said, "*Zingales* come here to sleep in winter, but not yet. They will be the only guardians needed for your paintings, Father. Look around, see how dry and clean it is. . . ."

After an abrupt ascent of several yards, the floor of the cave leveled out, its natural sloping dome rising a dozen feet overhead. It was indeed clean, a long cave, perhaps fifty to sixty feet deep, and uninhabited. At the far end was a projecting ledge of rock, much like a crude altar. In fact, the cave's interior simulated the ideal shape of a chapel. It was truly a fitting natural repository for the paintings. Here they would belong to the ages.

Father Miguel felt oddly relaxed and comfortable, almost light-headed, for he seemed to have come home. He did not need a visual sign from God that this was where he must leave his treasure. He simply knew by instinct that he must part with his precious chest here.

"Well, what do you think?" Mateo asked him as he placed the votive candle on the rock ledge.

"It is remarkable," the padre replied.

"No rain or snow ever penetrates here, no heat or cold. The cave is always as it is now, pleasant and secure. The *zingales* go into cracks in the left wall; they are not hostile here. And because the cave's entrance is sheltered by that overhanging stone outside, no snow can ever block the entrance; no rain will wash down because the floor rises."

Father Miguel nodded. It didn't really matter, he thought, whether his Order eventually retrieved the paintings and restored them to their rightful place, or whether the Franciscans or some other Order discovered them in the future, although that seemed highly unlikely. The fact that they would never fall into the greedy hands of spoilers or infidels was of prime importance to him. He knew that Mateo as guardian would see to this as long as he lived. He did not doubt this for a moment.

"We will bring the chest in here," said Father Miguel.

Mateo sighed with relief and smiled. "I am glad, Father. It will be safe. The villagers never venture up this way. Most of them don't even leave the village, and none would ever enter the cave, even if they found its entrance. They are still as much afraid of the spirit dead in caves as they are of snakes. . . ."

The wooden chest barely fit through the narrow cleft in the rock. Mateo carried it up the incline and across the cave and set it on the ledge. Father Miguel straightened it so that it sat broadside, with a votive candle at one end.

Mateo produced a second votive candle and lit it from the first, setting it on the opposite side of the chest.

Father Miguel knelt before the chest, intoning a soft prayer of protection. Then he crossed himself with great relief, as Mateo did, and the pair departed. Father Miguel did not look back as they walked away from the cave. By noon he had left Antelope Valley.

A party consisting of the padre, Mateo and Rain, his bride, soon to be called Maria, and the two faithful Mission Indian bearers, made the trip back to the coast. It was a far easier journey than climbing up to the plateau, but along the way Father Miguel came down with chills and fever.

After a day's rest the padre seemed better and insisted that they press on.

"I'm quite all right," he told the anxious Mateo, but he was not. Once at the mission he took immediately to his bed. The illness was typhoid fever. A perforation of the intestine occurred as the disease progressed, and a massive hemorrhage followed. Father Miguel wasted away despite the constant care of Mateo and Maria and the devotion of Father Jaime.

To Father Jaime's intense grief, his beloved brother in God went to his Heavenly reward shortly before Christmas. Father Jaime was still mourning the loss of Father Miguel when a Spanish ship from New Spain anchored in the shelter of Point San Jose, with a purpose inland.

Soldiers arrived at the mission early next morning with written orders to take the two Santo Tomas padres into custody. Father Jaime was evacuated, Mateo left in charge by the padre, along with two soldiers. In the tearful parting with Father Jaime, the wooden chest of Father Miguel was entirely forgotten.

Although Mateo made the trip up to Antelope Valley in late summer before the birth of their first child, so that Maria could be with her mother, he did not enter the cave. In fact, he could not.

Early one morning shortly after his arrival at the village an earthquake hit the area. The quake was of massive proportions, panicking the villagers. While there was nothing to shake down in the village, the rocky area to the west where Mateo's cave was situated had been dramatically altered—as had Mateo's life, for shortly after the earthquake Maria gave birth to a hearty boy, who was immediately christened by Mateo as Jesus Miguel.

When Mateo felt that it was safe to climb up to the cave's entrance, he found the terrain much changed. The overhanging slab of rock that had sheltered the cave's mouth from the elements had broken off. It had fallen neatly across the entrance, totally sealing it. The slab was enormous, and wedged as it was between two miniature perpendicular slabs, it could never be removed. Mateo realized with sinking disappointment that he would never be able to retrieve the paintings. There was no other access route to the cave, he knew, so he did not even search for one.

The earthquake was God's will, Mateo decided, sealing away Father Miguel's treasure forever. Now there was no longer any need to think about building a chapel to house the paintings. He would instead erect a small wayside shrine to Father Miguel's memory, a cairn with a wooden cross planted in it by the western shore of the lake. That would be most fitting.

Mateo said a silent prayer for the repose of Father Miguel's soul and went away, turning his mind to other matters, to his and Maria's little son, the child he would offer to the Christian God, once the new Order of padres arrived at Santo Tomas. . . .

NEW YORK
1846

1

BUSTLING, fast-growing New York City in the 1840s was a perfect product of the Industrial Revolution, a new, brisk kind of commercial chaos that was soon to become the hallmark of the American scene. The island city was not only the most modern metropolis in young America, it was the world's most energized. In the heart of it among four hundred thousand other souls lived the Lowell family, wealthy, middle-class and sedate, secure in their very comfortable existence.

The Lowells lived well within the rigid conventions of the times. They existed temperately, and they tended to believe that the only way their lives could go was up: the God favored enterprise and virtue and would continue to reward them for faithful adherence to the accepted mores of their times: loves of family, continence in all matters, sexual fidelity, respect for one's parents, and, of course, making money.

Banker-merchant James Lowell was a handsome man

of 42, already graying at the temples, putting on a slight paunch, but active, cheerful, shrewd in business and a man of diverse commercial interests. He was not only a banker but a financier who had taken over a failing business and transformed it into a flourishing textile mill. Lowell had only two non-business interests in life—his charming wife Fanny, two years his junior, and his two children, Beth, just 19, and Timothy, 15. These children were James Lowell's pride and joy, and he wished for only two things: a fine husband for Beth, and a fine education for Timothy that would send him off on a splendid commercial career.

Lowell ran the businesses and Fanny ran the house, supervising the servants that he provided for her and the children. Fanny was an efficient manager; she planned dinners and social events with dash and style, and saw to it that the children learned manners and propriety. On the side, Fanny did some needlework, read proper novels, went to a Protestant church every Sunday, and generally did what most other well-bred, long-married matrons did in New York with their lives. While the rush of the city flowed around her, Fanny didn't need to look beyond the shelter of her beautiful Gramercy Park mansion for fulfillment. She was still very much in love with her husband of 21 years, she adored her two offspring, and she couldn't see a cloud on the horizon, short of an Act of God, that would change her life one iota.

Fanny's daughter Beth was not a conventional young woman in any sense but the external one, although she had the intelligence to conceal her differences. A year out of finishing school, where she felt she had learned virtually nothing of value, Beth was bored with the routine life of New York City and the traditions dictated for her. She wasn't looking forward to marriage, primarily because she wasn't in love, and she was not looking forward to spinsterdom either, since she wanted children. The men of her own class, whatever that meant, were simply dull. All they ever talked about were business deals; and when they dined at the Lowell house, they brought more commerce with them than charm, certainly very little to stimulate someone of Beth's eager nature.

Then, suddenly one afternoon Beth's life changed dramatically. She came home from a shopping trip with her brother Timothy to find a business associate of her father's seated in the small front parlor, awaiting the arrival of James Lowell.

The young man, dashingly dark and handsome, smartly dressed, with blue eyes that would not leave her alone, attracted her from the moment she entered the parlor.

Michael Porter, all six feet of him, was on his feet smiling in an instant, introducing himself in a deep, pleasant voice.

Beth introduced herself and asked, "Have you been waiting long for my father?"

"Only a few minutes. I'm a bit early. Your father and I had an appointment at four o'clock."

"He's usually very punctual," Beth said. "I'm sure he'll be along soon. My mother's out. Would you like some tea? It's about that time."

"No, thank you, Miss Lowell. Your maid offered me some when I arrived. I'll just sit here and go through some papers I brought with me. Please, do what you have to do. I'll be just fine."

Beth had no intention of going about "business"—as the intriguing stranger put it.

"Where is your home?" Beth asked, with a directness she would never have employed beyond the security of her own parlor.

"The Far West," Porter told her with a genial smile. "California, specifically."

"California!" Beth sighed in rapture. "El Dorado! I've heard so many fantastic tales about it, but I've never met anyone who's actually been there."

"Some of the stories are true," said Porter, "but most are pure fiction."

"What is it you do in California?" Beth asked.

"Nothing very exciting, I'm afraid. I have a drygoods business in Los Angeles, a spot so small it's not yet on any map back here. It's in the south of California territory, and thus there is a lot of Spanish influence. Los Angeles is dusty, dirty, disorganized—very much a frontier town. I don't think you'd like it, Miss Lowell. It's rough and ready, with very little law and order and lots of violence. Nothing like New York, not by a long shot."

Beth tossed her blonde head. "You should know, Mr. Porter, that I find New York to be tedious, colorless and ever so boring."

"Really?" Michael Porter raised his eyebrows. "I'd have thought that a young lady in your position would have more engagements than she could possibly manage. How could life be dull?"

"It all depends on what you mean by engagements, Mr. Porter. If you mean parties with my former school chums, or the opera, the classical theater, recitals, that kind of thing—oh yes, there's plenty of that, and certainly no lack of escorts." She waved all this away with a flick of her wrist. "But it's so uninteresting. I spend a good deal of time alone, reading, or with my younger brother. It's much more fascinating to know about other worlds and other lives than to bury oneself in the monotonous social scene of New York."

"You don't sound like any of the other young ladies I've met since I've been here," Michael observed.

"Well, I'm glad to hear it," Beth said. "Now tell me, what brought you here to my father's house? I mean, what will you be buying? I know it's forward of me to ask, but I'm dying to know what you'll take West with you."

"I'm a merchant, Miss Lowell, plain and simple. I come armed with references and ready cash, vulgar though that may seem. I hope to purchase a fair quantity of goods to take West with me. That's about it."

"And then what?"

"I'm shipping the goods to New Orleans from the port of New York. They'll go from there up the Mississippi

River to Missouri, and from there by horse-drawn vehicle to Santa Fe, Mexico territory."

Beth sighed and said with real envy, "What a marvelous opportunity to see the world! The wilderness, Indians, buffalo. Dear me! And I'm supposed to be going to Europe next year with my mother and brother. But it certainly won't be as wonderful as stepping foot on the docks of New Orleans. I've read everything I could on Europe, I know it back and forth. But New Orleans—now that's a place with mystery and excitement."

Michael Porter grinned at the lovely young woman in disbelief. "You mean you're actually serious?"

"Of course I am. I like the unknown, the places that challenge the imagination. . . ."

Beth heard the front door open and close, and a servant in the hall speaking to her father. She jumped up from the chair opposite Michael, blushing. She'd hoped to slip away before her father arrived; now she was caught. And it was just possible that James Lowell would consider her too forward in chatting with the young man. Anyway, there was nothing to do about it now, so she called out gaily to her father, who came at once to the parlor.

"Father, this is Mr. Michael Porter, who says he has an appointment with you."

"Yes, my dear, we've met."

James Lowell smiled at Michael; the two men shook hands. Lowell turned to Beth. "Has Mr. Porter been filling you with tall tales of Indians and covered wagons and the California Trail?" he asked his daughter.

Beth had the good grace to blush. "Nothing like that, Father," she protested. "Mr. Porter has told me little about the West. I'm hoping we can all learn more from him at the dinner table one evening."

Lowell was used to his daughter's maneuvering, but this time he thought she had gone too far.

"Ah yes, of course," he murmured quickly. "Well, Mr. Porter, shall we get down to business?"

"I'll arrange for tea," Beth said tactfully, knowing that

her presence was superfluous. "It was pleasant meeting you, Mr. Porter."

"The same to you, Miss Lowell," Porter said soberly, nodding his dark, curly head at her as she left.

Beth met her brother Timothy in the hallway that led to the rear of the house. Timothy, tall and still growing, was just coming in from school.

"Who's with Dad?" he asked his sister. The two had an easy rapport; they rarely quarreled, but they were both tireless teases and never missed an opportunity to set each other up with an amusing situation.

"A Mr. Michael Porter," said Beth, unable to keep herself from rolling her eyes at Timothy.

Timothy leaned forward conspiratorially. "An adventurer, eh?"

"Oh Tim, please, not *that* kind! Just a businessman from the West. Father's arranging to supply his caravan with merchandise."

"You liked him. That's obvious."

"Yes, I liked him. I like you, too. I like Mother, and I like the new parlor maid, and I'm going to see her right now and order tea for Father and Mr. Porter. And that's all there is to it, so there!"

"Tea which you'd love to deliver yourself," Tim said mischievously. "I can see that telltale sparkle in your eyes."

"How would you know?" Beth retorted. "It's never been there before."

Timothy stepped back from his sister, in order to observe her better. "Well, well," he said, almost in a whisper, "I do believe my fair blonde sister's just given her heart away."

"Oh Tim, really! I've just met the man. But he *is* handsome and he *is* charming. Still, we know nothing about him. Ask me for a report later on."

"I see the wheels turning in your devious mind, dear

sister," Timothy observed. "You're as transparent as clear glass."

"It's time I went to order the tea."

"By all means!" Timothy made a sweeping, courtly bow. "I'm going upstairs. Join me for checkers? It'll calm your nerves."

"My nerves are fine, thank you."

"Look, your brow's moist, your delicate hands are trembling, your pretty green eyes are glazed over. You're all but a wreck!"

"Honestly, Tim, I've heard enough," Beth said, and flounced off to the rear of the house to order tea.

Tim ascended the broad, red-carpeted stairs to his room. On the way up he heard his father's voice and Mr. Michael Porter's. He paused, glancing in through the open door to the parlor. The stranger sat in Tim's direct line of vision, so the boy had a brief but thorough glimpse of the man. He was impressed. The fellow was easily the best-looking young man who'd ever set foot in the Lowell house, which was saying quite a lot. Tim liked Porter's deep voice, his easy smile, his general manner. Observing impartially, not balmy like his sister, Tim had to concede that this stranger possessed something very special, some kind of strength or vision. He didn't know what it was, but the quality made Porter unusual. Like Beth, though he'd never admit it to her, he hoped that his father would invite the man to dinner soon so he could ask him about life in the West. Tim would become the sought-after boy in his class. He would be able to recount tall tales of buffalo shoots, of Indian massacres, of the wild, rugged beauty and the incessant danger of the Far West. Even if he couldn't actually go West himself—and he knew his parents would never allow him to go, at least not until he was full-grown—at least he could lord it over his school colleagues with the stories he could tell.

Tim raced up the rest of the stairs to his room, threw down his books and began to make a list of questions he would ask this Michael Porter, for he was pretty certain

that he'd have his chance. He had never seen Beth react
to any young man the way she had to this first brief
meeting with Porter. And if he were any judge of his
sister's ability to wheedle, which was considerable, then
Porter would soon be dining at the Lowell mansion.

"There it is, sir," Michael told James Lowell, spreading
out his items list. "And I brought cash to cover in advance. It's there in my leather case."

"I'm impressed with your sense of business, Mr. Porter,"
Lowell declared. "Usually it's fifty per cent."

"Not in my case, sir," Michael said, waving aside the
compliment. "I've not done business with you before,
and you don't know me from Adam. I know your repu-
tation as an honest man whose prices are fair, and I
thought it wisest to bring the entire payment in cash. If
we continue to do business in the future, perhaps my
credit will have some substance. Right now, I prefer to
pay as I go."

"Sound thinking," Lowell said. "Now, let's get down
to business. . . ."

Lowell ran quickly through the list that Michael had
prepared. At last he said, "It's a rather large order. We
might have some trouble filling it immediately."

"Sir, I'm on a tight schedule," Michael pointed out. "I
must leave New York in three weeks on the *Indiana* for
New Orleans. Everything I intend to purchase in New
York must be ready to go with me. You've never sold to
muleteers like myself before, have you, sir?"

"That's right. I haven't."

"Well, sir, a cash operation means that we risk everything on the trail, but we stand to gain everything, too,
if we get through intact. Three weeks, sir. That's all the
time I have. I can't stay beyond the scheduled sailing. Do
you think you can meet the deadline?"

"We'll do it in two," Lowell promised, as the new
maid brought in a silver tea service and set it down in
front of the two men.

"Tea?" Lowell suggested.

Michael pulled an engraved gold pocket watch from his vest. "Thank you, sir, you're most kind, but I think not. I've an appointment at my hotel in half an hour. When shall I check back with you?"

"The day after tomorrow would be ideal, Mr. Porter."

"That's fine with me." Michael rose to his feet and shook Lowell's hand firmly. "I'll come by around four in the afternoon, if that's all right with you, sir."

"Perfect. I'll be in. By the way, if you don't want tea, how about a quick whisky?"

Michael brightened. "Absolutely, sir!"

Lowell went to a cabinet, took out a bottle of bourbon and poured a shot into a crystal glass. He handed it to Michael who accepted it graciously, downed it in one gulp, put down the glass and thanked his host.

As Michael turned toward the open parlor door, Lowell said, "You don't really need to leave your case. You can wait until I have news on the order two days from now."

"As I said, sir, I like to cover all purchases in advance. It's a California custom. It makes the deal easier all round. You are now the guardian of my entire fortune because"—he grinned at Lowell—"that's just about all the cash I've got in the world, once I've settled with the steamship company and paid a few other bills."

"Your advance is as safe with me as it would be in the bank, Mr. Porter."

"I know that, sir," Michael said, and left thinking, as the maid showed him out at the front door, that Lowell's lovely daughter had better be locked in a bank vault for safekeeping while he was near. Otherwise he might not be responsible for his behavior. She was just about the most luscious thing he'd ever seen. With her lovely fair skin and hair, her luminous green eyes and quick smile, her charming manner and voluptuous figure, her poise and intelligence, it would be easy to fall in love with her.

In fact, Beth had already taken the wind out of his

sails, Michael admitted to himself. But falling in love with her would avail him nothing more than a dizzy pulse and an aching heart, for she was quality far beyond his wildest dreams. Still, what harm would it do to see her again, to bask in the sunshine of her presence? He wondered if he could wait until the day after tomorrow before he had another glimpse of her. Already the time until then seemed an infinity. Thank God he didn't have to hold his breath until then; he couldn't survive. . . .

After taking leave of Michael Porter, Beth floated upstairs in a glowing dream. Instead of going to Tim's room, where they usually played games, she stopped in her own room to change into a simple shift she often wore around on the upper floor of the house. As she changed she wondered what she would wear when Michael Porter came again to the house. Something pink, demure and delicate? A dark green dress, with just a hint of sophistication to its cut? A turquoise frock? Her beige velvet theater ensemble with the white lace detail? Or the soft, pale blue lace?

Beth took the blue lace from her wardrobe and held it up against her, so that she could see its effect in the mirror, even though she already knew that the dress showed off her blonde hair and features to perfection. Yes, blue was definitely the right color. It set off her features and gave her a deceptively naive look. She would wear the blue, she decided, and put the dress away.

Since when, she reflected, had she taken this much time to consider the effect of one of her dresses on a man? Never. With her suitors, and there were several, she hadn't felt the need to prepare this far in advance. She knew she looked excellent, and took it for granted that they would too. But in the case of Michael Porter, there couldn't be too much thought given to her appearance. Even without knowing him better, she was certain that she couldn't let him go. Trails to the West be damned!

She'd keep him in New York even at the cost of her so-called honor.

Beth entered Tim's room in a sober, thoughtful mood, far removed from the little girl petulance she had exhibited downstairs earlier. Tim was curled up on the couch with a book. He glanced over its cover at his sister and immediately recognized her mood as a rare one. She was seldom so visibly introspective, and he could only conclude that she had some weighty problem on her mind.

"You look like you're loaded in a tumbril on your way to the guillotine," Tim observed.

"That might be one way of describing it," Beth replied, dropping down into a chair across from her brother.

Tim put his book aside. "Well—? Is it going to be a secret for the ages?"

"It's really no secret," said Beth. "You caught it downstairs."

"Ah! Thinking about Porter."

Beth sighed. "I'm afraid so. Now, how do I get to know him better without seeming too forward?"

"You're going to enlist my help."

"Am I?" Beth said, and laughed. "What could you possibly do to help me?"

"He's coming over Thursday, isn't he?"

"That's right."

"Then you can manage to stay around the house all Thursday afternoon. I'll have Mother meet me after school and go shopping. Father won't be home until four, so if you're there already you'll have another chance to talk to Porter. Suggest that he go riding with you in the park on Friday."

"You know Mother won't let me."

"I'm going along with you two, silly."

"Then how can I talk with Michael?"

"Leave it up to me. I'll invite Mary Tull along. She's a birdbrain, but she likes me. We'll be your chaperones, but far enough behind you so that you can talk undisturbed."

"Splendid. All I want is to find out more about Michael's adventures," said Beth, "on the big trails."

Tim winked. "I'll bet that's all. What else would a young woman want to know about a man? Details of his business, routes taken, Indians he's shot—"

"It sounds pretty ridiculous, the way you put it."

"Sort of. You know what the trouble is with young women like you?" Tim asked.

"No, smarty. Do make me wise."

"They're as transparent as glass. All they want is a man's freedom in exchange for their hearts."

"Dear me, you make it sound like some bloodthirsty game."

"It is," said Tim, "and you won't find me falling into the trap. Knowing you has given me a very clear perspective on the female motive in life—to trap a fellow. The best one available, of course."

Ordinarily Beth would have bridled at Tim's generalization and begun an argument that might go on for days, friendly but spirited. But this afternoon she was grateful to him for sensing in her a response that was anything but superficial, foolish or commonplace. Even though her enthusiasm might be unfounded, Tim understood that she was obliged to follow it through. She was of an age to marry; it was expected of her in the next year or so. She was supposed to leave no stone unturned in her quest for the best, wasn't she? And if that were an awkward cliché, stones applied to New York men, all right. But as for Michael Porter, she hadn't found him under any stone. He was a creature of light and air, a lone eagle, a prince, a knight, and he was just as liable to swoop down and carry her off to his lair as he was to dash off West.

Well, whatever, the game was there to be played, Beth knew, and Tim was willing to help her a little, bless him. The trick was not to let her parents know what was going on until she was sure of herself. Yes, the soft blue would do nicely for Thursday. As for Friday, she had a handsome new riding habit she hadn't even worn yet. Did she know something subconsciously, she wondered, to keep her from wearing the outfit before? Perhaps. It was a nice conceit.

"Well," said Tim, "ready for a game you can't win?"

"I'm ready for you anytime, little brother. Let's begin."

2

BETH Lowell sat in the front parlor having tea with Michael Porter. The door to the hall and foyer was open, and Beth was doing her best to crowd a carefully planned inventory of questions for Michael into the precious few minutes left before her father came home.

Beth got the distinct impression that Michael found her too young, too inexperienced, and consequently not very exciting. She was searching her resources for the right things to say, struggling desperately to cover his silences with bright chatter.

"You were born in Massachusetts, you said, but where were you educated?"

"My mother taught me to read and write very early," Michael said. "I was her only child. She was a trained teacher and only had a year at it when she met my father. I've had very little public school, but I've read a lot."

"Your parents took you West?"

"My father decided it was the only way to combine his passion for adventure with business. He became a hunter and a trapper. As you can imagine, we lived everywhere. I can't recall a time when we weren't on the move; it was a way of life. That is, until I was seven. . . ."

Michael glanced uneasily at Beth, not wanting to discuss this part of his life, but wondering how he could change the subject without offending her. She seemed so interested in his background, something no other young woman had ever given much thought to before.

"Miss Lowell," he began.

"It's Beth, please."

"Yes, of course, Beth. And you're to call me Michael— unless you think your father might object."

"He won't, he indulges me."

"Tell me, why is it so important for you to know my background? If your father inquired, I'd understand. But you are a young lady of fashion, the toast of your set quite probably, with position and money, if I may say so, and the opportunity to go everywhere you choose, do everything, see all. Why is my background so interesting to you? I'm deeply curious."

Beth snapped her fingers at him and laughed softly. "Curiosity, that's the key word. Can't you conceive that I might be bored to death with my life here in New York? That all the comforts and luxury my father can give us must ultimately pall?"

"On the contrary. I think most young women would envy you both your position of elegance and your beauty."

"Oh, come now," Beth said, blushing, "I'm not beautiful, I'm simply well-groomed. That's what money can do."

Michael wasn't prepared to argue Beth out of this half-truth. She would look marvelous in a flour sack, he was certain.

"Whatever," he murmured agreeably. "But the total effect is impressive. And it fits perfectly against the background of life in New York."

"Well, I'm far more impressed by life on the trail," Beth replied. "You were speaking of wagon tracks and ruts as hard as rock. You said you could see the track stretching away sometimes for miles ahead! I've never seen such empty space in my life. It's exciting. Tell me more about the caravans. You said the wagons would start out from Independence, Missouri. Why?"

"It's a crossroads, for one thing, and it's the absolute end of the present frontier. Between it and California is that great open space that takes your breath away."

"Untamed and vast," Beth mused. "And the caravans go all the way from Independence to California with their wagons, right through the thick of the wilderness?"

"Well, halfway," Michael explained. "You see, there are two legions of traders in the West. One group goes from the East to a rendezvous point in the West—Santa Fe—where it meets up and exchanges goods with its Western counterparts. Then the caravans turn round and go back to their points of origin. This year I'll be going all the way West because of my investment in goods, and also because I have a business there now."

Michael paused, then repeated his earlier question, "Do you really want to know the details? I can't imagine why."

"I already told you, I'm curious about you. I want to know everything."

"About the dirt and death, the real deprivation and misery of the trek? It's not a dream journey, you know," he said. "And the people are often pretty rough. Desperate folk, cursing bullwhackers who drive the ox teams on the Santa Fe Trail. It's not a pretty scene, and no place for a young lady of breeding."

"You can't disenchant me by telling the truth."

"That sounds as if you'd like to go along."

"But I would, I would. And I'd make it easily," Beth declared resolutely. "You think because I'm dressed in the latest fashion that I'm just a soft, silly female with a lot of fairytale ideas about life. Well, that isn't true. I'm strong-willed, hard-headed and determined. I refuse to be pushed around by life. I *know* I could make the journey as easily as your bullwhackers."

"Perhaps," Michael allowed, to humor her. "But let's continue. You wanted to know how the caravan gets going. Well, it assembles at the prairie rendezvous of Council Grove. There, the large groups are formed from the many smaller ones for travel to Santa Fe, about eight hundred miles West of Independence. While the caravan is moving West, another portion is moving East. They meet at Santa Fe. The way I usually travel is West to East and back again from Santa Fe, to Los Angeles."

"I'm fascinated," Beth admitted. "And I know exactly what you're taking with you. I did the unpardonable. I snooped at the lists you left with my father."

Michael was amused by her fervor. "Mr. Lowell might not like that."

"Well, I'm sure you won't tell him. I don't usually pry. You're buying textiles and household items that Father will furnish. I know that much."

"Correct. And the caravan that returns East from Santa Fe will bring back merchandise we've bought."

"What would that be?"

"You may find this hard to believe, but it's mostly mules. Prosaic little creatures, great numbers of them. They're bought and driven back East because they're extremely reliable animals that can't be raised successfully in the East. Also, there'll be Chinese silks and cottons, jade, spices from the East Indies . . . Now *that* should intrigue you."

"Oh, it does," Beth said dreamily, visualizing the size of the operation and the gigantic, pulsing life of it. This was better than all the armchair adventuring she and Tim had done together through the years.

"How far is it from Santa Fe to California?" Beth asked.

"Another nine hundred miles West."

"And you ride all that way on mules?"

"Sometimes, and even further," Michael said. "We have to bypass an enormous canyon in the earth, a deep gorge carved out by the Colorado River. There's no road around it, not even the usual endless wagon tracks. We just follow our instincts. But we always get through—we know where the West is, and the route."

"And what might that be?"

"The Old Spanish Trail," Michael explained. "It was originally charted by the early Spanish explorers."

"Did your father decide to stay out West after your mother died?" Beth pursued.

Michael frowned momentarily at the question. "He decided by taking a second wife."

"Oh! Well, do you have any brothers or sisters?"

"A half-brother named Joe, seven years my junior. He's my business partner in Los Angeles. Is there anything else you need for your dossier on me?"

"Oh, lots and lots of items," Beth replied airily, "such as your favorite dessert and a hundred other things! But I can see you've got other matters on your mind. I won't pry any further. Thank you for being so candid with me. You must know that most men treat women my age like children, and tell them nothing. At least that's been my experience up till now."

It was true, Michael reflected, that Beth lived in a rarefied, hothouse environment, due to her wealth and position. But it was also true that she was a restless, intelligent young creature with an insatiable desire to know all about the world beyond her door. Soon her parents would have her married off to some dull clod whose father owned a prosperous business on a par with the holdings of Lowell. In no time Beth would be saddled with a brood of children, her entire life proscribed. She would be forever stifled, frustrated and unfulfilled, never able to express her spirits again, and what was worse, never to do anything on her own. It was a crying shame, Michael decided, a monstrous pity. This perfect flower wasted on the sterile climate of New York life. For that's all it was—a self-consuming pattern that gave no man a chance to take a natural breath.

"No one should treat you as a child," Michael told Beth, feeling that even this was more than he ought to say. "I wouldn't treat you that way, not ever."

"I know that, Michael," Beth said seriously, just as they heard James Lowell entering the house.

"Well, another time," Beth told him. "Are you busy Friday?"

"A few odds and ends. Why?"

"Want to go riding?" Beth asked quickly. "We have horses."

"Of course," Michael said, "but—"

"Leave it to me," Beth whispered, and went to open the parlor door to greet her father.

"Good afternoon, my dear," Lowell said, kissing Beth on the cheek. "I see you've been taking good care of Mr. Porter."

"The best, sir," Michael said, standing.

"Father, before I go and leave you two alone to talk business, may I ask you a question?"

"Of course, my dear."

"I'd like to go riding in the park with Mr. Porter on Friday afternoon. With your permission, of course. Tim will be coming along with us."

"Riding?" Lowell seemed unprepared for the question. "Well," he said graciously, "I don't see why not. Although I should think that Mr. Porter gets enough of such exercise on the trail."

"I've never ridden in New York, sir," Michael said. "I would enjoy the novelty, I assure you."

"There's certainly no better companion than my daughter. She's an expert equestrienne."

"Then it's all arranged," Beth said jubilantly, turning to Michael. "Is two o'clock all right?"

"Two it is," said Michael. "I'll be here."

"Well then," Beth said, smiling, "I'll leave you to discuss your business matters." She went out, closing the door behind her, barely able to repress a shriek of triumph as she bounded upstairs to wait for Tim's arrival from the shopping tour with her mother.

"Wonderful young lady, sir," said Michael.

"High-spirited, we call her," said Lowell.

"Absolutely charming."

"Yes, well, sometimes she's a bit overwhelming. It's difficult to deny her anything."

"I can understand, sir," said Michael, and changed the subject. "Now about the white cotton yardage, I think I'll increase the order. I was a bit conservative about my original estimate and I've reconsidered."

"By all means," Lowell agreed, "let's change the order as you wish." He was thinking that perhaps he should have been more conservative about letting Beth go riding with this young Westerner. But then, he couldn't very well refuse Beth's wish in front of Porter, and besides, the event would reinforce business goodwill. The Porter account was a healthy one. A canter in the park was exactly the sort of innocent social pleasure that he himself would have enjoyed at that age with a pretty girl. And Beth's mother had been just as pretty as Beth was today. Too, the ride would give Porter something to remember when he was out alone on the trail.

There was the question of inviting Porter to dinner also. This had to be done, it was etiquette. So he would arrange for that with Fanny for Friday night, the night of the party. It would probably be the last time that Beth would see Porter, Lowell concluded. She would be too involved with Peter Enfield, now that the spring season was upon them, to give Porter more than a vagrant thought. At least Lowell anticipated this as he discussed the Porter order. Little did he think that things would work out quite differently, nor could he know the plan that was brewing in his daughter's mind. In fact, even Michael Porter had no inkling of the role he would play in the life of the Lowells.

"And the Indians?" Beth asked as they rode in the park on Thursday afternoon, Tim and Mary Tull behind them at a distance strictly specified by Beth. "Are they dangerous?"

"Well, they're armed," Michael said. "And yes, some

of them are. But the caravans always manage to get through, even if there's a shootout."

"How exciting to make the trip," Beth said with a sigh. "As if I hadn't said that already at least a dozen times. I know you find me a little daft to think so."

"*Unusual* would be the right word. Not many young ladies in your situation would care to go."

"Ah, we're back to that. You keep underestimating me, Michael."

"How so?"

"Well, you consider me a product of my background, without even looking beneath the surface."

"I have looked beneath the surface, Beth." He turned serious eyes on her, thinking how beautiful she was in her beige velvet riding habit with pert hat to match. In all his experience, he doubted that he'd ever seen a lovelier young woman. He wasn't even sure he could keep from falling in love with her, which would be painful, for there was really nothing he could do about it. He couldn't simply run off with her, take her along on the journey. He could never be her husband. He didn't think she had any such idea in mind; she was simply charmed by the idea of wagons West, as many of the young were. Anyway, it would be folly for him to entertain such a thought. He had a heavy task ahead of him.

"I consider you a remarkably bright young lady," he told her. "I only hope you find fulfillment in your life here."

"You mean, do what all my female friends do? Marry, and settle down to raise a family?"

"That's the role of women, is it not?"

Beth snapped back, "Only *one* of the roles, Mr. Porter. I was beginning to think that you were different from the men I know in New York. That your adventures might have given you a perspective on the feelings of others."

"They have."

"Well then, why must you relegate me to a standard category?"

Michael reined in his mount along the bridle path, so that Beth was forced to pause with him, as were the pair behind them.

"Beth," he said, "I consider you a very special person, with a unique kind of charm. I'm a stranger in your life. I could talk for weeks and you still wouldn't know me, anymore than I could know you really well in that time—our lives are so different. Yes, we're both exotics to one another. That's a dangerous relationship to maintain for very long. It leads to misunderstandings."

"Then we should talk more frankly."

"Perhaps we shouldn't talk at all," Michael suggested, then, catching Beth's hurt expression, was sorry that he'd spoken. "I mean to say, you have a dream, I know the reality. In short," he said uneasily, "we're walking on quicksand."

Beth grasped immediately what he meant. She stared at him for a moment, then smiled. Yes, he was just as sensitive beneath all that masculine bravado as she had thought. This was very definitely a man she could love with all her being; and yet some inner sense told her that the situation was, as Michael had just said, quite perilous, an impossible reality.

"Next year I'll be going to Europe. Have you been there?"

"Unfortunately, I've only traveled in the American West."

"I don't look forward to Europe much," Beth said. "I'd far rather be on the trail."

"But there's so much to see and do in Europe. Many feel that all the trail offers is endless monotony."

"Let me be the one to talk about monotony. Wherever we go we always carry our own environment with us," Beth said. "The beach in summer is no different from being at home in the winter, except our costumes are different in different seasons. We eat at the same time wherever we are, we see the same people from town if we're at the sea. We even say the same things each year. It's all so predictable."

"But you can't argue the comforts," Michael pointed out. "You live in luxury."

Beth suddenly urged her mount forward, so that Michael was obliged to follow.

"I'm not getting my message through to you," Beth said. "I'm simply dying to know what goes on in that big, brawling world out there beyond this *predictable* modern metropolis. I'd like to curse once in a while, and read books no 'nice girl' is supposed to know about. I'd like to meet people who've come up by their wits, whose fate is constantly changing."

"You're a headstrong young woman. Too much curiosity is a dangerous thing," Michael said.

"I can't help it if I'm that way. It won't kill me and it isn't unhealthy."

"It can get you into a lot of trouble."

"Oh pooh!" Beth exclaimed. "I'll take that chance. Anyway, it's time for us to go back."

"And we haven't solved the world's problems, have we?"

"Not even our own," Beth said sharply, wondering what it took to get to Michael as she spurred her mount so suddenly that she shot far ahead of him down the path. She was impatient with the man for being so thick-headed, for refusing to recognize what she was talking about. She was hopelessly in love with him, even if he couldn't see it, but she would have to be a lot faster, a lot bolder, or the weeks would slip away and he'd be gone. And yet, she couldn't throw herself at his feet, knock on his hotel door and offer herself to him.

Following her, Michael had a very clear idea of what she was up to, and he vowed, against all personal feelings, that he would do his best to put her off. She had a wild-brained idea about his life that wasn't true. But the situation with Beth wasn't something over which he could exercise sane, clear judgment. Plenty of young women in the past had thrown themselves at him and he'd accepted what they had to offer, carefully skirting any talk of commitments. This time he was caught. The dream that seemed to be forming in Beth's mind could not be realized without ruining her life. For all her fire, her brash spirit, she was a delicate hothouse flower. She would not transplant; she would wither and die in any other climate. No matter how much he wanted her, he refused to be responsible for a tragedy. And yet, he wanted her. The hunger gnawed at him.

3

THE supper party to which James Lowell had invited Michael was a regular informal Friday evening buffet affair given the first week of each month.

James Lowell took this opportunity to fulfill his social obligations to a small, select group of business associates, both old and new. These men were also Lowell's friends; business was friendship, so far as he was concerned. Fanny Lowell always invited a few personal friends to the soirees, and also attended to the wives of Lowell's business friends.

The children, Beth and Tim, were always allowed to invite one or two friends each. Tim didn't usually avail himself of this privilege, but Beth often did. This time it was Grace, a chubby school chum, bright and witty, the only counsel Beth kept among females when it came to her private attitudes, or at least some of them.

Beth had told Grace nothing about Michael Porter in advance. She wanted Grace to see him without any briefing, to view Grace's reaction when she met him. And she wasn't disappointed. Grace, usually poised and confident, was struck nearly speechless when she was introduced to Michael.

Later, drawing Grace aside, Beth asked what she thought of him.

"Splendid," Grace replied. "And knowing you, I'd say you'd already staked out a claim."

"Not precisely," said Beth.

"Precisely indeed!" Grace scoffed. "If you don't you're an absolute fool, and I know you're not that. Come on, Beth, confess to your old friend. You have serious designs."

"Very serious. But it's not mutual."

"What do you mean? I saw him drinking you in, eating you up with his eyes."

"Ah, lust is one thing," Beth said loftily, "and love is another. Anyway, he hasn't made the slightest move."

"He's a gentleman, he's biding his time. Wait until you get him alone, or he gets you."

"We've had tea together."

"Where?"

"In the front parlor."

"With the door open to the hall, no doubt?"

"Yes, of course."

"He's not liable to turn into a tiger under those circumstances."

"And we went riding in the park yesterday."

"Alone?"

"No, Tim and a schoolmate came along."

"Well then, you better make a quick solo move soon," Grace advised. "Tonight."

"How can I?" Beth said miserably. "Peter Enfield's due here any minute now."

"Oh, dear. But you're not tied to him," Grace pointed out. "I wish Peter had an eye for me. I could sweep aside the inessentials fast enough for the most eligible bachelor in New York."

"He's no beauty. And you get bad breath and boring

chatter along with the millions. I doubt if he'd strike sparks as a lover."

"You're shameless," Grace said, giggling.

"And so are you!"

"Now, hop to it. Spend your time with Michael. Look at him. He appears to be dying of shyness over in that corner."

Which was exactly the way Michael felt in the new suit he had purchased especially for the occasion. The brittle conversations around him could have been conducted in a foreign language, they were so alien to his knowledge and experience. Just when he wondered where to move next, Fanny Lowell glided up to him with a young man perhaps a year or two older than he was, and she was introducing him.

"Mr. Michael Porter, may I present Mr. Peter Enfield?" Fanny said. "You two will find your differences interesting."

Michael wondered why Mrs. Lowell had said such an odd thing as he shook hands with the slim, rather haughty fellow whose smile was at best cool. A rather foppish indoor type, Michael decided, but probably pleasant enough.

"Differences are always interesting," said Michael, as Fanny Lowell moved away.

"What's your line, Mr. Porter?" Enfield asked.

"I run drygoods caravans from Santa Fe to California. This year I've come to New York."

"Is that a regular business?"

"Not like banking or factories."

"Ah yes," Enfield said, seeming to have run down, lost interest.

"What's your occupation, Enfield?" Michael inquired, feeling entitled.

"Along with my mother, a considerable business woman, I manage the Enfield holdings," he explained. "It's a full-time job that leaves me precious few minutes for planning my social activities. If it weren't for Beth arranging events, I'd be spending most of my nights in our Gramercy Park study."

Michael felt a sharp twinge of jealousy. Beth had mentioned nothing about a steady suitor, or whatever role Enfield filled in her life.

"Work is really my basic existence," said Michael. "I'm on the trail twenty-four hours a day when I'm bringing in goods. Besides that, there's a store."

"Isn't the trail a dangerous way of making a living?"

"I suppose it is, but somebody has to do it. You get used to it in time. Anyway, I'm totally committed to the East. High-finance, a comfortable life."

"Are you married, Mr. Porter?"

"Not yet. Are you?"

"No, but I've hopes." Enfield smiled in Beth's direction. "Rather, I'm open to suggestion. It would depend upon a number of factors. One can't be too careful, Porter."

"A lifetime union is nothing to take lightly," Michael agreed.

"Exactly. One can't rush into the matter without considerable planning and forethought. How one's life will mesh with another, the social structure to support the marriage, the quality of the partner. A fellow must use his keenest judgment—if you know what I mean . . ."

Michael knew this much; that Peter Enfield was a damned snob. It chilled him to imagine the vibrant, warm-blooded Beth in the arms of this colorless ledger-book tycoon who apparently placed business and social values as the ultimate conditions for a marriage. It was done all the time, of course, but to Michael it seemed so cold and premeditated where Beth might be involved. Was she aware of Enfield's attitudes? She must be, poor thing, for she was very bright.

"Do you have someone in mind?" Michael asked Enfield.

"Oh yes, three young ladies, as a matter of fact. If the first fails to meet standards in the final summing up, one moves on to the next, and so forth. Quality is everything, don't you think, Porter? I certainly wouldn't sacrifice it for the most beguiling infatuation. One must use common sense; life's a serious game."

"You may be right," Michael said numbly, and wondered how in hell he was going to get away from Peter Enfield and his idiotic conversation.

Luckily, at that moment Beth joined the two of them. She was blindingly lovely in her white lace gown. She gave both her hands to Peter for a second, then turned and smiled at Michael.

"You haven't seen our garden, Mr. Porter, or our greenhouse. Every guest must." She smiled at Enfield. "Excuse us, Peter, won't you? We'll only be a few minutes."

Peter Enfield's ingrained sense of decorum forced him to acquiesce, although he looked surprised, and they left him standing alone in the corner.

Beth led Michael quickly out onto the broad terrace, away from the guests. The garden in full spring bloom lay below them, moist and fresh and sweet-smelling, deep in twilight shadows. Beth tripped down the wide stone stairs to the lawn's level, then reached out and gave Michael her hand.

"Come," she murmured urgently, "let me show you the greenhouse and Mother's exotic plants."

They got only as far as a concealing hedge when Michael pulled on Beth's hand.

"Wait," he said, "let's stop here a moment."

He swept her into his arms, giving her the first real kiss she had ever received. She thought as Michael held her that she would faint, that her heart would stop for good. It was the most satisfying moment of her life, yet after a moment she could bear his kiss no longer and broke away, taking steps backwards, nearly sitting down in a flower bed.

"Oh Michael," she said softly, "really—"

"I—I'm sorry," Michael apologized. "I let myself be carried away. I had no right."

"No," she said sharply, moving toward him, placing both

hands on his chest, "you only did what I wanted you to do, and have since the moment I met you."

"I'm not free with my kisses," Michael said.

"Nor am I," said Beth, suddenly amused by his awkwardness.

"What about—?" Michael paused.

"Peter Enfield?" Beth laughed. "He's no one I take seriously as a contender for my hand."

"I'm relieved to hear it," said Michael. "Beth, I might as well say it right out: I love you. I don't know what it can mean to us in practical terms, especially to you. But there it is, for what it's worth."

"Oh, Michael," Beth said in a thrilled whisper, folding herself into his arms, leaning her head against his shoulder, "I've been longing to hear you say that. I love you too, but I'm torn by a million considerations."

"Commitments?"

"Well, yes. Family ones."

"We'll have to give the matter deep thought. What about luncheon tomorrow? I'm staying at the Metropole. You could meet me in the lobby at noon."

"I'll have to think about that, too," Beth said. If she met him for luncheon, then she could just as easily be persuaded to take coffee in his suite afterwards, and things being the way they were with her, one thing could lead to another.

"Meanwhile," she said, putting both hands to his face and kissing him, "this is my pledge."

Neither of them noticed the soft approach of footsteps, but both heard the unmistakable voice of James Lowell and broke apart.

Beth gasped and turned toward her father.

"Beth," said Lowell in a cold, stern voice, "go back to your guests," and Beth fled across the lawn without a word of protest.

"As for you, Mr. Porter," Lowell continued, "I'm surprised and shocked at your cavalier attitude toward my daughter."

"Sir, I—"

"No explanations, please. I won't send you away from the party, of course, but I want to give you a word of friendly advice. My daughter's life is already ordered, no matter what she might have told you. I am the judge of what's best for her, and I don't intend anyone to come between Beth and her destiny."

"Sir—"

"Now, I'd like you to come inside with me as if nothing untoward has happened. Mingle with the guests, enjoy your dinner, live in our world for an evening, Mr. Porter. See what the truly organized life is like. I'm afraid you've been away from it too long."

"Sir, I'd just as soon go back to my hotel."

"Porter," Lowell said in a quiet, firm voice, "you want us to fill your orders, don't you?"

"Of course, sir," Michael said.

"Well, then, you must do as I say. You will not be invited to the house again. We'll do the remainder of our business at my downtown office. But being a man of my word, your order will reach the *Indiana* in plenty of time to load for sailing. Is that agreeable to you?"

"If it has to be, sir."

"It has to be," Lowell told him. "Believe me. Now come, let's go back to the party . . ."

4

THE next day as James Lowell was on his way to see Amanda Enfield, Beth sneaked out of the house and made her rendezvous with Michael at the Hotel Metropole, where they lunched at a table discreetly set behind potted palms. Their talk was intense and inconclusive. Michael was reluctant to say anything to Beth that would encourage her to disobey her father, for it was vital that he sail with his cargo on the *Indiana.* But what he felt for Beth transcended other considerations. He told her of a plan he thought might work when, with tears in her eyes, she said that she loved him enough to go anywhere with him.

"Anywhere at all," she said. "Even to parting with my beloved family, though I couldn't just run away. Maybe I can persuade my father to see things in a different light."

"I doubt that," Michael said, "but it'll be worth a try."

"We can't see one another in the meantime, but our new maid will get notes to you, and bring messages," Beth said. "Maybe when you return next year, we can think further of the future. You know now how I feel."

"Yes, I know," Michael replied, overjoyed.

Although reclusive Amanda Enfield hadn't attended the Friday evening party at the Lowells', her son Peter had told her about Michael Porter's attentiveness to Beth, and Beth's reaction. Something had gone on in the garden that was quickly interrupted by James Lowell, so when the banker came to visit her at noon on Saturday, she thought she understood his motives.

Lowell was plainly nervous as he sat down opposite the widow, severe in the eternal black silk she wore everywhere, a formidable lady with iron features.

"Amanda," Lowell began, "we're old friends, we understand each other. I don't think I need beat about the bush, do I?"

"Hardly," said the widow. "Go ahead and tell me why you're here, James. It must be a very pressing reason if the business won't wait until Monday morning."

"It's not business in that sense, Amanda. It concerns Beth and an adventurer with whom I am presently involved in a large business deal."

"Would it be the young man Peter mentioned meeting at your house last night?" Amanda Enfield asked.

"The same."

"Does it concern a possible romance?"

Lowell grimaced in distaste. "Fortunately, not yet. But the young man's obviously smitten with Beth. I'm worried that she might be over-impressed, shall we say, what with talk of the Far West and new horizons. The young man's a merchant from California." Lowell went on to explain something of Michael's background and concluded, "So you see, I'm impaled on the horns of a dilemma."

"Quite so. But get to the point, James."

"Dammit, Amanda, you're an intelligent woman, you know why I'm here. Peter cares for Beth."

"A great deal," Amanda agreed. "But the boy's inept where Beth is concerned; she's his Achilles' heel. He can't seem to get his message across, and I've begun to think he never will."

"He has more than a chance," Lowell assured the widow. "I'm here to make you a solemn promise, Amanda. A guarantee. I'll deliver Beth to Peter in marriage as soon as you wish it. And to put the seal of good faith on that declaration I am now willing to amalgamate our copper holdings, something I know you've wanted for a long time."

Amanda Enfield sat back with a quiet smile wreathing her plain features. "My, my," she observed mildly, "you are indeed desperately up against it. I had no idea."

"Nor I when I felt there was a chance of losing Beth to some stranger."

"About the particulars, James. Beth is still, I trust, un-sullied?"

"Naturally!" Lowell said with some irritation. "The child has a strong will, but her mother and I have imbued her with sterling principles. She's never run loose, and to an-swer your explicit query, yes, Amanda, Beth is a virgin."

"Well, I shall have to talk with Peter."

"I beg you, do it today," Lowell urged her. "There'll

be no point in all this if we lock the cage after the bird has flown."

"All right, James," the widow said, concealing her intense delight. As far as she was concerned, Peter and Beth were an excellent match. "Just so long as you think you can persuade the girl to accept Peter."

"She'll accept him, all right. She'll have no other choice. You've my word upon it. Good sense will prevail."

James Lowell rose and shook hands with Amanda Enfield and the widow watched him depart. She had always hoped that Peter would one day claim a suitable choice as his bride, but not in this manner. However, since Peter hadn't made the alliance, it was this way or not at all.

The widow sat waiting for Peter to come in from his usual Saturday walk, hoping to find a tactful way to break the news that he could now marry the girl he loved, even if she didn't love him. This wasn't the easiest task she would ever perform, but it had to be done. It was the way of the world. She herself had endured a marriage of great eventual empathy. Her husband Willis had been a man of integrity, gritty but adoring. She hadn't loved him at first. But when he was taken from her in death only three years after their union, for a while she was desolate. She had survived only by plunging into business management, raising Peter carefully, perhaps too much so, for she had taken the spice out of him, she sometimes felt. Now at least he would be married to the woman he so obviously loved, poor, inarticulate boy.

Amanda knew it should bother her that Beth had no love for her dull and proper son, but where Peter was concerned, Amanda Enfield wore blinders. He was her life; she would do almost anything for him. Practical and shrewd, she also envisioned a grand union with the Lowells, ending in a mighty merger of two estimable fortunes. Agreeing to a manipulated marriage didn't bother her at all. She saw no reason why it should.

Peter came in while she was still reflecting on the future.

"My dear," said his mother, "come and sit with me before you wash up for luncheon. I've something important to tell you."

Peter came dutifully to his mother's chair.

"Are you fond of Beth Lowell?" she asked.

For a moment, Peter's expression was fearful, then affectionate.

"Of course," he said slowly, "I love her."

"Enough to marry her?"

"More than enough, Mother."

"Well then, what would you say if I told you this can be worked out?"

"I don't think she loves me," Peter said. "I know she doesn't."

"I want the marriage, Peter."

"You've arranged it?"

"Let's say that James Lowell has. He just left. I'm to give him our decision as soon as I've talked with you."

"Very well, Mother. I'll do as you say."

"You don't seem happy. I thought you'd shout for joy."

"I know how Beth feels about me."

"Don't you worry, my dear. She'll come to love you. Let's have luncheon now, and this afternoon you can pay a formal call on James Lowell and advise him that you'll marry Beth. It won't be a long engagement, I'm sure."

"Is it because of her interest in someone else?" asked Peter.

"Whatever makes you think that?" Amanda said sharply. "Come, come, son, let's stop being so melancholy. You should be the happiest lad in New York. Beth is a prize."

"I know," Peter said wistfully, "and that's why I'm a little sad that she doesn't care for me."

"She will, my dear, she will. Give her time. I know about these things. Trust me."

"I trust you, mother," Peter said. "It's just that I don't think you can perform miracles."

* * *

James Lowell called to Beth as she returned from her luncheon with Michael.

"I want to see you, Beth," he called from the study doorway. "Would you please come in here for a moment?"

Please let it be something else besides the business with Michael, Beth thought. It was bad enough that she'd defied her father's orders and kept the luncheon date with Michael, although nothing untoward had happened, except for some hand-holding under the small table for two, and fervent conversation that had decided nothing.

"Yes, Father?"

Lowell closed the door, and waved his daughter into a chair.

"A decision has been made," Lowell said, "and an agreement reached. Peter Enfield will ask for your hand in marriage, and you will accept him."

Beth gasped in shocked surprise. "But Father," she protested, "I don't love Peter, of all people. He's just someone I see from time to time."

"Peter's credentials are impeccable," Lowell said. "He's an outstanding young man with a very bright future."

"That doesn't mean he's right for me as a husband," Beth argued. "He's dull and uninteresting."

"Beth, I'll thank you not to stand up to me on this issue. Enfield will make you a fine husband. It's my wish that the two of you be married."

"What about Mama's wish, or mine?"

"Your mother and I have had a long talk over this. She agrees with me."

Beth's heart sank. Her mother was easily intimidated by her father, Beth knew, and would always eventually knuckle under on important matters. And in this case Fanny had been as distressed to hear of Beth's impetuosity in the garden with Michael Porter as her husband was.

"I don't want to marry Peter," Beth told her father, frightened that her life had taken the kind of turn she would not have thought possible. At that moment she loved Michael intensely, even more than she had a mere two hours earlier. She would almost rather kill herself than submit to a lifetime with Peter. The thought was insupportable.

"Silence, Beth!" Lowell said sternly. "It's not for you to make such a decision. Your mother and I have decided, and that's the end of it. You'll be civil to Peter when he comes to make his proposal, and you will accept him. This is an order."

"I think it's horrid of both of you to do this to me," Beth said, tears in her eyes. "I'll run away," she threatened.

"You'll do no such thing," Lowell said. "You'll be confined to your room until you change your mind, dear child. You must decide what you want—confinement, or acceptance of the inevitable."

Beth had never seen her father like this, and she realized that both her parents had all along expected that she was interested in Peter Enfield and would marry him when the time was right.

"My answer is no, Father. I'll never accept Peter."

"You will, my dear," Lowell assured her. "You'll come to see the futility of your resistance. We all have to make compromises in life. So far you've had everything your way. Now your mother and I are asking you to put practical considerations before emotional ones. Your first duty is toward your family. Don't lose sight of it. You'll regret it if you do."

Beth jumped up; there was no point in arguing further. "I'm going to my room, Father."

"Where you'll stay until you've thought some sense into that head of yours."

"I'll never change my mind about Peter. I love someone else."

"You can't love someone you don't even know, dear child."

Words were useless. Beth stared at her father's set features for a second, then ran from the study.

* * *

That evening, the new maid Effie brought a supper tray to Beth's door and rapped for admission.

"Who is it?" Beth asked through the door. She hadn't let anyone in, not even Tim.

"It's Effie, Miss Beth, with something to eat. Let me in, please."

Beth wasn't the least bit hungry, but she opened the door to Effie. Her eyes were puffy from excessive tears, her hair in disarray, her dressing gown rumpled. But she didn't give a damn how she looked. What concerned her was a plan that suddenly could include Effie.

"You got to eat something, Miss Beth," Effie insisted, setting down the tray as Beth closed the hall door behind her.

"I'm not hungry," Beth said, "but there is something else. Sit down, Effie, and listen."

The young maid sat down, wide-eyed.

"Effie, if I swear you to eternal secrecy and offer you a bribe, will you do me a great and serious favor?"

"I don't need no bribe," said Effie, who was the same age as Beth, but timid and rather scrawny. Effie gazed up at her young mistress and was immediately captivated by the thought that she was being considered for a major role in a domestic intrigue, for she had some idea of what was going on with the Lowells. Beth was the only member of the household with whom Effie could truly identify, and she adored her.

"What's the favor, Miss Beth?" Effie asked rather timorously. "I got to know particulars. Don't want to get into anything that'll cost me my job."

"Don't worry," Beth assured her, "it won't. So long as you can keep a secret and move fast, no one will be any the wiser."

"I've a very tight lip and strong ankles," Effie said. "What must I do?"

"Very simple. Deliver those two envelopes." Beth nodded toward her desk where the two white squares lay.

"You know my sapphire brooch you've admired so often, the one Mr. Enfield gave me for my last birthday?"

"Why sure I do, and it's lovely."

"Well, it's all yours, Effie, if you'll deliver the two envelopes for me as addressed. One goes to my friend Grace Morley, just two blocks away, and the other goes to Mr. Michael Porter at the Hotel Metropole.

Effie rolled her eyes, and her jaw dropped open.

"Oh Miss Beth, I don't know—"

"Effie, you simply must help me," Beth urged. "I'm desperate."

"But your folks will kill me if they find out—"

"Listen to me, Effie. If you were in my place, would you want to marry somebody you didn't love, didn't even like much, just to please your parents?"

"I guess I wouldn't," Effie agreed.

"Well, my parents are forcing me to marry Peter Enfield, and I don't love him. I love somebody else. The details are too complicated to explain, but the fact is, I'm not allowed out of my room until I consent to the marriage. So you see, if I'm to work this out to my benefit, I need some help—yours."

"You could ask Master Tim."

"He can't go out nights. He'd be missed."

"Well—"

"Trust me, Effie. I know what I'm doing, it's not wrong. You just deliver the envelopes, put them into the hands of the addressees, and you'll get the brooch."

"I couldn't ever wear it around here, Miss Beth," Effie said dubiously.

"Of course not. Put it away in your hope chest. The right time will come. Wear it at your wedding."

"I'm not even spoke for yet."

"You will be, Effie. You won't be in domestic service all your life."

"I sure hope the Lord's kind to me," Effie declared, crossing herself piously for good measure.

"He will be, Effie. And especially so if you do this favor for me."

"I hope what you're asking ain't wrong."

"It's not. And I know you won't give me away."

"I'd never do that, Miss Beth," Effie swore, and the deed was as good as done.

An hour later, dressed for the street, Effie crept out the servants' entrance and delivered the first envelope into the hands of Grace Morley at her house. The second envelope she delivered into the hands of Michael Porter at the Hotel Metropole. She was back at the Lowell mansion within an hour. She collected Beth's tray, told her the news, was promptly given the brooch in a velvet box and retired to her room, locking the brooch in her suitcase. No one had even missed her.

5

The next afternoon Grace Morley dropped by for an impromptu visit with Beth. She contrived to spend a few minutes chatting innocently with Fanny Lowell, talking about trivialities, never once mentioning the current crisis in Beth's life.

Grace ended her brief chat with Fanny by remarking, "Incidentally, Mrs. Lowell, my mother and sisters and I are going to spend two or three weeks at the seashore down the New Jersey coast. Mother suggested that I invite Beth, since I'll be more or less alone there, little sisters being the pests they are."

"Why, that's a splendid idea," Fanny said innocently, glowing. It would indeed take Beth far from the local scene, give her a breather in which to make up her mind, remove her from the adventurer. "I'll speak to Mr. Lowell about it this afternoon and let you know at once."

"It would be wonderful to have Beth along," said Grace. "I'll give her the news when I go upstairs."

"She's—not feeling too well."

"Oh? She was fine Friday night."

"You'll hear more about it when you talk with her," said Mrs. Lowell softly. "I'll let her explain."

"But you'll speak to Mr. Lowell about our time at the seashore?"

"Of course," Mrs. Lowell promised. So when James Lowell came home unexpectedly in mid-afternoon hoping that his daughter had assumed the mantle of submission to his proposal, Fanny sprang the seashore venture on him. Lowell was pleasantly relieved and agreed at once to Beth joining the Morleys in New Jersey.

"Impeccable people," James Lowell said, "but to be on the safe side perhaps you'd best have a discreet word with Martha Morley and explain the situation."

"I'll do no such thing, James," Fanny replied stoutly. "I've had second thoughts about what you're doing to that poor child and I'm beginning to disapprove."

"Why?"

"Well, mercy me, she doesn't *love* Peter!"

"Lots of people marry without a scrap of love in the relationship, bear children, make a place for themselves in the world. At least without the illusion of romance there's no chance for disillusion."

"You're a good businessman," said Fanny, "but you aren't a philosopher. Beth will be safe enough with the Morleys, and glad to be out of the house. Mr. Porter won't know where she's gone, so there'll be no complications. And as far as I'm concerned, I don't think Peter ought to know, either. There's plenty of time for that when Beth returns."

Loving Fanny, loving his children, but wanting perhaps

a shade of the impossible for them, James had to agree
that his wife made sense.

"Do as you like," he said, "but don't blame me if the
Enfield holdings end up in another family."

"I think you're putting too much emphasis on the material, James," Fanny Lowell said, and went upstairs to
tell Beth she could begin packing for her trip. Fanny
found Beth dry-eyed, composed, and almost light-hearted
—a good sign, she thought. But she couldn't resist as
Beth began to bring out her clothes for packing in making sure that her daughter would behave herself at the
seashore.

"Darling, you won't do anything rash at the Morleys',
will you? I'm concerned for your future, and—"

"Mother, I wish you'd drop the subject of my future
once and for all. I'm resigned to consider father's suggestion. I might entertain it favorably."

This was more than Fanny expected from her daughter, and it made her faintly suspicious. "I'm only asking
that you act with decorum at all times and make me
proud of you."

Beth stopped folding dresses. "Mother darling, I promise not to do anything wrong. Anyway, how could I
manage? Grace will be my chaperone night and day, along
with Mrs. Morley, the cook, the girls, and Mr. Morley
on the occasions when he comes out from the city. Besides that, I'll write you at least every other day."

"Your father will approve of that."

"All right, my dear, I won't mention the subject again,"
Fanny Lowell promised, and departed.

Tim came in a few minutes later from school, surprised
to find his sister packing.

"Off to the great adventure?" Tim asked.

Beth knew exactly what he meant. "Well, if you can
call the Jersey shore a real adventure, yes, I'm on my way.
The Morleys invited me down to their place at the seashore for a couple of weeks." Beth yearned to tell Tim
what was in her mind, but had decided not to. There was

always the possibility that her father would question him, and Tim might break down and tell James Lowell what he knew.

"You'll make the most of it," Tim said. "I wish I weren't in school and could go along. But you'll have some good fun."

"I expect so," Beth said, "and I'll keep in touch."

"You'd better," Tim said. "I'll miss you."

Beth wanted to cry but grinned instead and threw her arms around Tim, embracing him emotionally.

"Hey, what's *this* all about? You're not on your way to exile in Siberia."

"Of course not," Beth agreed. "I just wanted to let you know I love you."

"I guess that goes for me, too." Tim said. "You have a good time, hear?"

"Oh, I almost forgot," Beth said. "Grace and I are doing scenes from *As You Like It* for her friends down there. I'll need some of your old clothes."

"That's easy, I'll go get them."

"A shirt, breeches, stockings, maybe a cap, and a light jacket."

"You'll still look like a female with your figure but you can have them anyway."

"Nobody will be looking at me," said Beth, "only listening to Shakespeare's verse."

The following morning a carriage arrived for Beth. She accompanied Grace Morley to the dock to meet Mrs. Morley and the other girls. There they boarded the small steamboat that would carry them down the New Jersey coast to their destination.

In the crowd on the dock Beth saw Michael Porter, standing in the shadow of a canopy, very much in the background but never taking his eyes from her face for a moment. Faithful Effie, Beth reflected, had certainly earned Peter's sapphire brooch.

* * *

Less than three weeks later the *Indiana* was loaded and
ready to sail. Michael Porter had made no attempt to visit
Beth at the Morleys', as was suggested by Beth, nor had
Beth and Grace made any excursions away from the seashore to rendezvous with Michael. Beth wrote to Peter
that they had decided not to do the scenes from *As You
Like It,* and that she would see him upon her return to
New York, whenever that was. Michael received one brief
note from Beth, as prearranged and addressed by Grace.
Michael replied to this through Grace. Mrs. Morley was
unaware that Beth had received mail from anyone besides
her mother, nor did she pay any attention to a letter to
Grace from New York, since Grace was always writing
notes to her friends.

The *Indiana* was scheduled to sail with the tide on a
Monday evening.

That morning at breakfast on the New Jersey coast
Beth was suddenly sick to her stomach. Pleading the standard female complaint, she retired to her room. This illness Martha Morley accepted without question, although
with some disappointment. Beth, the girls and Mrs. Morley were set to attend the annual gala spring picnic with
neighbors, an all-day affair. It was also cook's day off.
Mrs. Morley was reluctant to leave Beth alone, but at
Beth's insistence that she'd be perfectly all right, she decided to proceed with the outing as planned.

When the Morleys had departed for their beach picnic
an hour's coach trip down the coast road, Beth threw her
clothes into suitcases, sealed a last letter for her parents
and one for Tim, and climbed aboard the coach that was
arranged to carry her to the afternoon steamboat for New
York. She had already had an impassioned farewell scene
the night before with Grace on the beach when they took
their evening walk. Grace had cried and begged her to
reconsider her flight.

"I'm already upset enough," Beth told Grace, "so please
don't make it any harder for me than I'm making it for
myself."

"I'm so afraid this could be a tragic mistake. You have everything in the world to live for right here. You don't even know what's out there. You're a babe in the woods, Beth dear, you really are."

"Peter Enfield definitely isn't 'everything to live for'," Beth pointed out. "Anyway, I have the deepest, soundest conviction that I'm doing the right thing."

"Just as long as Michael won't let you down."

"He won't, Grace—he won't sell me into slavery, or any other such nonsense. He's a man of honor. Truly. I *know*. . . ."

"I hope you're right," Grace replied. "But you have such pure faith it'll probably all work out for the best."

"My prayers are bound to be answered," said Beth with such deep confidence that Grace decided maybe they would be. At least she hoped so, for Beth was a good person. Her father was the unfeeling one. How he could order her life as he intended to do was unthinkable; she hated him.

"I'll add my prayers to yours," Grace said, and embraced her dear friend, sobbing quietly.

Aboard the steamboat, Beth went immediately to a small cabin she had reserved in the first-class section. Here she changed into what she called her Rosalind disguise—the clothes Tim had given her.

While she had trouble convincing herself that she could pass at close daylight scrutiny as a stripling, what with her delicate, fair features and distinctly feminine figure, still she didn't think she looked too bad as she pirouetted in front of the full-length door mirror in the cabin.

Then she sat down to wait for the interminable voyage to be over, nervous and jittery, her throat dry, her nerves taut. She wondered over and over if she weren't making a horrid mess of her life. Despite her confidence with Grace she had plenty of misgivings. Even if Michael turned out to be an angel, she had no idea what she might be up against in the West, and ill-fitted for the life as she was, she might be unable to bear it. And there was no turning back once she boarded the *Indiana*. Her father and mother would cancel her out of their lives—at least her father would—and it was even highly doubtful that she would see her beloved brother Tim again. An enormous price to pay for what might turn out to be a wild goose chase.

She emitted a moan of relief when she sighted the shoreline of Battery Park through the porthole an hour later. The steamboat would be docking in another fifteen minutes. From there it was only a few blocks to her destination, her fate. She stole another glance at herself in the mirror and resigned her mind to the fact that this was the best masquerade she could manage.

Coming down the short gangway she scanned the crowd for familiar faces. Seeing none, relieved, she whistled to a porter with a small, rickety go-cart. Quickly he piled up her suitcases and took off at a surprising clip down the dock, forcing her to spring along in order to keep up with him.

The dock alongside the *Indiana* was empty save for three stevedores idly unloading crates of fresh produce, the operation being supervised by the galley chef.

Beth started up the gangway and was immediately challenged by a seaman on watch. She identified herself according to plan as Jimmy Garfield and was allowed aboard, instructed to go below and wait in a specified cabin; Mr. Porter would be with her shortly.

Beth had no sooner gone below and entered the cabin passage than a door opened and Michael stepped out into the corridor. It all happened in a few seconds. Michael recognized her instantly, gave her a look of warning, turned back into the officers' lounge, shielding her from its interior. Beth realized that he wanted her to hurry past; it was dangerous to linger. And she did just this, hearing as she scuttled past Michael's broad back in the doorway the unmistakable sound of her father's voice.

James Lowell was just about to leave the ship, the details of the Indiana deliveries all settled. There was more to it than just that, Beth was certain as she entered the small cabin to which she'd been directed by the seaman on duty, and shut the door firmly behind her. Her father was making sure in his own thorough way that she wasn't aboard the *Indiana*. Luckily she had managed to slip past him, although he must have caught a flash of her as she scurried along. Fortunately he hadn't recognized her.

She shut the cabin door, leaned against it faintly, her heart racing, then staggered to the lower bunk of the two-bunk cabin and fainted across it.

She came to some minutes later. Michael was kneeling beside her in serious concern, dabbing her forehead with a damp cool towel.

"It's all right, my love," he said, "your father's gone. I hadn't expected him. He had no reason to come down to the ship, except to look for you. We had a close call."

"Yes. Thank God it's over," Beth said tremulously.

"Thank God indeed," Michael agreed, and bent down to kiss her lightly. . . .

THE WESTERN TREK
1846-1848

6

ONCE beyond the harbor and into the open sea, the captain performed a solemn ritual in the officers' lounge—he married Beth and Michael.

Beth, dressed in pale blue, looked anything but radiant

during the ceremony, for she cried silently through most of it. Michael wore a suit of dark wool and sweated heavily throughout the entire procedure.

There was a dinner afterwards with champagne and many toasts before the happy couple retired to their double-bunked cabin where Beth had first fled in her boy's disguise.

Michael understood perfectly what Beth had gone through to join him in matrimony and he was not going to press his good fortune.

"I'm sleeping up in the top bunk tonight," he told Beth casually, and climbed up into it fully dressed, except for his boots. "You go ahead and get comfortable, dearest. I'll undress once you're in bed."

Surprised at the turn of events, Beth went about the business of changing into her nightgown. When she was in bed Michael climbed down and proceeded to undress in the semi-darkness of a shielded, low-burning lantern.

Turning on her side, Beth could see the silhouette of Michael's powerful physique as he stripped naked, and her heart began to pound unnaturally. Wide awake, she watched him start to climb up to his bunk.

"Michael," she whispered, "I don't want to be alone."

Michael sat on the edge of the bunk.

"I didn't want to press things," he said, his trembling hand finding her cold fingers. "I thought perhaps—"

"Forget what you thought," Beth said. "Sleep with me. I want you."

Michael needed no second invitation. He crawled into bed and took Beth in his arms, settling her against him. They lay close together for a long time, savoring the silent wonder of their union.

"I don't believe it," Michael said finally. "We're actually here together. I never thought it would work out."

"Nor did I," Beth said. "And I certainly didn't expect to see my father on the ship."

"He didn't recognize you. The disguise was a fine idea. You're full of ideas."

"I don't know about that," Beth said, "but I know one idea you'll agree to."

"And what's that one?" Michael whispered playfully. "I don't think I could ever guess."

Beth reached down and touched him.

"Make love to me, darling."

And Michael did as she commanded, slowly and tenderly, bringing Beth to a gentle, triumphant climax that left them both exhausted and deeply satisfied.

This was the beginning of their honeymoon, and it could only get better, Beth thought, lying awake long after Michael's regular breathing told her that he had fallen asleep beside her. It was only the beginning of a long and happy life together. The only depressing element of the moment was that she couldn't share her joy and certainty of a bright future with her parents, or with Tim. But apart from that, she held a deep conviction that she had done the right thing; running away with Michael was no mistake, of that she was certain. She had made the most sensible, the happiest move of her lifetime, and she went to sleep content with this firm knowledge.

The *Indiana* brought Beth and Michael safely to New Orleans in the damp, tropical opulence of late spring. It took Michael another two weeks of patient waiting and negotiating to secure the rivercraft that would carry his supplies upstream to Independence, Missouri.

During their stay in New Orleans, Beth had herself outfitted with sensible dresses for the trip West, at Michael's suggestion—although she might have done it entirely on her own had she not received his suggestion.

"You must have some practical garments that will stand up to hard daily use," Michael said. "Something that will wash easily, when we have the water."

Beth understood what he meant and went in search of a dressmaker who would be willing, in the fashion-conscious city of New Orleans, to sacrifice style for comfort and convenience. She found one in the person of a small French lady of middle years who ran an establishment in an old house, a Mme. Yvonne Bernard. She catered largely to women who worked as housekeepers, governesses, schoolteachers and the like. Her clothes were simple, practical and well-made.

Mme. Bernard was enchanted with Beth. She had never met a genuine New Yorker and found Beth a refreshing change from the women she normally sewed for. She made up eight dresses of simple design, easy to wash and store.

"Now, my dear," she told Beth in her heavily accented English learned in convent schooling, "you will be as well-dressed as any of the women who will travel with you in the caravan. But you must take something along for a special occasion."

"I'll take my blue dress, the one I was married in," Beth said promptly. She could not have parted in any event with her "standing-up" dress, but she shed no tears over the other accoutrements from her past. She gave these dresses to Mme. Bernard to use as models for young ladies' gowns.

Mme. Bernard served tea and pastries to Beth on the day before she sailed with Michael. The new dresses were already at the hotel, stored in a special lightweight trunk that would travel well. Beth was wearing one of the simple costumes Mme. Bernard had designed for her, a dark brown cotton dress with a long skirt, simple bodice, long sleeves, plain piping. Moreover, Mme. Bernard had designed a modified sunbonnet with a stiff visor that would protect Beth's delicate fair complexion from the cruelties of constant sunlight. She had also provided Beth with several pairs of dark cotton gloves, easily washed and extremely strong.

"I expect you to keep in touch with us here in New Orleans," Mme. Bernard told Beth. "I am most anxious to know how your life goes. The West is so far away and I shall be concerned."

"My life will go well," Beth assured the little dressmaker. "It has to. There's no other way."

"Yes," said Mme. Bernard, "I think you have the right attitude to make it so. Here, I have something for you."

Mme. Bernard produced a small silver cross on a strong silver chain. She held it out so that the sunlight streaming through the shop windows made its floral engraving sparkle.

"This was my mother's, Mme. Porter. I would like to pass it on to you."

"Oh, I couldn't take anything so valuable," Beth said.

"Its value lies in the heart of the wearer, my dear," Mme. Bernard said. "You will wear it even if you are not Catholic, and one day you will pass it on to someone dear to you, with your blessings. Please accept it."

Beth couldn't refuse, and Mme. Bernard put the chain around her throat, so that the cross lay against her dress and settled between her breasts.

Mme. Bernard stepped back. "There. Now you will remain attached to the memory of New Orleans, and myself."

"I'll keep in touch," Beth promised, strangely moved by the little dressmaker's kindness."

The small French-born dressmaker embraced Beth warmly as she departed. "Be staunch," she said, "for you have a long road ahead before you settle down for good. I am a mystic of sorts," Mme. Bernard went on, "and I see mountains, high and protective."

"They might be the Sierra Nevada mountains on the way to California," Beth suggested.

"No, no." The little dressmaker was emphatic. "I am sure not. These I see lie to the south, in the drier territory of New Spain."

"That doesn't sound possible, from what my husband has told me. But perhaps you're right," Beth said deferentially.

"I am always right about these matters. I shall pray for you, my dear." Mme. Bernard leaned forward, forgetting her tea. "Long ago I fled from France to come to

Louisiana to join my fiancé, against the wishes of my family. So, I know what you are facing. A long road lies ahead before you can settle down and face the past with clear, calm eyes. There will be some regrets, but they'll fade away with time so you can bear them easily. Let us hope that your life is a happy one, that it fulfills the secret wishes of your heart."

"I know it will," said Beth.

"I shall pray for you," Mme. Bernard told Beth as she rose to leave. "You are like the daughter I never had."

"That is the nicest thing anyone's said to me in a long time," Beth replied, close to tears. "I shall always remember it."

"God bless you," said Mme. Bernard, making the sign of the cross, opening the street door of the shop.

"Thank you for everything," Beth said, stepping into the street, turning away with a quick smile before she burst into tears.

Mme. Bernard watched Beth hurry down the narrow, balconied street. The lovely young thing had tragedy and hardship ahead of her, Mme. Bernard knew in her heart. Beth's destiny was inescapable. Not even the silver cross that had belonged to her mother could protect Beth from what would happen, but it would certainly help to ease the pain.

When Beth reached their suite at the hotel, Michael was waiting for her. He had returned early from the docks where he was supervising the last of the rivercraft's loading.

"We sail tonight," Michael announced.

"Oh Michael, how wonderful!" Beth threw her arms around him, delighted to be leaving New Orleans.

Michael noted the crucifix that swung from Beth's neck and held her at arm's length to inspect it.

"Where did you get this thing?" he asked, frowning.

"From Mme. Bernard, the dressmaker," Beth explained. "She asked me to stop in for tea this afternoon. . . . Why, is there something wrong with it?"

"No, not really," Michael said stiffly. "Except that you're not Catholic."

"Anyone can wear a religious symbol," Beth said firmly, "if he or she believes in God. I could wear the Hand of Fatmeh or the Star of David and not feel strange. Isn't simple faith in a higher being enough to allow me to wear a cross?"

Michael couldn't argue with her logic. "Of course, darling, you're absolutely right."

He swept her up into his arms and kissed her tenderly. The cross had reminded him of his brother Joe, who had a fierce devotion to the Church, something Michael had never accepted.

As Michael embraced Beth, she had half a mind to resist his caresses. But of course she knew this was impossible; she responded to his slightest touch and had never been able to feign indifference to his lovemaking, and probably never would.

7

THE prayers of Mme. Bernard were welcome and much appreciated on the voyage from New Orleans to the way-station of Independence, made via the broad, clay-colored Mississippi to St. Louis, then via the Missouri River to Independence. The side-wheeler that carried the Porters and Michael's goods to their water destination was a handsome rivercraft named *The Mississippi Maiden*.

The trip was long and would have been as tedious as the ocean voyage from New York to New Orleans except for the constantly changing shoreline panorama, dotted with small and rapidly proliferating towns, and for the variety of passengers making short trips up-river.

Though the river life was fascinating, and the life along the shore vigorous, Beth did not find all of it exciting. It was what lay ahead of her—the caravan and the trail—that she looked forward to. She hoped she wouldn't be let down. All the river settlements bore a monotonous similarity; the land on either side of the river was flat, verdantly green, but it never really changed too much. There wasn't the openness Beth expected. That would come, Michael assured her when she discussed the matter with him.

"You'll see," he promised. "You'll fall in love with it."

She hoped this was true, for so far she had been mildly disappointed.

From Independence to their water destination on the Missouri River was a voyage of several days. Then from the debarking point it was close to fifty miles overland to Council Grove, the point where the caravan would be assembling. Michael's sense of organization, and his command of men, impressed Beth more and more as they moved farther away from the trappings of law and order. She began to see a new Michael, still the devoted husband, but there was a new authority about him that impressed her, while at the same time it made her wonder just how ruthless he might be if the occasion demanded. Not only did Michael have the ability to give orders succinctly and effectively, but all manner of men seemed to respect him, and would obey his orders without question.

When Beth discussed this with Michael he told her, "I never ask a man to do any job I can't or wouldn't do myself. This impresses even the most stubborn and ignorant among them, believe me. Without this I'd only be a cipher in the West. A man must be respected and remembered if he's to make his way. And with you at my side," he said, squeezing her to him as they stood at the rail of *The Mississippi Maiden* one night nearing their destination, "there's little chance anybody's ever going to forget me. I'm the lucky man who happens to be your husband."

"Now you'll ask me what I see in you."

"I suppose I might as well," Michael said playfully.

"I see in you what I've never had from my life in New York," Beth said simply. "You've helped me to know a sense of freedom, a sense of doing something important. Because you're a man and not a woman, you may not understand what I mean, but it's always been my dream to be first in a new place, first in a new venture."

"I know what you mean," Michael assured her. "We were meant to be together."

"I've known that since I first set eyes on you," Beth said.

"You won't forget it, will you?" he asked, and Beth thought she noted a slightly anxious shading in his tone.

"How could I?" she said. "You're my husband, my lover and my life."

Council Grove was a veritable city on wheels. A pall of excitement as palpable as a dust storm hung over the place. Beth knew instantly that this was the beginning of the adventure. Everything that had happened to her so far—falling in love with Michael, marrying him, traveling from New York—had been merely a prelude to the real thing. In her wildest flights of imagination, even with the aid of Michael's description, she had been unable to create a precise picture of the caravan. Now it lay before her in all its teeming action, a hundred times more exciting than she had anticipated.

Beth was shocked at the rawness of some of the men and women, their actions, their language. She was also impressed with their toughness, and stimulated, though faintly intimidated and alarmed. She revealed none of her emotional reactions to anyone but Michael, however. The assembling of the caravan was no time to have misgivings. She had bitten off a large chunk of life voluntarily. Neither economic need nor enforced exile had prompted her to leave her comfortable life and the prospect of marriage to Peter Enfield and come West with Michael Porter to an unknown world. Love of Michael, love of challenge —these were her drives. She was finding them as natural as breathing, and she was determined to digest the new life carefully but totally, to make it an integral part of herself. She would make it her world, as Michael had done; she would be the kind of wife she saw the women around her being to their men—supportive, side-by-side helpmates, ready to pitch in and load a wagon, clean a rifle, cook a meal, tote water, make a bed, build a campfire.

Each night Beth went to bed with aching muscles, but she was not one to complain. The exhaustion she often felt was a satisfying kind of fatigue, and she took pride in it. One of the things she liked best was not having a moment's time in which to brood about her parents and dear Tim. On the long voyage from New York to New Orleans there had been anguished times which she carefully concealed from Michael for fear of making him feel unhappy. On the trip up the Mississippi there had been little time for reflected regrets, and now, of course, there was none at all. There would always be the ache of separation from her family and friends, but she would eventually write to Grace and through her she would learn what her family felt. And one day she would see them again—at least, she prayed that this was possible.

Finally the caravan was loaded and ready for departure. Even the animals seemed to have a sense of excitement on the day of leaving. Michael's supervision paid off through astute distribution of the goods he had purchased among the various caravan units, appointing lieutenants to look after his interests. The domestic chores were Beth's, and she performed them cheerfully and efficiently, learning from the other women what she needed to know.

Soon enough Beth saw signs on the plains of the rugged trek: hastily dug graves along the route, sterile, parched land as they moved West, water mostly unfit to drink. The men would go out ahead of the slow-moving caravan each morning on their horses in search of game with a great show of masculine bravado. Sometimes they bagged antelope, but rarely. Mostly they got deer, less fleet-footed than antelope.

Like all the other men in the caravan, Michael was soon as black as a savage from the spring sun. All the men let their hair grow, their whiskers go wild. The dirt of the trail seemed as natural to them as cleanliness might under ordinary circumstances. For a time Beth tried to apply some domestic order to Michael's clothing, but she finally gave up, at his request.

"No need to bother yourself about me, Beth," Michael told her one night. "We'll just get used to the smell and the dust. Don't let it worry you. . . ." And by degrees Beth began to adjust. She washed when she could and got used to wearing the same clothes day after day. Eventually this gave her no discomfort whatsoever. The conventions of her upbringing gradually came to mean little. She found herself with a hearty appetite and the ability to prepare whatever Michael brought in. Once it was a wild turkey, another time there were rabbits. And quite often, when game was scarce, they were obliged to subsist on jerked venison, boiled potatoes and pan biscuits.

Rumors of Indians nearby filtered back to Michael and the other caravaneers, brought by the scouts who rode out at dawn, then back at dusk. A passing U.S. Army company, bedraggled but spirited, assured Michael that famine among the hostile Indian tribes and the burden of their own wars would keep them away from the caravan, which was the case. However, they heard occasional stories of atrocities committed against white travelers, grisly news which came from wayfarers they met along the trail.

Without firewood, Beth helped to gather dried Buffalo dung as soon as they encountered their first prolific herds. After that the caravan had all the fresh meat they needed in the shaggy animals. Sometimes more were slaughtered than could possibly be used, and though Michael deplored this he couldn't prohibit it. Several times the caravan bogged down on the trail. Thundering spring rains made raging rivers of once-dry creek beds as they moved through the high plains into Mexican territory. Cattle were often found miles from camp, and wagons were marooned in deep mud after these horrendous downpours accompanied by high winds.

Sundays were observed with morning prayers. Although many of the personnel were raw types, there was a powerful observance of creedless religious feelings. Michael would attend the rough rituals in silence while Beth joined the women in singing familiar hymns. At these times she always wore her silver cross, the gift from Mme. Bernard, as a symbol of observance. During services she would send silent, loving thoughts to her family, praying for their good health and happiness, and to the continuance of her marriage she gave private blessings. Not that anything was wrong with her union to Michael. He continued to be the concerned husband, tender and ardent as a lover. He treated her with respect in front of the men and womenfolk of the caravan, although she had to allow that his attention was often perfunctory, since his prime interest was a continuous concern for the caravan's safety. Beth didn't mind being relegated to second place. In fact, she had expected it.

One way to endure the hardships of the trail, Beth soon learned, was to wave aside discomforts and concentrate strongly on the ultimate goal: California. Beth was forever plying Michael with questions about his life out West, and although Michael was eager to talk about general conditions there, he volunteered no information about his brother, Joe Porter, except to say, "Joe will be in Los Angeles when we arrive. You'll meet him then. I'm sure you'll like one another." But beyond that he would say nothing, which only whetted Beth's curiosity. Whatever it was that made Michael reluctant to discuss Joe would be for Beth to discover for herself, she realized. This was the personal side of Michael's character, she soon understood, and she would simply have to work this out for herself when she met Joe. Perhaps Joe would be able to put Michael together for her in an entirely new way, and she welcomed this, eager to learn more about her husband than she had already learned from his lips.

The weather grew warmer as the caravan moved further south, still without any major catastrophes. An old man traveling with his daughter and her husband died of a heart attack one night, and was buried alongside the trail next morning with a simple ceremony. A boy child was born to a young woman Beth's age, evening the vital statistics of the caravan. Beth was called in to help at the birthing, her first. She went reluctantly, with wildly beating heart, but found that she could assist without flinching, even savoring the attendant chores.

The weeks went by quickly. Days melted into nights, nights seemed like minutes. Actually, Beth was a bit disappointed that all had gone so well. Having heard dire tales from the caravaneers, men and women, Beth had expected one calamity after the other, sure that Michael had tried to paint a gentler picture than the reality. But whatever had happened to other caravans simply did not happen to the Porter party. Monotony was their only foe.

The scenery changed to more colorful landscapes. Presently the serrated peaks of the West began to take shape on the horizon, and finally, on a gloriously warm day that presaged the imminent arrival of summer, Michael said, "We're almost upon our changeover point: Santa Fe. With a little luck, we should arrive there tomorrow afternoon."

"Oh, wonderful!" Beth said with delight, scarcely able to contain her excitement, for the event meant that she was at last in the true West, even if it was New Spain.

Beth wasn't quite sure what she expected to find at Santa Fe. She knew that the governor resided there in his palace, ruling the territory with a Spanish hand. She knew that his name was Manuel Armijo and that Michael was on excellent terms with him. There was always some special gift set aside for the governor, whichever way Michael was going with his caravan. It was the Spanish way, *mordida,* Michael told Beth. "Otherwise we might have to pay even heavier taxes on our goods."

They left Apache Canyon behind them and moved across the wide, sloping plain with the Sangre de Cristo Mountains on their right, and Beth was unprepared for what lay ahead. The vast open beauty of sky and land, the distant sprawl of ash-pink adobe buildings seen through the clearest air she had ever known. The marked darkness of the mounted horseman who came out to greet the arrival of the creeping caravan impressed her deeply. Somehow she hadn't thought of the Spanish as being dark; but then, there was even darker blood mixed with the Spanish, she recalled Michael telling her.

As the riders came forward and stopped, waiting for the caravan to approach, one rider moved toward them at a gallop, shouting Michael's name. Beside the lead wagon in which Beth sat, she heard Michael's surprised, excited cry: "Joselito!" Michael rode out to meet his brother, Joe Porter.

Beth saw the two men jump down from their horses and clasp each other in a hearty embrace.

From a short distance Beth could see that her brother-in-law was shorter and sturdier than Michael, carefully dressed in Spanish cowboy fashion, his saddle silver-trimmed. Joe wore his wide-brimmed black *vaquero* hat with its silver-tipped cord round his neck, cord across his throat, hat on his back. His smile was electric. His gleaming white teeth and sparkling black eyes were set off by his deep bronze skin.

Beth reined in a wagon a few feet from the two men.

"My God, Joselito!" Michael said. "You're supposed to be in Los Angeles. What a surprise to find you here in Santa Fe."

Joe Porter glanced at Beth, who smiled at him.

"Who's the charming señorita?" Joe asked his brother.

Michael grinned. "She's no señorita, Joselito. Come." He took Joe's arm and led him over to the wagon where Beth was sitting.

"Meet Mrs. Michael Porter—my wife, Beth," Michael said with quiet pride. "We were married on the *Indiana* just after we sailed from New York."

For a moment Joe registered stunned surprise, then quickly recovered his poise, bowed low to Beth, took the hand she held out to him and kissed it gallantly.

"A joy and a delight," he murmured easily in strongly Spanish-accented English. "I didn't expect to meet my sister-in-law at Santa Fe. A pretty young lady in Miguelito's life, perhaps, but not a wife. I'm surprised. And I'm also impressed and pleased."

Beth laughed softly, careful not to overdo the geniality. She had learned on the trail that Michael was extremely alert to conversations she had with male members of the caravan, hovering nearby if he happened to be around. He was a man capable of deep jealousy, and apparently this jealousy could also extend to his brother.

Now, seeing the two brothers together, Beth thought she understood why Michael had told her so little about his brother, merely that Joe was several years younger and the offspring of a late union between Nathan Porter and a young second wife. What he hadn't told her was that the second wife had been Mexican, or perhaps Indian and Spanish, a mestiza. In any case, this was a subject that Michael had carefully skirted.

"You would make a conquest anywhere," Joe declared, holding her blondeness in his dark-eyed focus for a long moment. In a very different way, Beth observed, he was as handsome as Michael. And yet she found it difficult to accept that they were brothers.

"Well," said Michael, "aren't you going to congratulate us?"

"Only Beth," Joe replied. "Envy isn't congratulation. Do you have a sister, Beth?" he asked with mock-seriousness.

"I'm afraid not," Beth answered. "Just a younger brother."

"A pity. Where is your home, Beth?"

"New York City."

"And my brother managed to take you away from New York?" Joe exclaimed in genuine surprise.

"It's not that fascinating," said Beth. "I was easily persuaded." In due time Joe would learn about the elopement, and her estrangement from her family.

"Come, come," Michael interjected impatiently, "let's get the caravan into town. We've a lot of hard work ahead of us if we're to start off on the trail tomorrow."

"I didn't say anything about leaving tomorrow," Joe replied. "First we'll have a wedding feast and many fandangos. We can leave the day after tomorrow. That's my mañana blood speaking," Joe explained to Beth, with a broad smile. "You'll soon find out what a real Western welcome is like."

"Plenty of time for that when we get to Los Angeles and settle in," Michael said with a slightly irritable edge to his voice.

"You won't be settling in for very long," Joe declared.

"What do you mean by that?"

"Trouble brewing," Joe said. "We'll talk later. Right now what you both need most is a long, hot, soaking bath and a big bed with clean sheets to dream away the trail dust."

"A real bath?" Beth exclaimed. "I can hardly believe it!"

"It's true," Joe replied. "You've hit civilization again."

"Let's get going," Michael said, mounting his horse.

Joe bowed again to Beth. "It is nice to have a new member in the family."

"Thank you," Beth said softly, "I'm glad to be here," and meant it.

8

THE wedding feast and fandango dancing would normally have lasted several days, as Spanish custom dictated. Friends and relatives from miles around would descend on a hacienda or village, bringing food and gifts. There would be a joyous festival to toast the bride and groom, something they would remember with pleasure all their lives. But not this time. Michael was adamant about having only a short celebration, particularly after his private conversation with Joe that same night while Beth was preparing for the morrow's fiesta, in the only building that Santa Fe could properly call a hotel. In reality it was no more than a simple one-storey adobe with small guest rooms opening onto an inner patio, but it was heavenly for Beth.

While Michael and his brother talked in Joe's room, across the patio Beth was pressing her blue gown and fretting over her limited wardrobe. Michael and Joe were having a serious conference. Michael was becoming upset, Joe was almost glacially calm, prepared for what he was about to say.

"Explain how in hell you managed to antagonize the white settlers," Michael demanded. "They're our steady customers. Without them we're finished in Los Angeles."

Joe shrugged his shoulders. "Just being me, I guess. After all, I'm a greaser, not a gringo." Joe's expression was almost hostile for a moment. "Or have you forgotten?"

"Oh, for God's sake, Joselito! Don't talk that way to me. We're brothers."

"Only fifty-fifty," Joe reminded him. "Blood is a lot thicker than affection."

"Stop that nonsense!" Michael said sternly. "I don't want to hear any more of it."

"It isn't nonsense, dear brother. It's the hard, unvarnished truth. You seem to forget there's a nasty little war going on under our noses, even if it hasn't been officially declared by the American and Mexican governments. The Yanks want the Californios out so they can jump their holdings, take over the territory by the thousands, and extend the American empire."

Michael grunted impatiently. "Perhaps so. But you know as well as I that this is inevitable."

"It's also wrong," said Joe. "I don't like it."

"But Joselito, you're an American citizen, just as I am. Not a Mexican, but a true-blooded and born American."

"Am I?" Joe said guardedly. "What about my mother? A lot of people don't think I'm American. I've been shot at since you went away. Four times, to be exact."

"My God—"

"It's true. Some record for survival, eh?" Joe shook his head.

"It's shocking, that's what it is," Michael said.

"Well, Miguelito, maybe they didn't mean to hit me. Who can say? But they sure scared me into action." Joe paused, stroking his chin with one finely tapered bronze hand. "I don't know quite how to tell you this. I've joined up with a vigilante band to defend Americano rights."

"Joe, that's in a class with cattle rustling," Michael declared. "You're fighting against yourself."

"I don't see it that way. I consider it a call to duty," Joe said stolidly.

"Why are you always so damned stubborn?"

"I'm like you. I can't help it."

Michael sighed. "You're a Yank, Joselito, a U.S. citizen by birth."

"That's a fact, but it doesn't change my sympathies."

"I thought we'd be closer this time." Michael's tone was reflective, wistful. "We stand to make a lot of money over a year's time with the drygoods I brought."

"I'm impressed with the goods, of course."

"But the way you talk, it looks like the virtual dissolution of our partnership, or damned close to it."

"You can have my share."

"Damn, I don't want it!" Michael replied emphatically. "I want you working alongside me. How many times do I have to remind you that we share in the business equally?"

"You can manage my share, and take a percentage for the extra responsibility. Los Angeles just isn't safe for me any longer. You keep on ignoring the fact."

"So what's the alternative if I don't want to let you go?" Michael asked.

"Close the store, or sell it. Come south with me until the Mexican-American thing is settled."

"Where south?" Michael asked slowly, thhinking he already knew the answer: Joe's obsession.

"Into Baja California, of course."

"Down to your mother's place?"

"Exactly. Where else?"

"But it's a wilderness. What can we do down there?"

"Settle in, build ourselves a small kingdom. Think of the challenge."

"I'm thinking only of the hardships, Joselito. Don't ask me to take Beth there, not now."

"The war will come," said Joe, "and soon."

"You may be right. But I'll weather it out in Los Angeles."

"Neither one of us will give an inch, eh?" Joe observed. "So what's the alternative?"

"Before we make that decision, tell me—what's truly

behind this sudden desire to move south, to desert every-thing we've worked for these past few years?"

"I've been accused of rustling a thousand head of cat-tle, of driving them down into the Mexican mainland and selling them."

"Well, you didn't—did you?" Michael demanded.

"I could have, of course. But I didn't."

"Well then?"

"Miguelito, I can't go back to Los Angeles."

"Why not?"

"George Hearn and some others have put a price on my head. It's open season on me. I had to slink away like a coward and move like the wind to get here at all."

"Good God!" Michael gasped. "So that's why you came all this way to meet us. I thought it was just a happy coincidence that you were here and could meet Beth."

"I didn't even suspect that you'd have a beautiful wife to look after."

"She's not exactly a burden to me," Michael said stiffly.

"I didn't mean it that way."

"Joselito, what can we do?"

"You can go on to Los Angeles, I can go south."

Michael shook his head. "I don't like it."

"We don't have a choice."

"You'll get the usual share, half of all profit."

"I know that."

"This isn't going to be the happiest wedding party we've ever attended."

"It needn't be a sad occasion," Joe said. "Tell Beth I'm being called away to look after my mother's interests in Baja. That's part of the truth."

"I don't like running the store alone."

"You'll have Beth to help you. You won't miss me."

"Beth isn't you. She can't do a man's work."

"There's my cousin, Pedro. He's there now. He's re-liable and a hard worker, and our clerk, Garth Winslow."

"Damn, the business won't be the same without you,"

Michael said. "All the way across country I was thinking about you, how much you'd enjoy what I'd done in New York. Now you've taken all the pleasure out of our lives."

"Oh come now, the trouble between the United States and Mexico won't last forever. It'll soon be settled."

"That's just a guess."

"I don't think any group can resist the American tide for long. It's too powerful. It's driven me out."

Michael and Joe shared a common characteristic; when they made up their minds to do something, heaven and earth couldn't shake them from the decision. Michael saw that it was no use trying to argue with Joe, not to-night anyway. He would try again tomorrow. Put some good Spanish wine in him, get him to dancing and he might be persuaded to return to Los Angeles. Maybe. . . .

"All right," Michael said, "we've talked enough. I'm dog-tired. I need a bath and a good night's sleep to be ready for tomorrow."

"Sleep?" Joe grinned. "I wouldn't be doing much sleeping if I were in your bed."

"Thanks for the compliment," Michael retorted harshly. "From anybody else, those would be fighting words."

Joe reached over and slapped his brother's knee. "You don't change, Miguelito. You're still my big brother."

"And you're just the same as always. Only this time," Michael said wistfully, "I can't dig you out of trouble."

"No, you can't. And this time I'm completely innocent."

"I hope you are, Joselito, I sincerely hope so."

"I am, dear brother, I am."

For a quickly improvised celebration the wedding fiesta was a model of opulent colonial hospitality. This could never have transpired were it not due to a fortuitous coincidence. Preparations were already in progress for a birthday party in honor of Governor Armijo when the Porters arrived. The moment Manuel Armijo heard of Beth's and Michael's recent marriage, he ordered that his birthday celebration be shared with the bride and groom, a singular honor. The fact that Michael had brought Governor Armijo some handsome gifts—as Joe had from the West— certainly did nothing to restrain the governor's friendliness.

The fiesta was a splendid one. Tables groaning under the weight of Spanish delicacies were set along the shady arches of the governor's palace. Toasts were drunk by the dons, the lesser people, the bride and groom, the governor and his lady. His Excellency made an impassioned speech for the happiness of his young guests, and the party dissolved into a pandemonium of eating, dancing and conversation that lasted all day until evening.

That night Joe met with Michael and Beth to say his farewells.

"I'll send word to the store when I've safely arrived," Joe told them both, "so you won't be worried. And I'll stay down at Antelope Valley until I get word from you that it's safe to return. If it ever is."

Michael agreed that it might be some time hence.

"You must come to visit," Joe said to Beth.

"I'd love to," Beth replied. "It must be wildly beautiful there."

"It is that," Joe agreed. "Sometimes like an enemy, that country. Before it becomes your friend you have to prove yourself to it."

"When we get to Los Angeles I'll try to talk to George Hearn," Michael promised.

"It's a waste of time, Miguelito," Joe replied sharply. "He won't give you any satisfaction. He's not going to leave me alone until a war's fought and won. Maybe not even then."

"We'll see about that," said Michael, and embraced his brother in farewell.

Joe rode out at dawn, heading south on the trail that led down to the mainland of Mexico where he would cross the Colorado delta and then climb up into Baja's high country. There he would become as invisible as a lizard sunning itself among scorched rocks in summer, or the timorous rabbit that blended into the earth. Baja was a rugged fortress that would protect him.

The long march from Santa Fe to Los Angeles was accomplished in a much calmer political and geographical climate than would be the case for future caravans. The Apache and Pima Indians were amiable and fairly helpful along the trail, willing to sell supplies, including some water, and the spring weather held nicely, warm but not the parching oven heat of summer and early autumn. Beth loved the wild starkness of the landscape; she was fascinated by the Indians and didn't once complain about the inconveniences that the caravan's route forced upon her.

Very few women, Michael reflected as he watched Beth go lightheartedly about her daily chores on the trail, would be able to endure the trek as Beth had. This was particularly unusual considering the life of luxury that she had led in New York, where she had never had to wash a dish, press a garment or cook a meal in her life. But then, Beth had made up her mind firmly when they started up the Mississippi that it was time she assumed the responsibilities of the trail life, promising that she would never complain.

"I have to move forward in life, Michael," she told him, "and never look backward."

It was this pragmatic attitude that made all her duties, even learning midwifery en route from Los Angeles, bearable instead of onerous.

Los Angeles, too, was a place for which Beth had prepared herself. She accepted its dusty, ramshackle frame and adobe building smallness as she had accepted all else so far—a fact to be lived with cheerfully. She insisted on going to work in the store the day after their arrival.

"I need to learn all about the goods you handle, about selling across the counter and dealing with the accounts," Beth declared. "I want to know everything."

"Why?" Michael asked, knowing full well that he would

give Beth her wish, happy to have her involved in the operation. "You'll be raising babies before long."

Beth laughed. "Well, there's no sign of that so far. We'll deal with it when it happens."

Friendly to all customers, Beth made an excellent impression in the store, Michael found. The customers came to like and admire beautiful young Mrs. Porter, who wasn't afraid of toting a heavy item or of getting her pretty hands dirty in the process.

One day, Beth broke the news to Michael that she was pregnant. Michael was overjoyed. He was concerned for her though, and insisted she limit her activities to the two-room apartment they had at the rear of the store, working only on the accounts and ordering in her spare time.

During the months of Beth's pregnancy following their arrival at Los Angeles, General Kearny's army, such as it was, marched into Alta California territory from Santa Fe. Back in Santa Fe, Kearny had met with a bloodless surrender by Governor Armijo, but California was not quite so docile. There were intense street fights in and around the pueblo. The stubborn insurgents of Mexican blood refused to give up until they were either shot or forcibly driven across the border into Baja. During this period of unrest and violence, Michael was deeply thankful that Joselito was living in Baja, or he would probably have been caught up in the struggle and got himself killed. But being realistic, Michael knew that his brother wasn't remaining totally passive while all this was going on. That would be too much to ask of Joselito. Rumors reached Michael that one special band of Mexican commando bandits rode across the border between Alta and Baja, making raids on ammunition dumps, stealing horses directly from the American army, and slipping back into the safety of the high country before dawn, where no one could find them. Even Kearny's men had better sense than to try to follow.

On January 10, 1847, the town of Los Angeles surrendered officially to the American military forces, such as they were. Later to become the thirty-first American state, the territory of Alta California accepted defeat in the north around San Francisco and Monterey as well as in the south, and with docility assumed the yoke of American dominance. Thus, the conquest of California was over almost before it had begun. However, it would be over a year before the final peace treaty between Mexico and the United States was ratified, and another three months after that before the treaty would become fully operative in May of 1848.

A couple of months before the final peace between Mexico and the United States, a son was born to Beth and Michael. They named him Nathan after Joe and Michael's father. There was much cause to rejoice, the Porters felt. Michael sent off a message to Joe that he was now an uncle. Joe wrote back weeks later, the letter delivered by an Antelope Valley Indian.

"I am proud to be an uncle," Joe wrote. "One day I'll return to Los Angeles, but the time is not yet. There's much to be done, many wrongs to right. The war isn't over for me," Joe ended the message. Michael didn't know how involved his younger brother was, but hoped that Joe was not putting his life on the line as regularly as he suspected he might be.

Simply because a formal peace treaty now existed between Mexico and the United States, with California now a new American territory, the burning resentment of many proud Californios toward the new American regime and its settlers did not die out. Although law protected the old residents momentarily, the Californios knew with a sense of foreboding that their vast land holdings, undisputably theirs for generations, could not remain inviolate much longer against the growing tide of pioneer settlers whose prime obsession was to break up the huge Spanish estates and settle on the land, dissolving the Spanish land grants and developing small parcels for private enterprise.

Opportunists like George Hearn came early to Alta California before the Mexican-American War, intending to realize their ambitions at any cost. They were not content simply with taking over, legally or illegally, the rich legacy of land that the Spanish grants had so zealously protected. They wanted California purged of the entire Spanish and Indian population, and it really didn't matter how this expulsion was achieved—either by banishment or murder.

Hearn was a rabid xenophobe, with a searing, contemptuous hatred for anyone not of pure Anglo-Saxon blood. He was well-known around Los Angeles as a dangerous character, testy and trigger-happy. Some thought him mad, others said he was obsessed. In any case, Michael and Beth didn't like him coming into the store at all. He almost invariably reeked of whisky when he made an appearance, and he refused to let Pedro near him, demanding that only Michael or Beth wait on him.

One day not long before the final effective date of the Mexican-American peace treaty, Hearn slouched into the store for some supplies for his ranch, which was several miles south of the pueblo. He demanded Michael's presence, and Michael came from the back store office to attend to his needs, gritting his teeth to conceal his distaste for the man who had caused his brother to flee to Baja.

Michael had never found the right moment to speak to Hearn about the charges leveled against Joselito. It was true that cattle had been stolen, quite a few head from Hearn's own corrals. It was also true that Hearn had convinced several other ranchers of Joe's guilt in the matter, persuading them to put up a bounty purse against Joe's life. The matter had simmered down during the last year with Joe's absence. Several proven rustlers had been hanged, though this hadn't diminished Hearn's hostility toward Joe. He had talked openly in town saloons about killing Joe on sight if he ever so much as showed his face around Los Angeles. "Either I'll do the job myself, or one of my friends will," Hearn vowed.

On the particular day that Hearn came in, Michael

didn't have to bring up Joe, because Hearn did it for him, right after he'd paid for his purchases and Michael and his assistant, Garth Winslow, had stowed them in the bed of Hearn's wagon.

"By the way," Hearn said, "what d'you hear from your greaser brother?" Hearn was getting into his wagon. "Still leading a yellowbelly's life down in Mexico?"

Michael resisted the temptation to pull Hearn from his wagon and give him a good thrashing. He could do it easily; Hearn was middle-aged, drink-raddled, slight. But instead he clenched his fists together and said quietly, "I haven't heard from him in a long time, Mr. Hearn."

"There's still a goddam price on his head. We ranchers all know he's guilty, headin' them bandidos."

"He hasn't done anything, Mr. Hearn," Michael said. "He's not guilty of stealing your cattle or anyone else's. I know my brother."

"You don't know him well enough, Porter."

"He wouldn't steal cattle."

Hearn's eyes narrowed. "You callin' me a liar?" Hearn demanded with a nasty curl of his thin lips.

"You are only mistaken, Mr. Hearn," Michael replied evenly. "I'm saying there's no proof Joe took your stock."

"A couple of my trusted men swear they saw him in the hills at the time the cattle was taken," Hearn said. "Their word's good enough for me. The bounty's still out. You just tell him if he ever comes back here his life won't be worth a plugged nickel. You hear?"

"I hear, Mr. Hearn. And while we're at it, I'd appreciate it if you didn't come into my store again. I don't like you and I don't want your patronage."

Hearn grinned and spat tobacco juice on Michael's boot.

"All right with me, pardner. You just confirmed what I been thinkin' all along. You're no better'n your spic brother. I won't be back. I'll tell my pals to stay away, too. That good enough for you?"

"It's perfect," Michael said. Nodding curtly, he turned and walked into the store, aware that if the two of them had been pursuing this conversation on the open range, turning his back to Hearn would have been an easy way to lose his life.

Back in the rear of the store, Beth noted the angry flush on Michael's face. "What went on out there between you and Hearn?" she asked.

"That bastard," Michael growled in high fury, "that dirty, filthy scum! He's still after Joe's hide. He means to kill him."

"But Joe's safe in Baja."

"He isn't now," Michael replied, frowning.

"I don't understand."

"I should have told you. I got a message from Joselito yesterday. An Indian brought it to Pedro."

"And you didn't say a word," Beth observed.

"Well, I didn't want you to start worrying," Michael explained. "He said he wouldn't come into town."

"Thank heaven for that!"

"I'm to meet him."

"Where?" Beth asked.

"It's best you don't know, my dear. It's a few miles out of town, that's all you need to know."

"As you say," Beth replied. She was ready to accept any decision Michael made about his brother. Although their relationship had quite obviously undergone many stormy moments, there was a powerful love between them due to their father. Michael, Beth knew, was never able to accept Joe's family at Antelope Valley. He had gone down there once for a visit years ago. Feeling out of place and closed in, he'd never gone again. After all, it was Joselito's home, not his, and dominated by Joselito's mother, the once-beautiful, now middle-aged Luz Porter.

Upon Nathan Porter's death Luz Porter had returned immediately to Antelope Valley. There she was living out her life as the matriarch of the forty thousand-acre estate that had been in her family since the early Spanish colonial days. She headed up a community that was virtually a village, a mixed bag of Indians, relatives and retainers, hardly in regal Spanish glory, Beth could imagine, since the family was poor. But at least Señora Porter existed secure in the knowledge that her estate would never be stolen from her by rapacious American settlers—she lived in Mexican territory.

Later in the day Beth said to Michael, "Is it safe to go and meet Joe?"

"It's a chance I'll have to take. Joe needs money. He wants his share of the profits."

"But we're not doing that well. We've put his share back into the business."

"I'll have to work it out with him."

"You'll argue," Beth said.

"I hope not."

"When is the meeting?"

"Sunday."

"You ought to send Pedro. I don't like the idea that you're going by yourself. There are too many prying eyes in this town. *And* George Hearn."

"I'm not worried about him," Michael said, but in fact he was deeply concerned, still shaken from his conversation with Hearn, who was as deadly as a rattlesnake.

"Well, I am. Michael, please send Pedro."

"Stop worrying, Beth," he told her.

"That's impossible. Michael, let's go away for a few days, let Garth and Pedro run the store."

"Where would we go?"

"Over to the Coast. We could camp on the beach for a few days."

"You simply don't want me to see my brother," Michael said.

"It isn't that, it's the circumstances. After all, there is a price on his head," Beth pointed out in an even tone. "Send Garth to meet him, or Pedro."

"I won't have them running my personal risks," Michael said. "Now, I think we've discussed this long enough. I appreciate your concern but there's no need for you to worry. I'll take all possible precautions and I'll be back with you in a few hours. It's not like you to get this emotional, Beth."

"All right. Go if you must," Beth said, and walked out of the room.

Beth knew that there was no possibility of overriding Michael's determination to meet Joe outside of town. Dangerous or not, he would see Joe, and she could do nothing about it.

During the next two days Beth had fearful misgivings about the rendezvous. Everybody went around armed, and a man with Hearn's vile disposition and xenophobia might, after the conversation in front of the store, be waiting for Michael to make some move. The Sunday morning solo ride out of town could easily be interpreted as a sign that he was going to meet his brother. Hearn's henchmen roamed the pueblo at all hours—they had ever since the peace—and were as dangerous as a pack of hungry wolves.

Without Beth telling him, Michael was well aware of the risk in seeing Joe. He took what precautions he could. He rose early before dawn, saddled his horse quietly and was on the road, armed, before dawn's first pale streaks began to tint the eastern horizon. He looked forward partly with joy and partly with apprehension to seeing Joe. He was bringing Joe some money, but hardly the amount he had requested.

Worrying about Hearn as he rode out, he saw nothing to alert him in the pueblo. A dead Hearn, he knew, would be one hell of a lot less trouble than a live one. But Michael had never killed a man and wouldn't start now, except in self-defense. However, if the rotten little trouble-maker were dead, his colleagues would probably soon forget about Joe Porter. Hearn was the one who kept the enmity alive.

Unfortunately, one of Hearn's American ranch hands, Lefty Farrell, was just emerging from a night in a plaza brothel as Michael rode through the still-dark and quiet square on his way south to his rendezvous with Joe.

Lefty knew Michael by sight but did not make himself known and wasn't seen by Michael. The ranch hand rode immediately to Hearn's house to rouse the sleeping rancher.

"Thought you oughta know, boss. Hated to wake you up."

"You say you saw Michael Porter?" Hearn asked.

"I swear it, boss. And Porter wouldn't leave his pretty missus's warm bed for anything except his spic brother."

"I think you're right," Hearn said. "That's got to be it. Smart boy, Lefty. I won't forget this."

Hearn hastily threw on his clothes, collected his firearms and ammunition, saddled his fastest horse and took off down the south road out of town barely five minutes after sunrise. He rode alone because if he killed the two brothers he would want no witnesses. Later on, if Lefty Farrell so much as opened his yap, there wouldn't be any Lefty at the Bar "H" Ranch, just a small mound of rocks on a lonely hillside.

Hearn decided that there was only one logical place for Michael's rendezvous with his brother. It would have to be near the oak grove half a mile from the fork in the road where one track led southwest into Baja and the other southeast into mainland Mexico. Keeping the road ahead of him in full view at all times, Hearn moved toward his prey.

9

IT was a hot, beautiful morning. Just a hint of tangy-fresh sea breeze wafted up from the coast twenty miles west.

After an hour in the saddle, Michael nervously checked his pocket watch once again. He was due to meet Joe in another fifteen minutes. The meeting must be timed so that they would reunite inside the natural shelter of the rendezvous.

Ahead of Michael lay a route he had taken many times —over the broad flank of a hill and through a patch of oaks, then down to the rendezvous point that overlooked the junction of the southeast and southwest trails a couple of hundred feet below them and a quarter of a mile distant.

The rendezvous was a perfect natural meeting place. From the hill above or from below it looked like a large, solid cluster of grey boulders, similar to other rock formations in the area. But this arrangement was special. The fifty-foot-high boulders sheltered the small rendezvous point—an old Indian lookout—on three sides. At every flank they were too steep to climb. There was no need for a high barrier of boulders on the downhill side of the cluster, nor was there one. The ground dropped away precipitously below the rocky balustrade, so that the view of the road in the middle distance was unobstructed. Yet no one could look up into the core of the cluster from below, nor could anyone standing on the gently sloping upper hillside see down into the center of the boulders.

To enter this protected miniature valley stronghold, Michael would have to dismount and lead his reluctant horse carefully through the defile in the boulders that took them to the center of the lookout point.

In the shade of the oak grove, Michael made a last, cautious survey of the surrounding territory, turning slowly in all directions. To his eye the landscape was motionless, except for a single distant dust devil spiraling its capricious way west across the sunny land. It was silent, and strangely eerie. Perhaps the fact that it was Sunday had something to do with it, Michael decided.

Urging his horse on, Michael rode forward to the cluster of boulders. A glance at his pocket watch told him he was precisely on time. He dismounted by the boulders, saw the almost undetectable break in the rock wall, took his horse's reins and led it through the narrow passage for some forty feet of several abrupt turns, holding his breath as he emerged suddenly onto the flat surface of the lookout shelf.

There, suddenly, was Joe, gun in hand, which he holstered immediately at the sight of Michael.

"Miguelito!" Joe said, smiling and walking forward, his arms outstretched.

The two men embraced warmly.

"Thank God you're all right, Joselito," Michael breathed in relief.

"And why shouldn't I be?"

"You weren't taking any chances. You had me well-covered."

"I'm careful and suspicious these days," Joe said. "It's the only way to stay alive."

"I've been worried as hell about you ever since your message arrived. You had a dangerous ride up here."

"I take many precautions. Why would you worry any more than usual?"

"Oh, feelings in my bones," Michael said, "and tangible signs. I had a public argument with Hearn in front of the store a couple of days ago that's bothered me a lot. He wanted to know if I'd seen you recently."

"And what did you tell the scum?"

"I said no, I hadn't. And I also told him to take his damned business elsewhere."

"Good for you."

"He couldn't have known about your message to me, could he?"

"I don't see how. I take every precaution."

"That's what I kept telling myself, but still I've worried."

Joe smiled. "You always did, big brother, but you needn't have. There's not a disloyal man at Antelope

Valley," Joe assured Michael. "Besides, no one but Creek who carried the message to you knew where I was headed. And he'd never talk, not even under torture."

"I'm relieved," said Michael. "Hearn's a madman." He studied Joe carefully. "You're very lean, Joselito. Too thin." Thinner and darker, Michael observed. Joe's normally snug shirt and pants seemed to hang on him.

"I'm just fine," Joe replied. "Never mind about me. How are Beth and little Nate?"

"Excellent. And how is Luz?"

Michael had never warmed much to Señora Porter, although he admired her. He was unable to call her mama or mother, only Luz, which had never bothered her; she centered her interest in Joe. After all, Michael was nearing puberty by the time Luz gave birth to Joe, tall for his age, awkward, shy, scarred by his mother's untimely death from tuberculosis, his father's quick remarriage.

"Mother's well enough. But nobody at Antelope Valley is—" He broke off, then burst out, "Oh what the hell, we're practically starving! There's not enough to eat, Miguelito."

"Why haven't you told me sooner, for God's sake!"

"I didn't want to worry you. We've managed somehow, but the drought last winter's made it hard to raise anything. The rains weren't much more than mist, the springs were low. I hope to Christ you brought some money with you. I need it a lot."

"I brought some, but—"

"We have to feed about a hundred souls until crops come in again."

"Why didn't you say in your note what was wrong?"

Joe ignored this. "How much did you bring?"

"All I could spare. Here—" Michael reached into his saddlebag and took out a leather pouch. "Here it is." He handed the pouch to Joe, who opened it and quickly counted the silver and gold pieces.

Joe shook his head slowly. "Miguelito, this isn't going to be enough for supplies I must take back with me across the border. Have you any idea what the smugglers make us pay for supplies in drought time?"

"No, none at all. But the business isn't a gold mine, Joselito. We're just getting by. Prices doubled during the war. We haven't made a run in two years. And it doesn't look like conditions will be back to normal for some time—if ever."

"The business is still operating. You must be making something," Joe insisted.

"We're just barely getting by."

"I find it difficult to believe that my share's not two or three times this amount."

"I'm telling you the truth, Joselito. Look at me—" He took his brother by the shoulders and stared into his eyes. "Have I ever lied to you about anything? Well, have I?"

"No. I can't say that you have, but—"

"Then why would I start now? Just because I'm a father doesn't make me any less concerned for your welfare, Joselito. You're my brother, my father's blood and my closest friend. I beg you, don't distrust me."

Joe shook his head. "Go back and get me some more money, Miguelito," he said softly. "I *must* have it."

"Joselito, listen to me—"

"Look," Joe said in sudden anger, "I'm not fooling around! You ride out with more money and I'll meet you here the same time tomorrow."

"But that's foolhardy. The road will be filled with week-day travelers."

"All right then, I'll ride into town tonight and come to the back of the store. I'll be there right at midnight."

"It would be very dangerous for both of us if you were to be seen."

"Ah, you don't want me to come," Joe said suspiciously. "You're hiding something."

"Joselito, I'm hiding nothing."

"We'll see. I've ridden a hundred and fifty miles in the last two days. I won't go back without the supplies bought for border shipment," Joe promised firmly.

"Then it can't be true."

"What?"

"That you're heading a band of rustlers."

"Do you believe that lie?" Joe demanded angrily.

"Well, you wouldn't need money so desperately if it were true."

"I may have to join those desperadoes yet and be the thief Hearn thinks me. Unless you help."

Michael sighed, reluctant but committed to ease Joe's anxiety. The modest nest egg he had in the safe was even less than the amount he had already brought for Joe. Parting with it would force him to curtail the store's operation drastically. But if Joe really needed the money, and it was evident that he did, then he really had no choice but to hand it over to his brother. Joe was headstrong, quick to explode, impetuous, but never selfish. The need must exist.

"All right, all right," he said, "I don't know how you can sneak into town tonight without being seen, but—"

"I'll manage. I'm not part Indian for nothing."

"You better wait here until then."

Joe nodded. "Nearby, anyway."

"I'm shocked by the situation in Antelope Valley. Why didn't you get word to me sooner?"

"You were just about the last resort besides the desperadoes. And then Luz. You know how proud she is. She thinks God will solve all her problems by miracles. It just doesn't happen."

"I'd forgotten how religious she is. Well, Beth will be mighty pleased to see you again. And you'll meet little Nate."

"Yes, sure," Joe said, "I'll look forward to seeing them."

"Well, I'd better go. I don't want to be caught riding into town just as the churches are letting out. I usually don't go anywhere Sunday morning."

Joe stepped forward and embraced Michael.

"I hate being a beggar, dear brother, but I don't have any choice."

"We'll survive."

"You're not angry with me?"

"I'm angry at Hearn for what he is, and for keeping you away."

"Except for being separated from you, I'm beginning to like it a lot up at Rancho Cielo. Open sky, silence—another world I'd forgotten the past ten years."

"Rancho *what*, did you say?"

"Cielo—Spanish for sky. My new name for it."

"Very apt, I like it. But you're pretty much alone up there, except for Luz."

"Not a chance. There's a whole village around us. You know, Miguelito, I may just pick me a wife soon and raise a family. About time, Luz thinks. She's anxious for grandchildren to spoil." Joe laughed. "Me as a father. What a picture!"

"You settle into it one day and then wonder why you didn't do it sooner," Michael said.

"Well, I'm thinking about it generally. Let's go."

"Me first," Michael said, "nobody's looking for me," and moved into the lead position.

Passing out of the twisting defile, the brothers emerged single file onto the slope of the tawny, oak-dotted hillside.

Joe raised his head to make a rapid scan of the area above them by instinct as Michael threw the reins over his mount's neck. Beside him, Joe finished inspecting the landscape and turned to do the same, then stopped, suddenly frozen in his tracks by some incongruity he had missed at first.

Turning, his eye paused at the figure of a man crouched motionless against the trunk of a massive oak. Behind the tree stood a horse, flicking its tail. Both figures were in shadow. The man was sighting down the barrel of his raised rifle.

"Get down!" Joe shouted at Michael as he threw himself flat on the ground.

A shot rang out. Michael fell with a groan.

Joe scrambled to his knees and fired a shot at the figure beneath the tree as the man mounted his horse and raced off up the hill, over it and out of sight.

Joe's eyesight was as keen as a hunting animal's and there was no doubt in his mind who their assailant was. It was the rancher, George Hearn. Somehow Hearn had managed to track Michael from town undetected, discovered their rendezvous and settled down to wait his time. The shot, Joe knew, was meant for him, not for Michael behind him.

Joe knelt beside Michael who had fallen on his back. He didn't need to feel Michael's pulse to confirm that his brother was dead. The round, nearly bloodless hole in Michael's left temple told him all he needed to know. He had lost the human being who meant the most in life to him.

Throwing himself across Michael's inert form he started to cry in great, wrenching sobs. When he had wept himself dry he began to lay his strategy.

His first act was to carry Michael's body back into the lookout shelter. With a short prospector's spade from his pack he dug a rectangle in the soft sandy soil between the boulders. He wrapped Michael's body in a blanket, laid him in the shallow trench and covered him with earth. It wasn't the way he wanted to bury his brother, but the shelter would have to do as a gravesite for the time being.

Then, keeping the focus of his fury on George Hearn, Joe sat down to brood until dark. As dusk settled, he transferred Michael's guns to his own horse, tied Michael's mount to a lead line and set out for a hilltop vantage point he knew that lay east of the pueblo.

When he reached the prominence of hills that was his destination, he untied Michael's mare, pointed her in the direction of Los Angeles, slapped her sharply on the buttocks and sent her loping down the hill toward the lights of town. She was docile and true and would find her way to the shed behind Michael's and Beth's store. He tried not to dwell on the thought of Beth's anguish when she found the horse in the alley by the shed. He would deal with that element later.

From the hills, Joe took a route to the western flatlands and rode two miles through the night until he sighted the lights of George Hearn's ranch ahead of him. In the long, low ranch house a single light burned from a window; the bunkhouse was ablaze with light.

Joe tethered his horse to a tree about five hundred yards from the main entrance to the ranch house, approaching the low building from behind. He assumed that either Hearn or his henchmen, or both, could easily be waiting for him to appear, and they wouldn't hesitate to kill him on sight. With Michael dead, Hearn would be anxious to get rid of him too, silence the one person who could pin a murder on him, so he could blame Michael's death on Joe. Say he heard an argument between them, and Joe shot his brother—something like that.

Creeping forward slowly and with the great stealth he had learned as a boy from the Pai Pai at Antelope Valley, Joe moved toward the ranch house. His life depended upon total concentration; he moved with the tense skill of a mountain lion tracking prey.

Joe moved toward the lighted window. The oil lamp threw a square of light across the open window sill onto the front porch. Curtains moved gently in the breeze. The open window was now so close that he could see into the room; it was unoccupied, which meant that someone was waiting for him outside, expecting him to show his silhouette in front of the window.

Joe crouched silently beside a bush in the yard for several minutes, using his powerful instinctual training as a sensor to seek out the palpable presence of the enemy, one or more.

Once he heard boisterous laughter from the bunkhouse, a hundred feet or more from the house. Card games would be going on, or tall stories were being told. Anyway, this was an encouraging sign. It probably meant that Hearn was waiting for him alone, and close to the house.

Presently he heard a slight rustling movement not twenty feet away from him, and a soft clearing of some- one's throat, a man's. The movement came again, this time just below the level of the porch, well out of range of the open window.

Joe's entire body became one tense, coiled spring. He gripped his horsehair riding crop in both hands so that it could act as a lethal weapon. The sound came again, settling in the new spot. By straining himself, Joe could now see that a figure was hunched up by the porch, lean- ing against the porch's edge with one shoulder, placing the man's back to Joe.

Joe crept slowly around the bush until he was no more than ten feet behind the figure. Inch by inch he moved closer, until he could hear the man breathe. Joe could smell a sour whisky smell, and he knew Hearn was a heavy drinker. Then he saw the man's bulk clearly, and his head, bullet-shaped like Hearn's. He had found the ob- ject of his quest, he thought with deep satisfaction. Now only the act of retribution remained, and he vowed to succeed—even if he died in the process.

Silently he began a slow count of twenty backwards, knowing that he would have to move with lightning speed once the count was done, and that he would only have one chance, for Hearn would be in possession of at least one gun.

Twenty, nineteen, eighteen, on down to one . . .

At the count of one, Joe sprang forward. Using his crop as a garrote, he threw it over his victim's head, breaking his windpipe and strangling him. He held the garrote with savage force until his victim ceased to struggle. Then he released the body so that it slumped across the porch, fell forward until its features were faintly illuminated by the lamplight flowing over the window sill.

The man was Hearn all right, still clutching a gun in his right hand.

Joe took the weapon, stuck it into his belt, and crept away from the porch. He returned cautiously to his horse, secure in the knowledge that he would have time to do whatever else must be done before someone sounded the alarm. Even if there were other sentinels posted about, Joe had crept in and out of enemy territory without detection, he thought proudly. As for Hearn's death, it was a justified execution, nothing more. He harbored no remorse for the deed.

Joe walked his horse away from the Bar "H" Ranch. At a safe distance he mounted and rode at a gallop through the night toward the pueblo of Los Angeles.

Michael's mare was in the shed stall behind the store. Beth would be waiting for him, he knew, and knocked softly at the back door.

"Come in," Beth called out.

Joe entered to find the muzzle of a rifle pointed at his chest, Beth's finger on the trigger.

"Wait a minute!" He held up his hands and Beth motioned him into a chair. She was pale, her eyes red.

"Michael's dead, isn't he?" she said.

"Beth, I—let me explain."

"You make one wrong move and I'll kill you," Beth warned him. "Like you killed Michael."

"I didn't kill Miguelito, I swear. Would I be here if I had?"

"You're lying!" Beth said sharply. "You had an argument with Michael. You killed him, then sent his mare home. Now you've come for the money, is that it?"

She was hysterical, of course, Joe realized. Anything he said would only make her that much more trigger-happy. He would go slowly.

"Beth," he said gently, "let me tell you what happened, please. Michael met me as arranged at our agreed upon rendezvous point." He went on to explain in detail about their meeting. "And when we came out of the shelter, someone was waiting for us."

"Who was it?" Beth demanded, the rifle still trained on Joe's chest.

"George Hearn."

"Hearn?" Beth slowly lowered the rifle.

Joe nodded. "I don't know how he discovered about our tryst, but he did. Miguelito must have been seen leaving town in the early morning hours. Anyway, Hearn was aiming for me but he hit Miguelito instead. He killed him with one shot and took off when he saw what he'd done." Joe told her about Michael's burial among the boulders, of his trip to the ranch house after dark, sparing her the grisly details of Hearn's death.

"I don't have much time to get away," he said. "The first place Hearn's men will look when they find him dead will be here at the store. If you can give me the money Michael promised I'll leave."

"What am I to do here alone?" Beth said. "Think of that. If it weren't for you, Michael would be alive right now."

"We took every precaution we could."

"Oh, I don't doubt that," Beth retorted bitterly. "But you're bad luck, Joe. I'm sure you always have been. Look, you can have the money. It isn't much. I'll manage somehow, since you won't be any help to me. Go to your ranch in Baja, forget about us, little Nate and me. I have Garth Winslow to help with the store; he's loyal. And old Pedro. They won't let me down."

She stood the rifle against the wall and went into the other room to open the safe, feeling numb and used and past weeping. She brought the money to Joe. As Michael had told him, he saw that it wasn't much.

Embarrassed, he protested, "I can't take it."

"Why not? Michael promised it to you. It's what you came for."

"I—I can't take the bread from your mouths," Joe replied. "And I can't go away knowing that you aren't properly cared for."

"We'll be all right," Beth assured him. "Something will happen. I can't believe God will simply desert us."

"You could go back to New York," Joe suggested.

Beth stared at him as if he were some kind of idiot.

"Back to New York?" she echoed in surprise. "I'll never go back to New York. The West is my home now. I'll get a job working as a governess in San Francisco, or even as a maid. Anything rather than go East. I burned that bridge when I eloped with Michael."

"A woman alone in this pueblo is a target," Joe pointed out. "It's rough."

"Where else would I go? A solitary, defenseless woman with a baby? I couldn't even work in a brothel with a child around my neck."

"I don't want to hear you talk that way," Joe said sharply. "There's a sensible solution."

"It can't be any good without money."

"Maybe there's a way, if you can trust me. I'll take you to Rancho Cielo, my home in Antelope Valley. You'll be perfectly safe there with my mother."

Beth regarded him without comment, waiting for him to continue.

"I didn't kill Miguelito. You know that. I loved him, as you did. He was the most important person in my life."

"In mine too," Beth said. "I know how Michael felt about you. He told me many times."

Tears suddenly welled up in Beth's eyes. She resisted giving way to the sobs that were almost ready to claim her. She sighed deeply and wiped her wet cheeks with her fingers.

"I'm not at all sorry that son of a bitch Hearn's dead," Joe said.

"At least he left no children." Beth glanced at the crib where little Nate lay sleeping peacefully. He hadn't even awakened with Joe's arrival.

"Oh God, what am I to do?" Beth moaned aloud in a choked voice. "What in God's name will happen to me?"

"As I said, you can come with me to Rancho Cielo," Joe told her. "But time's getting short."

Beth looked thoughtfully at her brother-in-law. It was impossible to remain here in Los Angeles without Michael. She couldn't manage alone. There would be an investigation into Michael's death, Hearn's death. She would be questioned, intimidated, perhaps even ostracized, certainly at least put in a tenuous position that would make staying on uncomfortable. If Garth Winslow took over the store as he'd once suggested when she and Michael talked of going East with a caravan last year, then she would receive some revenue. Not a lot, but some. And she would be gone from Los Angeles, which would remind her constantly of her aloneness. Going with Joe, however, would only be temporary. The wilderness of Baja California was the last place she had expected to go, but at present she couldn't see that she had any choice but to accept Joe's offer.

"All right," she said quickly, "I'll come with you now. I won't say for how long. Later Garth can send along our possessions with Pedro."

"At least to the border," Joe said. "Creek and his men will pick them up at our regular station. How soon can you be ready?"

"It won't be long. I've got to pack and write a note to Garth."

"Hurry, please," Joe urged her. "Every minute we stay here puts us that much closer to the discovery of Hearn's body."

"I'll be quick," Beth said, and Joe watched her disappear into the other room and shut the door behind her.

He stood up and paced the room nervously, alert with one ear to the sound of Beth moving about in the next room, the other ear strained for any odd noise out by the shed in the alley. He knew he was crazy to risk being caught here. He would certainly be shot on sight, or at the least strung up at the edge of town. And anything could happen to Beth with the gang of rapacious human wolves that hung around Los Angeles, drifting through on their way to the gold fields up north. It was a rough frontier town, whether Beth thought so or not. Her shield had been Michael; now he would have to play the role. He wasn't even sure he wanted the responsibility.

Joe had many unanswered questions about this seemingly fragile, beautiful young woman who had impetuously married his older brother. Raised in great luxury, spoiled and overprotected, she had crossed the plains and desert with Michael and hadn't complained. In the store she'd worked side by side with him, and borne him a healthy son. Joe had only seen Beth twice in his life—at Santa Fe and now in Los Angeles. He knew nothing about her. She might hate it in the isolation of the Mexican sierra, and then what did he do with her? Well, for the moment he would do whatever he could; she was his responsibility. What concerned him as much as getting away from the pueblo instantly was how his mother, Luz, would react to Beth's arrival. Two such strong-minded women in the same rancho might pose problems, but this was a worry he hadn't come to yet. Where Michael used to plan his every move in advance, Joe seldom cared to look very far ahead, suiting intuition to the event.

Exactly ten minutes from the time she went into the bedroom, Beth emerged. She had changed into one of her prairie costumes. She was carrying a roll of clothes, and a sling in which to carry Nate. She wore a bonnet and a cape.

"I'm ready," she said, and bent down to pick up Nate, who didn't waken.

"I can take the boy," Joe said.

"Oh no," Beth replied, "he's my responsibility."

"We have a chancy ride ahead of us," Joe said. "I want you to know the risk. You could stay here, let Garth take the man's burden. Nate would be safe."

"I told you, there's nothing here for me any longer."

Beth set a folded note against the sugar bowl on the kitchen table. As she walked to the door with Nate he opened his eyes, smiled at her, yawned, and promptly went to sleep again.

Once Joe had made certain that all was peaceful outside, he led the two horses from the shed into the alley. He helped Beth to mount, handed up Nate, then mounted his own horse and led them by the most circuitous route possible, avoiding the Plaza, to the edge of the pueblo. So far, so good.

10

IT was midnight by the time Joe and Beth neared the boulder lookout where Joe had buried Michael. At first Joe hadn't intended to take Beth at all near the shelter. But as he made one of his regular pauses in their journey in order to attend for the signs of possible pursuit, he heard distant hoofbeats across the valley, too faint for Beth to note. While he could not distinguish their number, their approach was swift, he was certain.

"What is it?" Beth asked tensely, suddenly afraid from the alertness of Joe's posture as he bent forward in his saddle.

"A party from town. I can't tell how many."

"What will we do? If they're Hearn's men, they'll kill us."

"If we can make it to the shelter safely we'll be all right," Joe assured her.

"Is it close?"

"Not too far. Come."

Joe headed briskly east and away from the wagon road, toward the low hills that were darkly visible against the starry nighttime sky and a slender new moon. Climbing up the flank of the highest hill, they reached the massive boulder lookout in a few minutes, but not a moment too soon. Just as they gained the shelter, a party of several horsemen appeared on the road below them, riding rapidly south toward the border, hooves beating a steady tattoo on the hardpan of the roadbed.

Joe and Beth watched them race along in silence. When they had disappeared behind a hill Joe said, "We better stay here tonight. It's too risky to go on."

"I understand," Beth agreed, and Joe led the horses inside the ring of grey boulders. He made Beth and Nate as comfortable as possible under the circumstances, then stretched out near Michael's grave with his saddlebag as a pillow and went to sleep at once. They were as protected here as could be, was Joe's last waking thought. By morning their pursuers—or his, more accurately— would have taken the well-marked wagon trail that lay on the other side of the hill back to Los Angeles, believing that Joe had escaped them. And so he would in the morning, he promised himself, departing at dawn.

Half an hour after falling asleep, Joe was abruptly awakened by a muted sound. It was close by and similar to the mourning of wild doves which he quickly translated into Beth's muffled weeping a yard or so away from him.

He sat up. "Are you all right?" he asked in a clear whisper.

He received no answer, but the soft weeping abated immediately. He understood Beth's shy silence, realizing she had been overheard. She was refusing to let anyone share her grief at this point. Instead she would portion it out gradually, bit by bit, in private, poignant moments of sorrow. One day perhaps she'd feel like sharing her bereavement with him, Joe reflected, but she would have to choose her own time. He went back to sleep.

An hour before dawn Joe awakened again. This time Beth sat up when he did as they both heard approaching horses, the voices of male riders drifting up from below. Once little Nate gurgled, but fortunately the sound was brief and did not carry beyond the lookout. In a few minutes the party rode on, but Joe didn't sleep again until it was time to break camp and be on their way.

He crept out in the lightening greyness to scout the landscape. After convincing himself that it was safe, he led the horses from the lookout and they were on their way again.

They turned deep inland for safety, skirting mountains, riding through rocky defiles where few riders except Indians ever went, and across open range land that had been parceled out over a century earlier by the old Spanish land grants. After pausing in a wilderness of scrub oak for a two-hour siesta, and a stop at a cool spring hidden deep in a narrow canyon, they pushed on again in the late afternoon.

Little Nate in his papoose sling on Beth's back was bearing up well under the constant movement of travel. Joe offered to carry the boy for a while, but Beth was firm about her responsibility.

"I carried him for nine months," Beth said, "so the least I can do is carry him to safety now." She continued to breast-feed Nate, augmenting this with a bland porridge she cooked over the fire Joe made for her.

By sunset they reached a hacienda set in a bowl of tawny hills, whitewashed and imposing. Beth could hardly believe her eyes.

"It's like a mirage, way out here in the wilderness," she exclaimed. "Who owns it?"

"The Romero family," Joe said. "Raul Romero is my childhood friend. Our mothers knew each other. The Romeros will give us shelter, and protect us, if necessary. The men who are looking for me won't come this far."

"I don't want to be a bother," Beth said, "but it would be wonderful to sleep in a bed tonight."

"You will," Joe assured her. "The Romero hacienda will be your home. These are warm and generous people, much more so than any gringos. You'll see."

The atmosphere at the Romero table that night was festive and friendly. Beth and the baby were pampered by all. The fact that Joe had appeared was enough for Raul to break out his finest brandy.

Señora Romero was a silver-haired matron of great size and heart. In her limited English she questioned Beth about New York all through the long dinner of roast kid and wild fowl, fascinated by a city she had built up in her vivid and naive imagination into a fairy tale metropolis. Beth hadn't the heart to disillusion her gentle hostess, so she did her best to reinforce the señora's fantasies.

By ten o'clock, Señora Romero and Beth made polite excuses and left the table to the men: Joe, Raul, a younger brother named Salvador, and the ranch foreman, Eduardo, a distinguished old vaquero. The patriarch Romero was long-dead.

Later, in the study that Raul Romero used as an office, Joe and Raul fell into the easy intimacy that had existed between them since boyhood, where any question could be asked in Spanish and a reasonable answer expected, where no one took offense at the sometimes outrageous thoughts exchanged. Behind the banter there often lay serious ideas.

"So, you have brought Miguelito's woman with you," Raul said. "She is very beautiful."

"Miguelito thought so."

Raul shook his head angrily. "It was a senseless killing."

"And avenged."

"Yes," Raul said, "these acts are sometimes necessary. You'll take her to Rancho Cielo. What then?"

"I don't know. She couldn't remain behind in Los Angeles. And if she had, if anything happened to her I'd have to answer to Miguelito in heaven."

"She is lovely. There are not many fair-haired women in this southern country."

"She's a strong woman," Joe said. "She can work like a man, she's not afraid of it."

"She could marry down here," Raul declared.

Joe looked at him critically. "Are you entertaining any such idea?" he asked.

"Oh no, not at all. I was thinking of my cousin in San Francisco. It would be a good match."

"Beth's not Spanish," Joe reminded Raul. "She will have to decide in the future at her own pace what she wants to do with the rest of her life."

"From what you've said, I gather she comes from a wealthy family. If she doesn't want to stay in California, we could perhaps make up a purse and send her back to her family in New York."

"She won't go back," Joe said. "You don't know this, but she ran away from her parents' home against their wishes to marry Miguelito at sea."

"Mother of God!" Raul exclaimed in a shocked voice. "Not even married in church and against the desire of her family. That doesn't even make her union with Miguelito legitimate."

"Yes, some would think that way."

"Why, she's no better than—"

Joe cut Raul short. "She's no better and no worse than anyone else, Raul, ourselves included. I don't know her well, but I do know she's a fine woman."

"I meant no offense."

"You haven't made one."

"Well, she will certainly die of boredom at Antelope Valley," Raul declared.

"It's a place of great peace and close to the sky," Joe said so ardently that Raul decided to drop the subject. Joe, however, pursued it.

"Beth will have to suffer through long days at Rancho Cielo for a time," he said. "We haven't any money—you know how things are this year."

"They needn't be so bleak, Miguelito. Your money problems can be swiftly solved. A remedy is at hand."

"What remedy?" Joe asked, knowing full well what Raul was about to suggest.

"You killed a gringo the night before last."

"He deserved it."

"Beside the point. If there was a price on your head before—for deeds you never committed—think what the bounty will be now."

"At least you won't turn me in to the gringo cutthroats who mean to strip us of everything."

"You talk as if you're one of us," Raul said, with intent to provoke.

"I may be only half Spanish and Indian mixed, the other half Americano, but you know where my heart lies."

"Then you must declare yourself. I wouldn't turn you over to anyone, Joselito. I know that whatever you did, you did it for honor. Now you must reap the benefits of being an outlaw."

Joe grinned at Raul. "The persuasion is obvious, Raul. I know your turn of mind."

Raul shook his head soberly. "I am not being playful, I've put aside childish games. The war is over. While it went on, as you know, we were much put upon. The Americanos landed at Ensenada, La Paz, at Mulege. For a time it appeared that Baja as well as Alta California would be transferred totally to the United States. But the Spanish who now call themselves Mexicans put up a heroic struggle and drove off the American troops."

"Only because the Americans wished not to fight anymore," Joe said. "What's your point?"

"My point is, we've been robbed."

"Not exactly, Raul. You still have your one hundred thousand acres of rocky land, and beyond that, your cousin's property extends to the Mexican border, making the two holdings a virtual corridor to Baja, almost down to Rancho Cielo."

Raul snapped his fingers. "You have it exactly!" He poured Joe another fiery Spanish brandy. "You see what I'm driving at."

"I wonder if I want to see," Joe said doubtfully, raising his glass to Raul. "I also think I don't have much choice but to look and consider. To your health!"

"You've been stubborn too long. I'm relieved at your decision."

"It's not yet a decision," Joe pointed out.

"See how well we live, through drought, war and famine. Consider that, amigo."

Joe nodded. "Yes. A whole lot better than we do up at Rancho Cielo."

"That's precisely my point. You could live as we do in spite of crop failure. The prizes are there for the taking—for those who possess stealth and courage."

"Become a desperado? Someone who robs stage coaches and shoots passengers? Never. It's suicide. One can't hold the trump card each time out on the highway. I'm surprised you'd even mention such a thing. I'll leave that capricious life to men like this Joaquin Murrieta we hear so much about. It's said he's giving the Americanos a lot of trouble in the gold fields of the north."

"There's a lot to be said for Murrieta," Raul said. "He has guts. He takes what he wants."

"He'll have a short life, wait and see. One day the U.S. government will catch up with him and shoot him dead on sight."

"There's always that, of course. So why not work differently? As the Americanos say, what have you got to lose. Come into business with me," Raul urged Joe. "I need you."

"To join you in cattle rustling?"

"Now that you've put it so plainly, yes."

"I can't, Raul."

"Why not?"

"There may be a price on my head, but I'm innocent of crimes and I'll stay that way."

"High principles are all very well when you have money and independence. You have neither. You're a hunted man."

"No one saw me take care of Hearn. You and Beth are the only people who know I was there."

"All the same, you'll be marked from now on." Raul sighed, pouring out two more brandies. "Well, if you won't go rustling with me you can always change your name and work for the Californios. Besides good money, you'll be doing a patriot's job."

"How is that?"

"Ever hear of a man named William Walker?"

"No. Is he Americano?"

"More than an ordinary one. He's a young fanatic now recruiting Americano volunteers to organize a military expedition that intends to land at La Paz and capture Baja California, as Hernán Cortés did in 1535."

"You must be mad to think I'd join an army like that. What makes you think I'd be interested?"

"You're an Americano, aren't you?"

"By accident of birth only," said Joe.

"All right then, join our side. There's as much money in Mexico for the purpose of defending Baja as there is in San Francisco to launch Walker's proposed conquest," Raul explained. "Our cause has no millionaire like Cornelius Vanderbilt involved, but we do have many prominent citizens all through Mexico who'll come to our rescue with funds. You could be valuable there."

"I don't savor the idea of being shot for my political beliefs," Joe said. "Let Walker have his war. It will fail. No one has ever conquered Baja, and no one ever will. Remember, the Jesuits came after Cortés, in 1697. They failed. The Franciscans tried and moved on. Would-be conquerors come and go. There's no get-rich-quick formula in Baja. Like always, we are just bull-throwing, as the Americanos say, to stay alive."

"Then what do you propose to do with your life?" Raul demanded.

Joe had made up his mind when they arrived at the hacienda that he would be open to any discussion Raul projected. Even before their post-prandial drinks he had determined to go along with the best offer Raul would make him. He really had no choice. He couldn't go anywhere but out of Baja and Alta California on his own and survive. He needed to work with an organized group of men, and of course that meant something illegal, dangerous, and ultimately liable to be fatal. He had, however, prepared himself for the latter possibility. He didn't want his mother, Beth, little Nate, the people of Antelope Valley to go hungry. And there was really only one way to go: Raul's way.

"What will I do with my life?" Joe said with an elaborate show of nonchalance. "First of all, set up my order with your principals for seeds and supplies for Rancho Cielo. I have the money, don't worry. Then travel on to Baja with Beth, do the best I can there for my mother and the villagers until new crops are planted and Beth is settled in."

"And then, amigo?"

"Join you, Raul, in whatever you think is most profitable."

"You really mean it?" Raul asked in pleased surprise.

"Of course I mean it. You know me. When I say it you can count on it."

"Now you're finally talking sense! I'm delighted."

"I don't know whether I'm delighted or not with the way life must go, Raul, but I must accept what comes to me from friends and enemies alike. It's my fate."

"But you're also willing to nudge fate a little, like I am, eh? Well, partner, we are now a team. I shall ride up with the supplies when they come down and we'll discuss our future at Rancho Cielo. Is that agreed?"

"Agreed," said Joe, and the pact was made. They spent until midnight drinking brandy and discussing what the future held in store.

BAJA CALIFORNIA:
THE HIGH COUNTRY

11

THE journey from the Romero estate to Antelope Valley took five days of steady riding. All that time, Joe and Beth saw no other human beings. They traveled well off the beaten track to avoid any Americanos who might be around, even though they were deep into the Spanish land grant territory held by Raul Romero's cousin. This vast area was in a wild state, none of it having ever been explored or cultivated, merely held, since it was low, arid desert and practically worthless for agriculture.

Gradually the plains over which they rode, midway between what is now Tijuana in the West and Mexicali in the East, began to give way to sharp, jagged hills, deep ravines and narrow, stony defiles of imposing height. Due to the landscape's irregularity, they made slow progress. Not only did the terrain grow more mountainous with each mile gained, but the ground cover changed dramatically as well. Cardon, the giant of all cacti, rose impressively tall above the candelabra cactus in the lowlands. Chaparral, copal and elephant trees were supplanted by scrub pines as they climbed. Alpine flowers began to appear in the protected depths of ravines where nearly exhausted subterranean springs still flowed, if moderately, in this time of drought.

Little Nate got a daily bath at the springs, whether he liked it or not, in pure and clear water that was often cold enough to start him crying.

Joe's chosen trail followed a centuries-old Indian route that led from spring to spring. As the Franciscan fathers built their mission strongholds in California one day's travel apart, one from another, the Baja trail leading Joe and Beth and Nate toward Antelope Valley offered them an inviting place to rest amid cool surroundings and plenty of water to fill their saddle skins.

Joe's six pack mules carried basic foodstuffs such as beans, fresh bread, coffee, oranges, apples and the dried beef known as *charqui*, in the Quechua language. The slowness of the mules and Joe's concern for little Nate caused him to make the trip at a far slower pace than he would have set normally by himself. Alone he could manage nearly thirty miles a day in country that would have defeated any rider unfamiliar with its geography. Riding all day and part of the night, Joe could make it from the Romeros to Rancho Cielo in two and a half days easily. With Beth the journey took the better part of five days.

Along the trail Joe pointed out fleet antelope in the small valleys, bighorn sheep dotting the impossibly high crags of the mountains. As they crested the first high trails of the Sierra de Juarez range, Beth saw eagles soaring loftily against the pale overhead sky, and below them hawks circling.

On their second day out they passed through a brilliant red rock formation.

"We move carefully from here on," Joe cautioned Beth. "It's just about time for the red rattler to come out of winter hibernation. They're hungry and mean at this time, and extremely dangerous."

Beth didn't have to be told twice about rattlers. She'd always had a strong fear of snakes, far stronger than her fears of savage Indians or gun-toting desperadoes.

On their third day at siesta time Joe had occasion to fire his gun. He shot a feisty red rattler fully six feet long who thought the party was encroaching on its territory. The snake was as thick as a man's wrist, gliding forth swiftly from the leafy shadows of a spring to confront the trespassers. It coiled for a strike behind Joe, by his horse. Beth saw it before it shook its warning, and screamed. In seconds Joe was on his feet, rifle in hand. He blasted the snake's head off with one well-aimed shot.

This was the only time during the trip that Joe used his firearms. Since they were carrying all the food they needed—as well as other emergency supplies for the valley—there was no need to shoot mountain animals for food.

Joe picked up the snake and threw it down the hillside, pointing out that where necessary in times of famine the red rattler could make a very tasty stew. "It's much like albacore," he explained, "the tuna fish that's so plentiful along the Pacific coast."

Beth shivered at the thought of having to eat snakes. "I think I'll just stick to dried beef this trip," she said, relieved that the crisis was past.

Joe moved them on immediately, just in case they were being followed by some enemy from Los Angeles, which seemed unlikely. On the trail Joe left nothing that he could control to chance. Guns echoed down mountainsides for miles in the clear, still air of high country. Joe was understandably cautious about exposing himself, Beth and little Nate to any unnecessary danger.

A campfire was necessary each night, however, to ward off the chill that settled quickly over the dry landscape after the intense, burning spring sunshine that beat down on them all day long as they moved. Joe built his campfires of dry chaparral and deadwood strewn about the dry washes, cast there by floods in good winters.

After leaving the Romeros' warm and comfortable hospitality, Beth soon became aware of the isolation of the country through which they passed. Quite gradually she felt they were leaving the civilized world as she knew it and moving backwards in time to some prehistorical reality. It had nothing to do with the bustling, brawling newness of southern California, the burgeoning Los Angeles pueblo, or the brash pioneers who were flocking into California by the thousands in pursuit of fortunes in the gold fields.

Having spent her formative years in New York, Beth was doubly impressed by the glorious openness, the somber solitude of the high country. Rough as it was to travel, to keep little Nate comfortable, every new turn in the trail offered Beth another breathtaking view of Nature's caprices. This was indeed a land that time had forgotten, and she could not imagine it ever being populated and developed, what with its extreme aridity and its remoteness. Over eight hundred miles long and only 125 miles wide at its broadest point, Baja was a land locked in the eternal struggle between the conquerors of climate and terrain, and the conquered, those who chose to struggle against these usually insurmountable enemies.

The second night out, Joe and Beth lounged around a warm, cheery blaze of tesota, or ironwood branches. This hard, heavy wood gave off a low, intense flame that burned for hours. As Beth warmed her hands at the fire, little Nate sleeping peacefully beside her, Joe asked, "How do you like Baja?" They had passed over the border from California late that afternoon.

"It thrills and terrifies me," Beth admitted. "I'm thinking of that venomous snake, so ready to bite a human being, and how terrible that would be. And I keep looking over my shoulder for the mountain lions you say are here."

"Oh, they're here, all right," Joe assured her. "They're close to us in the night, but we'll never know. Stealth is a fine art with them. Not even the most sensitive Indian scout on the whole peninsula can outwit them with their keen sight and smell. They avoid us as much as possible and prey mostly on sheep, wild or domestic. 'Puma' is what we call them."

"I think one has to feel subservient to Nature here," Beth observed. "I will be, anyway."

"A healthy respect comes in handy," Joe replied, stimulated by her reaction. "You might come to appreciate Baja yet."

"I'm looking forward to Antelope Valley," Beth said.

A new life, away from memories of Miguelito, Joe thought to himself. "It won't disappoint you," he told Beth, "not if you accept it as it is. It can't be changed much."

Beth knew what he meant. She would have to make friends with Luz Porter, with the villagers, mostly Spanish-Indian descendants of the early Pai Pai, there long before the Jesuits arrived in Baja. And she would have an even harder task rearing little Nate. But these were all problems she considered it unwise to discuss with Joe at the moment; their time would come. Joe obviously had enough on his mind already, worrying about returning to Antelope Valley without the funds he'd hoped to bring back from Los Angeles. Most likely, the whole community was holding its breath. Beth could only guess at the burdensome responsibility of Antelope Valley, and she wouldn't add to it. She would do all she could to help, once she settled in.

Joe was in a talkative mood by the campfire, after being moody and silent on the trail all day. Now he began to ply Beth with questions about life in New York. Although she really didn't care to talk about it at this time, she felt she should try to divert his mind before sleep came.

"What can I say about New York to make you see it?" Beth mused. "New York's the absolute opposite of Baja. Whereas here everything seems a million years old, changeless, in New York everything's still growing—you can hear the sounds of change. In a few years it will leap up even higher into the sky, move much faster and spill over with people."

"I don't think I'd like it," Joe said with polite disinterest. "It doesn't sound interesting."

"It isn't, in retrospect," Beth replied, thinking that if she talked much longer in this light, seemingly carefree manner about her forsaken home she would burst into tears. She had sacrificed a richness and a security that most young women would give their all for, and in place of it she had gambled on a future with Michael. And for a time it had been exciting, bright and full of promise. Even the store in Los Angeles, the hard work she put into it, the relative monotony of the West—none of this had discouraged her.

When little Nate came, she and Michael counted him a golden nugget of a blessing. And then, tragically, it was all over. Her sweet and beloved Michael was dead and buried in a matter of hours. She was suddenly here in the wilderness with a man she scarcely knew, not even linked to any longer by marriage, and whose motives she might never be able to fathom. A man who looked and dressed foreign—Mexican, Spanish, whatever—but who talked almost like a regular American.

She made an effort to smile at Joe and said, "I shall have to write some letters when I get to Antelope Valley. Is there a way of getting them out so they'll travel East?"

"Oh yes, there's always a way."

"Good. I haven't written home before—but now that Michael is dead and there's little Nate, I must get in touch with my family."

"Letters," Joe said. He had never written a letter to anyone in his life. "To New York. . . ."

"Yes," Beth said, "to my parents, my brother Tim and a school chum, Grace Morley. I think it's time I broke the silence and let them know where I am, that I'm alive and well and have little Nate."

"You're thinking of going back?"

"No, I'm not," Beth said emphatically. "Only forward."

"That's a sane attitude."

Beth got to her feet. "Goodnight, Joe. I think I'll turn in." She picked up Nate, walked over to her bedroll, turned it back to check for snakes, then settled herself and Nate for the night.

Joe remained by the campfire until it burned down to glowing coals. Then he spread his bedroll on the ground on the opposite side of the campfire from Beth, as he had done on the other nights. He lay there wide awake, staring up at the glittering night sky, so seemingly close he felt he could almost touch it.

He wondered if he hadn't made a mistake in taking Beth away from Los Angeles, that he may have forced her to make the decision. But then, she had seemed willing enough to come with him, even though she probably could have continued on with the store by herself, managing somehow to make a living, eventually meeting some man who would want her for a wife, even with little Nate. Beth was a lovely woman, bright and quick. Joe was attracted to her; she was the only fair-haired American woman who had ever caught his eye. Of course, this didn't mean he was interested; it was just a natural response; he had other commitments. He had admired Beth, however, from the first moment he saw her on the Santa Fe trail with Miguelito. And later he had seen her, resplendently feminine, beautiful, in her hour-glass pale blue lace gown at the Governor's party, which had merely served to reinforce his strong first impression.

But enough of that, he thought. His present worry was, could Beth adjust to life at Rancho Cielo? Would she accept Luz Porter with docility, and would she be accepted by Luz? Would Luz feel that Joe was challenging her authority by bringing Beth to live at Rancho Cielo without first asking her permission?

After all, Antelope Valley was Luz's world—she owned it. Maybe he was being presumptuous in assuming that Beth could easily don the mantle of remote village life and stay with it. Privately he wasn't too confident about Beth's future at the rancho.

What really troubled him most, he decided, was how Carmen Aguilar would accept Beth. Carmen was sixteen, nearly seventeen, a full-blown woman, fiery and spoiled, brought to Rancho Cielo by her guardian uncle who took her in tow when her parents died in an influenza epidemic four years earlier at San Diego. Carmen had blossomed exquisitely from a moody adolescence into voluptuous womanhood at Rancho Cielo. Next to himself, Carmen was Luz's most treasured possession.

Well, there was nothing he could do to prevent Beth being introduced to the tightly-knit society of Antelope Valley. If he had made a mistake he would be told soon enough. But whatever would happen he couldn't waste time worrying about it. He rolled over on his side and was fast asleep in a minute.

"There it is," Joe said, barely able to suppress the proud excitement he felt at being back home. He and Beth paused at the summit of the narrow trail that led into Antelope Valley, their journey almost over.

They had climbed to the six-thousand-foot crest of the sierra in the bright, dazzling air to arrive at their destination. Now they would have to descend into the valley.

"It begins just below us, but the Rancho Cielo stretches in all directions, almost as far as the eye can see," Joe told Beth.

Antelope Valley was about four miles long and two miles wide. It was not a deep valley, nor were the peaks that enclosed it very high. They rose five to six hundred feet above the valley floor that was a gently sloping basin, its lowest, most distant portion a marshy lake in wet years. During the rainy season it was drenched regularly by a series of tropical storms moving up from the Pacific waters of Mexico and Central America. After a period of intense saturation, the lake would fill and the lush, alpine meadows would turn green and blossom. Even in times of drought, Antelope Valley was still a haven, fed by springs that at least made it habitable.

One could feel very possessive about the place, Beth realized. Its very isolation was comforting, self-containing.

"Why," Beth exclaimed, "it's absolutely beautiful! I had no idea it was so big."

"Usually in spring we have cattle grazing on the far meadow by the lake. But not this year, sorry to say."

Beth studied the village below them, a collection of low adobe structures laid out neatly around a central plaza. A whitewashed wooden cross peaked the tiled roof of a small building that was obviously a chapel, Beth noted. Behind it lay a small graveyard. In the village and beyond, people were moving about in the landscape, although they were too distant to distinguish details.

Joe pointed to an impressive house, the largest, which was removed from the village cluster.

"My mother's place," Joe said, "where I was born. Luz shares the house with Carmen."

"Carmen?" The name was new to Beth. Joe hadn't mentioned anyone by that name on the journey to Rancho Cielo.

"Carmen Aguilar," Joe said. "My fiancée."

"Why Joe, that's wonderful! You should have told me sooner," Beth said generously. In one sense, she felt much easier with Joe because of his being affianced. Along the trail to Rancho Cielo there were moments when she felt Joe's eyes on her, and feeling was more than just mere speculation. Not that she expected Joe to behave in an unseemly manner—he was much too decently bred for that. But something existed, whatever it was. Now she wouldn't have to worry, she thought, relieved.

"Carmen is a fact of life," Joe said simply. "I have a Latin-Indian attitude toward the situation. It is something that's best for me. I don't question further. If it was bad, I'd know. It's good."

Beth wasn't sure she understood what Joe meant, but she had all the time in the world ahead of her to sort it out. Now her heart filled with the excitement of anticipation, she rode behind Joe, little Nate strapped to her back, down the mountain trail to meet her immediate destiny. She wasn't fearful nor was she particularly hopeful. What she kept strongly in mind was that the worst of life had already happened with Michael's death. There would be a long, reflective time in which she would learn and become wise. At least she was hoping this would happen.

And after that, who could say? She would accept what seemed right, whatever it was.

Joe and Beth were spotted the moment they appeared at the summit approach to the valley. Creek came running to Luz Porter's house with the news that Joe and a companion were entering the valley.

Luz came out of the house, trained her field telescope on the slope and was surprised to see a woman riding behind Joe. The woman had a baby strapped to her back, in papoose style. The strangest thing was that the woman was obviously a gringa, her fairness plainly visible.

"Carmen!" Luz called into the house. "Joselito is here!"

Carmen strolled onto the covered porch and leaned against a post. She was indeed voluptuous beyond her years. She had magnificent black hair; her eyes had the depth of obsidian, her skin was creamy beige. Carmen moved with a lazy walk, excited by the prospect of Joe's return but unwilling to display her enthusiasm. There had been little to do at Rancho Cielo with Joe gone, she resented every day of his absence and refused to articulate her delight over his return. Let him think she hadn't missed him.

Carmen squinted up at the trail.

"Who is with him?"

Wordlessly, Luz handed the telescope to Carmen.

"A woman," Carmen said, "he's brought a woman. An American woman! Who could it be, Mama Luz?"

"I have no idea," Luz replied, thinking that Joe would never have the gall to bring home an American bride, or even a female consort he may have found somewhere, knowing the reception he would get. The only other person this could possibly be was Michael's wife and child, and if it were then something grave had happened to Michael.

The villagers began gathering in the plaza, ready to welcome Joe upon his return. Joe and Beth left the trail and crossed the floor of the valley, riding slowly toward Luz's house.

Creek came up to Joe, held his horse as Joe dismounted and helped Beth from the saddle.

"I'm afraid," Beth said in a whisper, pinched lines made her doubtful expression into a frown.

"Don't be," Joe said, "they'll love you. Smile! You come out sunshine when you smile!"

Quick to respond, Beth put on her most amiable mask and walked quickly forward with Joe to be presented to a small, wiry woman with extremely dark skin, regular features, and silver hair that was parted in the middle and brought back into a tight chignon. These features were absorbed in a moment, along with the black shroud of a dress that Luz wore. What intrigued Beth most was Luz's penetrating gaze, the deep, dark eyes probing to her very soul. For a moment she was intimidated, but only a moment. Luz suddenly smiled at her, with such an intensity of welcoming warmth that she felt embraced by the emotion.

"Welcome to Rancho Cielo," Luz said in careful, accented English.

She stepped down from the porch and advanced toward Beth, holding out her two hands to her, then drawing Beth down and kissing her on both cheeks. Almost in the same gesture Luz reached around to see little Nate.

"He's a handsome child," she observed. "He looks like his father."

Then Beth found herself embracing Carmen, who had been studying her every movement with those enormous jet-black eyes, drinking her in.

"His father—" Beth began and couldn't finish. Tears welled up in her eyes, spilled down her fair cheeks.

No one seemed to know what to do in this awkward, unguarded moment, except Carmen, who stepped forward and took Beth's hand, as Luz relieved her of little Nate.

"Come," Carmen said in Spanish.

Beth understood that much and allowed herself to be led into the house, to a simple room with a narrow bed, a cross on the wall above it, a spread of Indian design gracing the bed. An Indian rug covered most of the brick floor.

Carmen threw open a window. "There," she said, "you are at home!" and left smiling.

Beth closed the bedroom door, threw herself across the bed and cried herself out. She had entered a world that might well be the extent of her future, with only Nate and the warmth of these well-meaning strangers to support her. The terrible strain of crossing over into alien territory had been too much for her. But only this once would she collapse in a flood of tears, she promised herself. From here on in she would go dry-eyed to her grave. She had made her couch among thorns and she would lie upon it without complaint. But she would honor sorrow in her own way.

Dinner that night was well-served by two silent, watchful-eyed Indian village women padding about barefooted on the tiled dining room floor. The dinner was simple—saffron rice, refried beans, flautas with wild fowl, and a simple brown sugar flan for dessert. There was a special treat of meat as the main dish. Two village Indians had gone out onto the range that afternoon looking for wild game. Antelope and bighorn sheep, normally shy and fleet, were already coming down to the valley for water and forage, since the rocky higher country yielded nothing for them in the drought. The Indians managed to chase two antelope into a cul-de-sac, killing them with one shot each. Though thin, they were still tasty when basted with herbs and roasted like kid on a huge spit in the cookhouse.

Luz donned her best black lace dress for the occasion, and a simple gold cross on a heavy chain for ornamentation. Carmen was dressed in a soft pink shift that clung to her generous figure, admired repeatedly across the table by Joe. Beth wore a dark, plain dress, one of three she had brought along, against which her silver cross stood out bright and bold.

Inspecting the pendant several times during dinner, Luz finally said, "You aren't Catholic, are you?"

"No," Beth replied. "At the milder end of the Protestant church, I'm afraid. My parents were Presbyterian, although not devout church-goers. I was sent to Sunday school, but my father allowed me and my brother to make up our minds about attending church. My parents felt that supporting your church financially was the important thing. We were Sunday Christians; church wasn't a way of life. If you gave generously you were allowed the sin of omission."

Luz looked mystified instead of shocked.

"But you're a believer," she pointed out. "You wear a cross."

"It was a wedding present from a Catholic lady I met in New Orleans during my honeymoon with Michael," Beth explained. "She gave it to me to wear as a talisman."

"It should be blessed," Luz declared.

"Well, perhaps," Beth said easily. "She didn't expect me to respond to it as a Catholic would—or so I feel."

"The Church is a great comfort," Luz said. "When it's possible we invite a traveling priest to come to Rancho Cielo and spend some time with us. It is a great joy to hold Mass in the chapel. There are times when I could not have survived without prayer," Luz added, and crossed herself, Carmen following her example.

"Ah yes, prayer," Beth murmured reverently, not knowing what else to do.

Carmen remained watchfully intent at the table as the two women talked. She was trying with all her concentration to glean some sense from the conversation with her little knowledge of English. Every so often she would utter soft and rapid phrases to Luz, who replied succinctly to all her questions without glancing at her.

The conversation drifted, as Beth knew it inevitably would, to her life in New York. Beth carefully skirted all personal comments about her family, about the schism over Michael that had caused her to elope. In fact, she revealed nothing of her relationship to Michael except the bare bones of their odyssey from New York to Los Angeles. She talked of life along the Jubilee Trail and the Santa Fe Trail, discussing the rhythms of that life, the dangers, the deprivations, but almost, she realized objectively, as if she were lecturing on a dais. She did not intend for Luz, Carmen or Joe to dig into what was her private domain. She had loved Michael and not found him wanting; she intended for his memory to remain that way. Later on, when she knew Luz better, and when she had a stronger grip on her emotions, she would be more easily able to deal with questions. She didn't wish to reveal too much about herself at any time, and she couldn't really say why; it was just the way she felt.

When the after-dinner conversation had wound down, Joe pushed his coffee aside. "If you ladies will excuse me, I'm going out for a breath of air and a smoke," he said. Luz gave him leave, he rose and left the table, off to visit Creek.

Perhaps, Beth thought, to share that bottle of brandy Raul Romero had given him. Just Creek and a few of the village men talking about Rancho Cielo matters that certainly did not concern three women: about hunting, crops in the autumn, young girls entering adolescence and the marrying age, children and their obedience training. Being with his familiars was one forceful way, Beth thought, for Joe to assert his masculinity. His understated yet worldly machismo made him the dominant male figure in the valley. With Luz ruling on domestic matters, they were a team. It was clear, Beth thought, that Luz considered her only son in two roles: that of patriarch to her matriarch, and someone she could influence, mother to son. What it boiled down to, plain and simple, was that Joe didn't have the kind of independence Beth had imagined was his at Antelope Valley.

There were many matters to sort out, she reflected in

her room that night before going to bed. She would have to consider becoming Catholic—*consider*, not necessarily become. But before this could happen, she had another plan in mind. With little Nate in a crib that Creek had brought her, taken from one of the Indian houses around the dry marsh lake, her life was tranquil, she thought sleepily, but it would never be simple in so small a place. Nonetheless, she was here, and for the moment this was to be her world. She promised herself that she would surmount all difficulties, and with a deep sigh drifted off to sleep. . . .

12

"WHAT is she like, this American woman?" Creek asked Joe in Pai Pai as he passed back the brandy bottle.

Joe shrugged. "Who can say?"

"But you traveled with her from the pueblo, you ate and slept with her," Creek insisted.

"Around a campfire," Joe said. "I didn't sleep with her."

"Ah, but she is beautiful."

"She has a complex mind. White women are not like Spanish women, or your Indian women."

"A woman is a woman. They are all the same."

Joe realized that it was useless to bring white values to Creek, just as it was impossible for him to explain how he could escort Beth and Nate from Los Angeles and not possess her. Not, of course, that he hadn't thought of it.

"Do *you* know what's in the mind of a Pai Pai maiden?" Joe asked old Creek, who had been his confidant since he was a boy, and his advisor in all Indian matters.

Creek threw back his head and laughed, showing stumps of teeth. "You are right," he acknowledged with a brief nod. "No man can know what goes on in a woman's mind. But tell me—will the señora stay with us at Rancho Cielo?"

"For the time being she will. She has no other place to go."

"But you say she comes from New York, the biggest city in the world."

"Not the biggest, the fastest-growing," Joe replied. "Anyway, she won't go back there."

"Then she will have to marry again."

"Your way of thinking, not necessarily hers."

"What about *you*?" Creek asked. "You are still unmarried."

Joe scowled at Creek, anger in his expression.

"What about *me*?" he demanded. "Don't go stirring up the bean pot, old man. There's no chief in this village but my mother, as we all know. This is her empire, she'll die here. It's only our sanctuary. We're all guests, just as Beth Porter is. Sometimes you forget that, just as I am wont to do. But we mustn't, ever. . . ."

Joe passed the brandy bottle to Creek. The old Indian was quite drunk now, dreamily so, and his rheumy old eyes were barely able to focus on the walls of Joe's single-roomed house.

Creek took a light swig and fell silent, having no comment to make on Joe's observation. It was all too true. He had accommodated himself all his life to the whims of Luz Delgado, first when her parents were alive and she was a young girl, all of them spending their summers in the high country. And later, when the Delgados were dead and Luz had married Nathan Porter, who had spent as little time as possible in the valley, and was always off somewhere with business as an excuse. Like his two sons: Michael, the elusive one, and Joselito, almost like one of his own.

Creek made no distinction between Luz, of Spanish

blood, one-quarter Indian, her mother half-Indian, her father full-blooded Spanish, and a true mestizo like Joe.

His own clear Indian heritage went back to an ancient time before the Jesuits arrived to proselytize for the Church. There had been no arranged mating of his women to the Spaniards. Even if no one else recognized it, he was of royal blood. In the old days if an Indian woman took on a conquistador, and a child came of the union, she had no choice but to become a pariah. When the pregnancy was obvious, the woman was sent away to higher ground above the valley to live in a cave known to be the hibernating refuge of red rattlers. She had the option of either starving herself to death, or of being fed but having the child taken from her at birth, and then destroyed. After that, she could return to the village if she wished, but none of the braves would ever marry her.

Today no one who called himself Mexican cared very much when Spanish and Indian blood intermingled, Creek thought, and introduced a change of subject.

"Now if the rains will come early this autumn," he said, "the seeds you brought from Romero's will make up crops. What have you decided to do with your days until planting time, Joselito? I notice a change in your eyes since your return. It wasn't there when you went away."

"You read too much into everything," Joe said briskly. "You speculate too much, old man."

"I read only what is there," Creek replied. "You are restless."

"Yes, I'm that, all right," Joe agreed. "And now that I've brought the señora—"

"You will be going away?"

"I think so."

"Have you told them at the big house?"

"No, but I shall have to."

"Do it tomorrow, before you are asked any questions."

"You sound like my father used to. Jump in, he'd tell me. Don't wait for anyone to anticipate you."

"I am only trying to sound like myself," Creek declared. "Somebody must tell you where your obligations lie, Joselito. You would rather ignore them."

"Oh, for God's sake, I'm no longer a small boy, Creek," Joe said stiffly, feeling the numbing effect of the brandy beginning to spread through his body. "You always think of me as about eight years old."

"Maybe ten," Creek conceded with a chuckle.

"I know what I'm doing," Joe said irritably.

"I hope you do," Creek said with a woeful look. "And you must do it soon . . ."

An hour later the brandy bottle was empty. Joe helped Creek to his house where he began to snore the moment his head hit the floor pallet. In the morning Creek would regret his fondness for brandy, but at the next opportunity to have a few drinks he would get drunk again. Drinking was a white man's excess that he had acquired in his old age. His other weakness was for a pipe of tobacco laced with loco weed.

Joe walked out into the chilly spring night to clear his head of the brandy fumes, admiring, as he always did, the vast, glittering dome of stars pulsing overhead. The slim moon had already set; the stars were so bright they shed an even, silvery light over the entire valley. Nowhere else, of course, were stars to be seen as clearly as at Rancho Cielo, Joe thought for perhaps the hundredth time. It was a shame he couldn't move the valley intact to the lowlands, sky and all. While the valley had rugged beauty, nothing happened in it. The lowlands, however, were always lively and lucrative.

For example, it was only ten o'clock, yet the whole valley was already fast asleep, making him feel restless, landlocked, with an impatient surge in his groin, and no place to bury it. Yet each time he attempted to live outside of Antelope Valley, sooner or later he couldn't stand it any longer and was forced to make the tedious journey back up to the oasis. Yes, that's what the valley was, a time-forgotten land sealed away from the rest of the world, a tiny universe unto itself, as simple and basic as the legend of creation. Antelope Valley had nothing to do with the current westward migration, with the invasion of California by white-faced pioneers determined to wrest the Californios' world from them. The valley was a paradise, except for one flaw, its fragile lifeline. If God failed to smile upon it for even one year, if life-giving rain did not fall, then Rancho Cielo was in serious trouble, quickly victimized. Only rain could rescue it. If the rain didn't come this fall, they would be approaching famine conditions.

As Joe mused about the situation in Antelope Valley, he found himself slowly walking toward his house, situated behind Luz's hacienda. Approaching his door, a figure detached itself from the shadow of the house and moved toward him.

For a moment he stiffened, but then a voice hissed "Joselito!" and he knew it was Carmen.

She ran to him, barefoot, clad only in a dark shift. As she embraced him he could feel her nipples hard against his chest, her pelvis thrust against him. She reached up and brought his face down to hers with both hands and kissed him passionately. After a moment he held her away. Her face was radiant in the starlight; he had forgotten how beautiful she could be.

"You shouldn't be out here," Joe said softly. "Luz might find out."

"We've met before after the village was asleep," Carmen reminded him.

But it was a year ago or more, Joe recalled, before Carmen had blossomed into stunning womanhood. Ever since then, or until a priest would consent to come to Rancho Cielo, and bind them in holy matrimony, he had stayed clear of her in compromising situations. He knew what he would do, if given the chance.

"Go back to bed, Carmen," he said, trying to be sensible. "You'll catch cold in that flimsy thing you're wearing. What is it?"

"My wedding nightgown," she replied, "I sewed and crocheted it myself. See how thin and soft it is . . ." Carmen took his hands and placed them over the hand-worked bodice so that he could feel the heart of her firm, full breasts through the lacy material.

Joe's head began to throb. He pulled his hands away.

"You shouldn't be here!" he said harshly. "It's dangerous."

"I don't care. I'm tired of all the games. I want you, Joselito. We've waited too long."

"We'll have to wait longer until the time is ripe."

"To hell with the time!" Carmen said. "*I* am ripe and waiting."

"Don't say things like that."

"Why do you always treat me as a child? You didn't treat Beth that way—I saw you at the table tonight. You were all smiling manners and courtesy."

"Beth Porter has been through a terrible ordeal. She is in bereavement here, an honored guest."

"Ha! We've had many guests before—the Romeros and others. You've never treated anyone else like that. Besides, Beth isn't a guest; she's to live with us, be part of the family."

"I'm not going to argue with you," Joe said severely. "Go back to the house and go to bed. You mustn't be seen out here in your nightgown."

"My *wedding* nightgown—" Carmen stepped lightly toward him, saying, "It doesn't matter, Joselito. I am your bride-to-be. You *must* make me yours, and tonight!"

Joe had seen this mood of Carmen's coming for a year, at least. It was Beth's arrival, of course, that had triggered an emotional outburst. Before he could protest her nearness, Carmen reached down and boldly caressed his crotch, squeezing him gently. Already excited, half-aroused, he grew to full response as Carmen continued to massage him, until he could stand it no longer.

He reached out for her and swept her into his arms, put his mouth on hers, exploring her with his tongue.

When he realized that another moment of kisses would mean the difference between control and total abandon, he pushed her roughly away, so that she stumbled backwards over a rock in her bare feet and nearly fell down.

"Why do you reject me?" she demanded hurtfully. "I haven't done anything wrong. Have you met someone else?"

"There's no one," Joe said truthfully. "If I can wait until we're married, so can you."

"I won't wait," Carmen burst out. "And if you refuse me I'll run away. I've made up my mind. I have no life at all here. I'm buried alive; I might as well be dead. You come home for a few days, then you go away again. I never know when you'll come back. It's all right for you—you can please yourself wherever you are because you're a man."

"Stop it, Carmen," Joe said patiently. "This is foolishness."

"No, it isn't, it's tragedy," she retorted. "And if you won't take me, there are plenty of men who will. I'll go to Los Angeles, even to San Francisco. I'll find me a man, a good, rich one who'll appreciate me."

Joe knew that she could find a man anywhere. Men were no problem for her; they'd always looked at her with lustful eyes. She was an undeniably luscious prize, but the fact remained that she was still a child to him. He liked her, he even loved her in the detached way that he might love a younger sister. Marriage did not have to mean love, he knew. Long ago he had accepted Luz's sensible wish for his marriage to Carmen. Although it was not necessarily his wish, he intended to honor it. Rancho Cielo was involved; it must be kept in the family at all costs. Carmen was an orphan, now a ward of Luz's; everything was in order for the marriage.

"You are talking absolute nonsense," Joe told her with growing impatience.

"It isn't nonsense," Carmen insisted. "Look—"

Suddenly she bent over and grasped the hem of her

nightgown. She lifted it up, pulled it over her head and flung it on the ground. Then she tossed her long, ebony hair and threw out her arms to him.

"Take me," she dared Joe. "Take me or I'll scream and bring Mama Luz. I swear I will, so don't tempt me."

Joe had known Carmen long enough to be certain that she would not hesitate to create such a spectacle. Joe hated scenes with women, he never seemed to know how to handle them. Anyway, he rationalized, they would be married soon enough. Why was he reluctant to take what was already his? He would be going away almost immediately, and this time he'd return in a matter of weeks with a priest to marry them—even if he had to kidnap one. So what did it matter if he eliminated a touchy situation by terminating Carmen's virginity and at the same time satisfying himself?

Without a word, he walked over and picked up Carmen's nightgown, went to Carmen, lifted her into his arms and carried her into his house. He laid her on his bunk, threw her nightgown across a chair, shut the door and undressed quickly. He lay down beside Carmen and covered her eager warmth with his body. Before common sense could take over he made urgent love to her.

Standing against the wall of the hacienda, in the shadows, Beth witnessed the closing of Joe's door. She had come outside into the silvery starlight because she couldn't sleep. Michael was heavily on her mind, and the burden of her future was nagging her. She refused to dissolve into tears, so she rose from her bed, put a shawl around her shoulders, stepped into slippers and went outside quietly, careful not to disturb the sleep of little Nate or the other members of the household.

Coincidence had brought her to view the meeting between Joe and Carmen as she came out of the house. She waited in the shadows for nearly an hour, surprised at her own curiosity, until Joe's door opened and Carmen emerged, going quickly into the big house. Beth waited a reasonable time until she was certain that Carmen had gone back to bed, then returned to her own room, unnoticed. She wasn't sure what she thought about the lovers. She was not shocked. She could understand a passion that made two people take chances. She had followed her own instincts where Michael was concerned, but the price had been high.

As she lay in bed she resolved that she would throw herself wholeheartedly into whatever opportunities offered themselves to her at Rancho Cielo. She would also write to her parents and Tim and Grace Morley as she had promised herself. As for what had happened tonight between Joe and Carmen, it was, she hoped, her first and last secret at Antelope Valley. She wasn't comfortable with mysteries or intrigue, having had little experience of them. Somehow she would work out a life for herself and little Nate that would put the resources of Rancho Cielo to good use. After all, no matter how tenuous the connection, she was already involved in her new home. She could not reject the challenge that it offered to become part of the place.

Luz Porter had no idea how to deal with Beth. She had never met anyone quite like her before. Luz's exposure to American women had been limited. She had met a few pioneer types while traveling with Nathan, and had seen loose women, girls of fortune, in Alta California. She also knew several Anglo-Saxon women who had married Spanish men and looked down on her for her mixed blood. But Beth was like none of these.

The fact that Beth had accepted her without reservation and treated her as an equal had melted the composure Luz employed as a facade to avoid being hurt. She still dealt cautiously with Beth those first few weeks, but it was soon plain to her that Beth meant only good, that she intended to help rather than take over, and that she was an asset to Rancho Cielo. In fact, Luz decided privately, Beth was a veritable fountain of industry and goodwill. No one like her had ever been seen in Antelope Valley, at least not in Luz's memory.

With Baja California in stasis from the driest season anyone could remember, activities at Rancho Cielo had slowed to a virtual crawl. Luz, however, had not expected Beth's inventiveness, her will to get things going, or her refusal to sit back and let others serve her.

On the second day of her stay at the hacienda, Beth came to Luz with her first idea.

"Mama Luz, would you object to my using the chapel as a schoolhouse?"

Luz studied Beth's friendly, open features, her gentle sage-green eyes and blondeness and saw clearly in a passing instant what Michael must have seen in her: warmth and earnest sweetness, sincerity, and a strong character.

"School?" Luz echoed. "We have no teachers here at Rancho Cielo."

"But you do. You have a teacher in me. And there should be no lack of pupils."

"How do you mean?" Luz asked guardedly.

"Well, for example, Carmen reads and writes some English, doesn't she?"

"Yes," Luz conceded, "to a degree. But Carmen is hardly the studious type."

"That's not important if she has a true desire to learn. Joe mentioned that several people in the valley might care to learn the English language, Carmen among them. I know something of English grammar. I can teach them. And in the process I shall be able to improve my Spanish."

Luz saw the possibilities of a limited school and brightened for a moment, then, considering the situation, said, "I wonder if it is necessary for Carmen to learn English? She will spend most of her life here."

"It's not a question of practical application," Beth said. "She may simply want to learn for the sake of learning," Beth pointed out reasonably.

"But Rancho Cielo is her life. Spanish and Pai Pai are enough."

Beth was not to be put off in this manner. She smiled amiably at Luz and said, "Well, there are other subjects of a more practical nature to learn. I know how to cut patterns and make clothes, and I know something about American cookery. What books do you have?" She'd seen none about the house.

Luz could be indifferent no longer to such clear enthusiasm. She was obliged to respond.

"Come," she murmured, and led Beth to a locked door which she opened with a key she wore around her neck.

Beth entered a small, neat study furnished with a desk, a straight chair, shelves containing at least two hundred books, she estimated. A candle lamp sat on a circular wooden table; a book lay open beside the lamp, almost as though the unseen occupant had gone out into another part of the house for a moment but would soon return.

"This was Nathan's sanctuary when the quiet and inactivity of Rancho Cielo began to pall," Luz stated with a faint smile. "He was only an outdoor man when he had a project in mind. It was his dream to do great things here at the rancho, and mine too." She sighed. "None of his ideas came to maturity. But this was his source of joy."

"He was a student," Beth observed, "from the looks of things here."

"A dreamer," Luz amended. "We lived at the hacienda several different times, all of them briefly. When matters collapsed down in the lowlands, we retreated to Rancho Cielo. He would then spend many hours behind this closed door, reading, writing, studying. I have no idea what he was planning in his mind; he never discussed matters with me, even though he taught me English for this purpose. His death left many loose ends."

"I can't believe how many books there are here," Beth said.

"Look them over," Luz told her. "I don't know what's

here, but you may take what you want." A gentle melancholy claimed her as she thought of her dead husband. "Nathan always said I should become truly expert at English, but somehow this never happened."

"Your English is excellent," Beth said sincerely. "But you can learn more with me. You can help me with Spanish, and I'll help you with English. It doesn't only have to be Carmen who's learning."

"You've given me an idea," Luz said suddenly. "I have never known my multiplication tables, or long division, systems like that, but numbers have always fascinated me. Oh, I can count pesos and dollars all right, but beyond that—"

"I can teach you arithmetic," Beth said. "And what about the Indian children? They might like to learn their three Rs too."

"A few here are of school age," Luz said. She explained to Beth that the males would leave Antelope Valley in early adolescence to seek work in the lowlands, mainly as fishermen on the Pacific coast of California, or at the growing villages scattered along the western shores of the Sea of Cortés. And, Luz went on to say, when most Indian girls had passed their first menstrual cycle they departed for the more populous areas to work as domestics. Thus, they were eventually absorbed into Spanish culture, or the American. In some cases they would marry mestizos, their blood adding a further mix to the people of upper and lower California. Occasionally, a few girls and boys would remain behind to marry and live in the valley, preferring it to the outside world they had never seen—although today this was rare, since there was no pressure on them to stay, and no money to support the valley's economy in times of crop failure.

"Over the years," Luz explained to Beth, gushing a bit, excited to have an audience, "the Pai Pais have been considerably reduced, until now few remain in permanent residence. Only the very young who cannot yet leave, or the very old who know no other life. There is nothing to keep the others in isolation when the world beyond offers such rich enticements as gold and freedom. Actually, Rancho Cielo *is* freedom of the purest kind, but the young people won't accept this. Having no other experience they do not believe what they have is best."

"I have noticed that men like Creek understand what a haven Antelope Valley is," said Beth.

"Creek is one of the few who's always lived here and would live nowhere else," Luz replied. "He appreciates what my father, Jaime Delgado, brought to this grant of ours, how he built it up, carrying what we have in from the outside over many decades, piece by piece. And of course I am one person who will never leave, being the last of my family to love the land. Alas, Joselito is different. He does have a feeling for the valley, he was born with its blood in his veins, but he is restless. He cannot settle anywhere."

"I know the outside world," Beth said. "This one is splendid by comparison. Not only is it wild and beautiful, its flora unique, but it is remarkably self-contained by Nature. I think it will be a good place in which little Nate may grow up and develop. He will be privileged. And I shall teach him."

Luz, in an abrupt gesture of affection, placed her hand on Beth's arm. Miguelito's widow was *simpatica*.

"My dear Beth," she murmured, "you are an exceptional woman. Please make the most of Nathan's facility. I am content at last that someone with knowledge will be handling these pages and papers again. I am glad now that I kept the library just as it was when Nathan was alive."

Luz took the key to the library from her neck and gave it to Beth. Her usually somber eyes sparkled.

"You may come and go as you wish," she said, "beginning now," and went away to issue household orders to the Indian servants.

Beth sat down immediately and began to make a list of Nathan's books. She was delighted to find among the volumes various histories of the world, an atlas, Gray's

Anatomy and various medical references. There were a couple of English grammars, a well-worn Spanish-English dictionary that Beth considered a priceless find, and a thick set of technical books on engineering and machinery. Occupying the top shelf above a wide range of classical novels was the 1821 Variorum Shakespeare, including the plays and sonnets.

If Nathan Porter had not been a formally educated man, he was a serious seeker of knowledge, Beth decided. She blessed him for that, noting for the first time a small leather case on top of the shelves. She picked it up, unsnapped the clasp and opened it. Inside was a daguerreotype of Nathan. In the photograph, already fading from the copper plate, there appeared a bearded, rather stern-faced man of about forty-five years. He had wide-set eyes, serious and penetrating, looking right into Beth's. Nathan Porter had given his strong chin to Michael and his warm, almost voluptuous mouth to Joe.

Strange, Beth thought, that Luz hadn't pointed out the daguerreotype to her, letting her discover it for herself. But that was Luz's way, as she was finding out little by little—opening a threshold, letting one make the discoveries beyond, such as the crystal paperweight and magnifying glass that held down the handwritten notebooks near the candle lamp. Etched on its base was *MY LOVE —LUZ*.

Beth shut the library's open door that led onto the covered inner patio of the hacienda. She sat down in Nathan's chair, at his place of study, feeling his presence, trying to imagine the countless times that he seated himself in this same chair and prepared himself to enter the world of ideas and books, traveling to far places he would never have known otherwise.

Closing her eyes, hands folded on the table, she was unaccountably claimed by a mood. She felt very close to Nathan, and then to Michael. Thinking of Michael's sudden, needless death, she was overcome by a torrent of emotion, a sense of loss so sharp and painful that it triggered a surge of tears that she could not restrain.

As the tears coursed down her cheeks, she resolved that she would dedicate herself to the people of Antelope Valley, with the help of Nathan's library. This dedication would reflect on Michael, become a living tribute that would never be diminished. The memorial would also be for Luz, of course, and for Joe. Even though the brothers were born to different mothers, they each shared in the history of Antelope Valley. Joe might be the rightful blood heir, but Michael's presence was here in the high country too.

It took Beth a while to compose herself, to wipe her eyes dry of tears. She realized that she was marking a change in her life, a settling in, achieved a step toward maturity. She understood that she had somehow undergone a powerful purging and would now be forever free to get on with her life in a place she could honestly call home. As for direction, it would be determined for her. The future was a bridge she'd cross whenever it appeared on the horizon. Until then, she would let work claim her, and the education of little Nate.

13

THE following day Beth started to set up her school. Meanwhile, Joe was out with Creek studying the possibility of a rock and earthfill dam. It would contain a spring-fed stream that was one source of nourishment for the marshy lake at the valley's northern end.

At first, Beth took only Carmen and Luz as pupils. With plenty of help to look after little Nate, even a wet nurse, and without kitchen chores or any other household duties to burden her, Beth was happy to be able to devote several hours each day to classes held in the chapel.

Luz and Carmen were excellent pupils, eager and quick to learn, a joy to teach. During the next few weeks Carmen began to pick up English with remarkable ease. Luz learned her tables and long division, then insisted that she go on to learn algebra, since among Nathan's books was a text on the subject.

A month after Beth started teaching in the small chapel, she had more applicants than she could handle. She decided that perhaps the best thing to do where the Indians were concerned was to turn their abilities around and make them work for the community.

"Weaving seems to be a lost art around the valley," Beth observed to Luz and Joe one evening at dinner.

"Very little has been done in my lifetime," said Luz. "Some leather work is still done, but it's more or less a lost art."

"These things ought to be preserved as an industry," Beth declared.

Both Luz and Joe stared at her, making her feel a bit foolish that she harbored ambitions for just about every facet of valley life, even in a decidedly off-year, and just as the hot weather was closing in for the summer.

"There's no natural talent for this among the Indians," Luz said. "Not any longer, it seems."

"I know of something," Joe volunteered. "The rock drawings that the Pai Pais made in the past can still be seen in the valley's caves. These could be copied."

Beth was excited by the idea. "I must see them! When can we go?"

"Tomorrow if you like."

"After classes would be fine."

So the two of them rode out to see the cave drawings in the afternoon when everyone else was taking their siestas. It was the first time that Beth had been out alone with Joe since their arrival at Rancho Cielo. Beth found Joe much subdued. His natural, flinty exuberance and resourcefulness, in ample evidence on the trail, gave way to taciturn moods when he was in the presence of Luz and Carmen. He would always return from a day spent in the outdoors with Creek in good spirits, but an hour in the hacienda generally made him gloomy.

Joe and Beth rode to a spot about a mile from the hacienda, an area of immense boulders, dwarfing those of the lookout shelter where Michael was buried. Among these were the caves where the drawings had been placed. The caves were not true caves, more a haphazard, scramble of large, fairly flat rocks jumbled together, but wedged tight enough to provide smooth, sheltered surfaces on which the Indian artisans lined out their stories in pictures.

The first cave Joe showed to Beth was the most detailed, he explained, of all the caves. On a broad, even granite surface a large parade of wild animals was drawn: sheep, leaping antelope, coiled serpents, and pumas crouched on high prominences, waiting for passing victims. Many birds graced the upper portion of the mural-like panorama. One particularly large bird, flying above all others with an enormous wingspread, probably ten feet wide in the drawing, captured Beth's attention.

"What is that huge creature that seems to lord it over the others?" she asked Joe. "It looks like some mythical feathered dragon from the legends of the Middle Ages.

Joe chuckled at her image. "It's no dragon, Beth. It's the California condor, found all along the Pacific coast, and no further inland than our sierra."

"Is it some kind of hawk?"

"No, it's from the vulture family and it's the world's largest living bird, or so it's said. There aren't too many around today. To the Californios and Americanos it's a pest. It preys on young calves when it can't get deer and antelope or smaller animals."

"It's magnificent."

"It is," Joe agreed. "Black bodies, white wings, and a ten-foot wingspread in flight that makes it nothing short of majestic. It nests on high crags difficult to reach, and takes off by actually falling through the sky until it hits an updraft of air. Then it soars for hours, or as long as it takes for its keen eye to find prey far below on the ground."

"A formidable creature," Beth declared. "I'd love to see one."

"Well, they nest in impossible places, as I said."

"I mean, just to see one soar."

"You may someday," Joe said. "They've been seen right around here. You know, this is a place where none of the Pai Pais will go."

"Why not?"

"It's taboo for them."

"Oh? Why?"

Joe crouched on a ledge at the entrance to the wide, open cave and grinned at Beth, as if he was skeptical of the tale he was about to tell but at the same time couldn't deny that there might be some truth to it.

"Well, the Pai Pais think this area is cursed, and the condor and rattlesnake are the natural guardians of some great religious secret. I've heard about this all my life. but nobody knows more than what I've told you. That's enough to keep the Pai Pais away."

"If this area's taboo, then we can't expect the Indians to reproduce these early drawings," Beth said logically, with some disappointment.

"There are a couple of other caves with Indian art. We can see those, if you like."

"Where are they?" Beth asked.

"Not far. Five hundred yards from here."

"With animal designs?"

"No, only geometric."

"Arabesques?"

"I guess something like that."

"Yes, I'd like to see them," Beth said. "Aren't there any human figures anywhere?"

"No, no, nothing like that," Joe replied. "The Pai Pais are superstitious about representing human figures in drawings. They believe a likeness captures the soul forever. Come." He led Beth through a narrow pass to a cluster of rocks.

"It would be wonderful to have enough sheep in the valley to produce rugs and serapes," Beth said wistfully as they reached the rocks.

"It would be," Joe agreed, "but impractical. Even in wet years there's not enough forage for domestic sheep."

"If we had a fairly large herd we could do some wonderful work and export our products," Beth persisted.

"I suppose so. We haven't had grazing sheep since I was a boy. After we slaughtered all the sheep one lean year, we gave up. When we want lamb we hunt antelope and bighorn sheep. It's much more practical."

The drawings in the cave shelters were small, the work undistinguished, similar to the designs that appeared on the garments of the Pai Pai women. Not very striking, Beth reflected. However, several of the motifs could easily be adapted to basket-weaving. She sat down to copy the designs into one of Nathan Porter's old notebooks.

Joe watched her, fascinated. "You sketch too," he observed with such a serious tone that she laughed.

"Only so-so. I have a deep appreciation of art but no talent, alas. But I suppose its better than being a mediocre artist."

"You never cease to surprise me," Joe said, as he escorted her to the next cave.

Sitting on a ledge outside the last cave they visited, Beth decided to bring up the subject of Carmen. She didn't know quite what tack to take, since she didn't want to give away the fact that she had seen Carmen go into

Joe's house. She opted for Carmen's progress in English as an opener.

"I'm very pleased with Carmen," Beth said after commenting on Luz's almost girlish enthusiasm over her progress in arithmetic.

"She's never had any advantages," Joe said. "She's eager to learn."

"Her English will soon be excellent. One day I suppose she'll want to move from Antelope Valley and see something of the outside world."

"She already does," Joe said. "She pesters me for information. She talks of going to San Francisco."

"And what about you, Joe?"

"I have dreams," he said evasively, but Beth wasn't to be put off by any such remark.

"Do they include going away soon?"

"Fairly soon."

Beth felt a flash of resentment toward Joe, who looked handsomer than ever in his home setting. He could decide on anything and do it, but poor Carmen was trapped.

"Will you marry her soon?" Beth asked boldly.

Joe's expression was dark. "I am not at all sure. But perhaps."

"You'll need a priest," she pointed out.

"Sure, I know. I'll get one when the times comes," he replied, and stood up, terminating the conversation. "Let's go. It's getting late."

It wasn't, but Beth knew him well enough to drop the subject. Still, something in his relationship with Carmen was obviously troubling him, and she was deeply curious to know what it was.

That night in her narrow bed, with little Nate peacefully asleep in the crib alongside her, Beth found herself wide awake. Her mind raced with plans for Antelope Valley, these plans doubly attractive by the fact that money and distance from all supply sources lent her several planned projects an air of frustrated fantasy.

She knew, however, that her plans were practical and could easily become realities—the cottage industries of weaving, pottery, needlework, leathercraft. These would all happen one day, Beth promised herself.

Then her mind darted to Carmen and her unsatisfactory conversation about the girl with Joe that afternoon. Was Joe still sleeping with her, Beth wondered, and wouldn't this eventually be discovered by Luz or the Indians and cause a major scandal? She knew from her brief exposure to Luz that while she was permissive and open about many things, her rigid Catholic principles did not include the right to total intimacy before marriage, even if the partners were engaged. Were they still? Beth wondered. On this note she got up, draped a shawl around her shoulders and crept through the house on bare feet. She crept outside through the rear door and stood in the shadows of the cookhouse staring over at Joe's house. She didn't know what she expected to see, knowing that there couldn't be another coincidence like that first one, seeing the lovers together. She remained in the shadows until she began to chill, then turned to go back into the house.

It was then that the door to Joe's hut opened and he emerged with Carmen, draped in a dark coat.

Beth shrank back against the shadowed wall of the cookhouse, praying that she wouldn't be seeen. Once Carmen had crept into the house and Joe had gone into his abode and shut the door, Beth thought it safe to return to her room.

In the dark hallway, moving slowly, she was suddenly aware of someone, a blurred silhouette, standing in her path. She stopped with a gasp. At that moment a match was struck on the floor, a candle lighted. Luz stood there, in her nightcap and gown, wide-eyed and stern-faced.

"I thought I heard you come in a moment ago," Luz said.

"Come in?" Beth faltered, trying to sound casual.

"Your door was open, little Nate was sleeping soundly, but you were gone," Luz said. "Since there was no light in your room, I assumed you'd gone out on the front porch. But when I went to look for you, you weren't there."

Beth saw immediately that one lie would beget another; the last thing she wanted to develop with Luz was an atmosphere of intrigue. It would destroy what she was trying to build. She said honestly, "I couldn't sleep, Mama Luz, I needed some air. I went out back for a short walk so I wouldn't disturb you and Carmen at the front of the house." Which was partially true.

"Well, next time take a candle lantern," Luz advised. "It's not a wise idea to go prowling around in the dark."

"I'm not afraid of wild animals."

"It's not wild animals I'm thinking about," Luz replied, ambiguously. "Now I bid you goodnight, Beth." She turned back toward her room, and disappeared through the door.

Beth breathed a sigh of relief as she slipped into her bed. Her project for tomorrow was lined out, she decided, as she drifted toward drowsiness. She would talk to Luz seriously about Carmen's future, and without making any inferences as to what might be going on between Joe and Carmen. And she would talk to Joe, later, and tell him what she knew. No more tiptoeing around, a detached observer. She was part of Antelope Valley now, and she must figure actively in its destiny if she intended to remain and be of use to its people.

Events did not work out quite as Beth had hoped they would. The next day, after Beth's regular sewing class for the Indian women, Carmen came to her in the chapel about a minor syntax problem with an English language composition she was writing. At intervals throughout the session, tears would well up in Carmen's eyes whenever Beth suggested the simplest corrections. This had never happened before. Carmen had a fairly thick skin and would usually giggle hysterically over her silliest errors, make jokes about them and write in the necessary changes, then go on to other problems. But not today.

Finally Beth asked in a gentle tone, "Is something bothering you, Carmen?"

Beth had an idea what it might be, but was almost afraid to pursue the matter for fear of having her suspicions confirmed.

Carmen nodded vigorously in affirmation to Beth's question, biting her full lower lip, her large dark eyes shifting and downcast.

"Well then, perhaps you'd better tell me what it is. Maybe I can help you. Whatever you say is strictly between us," she said to give Carmen confidence. "Do you understand?"

"Yes. But I—I don't know if I can tell you, Beth."

"Carmen, dear—"

Beth put her book aside, sat down on the chapel bench and took Carmen's hand. The fingers were icy cold, her brow beaded with sweat. The flesh around her mouth was bloodless from tension.

"Are you feeling all right?" Beth asked.

"I think so," Carmen said faintly.

"Well then, for heaven's sake, tell me what's wrong."

Carmen rose slowly to her feet, opened her mouth to speak, then turned away from Beth unsteadily. She took a few tentative steps toward the outside chapel door, as if she intended to run out of the building but didn't know if she had the strength.

Then, abruptly, a violent tremor seized the girl. It seemed to ripple through her voluptuous body with almost supernatural force. Wordlessly, she crumpled to the floor, full-length on her back, as the convulsions began to flail her head and limbs.

Carmen thrashed helplessly back and forth on the brick floor of the chapel as Beth watched in dumb horror. Froth collected at the corners of Carmen's mouth, and a trickle of blood ran down her chin.

Beth remembered witnessing an identical incident at school years before. A schoolmate had been taken with just such a seizure during recess in the school yard. While all the little girls looked on in terror, their teacher had knelt quickly and thrust a wooden ruler she was carrying between the girl's upper and lower teeth so she wouldn't bite her tongue off as she convulsed. Later Beth had learned what the seizure was: an epileptic fit called a grand mal. These terrible seizures were often hereditary, her father had told her, or else caused by some early physical illness, a traumatic injury, or a tumor of the brain.

Beth had no ruler handy, but she did have a crude pointer she had cut for herself from a pine tree and which she used sometimes while teaching. She took this and thrust it between Carmen's clenched jaws, straddling Carmen's body so she could keep her from thrashing about and injuring herself.

Fortunately the convulsion was brief, over almost as quickly as it had begun. When Beth was certain that the girl was not going to have another seizure, she removed the stick with great care, at the same time peering into Carmen's mouth to see if she had swallowed her tongue. She hadn't, but she had bitten it slightly, which would account for the blood Beth wiped from the girl's chin with a handkerchief.

Carmen seemed to lapse into unconsciousness for a few minutes as Beth squatted beside her. When she opened her eyes she blinked up at Beth and said, "Where am I?"

"You're here with me, Carmen. Stay quiet. Don't try to get up yet."

"What happened? Why am I on the ground?"

"Don't you remember?"

"Nothing," Carmen said dully. "I recall nothing."

"You had a seizure and you fainted," Beth said.

"Oh, *Dio*!" There was fear in her eyes, her hand fluttered to her breast. She struggled to raise herself on her elbows. Beth helped her to a sitting position.

Carmen pressed her hands to her temples. "What has happened to me?" she murmured.

"I thought you were, you might be—" Beth paused. She couldn't use the word pregnant, since this wasn't in Carmen's vocabulary yet, nor was she familiar with the exact Spanish word. Carmen supplied it.

"*En cinta?* No, I am not that. There are ways of being careful."

"What ways?" Beth asked.

"Indian ways. Very old medicine. Wild herbs in a potion." Carmen stared at Beth with widening eyes. "So, you know about me and Joselito?"

"I suspected," Beth said discreetly.

"I hope Mama Luz doesn't know as well," Carmen said.

"I would hope so too," Beth agreed. "Well, needless to say, Joe will have to marry you. And the sooner the better."

Carmen shook her head. "No, it mustn't happen."

"Why not?"

"I love Joselito, but he doesn't love me. And besides, I am not well. I have had these spells before."

"Do you know what it is?"

"A doctor told my guardian about it before I ever came here. This is the first time it has affected me in a long time. The high country is good for me. My health has been fine here. I thought it had gone away. The doctor said it might."

Carmen's plight was pitiful, Beth reflected. Her heart longed to help the poor girl, but there was nothing she could do except to console her. Epilepsy, the grand mal, the horror, was obviously little understood by Carmen. And what about Luz? She must know something of it, or more accurately nothing about it, since she was countenancing an engagement between her son and Carmen. What a hideous cross for Carmen to bear. Whatever way the girl's life went, it seemed she was already under pronouncement of doom.

Well, there was nothing she could do, Beth realized, except hope that God or fate would intervene and make Carmen whole again. She would say nothing about the seizure to Luz; she really didn't know how to handle the matter, and for the time being would have to pretend that it hadn't happened.

"This will be our secret," she told Carmen.

Beth helped Carmen to her feet. Carmen flung her arms around Beth and clung to her in melancholy gratitude.

"I said I loved Joselito," Carmen said, "but I have to confess that I do not love him as I should. It's an arrangement of convenience—for me, for Joselito, for Mama Luz. Marriage is a way of burying me. I wish that God had never sent me to this desolate and forsaken place. You should go, Beth, while you still can."

"I love it here," Beth replied, voicing what had been in her mind for some weeks.

"You will hate it in time as I do," Carmen predicted. "It will become a prison. . . . Thank you, Beth." She turned away; brushing the dust from her clothes and hair, she walked unsteadily out of the chapel.

Beth glanced up at the large wooden cross that hung above the plain, unfinished altar. The cross was ornamented with gilt medallions, too massive for the tiny chapel. Beneath it the devout among the Pai Pai came daily to pray. Every Sunday morning, mass was muttered in garbled Latin by a middle-aged Pai Pai who once had been an altar boy at the San Diego Mission.

What kind of a God was it, Beth thought, who inflicted his worshippers with such agony before they'd even had a chance to live, like Carmen? Beth wished she knew and could do something about it. But for all her organizing skills, her push and drive, she didn't think she could reach an understanding through religion. To her it was a vacuum within the core of Nature. God, of course, was there whatever one believed, but religion only

made God more difficult to know. Yet she had to respect
the single-minded ardor of the blindly faithful.

Just to be on the safe side with her blasphemous
thoughts, she touched her silver cross with her fingers,
and crossed herself as she turned away from the altar.
She had never done such a thing before, she realized.
Maybe Yvonne Bernard's cross had special powers; she
certainly hoped so. She needed all the inspirational
strength she could get.

14

As the months rolled on toward September, it became
increasingly clear to Beth that Rancho Cielo had been
waiting for the arrival of someone just like herself. It had
existed as a community enclave in the highlands of Baja
California for a long time, but it had indolently dismissed
"progress" as anathema to its preservation. Now Beth
was convinced that a certain controlled growth was all
that would allow Rancho Cielo and the valley to survive.
In fact, slow starvation and disintegration were inevitable
without growth and change.

Beth continued to reflect on progress as the summer
heat made the days burning hot, the nights quite balmy
and pleasant. Beth found that wherever she turned her
attention, crying needs existed. She supervised the building of a new outhouse and a bathhouse for hacienda residents. In anticipation of heavy autumnal rains, a water
conduit system on a small scale was built to contain a
subterranean supply. This construction was a tiny lake

open to the sun which would provide solar-warmed water on cold, bright winter days, or so Beth anticipated, and in other seasons as well. The system was fed by gravity flow from perennial springs of pure water bubbling up from granite depths not far from the hacienda.

From basic sewing classes it wasn't difficult for Beth to teach the female community simple dressmaking. When Beth's New York letters had gone East via caravan from Los Angeles, a note to Garth Winslow begged for yard goods to be sent up.

Garth was without funds to buy the Los Angeles store for himself, and there were no other takers in the pueblo, but he continued to run it for Beth and Joe, taking a modest percentage of the profits for himself, being quite meticulous and scrupulous about the accounting of business, as Beth knew he would be. One day Beth hoped to be able to settle with Joe and then hand the store over to Garth, if Joe would approve of this exchange, which she was sure he would. He hadn't figured in the actual operation of the store since it opened, and Garth had earned the right to own the business.

The yard goods reached Rancho Cielo in good time, sent first to the Romero estate, along with Beth's and Michael's personal possessions. Joe brought them up by muleback from Rancho Romero to Antelope Valley. Michael's clothes were distributed among the Pai Pai women, who were soon taking them apart and reassembling them into suitable garments for their children. Pants became dresses, coats became baby blankets. Boots and belts went to the Pai Pai men, and shirts were tailored to size. All were delighted in these transformations, adding color and difference to the usual drabness of the Indians' attire.

Joe seemed different upon his return. There was a faraway glaze in his eyes constantly. Beth read this as boredom with Antelope Valley, but that was only part of it. He was involved, she suspected, in some other imminent project and wouldn't be around long. She accepted this as an indisputable fact of life.

Toward Carmen, Joe exhibited a stolid indifference. The girl sensed this and stayed clear of him whenever she could during the days. Nights she sat at the table with him but for the most part said almost nothing, avoiding his glances whenever possible.

Joe took to riding in the hills all day with Creek. His moodiness at meals was overlooked by Luz, who acted as if nothing had changed.

To Beth's knowledge, Carmen did not have another seizure. She came to Beth's classes each day, and was proving a great help to Beth as translator for the Pai Pai women.

"By the way," Beth said casually one day to Carmen, "when the time comes we'll be able to make you a handsome wedding dress."

Carmen said nothing, so Beth went on. "I have that soft pink cotton. It will look charming on you." Carmen smiled, as if to say *if* such a time ever comes, which may never be.

Luz was silent about the situation between Joe and Carmen. Whatever she thought, she seemed to be waiting to see what would happen between the two young people. God's hand would decide their fate. She had set up the possibility, and that was all she could do.

Once, however, Luz did bring the subject up with Beth.

"We are waiting to see what will happen," she said impulsively to her one day as they sat together in Nathan's study. But before Beth could pursue the subject, Luz had turned to details of the new bathhouse, wondering if perhaps next year they might build a similar facility for the Indians near the lake. The men would use it, she was sure, even if the women were too shy to at first.

In late summer, Salvador Romero, Raul's younger brother, rode up to Rancho Cielo from Rancho Romero to see Joe. The men sat up most of the night drinking brandy that Salvador had brought with him. Their steady raucous laughter drifted across from Joe's house and in through Beth's open window, keeping her awake. She took Salvador's arrival as the sign Joe had been waiting for, and assumed as she lay in bed that Joe would soon be leaving Rancho Cielo on some secret mission whose nature she preferred not to know.

On the last day of Salvador's visit Beth encountered Joe near the stables. Joe was getting his riding gear in shape.

"So, you're going away," she observed. "You and Salvador have a commission."

"For a few weeks, yes." Joe looked surprised. He'd said nothing to Beth about his plans to leave early the next morning. "Things to take care of," he added vaguely.

"That's unfortunate," Beth replied. "Your presence is needed here. Unless, of course, you'll be earning much-needed money to bring back to the valley. As you know, the store isn't making a mint, though Garth does the best he can."

"He's all right," Joe said. "Anyway, I can't go there to lend a hand. You know the reason well enough."

"I wasn't asking you to. Only that you help Mama Luz out if you can by returning here as soon as possible. And as for the store, I think we might as well give it to Garth."

"That's not a bad idea," Joe said. "He could pay for the goodwill and merchandise he takes over in easy installments. That's with the proviso that we're able to maintain the right to order merchandise at cost and sell through the store whatever goods we produce up here, if that ever happens."

"Good! You've been of some help for once," Beth said without a trace of irony in her voice.

Joe grinned. "You know, Beth, you're a very difficult woman to read. Usually I haven't the remotest idea what you're thinking."

"It takes two to play that game," Beth said, amiably enough. "Now, about the store—"

"Oh, do what you like with it," Joe retorted. "I'm not interested. It's entirely in your hands."

"That's where it's been since Michael died," Beth pointed out quietly, and closed the matter for the time being, taking up a more personal one.

"Carmen needs you," she said bluntly. "Don't be away too long." She was about to tell him of Carmen's seizure, then decided against it.

"Carmen doesn't need me," Joe replied, "even if my mother does. She doesn't love me, she sees nothing interesting in my life. If I don't come back she won't pine away, nor will she get herself to a convent."

"You're away on dangerous negotiations, is that it?" Beth asked, not expecting a direct reply.

"Sort of. It's true there's an element of danger involved," Joe admitted.

"I have no right to say this," Beth began.

"But you'll say it anyway," Joe replied.

"I'm not even related to you by marriage, now that Michael's gone. But I must say I think you're irresponsible. You refuse to be mature. This whole valley is your sacred responsibility, Joe, yet the moment a challenge arises you find some excuse to drift away. Or so it would seem."

"That's your opinion, but what I do is none of your business," Joe said testily. "I'm head man here, and I do what I must."

"Well, I hope you'll bring home some money. We could use a little around here. The valley's down to poverty level."

"You don't have to remind me. You know, Beth, you take this place more seriously than my mother does."

"You should be more serious yourself. After all, Antelope Valley will be yours one day. You don't seem to care about it."

"I thought you knew it was already half mine."

Beth was staggered. She'd assumed that Luz was the sole owner, that the property would only pass to Joe as sole heir on Luz's death.

"It's Spanish law," Joe explained. "Actually, Miguelito

never figured at all in the ownership, or didn't you know?"

He was implying, Beth realized, that she was after the estate.

"No, I didn't," she admitted. "As for my interest in Rancho Cielo, it isn't proprietary, it's purely emotional."

"That's just as well."

"Why?"

"No gringa will ever own the grant of Antelope Valley and environs. The Mexican government wouldn't allow it."

"But you're a gringo," Beth said.

"No, I'm a half-breed," Joe replied. "Half Anglo-Saxon, half Spanish, or with half Spanish and Indian, the mestizo blend. Fortunately, Delgado is a name that impresses the government, so as my mother's son I'll be allowed to keep the grant. Until there's a revolution or greed wins out. But that's enough of personal matters."

"They're at a deadend," Beth agreed. "I wish you well, Joe. You know I mean it. Godspeed, safe passage, whatever is proper. I want you to come back soon. Don't fail us. We need you."

"With God riding beside me, I'll return," Joe promised her confidently. He took her by the shoulders and kissed her lightly on the cheek. "Look after Mama Luz and Carmen," he admonished, then turned and walked away and did not look back.

This was the last personal exchange they had before Joe left. Beth wasn't sure whether she liked the idea of his kiss, but she did know that it was his way of thanking her for being there, a manner of acknowledging that she belonged. She decided she could accept that.

That night the dinner was slightly more festive than usual. Salvador and Joe had brought in a young deer that morning. There was roast venison on the table, a couple of bottles of good Romero red wine, the linen and the silverware were Luz's finest. Carmen was almost demure in a new pink cotton dress she had made in Beth's class.

The girl glanced obliquely at Joe throughout dinner, but he resolutely ignored her.

By dawn the two men were on the summit trail that led out of Antelope Valley, en route to a less austere civilization.

On first awakening Beth had a sense of loss. She rose hurriedly to look at little Nate, still asleep in his crib. Later in the morning she was assailed with self-doubt, by a lack of purpose to her life at Rancho Cielo. It was all circular, she told herself. Nothing seemed to lead any-where except back to this sterile house inhabited by three women in lifelong confinement. As she went about her chores she had to admit to herself that she would miss Joe a great deal. She had learned to eschew dependency for some time. She was surprised to find that she felt it so sharply today. But it existed and there was nothing she could do about it except keep busy. She threw herself into her work frantically, bustling energetically about the chapel, immersing herself in forgetfulness.

After Joe's departure, Carmen brightened appreciably, although Mama Luz went about moody and somber. She spoke to Beth only when addressed and appeared unin-terested in everything, including the construction of a new corral near the hacienda. This was a project that Joe had sketched out and started two weeks before his departure. A corral would be necessary if they were ever able to afford to bring in cattle once more as a food supply. Using fieldstones with wooden posts made from ironwood and strung with wire along the post tops, Creek and his crew made slow but sure progress, almost as if they were on a definite time schedule, Beth thought. She would go out each morning to see what had been accom-plished the day before, which progress Creek would cite with modest pride. She had to give credit to Joe, for even in his absence the work went on. The Indians, Beth realized, had accepted his word as some kind of law. She supposed she was entirely too Anglo-Saxon in her quick

judgments and promised herself to be more understanding
in the future.

Months before Beth wrote to her family and Grace
Morley, she had brooded frequently on the welfare of the
Lowells in New York. She imagined that they had suppressed their anger and dismay over her desertion, that
her father had kept a bland public face but had forbidden
any mention of her name in the house. But she did not
think she was that easily forgotten, not even in the busy
opulence of New York City. Peter Enfield had felt her
absence, and others, although the rhythm of the Lowell
household would not be much changed.

Her letter to James and Fanny Lowell, and the one
to Tim, had outlined briefly her happy marriage to
Michael and the route they took from New York to the
pueblo of Los Angeles. She wrote several pages describing little Nate to his uncle and grandparents; she spent
no time with the particulars of Michael's death, or of
Joe's feud with rancher George Hearn. She glossed over
the facts and merely stated that Michael was shot by
accident while on a business trip into the countryside. She
stressed the sorrowful aspects. She was staunch, saying
that such things did happen in the West.

At the close of her two letters, she stated quite clearly
that she was truly content to remain where she was indefinitely. While Antelope Valley was surely isolated, with
none of the amenities of New York, it was a wild and
beautiful spot and she was enthralled with it. A healthy
atmosphere too, she added, in which to raise little Nate,
at least until his age demanded a wider horizon.

This general recasting of her personal history was dictated by pride, on the one hand, and on the other by
the ineradicable reality that she had deserted those who
loved and counted on her, causing great anguish through
her selfishness.

In Beth's letter to Tim she told him that if he cared
to visit Baja California, Antelope Valley would welcome

him Although she didn't believe he would ever make the long trip, she asked Mama Luz's permission for him to visit before she wrote to extend the invitation. Luz had given her consent gladly. Except for one of the Romero brothers, visitors were all too rare at Rancho Cielo.

Beth expected no answers from anyone, least of all from Tim, who had never written a letter in his life, so far as she knew. Her mother would want to write, of course, but her father would forbid it. And Grace? Well, Grace might write, but again, perhaps not. Nevertheless, she instructed Grace to tell Tim where she was, in case her letter might not be delivered to him. And if he could get to Los Angeles, Garth Winslow would have him guided through the lines to Baja and Rancho Cielo.

After the corral was completed, Beth spent most of her time thinking about the next valley development.

The Indians had worked very hard on the corral project, showing exceptional industry. She hadn't dared to hope for as much. Now that Creek had the men and women organized, it was a pity to let them remain idle. Beth saw that she had to be the mover of ideas and would have to determine the nature of a new project immediately. But what?

She consulted Luz.

"Do what you like," Luz told her. "You have already worked miracles at Rancho Cielo."

"Why not do something connected to agriculture?" Beth said. "It's our most important concern."

"Excellent!" Luz's weathered countenance lit up. "Nathan would have had some ideas, although I doubt if he could have started them going the way you do with your work. You amaze me, Beth. You truly love it here. A beautiful young woman like you—well, life isn't over. Maybe you should be living in San Diego or San Francisco, married to a rich Americano."

"Mama Luz, I wouldn't have the freedom there I have here."

Luz smiled gently. "I'm glad you feel that way. It pleases me. I think of you as a daughter, my dear, and of little Nate as a grandson."

Beth delegated her various classes to a well-tutored Carmen who responded with delight to the responsibility. Early in the mornings Beth would ride out before the heat became unbearable to look over the valley. One morning at the edge of the dry lake she had a flash of inspiration, wondering as it possessed her if Nathan had thought of the same thing at one time. To make farming more than a haphazard operation in the valley, something must be done to prepare a permanent growing area. What better than to build farming terraces against the high sierra flank at the northern end of the valley, west of the lake?

She returned that day to the hacienda, filled with the idea. Going through the technical books of Nathan's she ran across a construction system that would enable the Indians to grow crops almost the entire year round by clever use of the water and land. A dam above a system of stepped terraces, nourished by a spring-fed reservoir, was the answer.

Excited, she began to draw up a plan. Encouraged by Luz's reaction to her drawing, she conferred with Creek. He was all toothless grin and enthusiasm. Beth had never seen him this affable.

"You are doing something that should have been done years ago, señora," Creek told her in Spanish. "Joselito has talked of such a construction, but it was only talk. You mean to do it."

"It will have to be a community effort in which everyone pitches in," Beth pointed out.

"Don't you worry, I'll get the whole village to work," Creek promised.

Beth's plan was first to build a rock and earthfill dam to contain the springs that bubbled up at the base of two high, rocky projections. These were year-round springs. In the wet season their flow was considerable and the water made its way easily down the hillside stream bed to the shores of the marshy lake. Even in the dry season the springs fed the small pool at the base of the rocks, but they hadn't the force to survive the fall to the lake and evaporated en route in the arid climate. A reservoir was the answer.

Creek supervised the building of the rock and earthfill dam and it was done in three weeks. It was not an exceptionally skillful piece of work, Beth observed during its construction, but the dam was solid, and did the job it was built for. Now there was a fairly deep fresh water pool from which to irrigate the terraces that were constructed next. The terrace embankments of stone were filled with the rich soil sediment of the dry lake bed. Even heavy rains, Creek promised, wouldn't disintegrate them. They would be in place for a long time to come, more or less impervious to occasional winter downpours.

During the construction of the terraces it became Beth's task to involve the Indian women in a continuous work pattern. It was not the Pai Pai custom to plunge into a task and have it done quickly. The Indian method was a casual one, not quite haphazard but certainly not regular. Beth introduced a system that was a continuous conveyor belt. The Indian women would load up the sturdy pack mules with saddlebags of lakebed soil at the lower terminus of the work path. The Pai Pai men would unload the soil brought up by the mules at the base of the reservoir, filling in the terraces to the level of the stone embankments they had built.

The work on the system was monotonous and uninspiring, so Beth devised a solution to relieve tedium. She offered first, second, and third prizes of yard goods to the three women who did the best work. "Best" meant fastest, Beth explained to all. Surprisingly enough, the Indians caught on to the idea of Beth's extremely American competition at once and responded with laughter and good-natured smiles to the challenge.

The heavy stones that formed the dam and the embankments were, of course, placed by the Indian men. Their ability to find stones that matched with nearly the precision of the ancient Aztecs amazed Beth. The reservoir when completed was not only a practical construction, but it was handsome to look upon.

At a gathering of the Pai Pai at the hacienda, Beth gave out special rations of cornmeal, flour, rice and *charqui*, although the packets were small. These went to all the Pai Pai who had actively contributed to the construction program. To the very few Indian ancients who were unable to work, special rations of imported China tea, much prized, were given as a token of respect. Beth made several batches of brown sugar and cinnamon candy sticks for the children, who were ecstatic over this surprise. They had never before tasted such a luxury.

The dam and terraces had been created in an extremely short time, a matter of only a few weeks. Now it remained for the first rains to roll up from the southwest. These storms would test the soundness of the construction.

While the three women in the hacienda simply waited for the rains to come, the Pai Pais prepared for them in a different way. They concentrated on an early downfall by muttering lengthy primitive prayers around special fires built along the lake shore at midnight. They begged the rain spirits to come quickly and extinguish the fires. Mixed with homage to the rain spirits were simple prayers to the Catholic deity, to madonna and child. Within the Pai Pai remnant of the Sierra Indians' society, the Christian legends had long been mixed with the Indian myths, so that they were interchangeable. No one seemed to think it at all odd that Christ and the rain spirits were to be venerated equally. The same Pai Pai who said Mass in the chapel on Sundays performed the midnight fire ritual on the lakeshore, giving both ceremonies equal devotion.

During the weeks of the agricultural project's construction, no word reached Rancho Cielo about Joe

Porter—but then, none was expected. Beth thought she could pretty well guess what Joe was doing. She was worried that he was probably involved in the dangerous and highly illegal operation of cattle rustling. And while George Hearn was no longer around to settle scores, imagined or real, other Americanos would make short work of Joe and his accomplices, once they were caught. Rustling was a crime that called for summary execution.

Beth became faint whenever she thought of the peril to which Joe must be subjecting himself. The fact that he probably gained immense satisfaction in bringing the stolen livestock across the border with the Romero brothers only reinforced Beth's judgment of Joe's immaturity. He could be shot dead at any time, gunned down as Hearn had meant him to be when her Michael had become the victim in his place.

Beth spent hours in Nathan's study trying to glean inspiration for another project from the notes that Nathan Porter had left. This helped to divert her active mind from Joe, since an incongruity had been developing ever since her farewell to him down at the stable. She wanted to beg him not to go away, and yet this made no sense in the present pattern of her life. She tried to rationalize this feeling as loneliness for Michael, but she was too sensible to seduce herself in this way. She knew she was making Joe a surrogate for Michael, and that this was not only foolish, but would lead only to unhappiness.

Little Nate was beginning to walk and talk. Soon, she knew, his simple phrases would turn into questions which she must answer. Time had a way of moving ahead swiftly. She had obligations, and while they bound her to Luz and Rancho Cielo, Joe's indifference placed him outside any obligation. If anything, Joe owed her his concern. But she was far too proud and independent ever to ask for it. She hadn't even asked for his help when Michael was killed; it was Joe who had solved the immediate problem, offering to escort her to Antelope Valley.

One morning as Beth was reading in the relative coolness of Nathan's study, Luz burst into the room in a state of high excitement, most unusual for her.

"Come at once! Creek says there are visitors at the summit trail," she cried. "Two horsemen. They will soon be down in the valley."

"Could they be looking for Joselito?" was Beth's first chilling thought.

"They'd never come here boldly by day—not a mere pair of riders with mules," Luz pointed out reasonably. "There would be a posse of many men, heavily armed."

Beth wondered, for the first time, if Luz was aware of what dangerous actions Joe might be involved in.

Luz continued. "Anyone who knows anything at all about the Sierra de Juarez must have the instinct or the guides to find us up here. They would be well aware that the Pai Pais are excellent scouts, fierce when aroused and as dangerous as the puma when cornered. Ah yes, there would be many more men than just two."

"Then who could they be? Not casual travelers."

"Bring the spyglass you had sent up with Miguelito's effects," Luz said. "We'll go and have a look."

The two women joined Carmen outside on the rise of ground behind the hacienda and near Joe's house. Beth trained the spyglass on the distant mounted figures just beginning to descend the rocky trail that would bring them to the floor of the valley trail a quarter of a mile away.

The forward rider was an Indian, Beth observed, or possibly a mestizo, hard to tell at this distance. He blocked out her view of the second rider.

Then, as she watched, the order of the riders was reversed as the first horse shied on the narrow, stony path, allowing the second rider to move into the focus of Beth's spyglass, the two accompanying pack mules lagging behind.

Beth gasped in surprise when she saw the second rider clearly.

"Dear God!" she cried out. "It's my brother, Tim!"

She handed the spyglass to Luz and began to run toward the end of the summit trail to greet the riders as they made the final descent to the valley floor.

15

SEVERAL inches taller, filled out into early muscular manhood and deeply bronzed by the sun, Tim seemed almost a stranger to Beth as he called out to her in a deep adult voice. Not until he smiled, dismounted and held out his arms to embrace her was he the Tim she had known.

"Oh Lord, it's good to see you, sis," he told her. "I thought we'd never get here. This is really the wilderness."

"You got my letter," Beth said. "Thank God!"

Tim nodded. "I left New York a few days afterwards."

She was obliged to ask the question she feared to pose. "How are Mother and Father?" she said.

Tim hesitated a fraction of a second, just long enough for Beth to suspect that all was not well. Then he sighed, as if he'd already rehearsed this scene a hundred times and was deeply troubled by the responsibility it put upon him.

"Mother's all right, considering—" he muttered.

"Something has happened to Father!"

Tim inhaled slowly and nodded. "He's dead, Beth. He had a heart attack and died very suddenly, at home in his study one afternoon. It was only about three months after you—after you went away. It could have had something to do with Amanda Enfield and the copper holdings. The widow put a lot of pressure on Father after you left. She was plenty mad about you rejecting Peter. The stock plummeted. Talk was that the widow engineered it, and she may have. Anyway, he lost a great deal of money and it preyed on his mind."

"Oh, no!" Beth started to tremble, tears filled her eyes. She had great difficulty in not breaking into sobs.

Tim took her firmly by the shoulders. "Look, sis, you mustn't feel that it was your fault—" he began.

"But wasn't it?" Beth broke in. "If I'd stayed and married Peter, Father might be alive today."

"That isn't necessarily so," Tim replied soberly, his bright blue eyes studying her. "You mustn't blame yourself. You did what you had to do. Mother understood your elopement, even if Father refused to."

"She understood?"

"Of course," Tim said readily, as if he'd gone over and over his responses. "And she understood your choice of Michael. Our parents had some lengthy arguments over that. What grieved her was that you didn't write sooner."

"Bless her dear soul! Then she let you go without any fuss?"

"Well, not without considerable sadness," Tim said, "or regrets. But with love and good wishes. She knew that nothing would keep me in New York once I heard from you, sis. And she's in good health, she's a strong woman. How strong I never knew until Father died. She marched right in and took over immediately—lawyers, the disposition of the will, all kinds of business matters. Amazing woman. You wouldn't believe how tough she's become since Father passed away. Naturally, there is not a lot of money now, but Mother's got what was left in good shape."

"Then she's not bitter about me," Beth said, still finding it difficult to believe that her mother could handle her husband's death so well."

"No, and she sent her love."

"Is there something else you're not telling me?"

"You know Will Forrest?"

"One of Father's lawyers, of course."

"I think she's going to marry him."

Beth was aghast. "Mother, marrying again!"

"Why not? She's a lot younger than Father was. We're both out of her hair now. Forrest travels to Europe every year, has a summer house in the Hamptons, the town house in New York. Why not?"

"Yes, why not indeed?" Beth reasoned. "If it will make her happy. Just the same, I wish she weren't involved there. She could come West."

"She'd hate it," Tim said simply. "You know how she adores the amenities. Besides, she's become quite brisk since you left. I don't think she cares for putting up with hardships. This place isn't exactly Saratoga Springs."

"How did you come out?"

"By the Santa Fe Trail," Tim said, "the same route you took."

"The trip seems to have agreed with you, Tim. You're in fine health."

"You're looking wonderful yourself."

"I'm feeling the best ever, truly wonderful," Beth assured him sincerely. "And so is little Nate, your nephew."

"I can hardly wait to see him," Tim said. "So, how are you doing, sis?"

"All right, everything considered. They're very good to me here. They're warm people. Rancho Cielo is better than living in the pueblo alone. I dreaded that idea. Naturally, there's a deep void in my life since Michael's death. I miss him terribly, though the pain of loss recedes bit by bit every day."

Tim hugged her. "Good, I'm glad to hear it."

"I can't get over how you've grown. You're a giant now, strong and tough."

"I wish you'd said 'matured' instead of grown," Tim said with a grin. "I'm sure as hell no gangly boy anymore. I've acquired a man's zest for living."

As Tim spoke he glanced over Beth's shoulder at Luz and Carmen who stood at a discreet distance from them, the old woman in traditional black, Carmen in a simple

white blouse and dark skirt, bare-legged. Pablo, the Indian guide from the Romeros' hacienda staff, had dismounted. He stood holding the reins of the two horses.

"I must meet the ladies," Tim said. "It's Mama Luz
and Carmen, Joe Porter's girl, is that right?"

"Yes. Come, let me introduce you—"

Taking Tim by the hand, she led him over to the two
women. He swept off his dusty, sweat-soiled Stetson and
bobbed his head.

"A pleasure to meet you, ladies," he said with a smile.

Luz extended her hand. "Welcome to Rancho Cielo,
Señor Lowell."

"It's Tim, Señora Porter," he corrected her in polite
Spanish, which surprised Beth until she recalled that Tim
had been as quick to learn Spanish as she had to absorb
French.

Mama Luz gave Tim a warm smile. "Rancho Cielo is
yours," she said softly. "I am Mama Luz to you. And
this is Carmen Aguilar."

Carmen allowed her small hand to rest in Tim's huge
one. She looked up at him through thick, dark eyelashes,
her bright eyes glittering with discovery.

"I am happy to meet you," she told him in Spanish.
"Beth has spoken of you so many times, saying much
about you. But I supposed you would be much smaller."

Tim laughed. "I was, considerably, when Beth last saw
me. It's your benign climate out here—it's made me shoot
up!"

"Can climate do that?" Carmen wondered aloud, not
sure that he was joking.

"You'll have to get used to Tim's sense of humor, Carmen," Beth said, laughing happily.

"Come, let us go into the house," Luz suggested. "Pablo
will take care of the horses and the mules. You've had a
long, tiring journey."

"Long," Tim admitted, "but not tiring. I have the
strength for it." To Beth he said, "I wonder how you
managed so well."

"Pioneer fortitude," she replied, "female strength and resourcefulness."

Tim spread out his arms. "It's great to be here in this strange place," he said, walking toward the hacienda with the three women.

"It's marvelous that you're here," Beth said, thinking how much happier the reunion would have been if Tim hadn't been the bearer of sad news about their father.

At dinner that night, roast game hen and saffron rice were served, along with a dry white California wine from the Romero vineyards. Mama Luz was uncharacteristically expansive, savoring Tim's good looks and jovial, open charm almost as much as Carmen did. The girl smiled and laughed and hung onto Tim's every word, quite a change from her usual behavior in Joe's presence, Beth thought.

Tim regaled the ladies with tales of the journey West from the Mississippi. He had come part of the way from New York by railroad. The through-Mississippi connection, however, was incomplete and wouldn't actually be finished until 1853. Tim had bought a series of different horses on his journey West, replacing each when exhausted with a fresh one.

"I was determined to make record time," he explained. "No wagon trains for me. So I was on the trail sometimes for as long as twelve hours a day."

"By yourself?" Beth asked.

"Well, sometimes. I'd meet other travelers from time to time who were dependable, and I'd ride with them."

"You weren't afraid to trust yourself to strangers?" Carmen asked, impressed.

"I might in this country," Tim said. "But I wasn't while I was on the trail. At least not often. I took chances, riding at night. But a little excitement never hurt anyone. Right? And not much goes on up here, does it?"

"Wait until Joselito gets back," Beth said. "He'll brief you on the excitement of Baja."

"If he's not due in soon I may not meet him this trip," Tim said.

Beth glanced sharply at him. "What do you mean?"

"I'm not staying, sis. This is only a token visit."

"But you can't go. You must stay a long time with us," Luz said.

Tim smiled at her but shook his head. "I'm going to San Francisco, then heading up toward the gold fields. I can't stay long."

"What nonsense," Beth said. "You're staying and that's all there is to be said."

"You see," Tim said to Luz and Carmen with a tolerant smile, "she hasn't changed a bit. She's still my big sister."

Later that night after Carmen and Luz had retired, Beth went out walking with Tim.

They strolled arm in arm, serene and comfortable in each other's company after such a long time apart. Hundreds of small details were discussed—family trivia, the facts of James Lowell's death, Michael's killing—until Beth realized abruptly that Tim hadn't even mentioned Grace Morley in passing.

"I wrote to Grace," Beth said, "but I've heard nothing. Did you see her before you left?"

"Only on the street one day," Tim told her. "She's married, Beth."

"Married!" Beth exclaimed in startled surprise. "How wonderful! Why didn't you tell me right away? Who's the groom?"

"Peter Enfield."

"Peter?"

"Does that surprise you?"

"Yes, in a way it does. And in another way it explains her silence. How are they getting along?"

"Grace is pregnant. She was very smug about that. She said to tell you. I wasn't sure if you might not wish you'd married Peter."

"I didn't love him," Beth said. "So, Grace is happy. That's nice."

"She seems happy enough. For a fact, she's now rich enough."

Tim halted and looked down at his sister, her clear features glowing silver in the pale starlight.

"Tell me honestly, do you regret having given up city life?"

"Honestly, no, dear Tim. You shouldn't have to ask that question after meeting your nephew."

"I mean, about Michael's death."

"Well, since I've come to stay at Rancho Cielo I've taken on a different philosophy of life. I wouldn't say it's a religious one, but close to it. Let's call it fatalism. I accept what would be impossible to clarify, or spell out."

"I don't quite understand."

"I have the powerful conviction that my life—and yours too—is foreordained."

"Now, sis, that's a pretty big idea to digest easily."

"I didn't say it was easy. It comes partly from the religious credo of Mama Luz and Carmen, and partly from the Pai Pai Indians. Living as we live here, depending on what fate brings, one comes to accept what can't be changed."

"That's a far cry from what you used to think," Tim observed. "You were eager to move mountains back in New York. Otherwise you'd never have come West with Michael."

"That was in New York, and then," Beth answered. "Now I believe that one serves life instead of the opposite."

"Almost an Eastern philosophy."

"No, a Western one—Indian and Spanish."

Tim reached down and touched an index finger to Yvonne Bernard's silver cross that hung against Beth's bodice.

"Have you taken up Catholicism?" he asked.

"I haven't given it much thought," Beth said, "but it's

not an uncomfortable idea. A French woman in New
Orleans gave me the cross; she said it would protect me.
I don't know if it's done that, but it may have made certain events easier to bear. Such as the news you brought
me about Father."

"If he hadn't been so stern about your future and tried
to force your hand, you might eventually have married
Peter," Tim speculated.

"No, I think not," Beth protested with conviction.
"That wasn't written for me. But Antelope Valley and
Rancho Cielo were already destined for me. I feel completely at home here, in a way I'd never have felt being
married to Peter."

"Perhaps," Tim agreed. He knew from experience that
he'd get little more out of Beth at this time. She had a
way of stating her case and closing off the subject until
she wished to start it up again.

"I won't marry again, I promise you, if that's what
you're thinking, and I'm sure you are."

"Well, I've given it some passing thought since my
arrival," Tim admitted. "What about Carmen? Will she
marry Joe?"

Beth was tempted for a moment to tell him that Carmen and Joe were already married, in a sense, but decided against it. She would keep her own counsel about
their being lovers, and about Carmen's illness. Something
restrained her from telling Tim and she couldn't pinpoint
the reason.

"It's expected one day," was all she would say to Tim.

"Do you like him?"

"Joe? Yes, I like him. He has some very good qualities.
He's very different from Michael, though they had the
same father. And he's away a lot of the time, which is
hard on Mama Luz. She's getting along, but she's growing old. She's rather frail and I worry about her. As for
Carmen, she's a pretty young thing who needs a strong
guiding hand."

"What's Joe up to while he's away?"

Beth said, lowering her voice, "Out with the Romero brothers. It's anyone's guess where they are."

"I didn't meet them at the rancho. Something to do with border traffic, I gathered from speaking with Pablo."

They were now far enough away from the hacienda for Beth to say what was on her mind.

"I'm not certain," she said, "but the indications are there that Joe is with a gang. I think they steal cattle in Alta California from the Americano ranchos and sell them in Baja. I'm fairly certain Joe wasn't doing this before Michael was killed, but I'm sure he is now. He's been concealing his bitterness about Michael's death, but he hasn't forgotten. His vengeance goes deep."

"I can't blame him for becoming a renegade," Tim said, "if that's what he is. In fact, I admire him in a way. It takes great guts to be an outlaw with a price on your head."

"You've grown up, all right," Beth said with intended sarcasm. "You've acquired all the traditional masculine values, I see."

"Sis, let's not argue about that."

"I don't want you engaged in any nefarious trafficking," Beth told him severely.

Tim put his arm around Beth. "Don't you worry about Timothy Lowell, Adventurer."

"What are you saying?"

"I've the whole of California to explore before I make up my mind what I want to do with my life."

"You're not planning to go back to New York then?"

"Not right away. Mother's all right. She can always stay busy, as you know. And once the railroad goes through, she might even change her mind and come out. But that's a matter of time. Meanwhile, I've got a surprise for you. I've been saving it for this exact moment."

"More gifts? Tim, you've already done too much." Tim's two pack mules were loaded with foodstuffs and gifts purchased from Garth Winslow at the Los Angeles store.

"Something to tide you through until you get the rains

you need so badly," Tim replied. "A letter of credit to the New California Union Bank in Los Angeles. For two thousand dollars."

"Where did you get that much money, Tim?"

"Not from robbing the Pony Express," Tim assured her. "I talked Mother into giving you some of your inheritance in advance. I told her it was a belated christening gift for my nephew Nate. She couldn't refuse."

"How marvelous!" Beth was thrilled. "The money will see us through until we have crops coming in and can be self-sufficient once more. We won't have any more worries. The rain must come this year!"

"Seriously, Beth, I was thinking maybe you'd keep some of it for Nate's education."

"Oh, that will take care of itself," Beth said airily. "I'm presently concerned with the state of the valley."

"I should say you are," Tim agreed. "I guess I'm still a little surprised that you're so settled down."

"What you're saying is that you couldn't be?"

"Wings on my heels," Tim said, yawning. "And dog-tired."

Beth turned him around and they started back to the hacienda. "We'll talk tomorrow," she said. "There's worlds of time for it."

"Tomorrow I want to see the valley."

"I anticipated that. But," she warned him, "you'll be plenty tired of it by the time I've given you a guided tour."

"At least I'll know what will someday be yours."

"Oh, I hardly think that's likely," Beth said. "Anyway, I don't look that far ahead, not with Nate to consider. I must do what's best for him."

"Talk about my growing up," Tim said. "Look at you."

"Poor Mother," Beth said, "having to go on alone without you."

"But Mother's no more alone than you are," Tim said. "She's busy and content, she has friends, money—she's settled, as you are. You've both found appropriate niches, I'd say."

"Yes, I'm particularly rich in friends. I have Mama Luz, Carmen, and Joe too, I suppose—and certainly you, dearest brother."

"By the way, Mother wrote you a letter."

"A letter? Why didn't you give it to me at once? I can hardly wait to read it."

"First I wanted to see how you'd take the news of Father's death, and the letter of credit," Tim said, which was only part of it.

When they returned to the hacienda, Tim gave Beth the letter. She carried it quickly to her room, lighted a candle and sat down on the bed to read it.

Dear Daughter, her mother wrote, *Timmy will deliver this to tell you that we were grieved by your elopement.*

As you will appreciate, your father left you nothing in his will, nor to Tim. Everything came to me. I am settling the sum of two thousand dollars on you for support of your son.

I am no longer in deep despair over your father's death. There are ways of dealing with widowhood. My solution may come as a surprise to you. It even may not please you, but here it is anyway. By the time you read this letter I shall be married to Will Forrest, whom you met at our house with his wife at various times. Mrs. Forrest died over a year ago. Will and I have been graced with a mutual affection that has led us to marriage.

Concerning my estate, the bulk of it shall go to Will, if my death precedes his. There will be nothing for you, which I fear was your father's wish. Tim and I have agreed on a settlement for him, part of which will go to you. He does not wish to live longer in New York, but will go to you.

I was grieved to learn of your husband's death, but cheered to learn that you have a son, Nathan, and I a grandson. Perhaps the future will bring us together. We must wait and see.

May your health remain good, and the boy's.

Your mother

Beth put the letter aside and stared at little Nate as he slept.

Her first reaction was one of bitterness toward her mother for treating her with so little compassion. Her father's death wasn't her fault. His heart problem had existed since she was a small girl and he had always chosen to disregard it. As for the inheritance, she saw her mother's reasoning, although she considered it specious.

Fanny married to Will Forrest was an inconceivable match, she thought.

She went to bed with a heavy heart, hoping that tomorrow would bring her to a less emotional viewpoint. If she believed in fate, as she claimed she did, then this was the way that her life must go. Her real concern was to find some way to make Tim stay on at Rancho Cielo. She doubted her possible success, since Tim had only begun to travel and live. He wouldn't settle down until life forced him into it.

Beth lay wide awake until the sky grew pale in the East. She thought about her father, dying alone in his study, gasping out his last moments in excruciating pain. Guilt claimed her, despite her resolve not to let it, and she began to cry. She cried softly and steadily until she had awakened Nate, who began crying too.

She got up, brought him into her bed, letting him wrap his arms around her neck, half-smothering her, sleeping again. Somehow his nearness was a sedative, calming her from the excitement of Tim's arrival and the news he had brought. She had only the future to look forward to, she reminded herself, and finally fell asleep, comforted by the thought.

16

IN the morning Beth decided to take Tim on an inspection tour of the valley, and to see the work that had been done in preparation for the coming of the rains.

Mama Luz packed a simple luncheon of tortillas, refried beans and *charqui*, along with a bottle of spring water and a wineskin.

Beth and Tim rode south to the lake where the Pai Pais lived in their tents during the hot season. In the cold months, she explained, they moved to the adobe houses near the hacienda.

Tim was deeply impressed with the crop terraces and the reservoir that contained the spring flow.

"They're fine," he told Beth. "You're to be congratulated. Looks to me like they'll hold up under storms. Your only problem is the water supply, isn't it? With that, the valley could be self-supporting."

"Almost. I've dreamed of much more though—wells and windmills—but of course they aren't practical, inaccessible as we are. The roads needed to bring in proper equipment don't exist, and there's no money for them anyway. But even worse is the apathy. I haven't the energy to fight it all by myself. This is where I become a little less than fatalistic and a little more American than usual. But even so, one person can't do it all alone."

"You haven't changed," Tim said. "You're still a mover and a shaker. You always will be."

"Well, I wish I could do the valley some real good—like making it rain. My worry is, what will happen to us when there's barely enough water to drink, and still no rain?"

"You worry too much. You can't concern yourself with the whole world's fate."

"This *is* my world, Tim," Beth said quietly. "That's what I've been trying to tell you."

Beth found a shady spot for their picnic beneath a boulder overhang not too far from the cave drawings. They dismounted and settled down in the shade to eat, with a clear view of the valley a couple of hundred feet below them.

Tim had to admit that Antelope Valley and Rancho Cielo had a certain rugged charm that could probably become an acquired taste in time. He didn't believe it would work for him, however, but considering what Beth had gone through—the long trek West, the birth of her child, Michael's violent death—it was reasonable to accept her passion for a place that was mainly scruffy Indians without education or ambition, vicious red rattlers, some wild sheep, lizards, grotesque cactus, a few wildcats and rocks everywhere.

"The Pai Pais say rain definitely will come this winter," Beth continued, "but what if it doesn't?"

"All of you will have to pack up and move down to the Romero estate. Plenty of well water there, and enough food. They live like kings, with ham, turkey, or roast beef on the table every day. And plenty of wine."

Beth shrugged her shoulders disdainfully. "Yes, and how do they come by it?" she demanded. "Easy to say moving down there is the answer, but it isn't easy to do."

"Why not?"

"Mama Luz wouldn't go. She's lived here almost all her life. She says she won't leave, she'll die here. Besides, she wouldn't be a guest of the Romeros. She's too proud to leave Antelope Valley. Besides, Nathan Porter is buried in the small cemetery near the hacienda."

"Your life's fast becoming contained here, too," Tim told her. "Why don't you just give it all up, Beth, and come with me to San Francisco? Do you realize how long you've been in California without having seen any of it except the pueblo and this place."

"This isn't California, it's Baja—quite a different thing," Beth said, ladling out beans for Tim.

She was still deeply disturbed by her mother's cold, formal letter. Its tone was guilt-inciting and blameful. She couldn't run from it here, she had too much time on her hands. She had a sudden impulse to go away with Tim, at least for a while. She could always return to the valley. But as soon as this thought entered her mind she began to rebuke herself for being disloyal to Mama Luz and Rancho Cielo. She had made her destiny; she would simply have to live with it.

"What would I do somewhere else?" Beth said.

Tim chuckled. "God, you're so dense sometimes. Beth, you're still a beautiful woman. Seeing you after all this time apart I realize that more than ever. You're still young, you're bright. I guess what I mean is, you could marry again."

"Don't talk nonsense. I have little Nate to think of—I'm not free to do as I like."

"That's twaddle and you know it. You can do as much or as little as you like with your life. It's ahead of you, not behind. I don't understand you, Beth. Passive acceptance just isn't your role; you've always been a fighter. You up and ran off with Michael, for God's sake, and left a whole world behind. Now here, where you've got nothing, you're reluctant to leave. I don't know what to make of it. In the last twenty-four hours since our reunion you haven't stopped talking when we're together like you're a hundred years old and your sacred duty is guarding the portals of Heaven."

Tim tilted the wineskin to allow a stream of ruby-red

burgundy to course down his throat. He performed the operation without accident, a trick he'd been quick to learn at Rancho Romero.

"What I don't understand," Tim went on, "is why you and Carmen waste your lives here. You could both go away."

"As I've told you, Mama Luz won't leave, and Carmen's engaged to Joe. She can't run off on her own."

"I think it's more than Mama Luz and Carmen that concerns you," Tim teased her. "I'm beginning to get the picture. You want the ranch for yourself and little Nate one day."

Tim's remark made her bristle, but she controlled her rising anger, reminding herself that her brother was needling her. "Tim, I don't want to *own* Rancho Cielo," she said. "Anyway, it's not possible. I'm an Anglo. There'd be quite a ruckus over me as an owner, even as inheritor. Antelope Valley will belong to Joe Porter one day, not to me."

"Ha! The legendary Joe Porter. When in hell do I ever meet him?"

"When he gets back from wherever he's gone."

"That could be weeks or months."

"It could be," Beth agreed. "But you can wait. You've brought some staples with you to help out here. We have enough in dry supplies to subsist on if we live frugally until the rains come. You can go hunting with Creek; he'll show you the range. Wait and meet Joe. Please keep me company. *Behave!*" A key word she hadn't uttered since Tim was a small, mischievous boy and she'd occasionally lord it over him because she was several years older.

"Oh sure, *behave!*" Tim retorted. "That used to be your magic wand when you thought you were the fairy princess. That was yesterday, sis. It won't work on me today, *now*. I'm a man now, and I make my own decisions. I love you, and I'll stay on a while, but I mightn't be so charming in the process. I've developed a temper since you last saw me. Sometimes it surprises me."

"You sound like Joe Porter."

"Maybe I should stick around and meet him. Sounds like we have a lot in common."

Beth couldn't help smiling at him. Tim had turned out to be handsome and shrewd; he was indeed a grown man, she thought, as she nibbled on a stick of charqui. Acting snappish was Tim's old way of saying he would acquiesce to her wishes. But she knew better than to press her luck, to try to extract a promise. She began to gather up the remains of the picnic.

"Come," she said, "I have something to show you."

They rode further up into the hills until they came to the first of the cave drawing sites where Joe had taken Beth and where she traced the designs for weaving. Tim was politely impressed with the primitive wall graphics but not wildly excited. Art wasn't a passion with him. In any case, he preferred the American landscape artists; their vision coincided with his own romantic notions about the mythical pioneer horizon.

"What are the animals and configurations supposed to mean?" he asked Beth.

"Antelope Valley was once an extremely fertile area, as it will be again. The profusion of animals means just that."

"That isn't reason enough to wait around hoping, sis. I see it differently. A civilization that might have been self-sustaining once functioned here. Your Pai Pais are the remnants. Nothing is left; there is no chance for the future."

"It will all come back," Beth said confidently, "once the preparations are made. Rainy seasons come in ten to twenty year cycles, Creek tells me. We're now at the lowest point of a long dry cycle. The rains will begin to increase starting this year."

"How can you be sure?"

"The Pai Pais know about such things, more than we can ever realize. They're closer to Nature."

"You can't build your future on that kind of thinking," Tim said, but went no further. There was no point in arguing with her. He cared a great deal for Beth and her present stubbornness disturbed him deeply. He knew that he had a responsibility he couldn't shirk by running off; his conscience would go with him. So, he'd have to hang around until something happened to modify Beth's views—the coming of the rains, Joe's return, whatever. It was the "whatever" that worried him. Even in the revealed open barrenness of the valley, a brooding apprehension lurked. Perhaps riches did exist here, gold and silver, precious stones. But even if he were able to accept Beth's quixotic allegiance to Antelope Valley, it was only a way station on his odyssey for Jason's treasure. His own pot at the rainbow's end was more likely to lie to the north of Baja, and he'd get there when the time was right.

"So, have you decided what you will do?" Beth asked him on their way back to Rancho Cielo.

"I'll be here for a time," he told her. "Not forever, mind you. I've got things to see and do out there in the other world."

"Thank you, little brother."

"Don't thank me, sis. You wore me down to it by making me curious."

"Curious? About what?"

"About why you've changed so. . . ."

Beth had no reply for him. She refused to search her heart now for the answer.

That evening, in the luminous twilight of the mountain valley, Tim promenaded with Carmen, in full view of the house.

The girl was bubbling over with pleasure at having a male companion of such personable demeanor with whom she could converse easily.

"Tell me all about New York City," Carmen begged Tim in Spanish. "I want to know everything."

"Everything? That would take some time."

"I want to know how tall the buildings are, and how many horse cars move on the wide streets. What the people look like, what the restaurants and theatres are like. And romance! Are there early marriages or late ones, and are they arranged? I want to hear it all!"

Tim could only guess at what might please the girl, so he offered her general statistics from memory, talking impersonally about public places, museums, parks, hotels, and staying away from the gamier side of life—the bawdy houses, the streetwalkers, the near-starving, the crowding that went on among the very poor. When Carmen seemed to accept everything he said with placid nods of her head he realized that she could never understand what he was saying, being a simple girl who had spent her entire life here. It also occurred to him that she was only asking these questions so that she would have a legitimate visible reason for being alone with him. Or, that is, almost alone, for Mama Luz sat in a straightback chair on the rear portico, arms crossed over her breasts, black shawl around her shoulders, watching their every step with her penetrating condor's gaze.

Yes, Carmen was a simple girl, Tim decided, with her lovely features and clear complexion, her voluptuous woman's figure that needed no imagination to appreciate. She moved gracefully, catlike and vibrant beneath her simple, skin-tight bodices, the hems of her full skirts swishing against her shapely calves. Her long wavy hair was as black as a raven's wing, and hung down to the small of her back. At dinner she swept it up into a neat chignon and secured it at the nape of her neck with a tortoise shell comb encrusted with rhinestones, a gift from Joe. Her lips were full, naturally red, not like the women's mouths Tim had seen on the plains in those sober pioneer faces blurred from dust, grimly set toward a better future. Nor was she painted as were the frontier harlots from the Mississippi to Los Angeles. Carmen's was a natural beauty, enveloped in a cloud of unfamiliar Spanish musk that intoxicated him.

Tim's walks with Carmen became a regular thing, and he found himself forced to observe her qualities with gentlemanly restraint and decorum. Since their evening promenades were monitored by Mama Luz and even sometimes by Beth, Tim was obliged to use his softest manners.

Though the girl was extremely desirable, Tim tried not to take his walks with Carmen too seriously. After all, Joe dominated Carmen's life, that phantom Joe who was absent more than present at Rancho Cielo. It was no wonder, Tim reflected, that the poor little thing was so hungry for company. Between the severely conventional Mama Luz who nurtured Old World traditions which should be long-dead, and Beth's staunch American breeziness in the face of the abyss, what had Carmen to amuse her? Certainly not old Creek or the mute Indian faces in the community by the lake, or the jumbled scenery, spectacular though it was. Carmen wasn't even allowed to go out riding, as Beth could in her divided skirts.

Carmen was, by custom, sequestered, virtually a prisoner of Spanish mores. It was all very well for Beth to lean on preordained fate as the shaper of her own life, but what about Carmen? Tim wondered. There were moments when he wanted to sweep her into his arms, kiss those ruby lips, bury his face in her fragrant hair, make her forget her life and its cruel restrictions. He couldn't, of course. He owed propriety to Mama Luz, his hostess, to Beth, and to Carmen herself. So he kept issuing admonitions to himself as he walked with Carmen; it was not an easy assignment.

He would retire nights in a state of feverish excitement, wide awake in the darkness, imagining what he might do with Carmen if he could only creep into the hacienda and climb into her bed. And if he happened to be lucky, he finally fell asleep to have an erotic dream involving the girl, wakening to find that Nature had neatly solved the situation with a climax. After two weeks of exposure to the evening promenade and its predictable aftermath, Tim would often lapse into sullen irritability and go off by himself to talk with Creek by the dry lake.

Creek introduced Tim to a new kind of tobacco. It was a weed, he said, that grew in abundance throughout Baja California. "Something we Indians smoke for comfort and peace of mind," Creek told him, seeing his agitation, and guessing that it might be the luscious Carmen. "Say nothing to Mama Luz or to your sister," Creek warned him. "The weed is forbidden among the Spanish, and Americanos are the first to condemn it as pagan. Silence, I beg you."

Tim had no desire to challenge convention, so he kept his mouth shut and went off each afternoon riding alone, leaving the women behind. He and Creek would go up into the hills, smoke together, sit in the sun on flat grey rocks gazing dreamily off into the valley. It was during one of these times that the old man told Tim of a mysterious figure painted on a rock wall.

"It marks the sealed portal to a cave," Creek explained. "Something important, something sacred, is in the cave."

"What?"

"I'm not sure. It is a story that was passed to me by my father, and by his father to him." Creek crossed himself quickly.

"Take me there," Tim urged.

"No, señor, I cannot. It is taboo."

Tim questioned Creek further but could get no more information from the old man than what he had already learned. The significant object in the cave was meant to stay there, it must never be disturbed; and Creek would not reveal the cave's whereabouts.

One morning Tim rose before dawn and rode to the lake to help Creek and his Pai Pai assistants complete a major project. This was the placing of the roof on a communal house for Indian males, already half-built on a rise of ground above the lake's shoreline. The project had been left unfinished because the Indians had not mastered the technique required to suspend a series of triangular roof frames to which roof poles would be lashed. On top of the cross poles would then be stretched a membrane of cured animal hides, and over that a layer of clay. On this foundation would be laid two layers of rush matting, and over this another membrane of hides, forming a sturdy, waterproof roof that would easily endure a couple of decades of sun and rain.

The job was completed at dusk and Tim arrived back at the hacienda too exhausted to sit down to the evening meal. He carried a light snack out with him to Joe's house, where he was living, foregoing his usual promenade with Carmen. As soon as he'd eaten he undressed and fell into a deep, dreamless sleep

Around midnight he was awakened by a slight rustling noise in the cabin. He sat up in bed, and saw the silhouette of someone against the window.

"Who's there?" he called out, reaching for matches to light a candle.

"Shhh!" said a whisper close to him. "Don't say a word!"

It was Carmen's voice. Before Tim could say anything, Carmen was shedding her nightgown and getting into his bed. Too sleepy and surprised to protest, and hardly reluctant, he accepted her kisses, warm and passionate.

"You shouldn't be here," he told her after they had made love. "It's too dangerous."

"I know." Carmen giggled softly. "But if I waited for you, nothing would ever happen. It is safer for me to come to you."

"It can't be safe at all. What if Mama Luz found out, and my sister?"

"Mama Luz is asleep, she sleeps very hard. And Beth is asleep as well."

"You can't be sure."

"I am very quiet when I move," she said. "Don't

worry." She snuggled against him, soft, fragrant and deliciously comforting, pressing her voluptuous flesh against his, urging him on once more.

"No, Carmen," he said flatly, getting up out of bed, covering himself modestly, even though it was dark. "You must go now."

Carmen exhaled in disappointment. "But why? It's hours before dawn. We can make love again, can't we?"

"No, we can't. As I told you, it's too dangerous. We mustn't be discovered."

"You don't love me," Carmen pouted, running her hands over his body, finding an instant response.

Tim caught her hands in his, pulled her out of bed, brought her against him.

"I like you very much," he told her. "Too much." He was reluctant to call it love, but he knew he was perilously close to that emotion. "You're wonderful, Carmen," he said, "but we can't do this."

Carmen laughed softly. "We already have," she reminded him. "And we will again, many times."

"You mustn't ever come here at night."

"Well then, let us meet up in the hills. By daylight," she said boldly.

"You're crazy!"

"No, not crazy. I used to go walking by myself at siesta time instead of napping," she explained. "I can do it again, and no one will think it unusual. And you can sneak out of the cabin, follow the long trail around, and meet me. We will do it tomorrow, yes?"

"Make it the day after tomorrow. I have to meet Creek and Red Deer at the lake tomorrow. I promised to be there."

"Ah well then, the day after tomorrow, if it must be. Here's how you get to the rendezvous. No one will follow you. The Pai Pais think it is under a spell." She explained the geography carefully to him, and the markings along the trail, so that he would not get lost.

He stood in the open door of the cabin and watched

her, fleet of foot, skim silently over the ground to the hacienda. She disappeared, wraithlike, into its shadowy interior. He hoped and prayed that Beth, who had always been a light sleeper, hadn't heard Carmen come to him, nor watched her return to her room.

When he was satisfied that Carmen would be safely in her room, he went back to bed, worrying over what an impulsive fool he'd been. But on the other hand, he hadn't initiated the love-making. Why shouldn't he savor what was offered so readily?

Hell, he rationalized, it had been too long since he'd enjoyed the favors of a desirable woman. And Carmen was more than just a receptacle to please; she was a joyful, carefree, zesty creature who had illumined this dull valley for him, gracing his time. She had offered herself eagerly to him, with expertise, and it was obvious that she wasn't a virgin. Even if she did already belong to Joe Porter, in a physical sense as well as by formal promise, she seemed to feel that generosity was the better part of infidelity. The girl had a rich, pagan enthusiasm for passion, and apparently no qualms where he was concerned.

The next day Tim worked with Creek and Red Deer on a new type of light weather shelter for the Pai Pais. Easy to erect, quick to dismantle, its design was an oval base of rough poles lashed together at the top and covered with rush mats, brushwood, or grass. On his trek West Tim had seen the Indian shelters in climates with extreme winters and was impressed with their toughness. Sometimes these structures could endure several years of punishing winters. They were made with an arched framework of poles overlaid with bark, rush mats, buffalo hides. The design was far more practical for the Pai Pais than the fragile wickiup so common along the Pacific Coast. Tim spent the entire day helping Creek and Red Deer and a crew to construct several of the wigwams, clustering them along the lake's shoreline for the family groups that did not wish to lodge through the winter in the huts near the hacienda.

As Tim worked with Creek and Red Deer, he thought intermittently of Carmen. Each time he would dwell on the particulars of last night he would grow agitated, dizzy, with desire. There were some moments when he wondered, hot with lust, if he could last until noon the following day to bury himself in her tantalizing body. And at the same time, a part of him that grew from puritanical American values was shamed at the kind of folly in which he had involved himself. To go out in broad daylight on a sunny autumn afternoon, to make love to a woman who was already committed to marry his absent host—he couldn't help but feel shocked at his temerity.

Tim's sexual experience had been limited to a couple of attractive demimondaines in New York, aspiring actresses who had granted him unqualified favors in exchange for which gifts were offered. And on the journey West he'd had a whore in a small, nameless frontier town. But until Carmen, Tim had never truly experienced the mysterious chemistry that is usually called love, the force that brings two people together beyond rhyme or reason, making them behave sometimes nobly and wisely, though most often incautiously and without good sense.

Tim decided as he worked that what was happening to him with Carmen wasn't love, and he felt protected with this thought. Instead, what he felt he called alchemy, that medieval blend of chemistry and credo, with a dash of peppery witchcraft thrown in for good measure. This bubbling force could not only turn base metal into gold, he had read, but it possessed the power to cure all disease and to prolong life. Most significantly, however, alchemy was supposed to have the power to transform something ordinary into something precious and unique, even profound.

At supper that night in the hacienda, Tim was distracted at the table, Beth noticed, and Carmen appeared nervous. Beth wondered why. Perhaps Tim was getting bored and restless at Rancho Cielo. It occurred to her, too, that perhaps Carmen might be interested in Tim, a handsome young man of considerable presence and charm. In that case, Beth hoped that Carmen would not be as indiscreet as she had been with Joe—which in Joe's case was their business, not hers. But if Carmen and Tim got involved, and Beth found out, she would have to ask Tim to leave the valley at once.

At noontime the next day Tim managed to get away after luncheon, saying he was going to ride down to the lake to see how the Pai Pais were coming along with the construction of their wigwams. He was relieved that Beth didn't ask to come along; she had a sewing class at the chapel.

Tim followed the long trail that Carmen had so carefully described to him, finding each of the trail signs just where she said they would be. Finally, he came up onto a high cliff overlooking the valley. The rock shelter Carmen had chosen for their tryst lay a few yards beyond that, in a rough amphitheatre of boulders.

Dismounting, Tim tethered his horse to a scraggly ironwood tree and made his way into the cul de sac, scanning the ground for rattlers.

Carmen had not yet arrived, so he advanced into the welcome shade of the rock overhang. Directly ahead of him was the painting on the rock wall, so impressive that he couldn't suppress a gasp of surprise.

Larger than life, possibly ten feet tall, the human figure in the shape of a cross seemed to fly above him, condor-like. The vivid, staring eyes in a shadowy face suggested to Tim a watchful sentinel, a mystical guard. He could not tell from its seemingly fresh black and rust coloring how old it was. But of course it must have been there for centuries. The figure was clad in an ankle-length garment, its long full sleeves straightly horizontal, square fingers protruding, the feet square stubs. The figure's head was outlined, without a halo. No attempt had been made to paint in features; the eyes were grimly outstanding, daubs of rust-red against the somber shadows.

As Tim stood in silent contemplation of the crude

graphic he heard a noise behind him on the approach path. He turned to see Carmen hurrying toward him, out of breath, her features flushed but determined, her jaw set in his direction. She came running to him with open arms. She flung her body against his with such ardor that he nearly lost his balance.

"I can't wait," she murmured, reaching for his belt.

He held her at arm's length.

"Carmen, catch your breath," he commanded. While flattered by her passion for him, he was also intimidated by its intensity.

"I need you!" Carmen breathed. "Please don't torment me, Tim. Let's make love!"

They did, immediately, in the shadowed arch of the overhang, beneath the palpable presence of the figure. Somehow, and Tim couldn't say why, he had the peculiar feeling that they were being watched.

When he had satisfied Carmen's needs and his own, he sat next to her on a rock ledge, with the towering figure behind them.

Without looking at it, Tim asked her if she knew the significance of the figure.

"Creek says it is religious," Carmen told him. "He says it was put there to remind the Pai Pais of God and the Church."

"When?"

"According to Creek, the mission Pai Pais painted it around the time the Jesuit padres were driven from Baja California."

"That was almost one-hundred years ago," Tim said. "I wonder what the figure is supposed to be doing."

"He is protecting Antelope Valley from evil spirits, Creek says." Carmen reached for Tim's hand and pressed it to her breast. "When are you going away, Tim?"

The question Tim hadn't realized he was dreading until she uttered it was finally out in the open.

"Soon," he muttered, "soon. What makes you ask?"

"I am going with you," Carmen announced.

"What do you mean by that?"

"Just what I say—I'm accompanying you."

"You can't, Carmen. I'm on my own, I have to be. I can't be responsible for anyone but myself. I have places to see and things to do in a man's world. There's no room for a young woman like you, as much as I'd like it. Besides," he added quickly, "you are engaged to Joe."

She pushed his hand away.

"I don't care a damn in hell for Joe," she replied fervently. "I care about you now. I love you, Tim."

"Love," he observed, "is something that has to work itself out over a long period of time."

"We could marry and let it work out itself," Carmen pleaded. "You can take me to San Francisco as your wife."

Good God, thought Tim, the girl was hysterical. Could there be something really wrong with her?

"Banish that thought from your mind," Tim said, deciding instantly that the sooner he left Antelope Valley— alone—the better off he would be. If he remained, Joe would soon return and there would have to be a showdown.

He couldn't see taking Carmen with him. There were hordes of lovely women out there who would find him attractive, and he didn't want to be saddled with one woman whose possessiveness would grow greater the further away she got from security.

But it was true, he thought, that Carmen was a marvelous lover, sweet and tender, and utterly devoted to him. Having her around might not be such a bad idea. It was clear to him that she didn't care a fig for Joe, only for him. The more Tim thought about it, the more the idea of taking Carmen seemed like a good one.

If he did decide to take her, he wondered how he could broach the subject to Beth. He would have to tell her tonight. No, tomorrow. Tomorrow was best. He realized that he was getting more like the Californios every day, putting off until tomorrow any task that was either large or onerous, or both.

"I'll think about it, Carmen," he said finally. "You think about it, too. It's a serious decision to make."

"I know, and I don't need to think about it," she said resolutely. "I already have. I'm going with you. I will be yours alone."

17

ALTHOUGH Tim had expressly admonished Carmen to remain in her room and not come to him, that night she came anyway, around midnight. They were half-undressed, about to make love, when there was a knock at the cabin door. Carmen crouched down beneath the bèd as Tim hastily pulled on his pants and opened the door.

Beth stood there in her nightcap and gown, looking for all the world, Tim decided, like a puritanical matriarch about to uncover a shocking scandal.

"She's here, isn't she?" Beth said sternly, a statement, not a question.

"You spying on me, sis?" Tim said, trying to be nonchalant. Now there'd be a showdown which he had tentatively decided to avoid by sneaking away with Carmen the following night, leaving Beth an explanatory note instead of telling her in person.

"I know what's going on," Beth announced. "Carmen is here. I saw her sneak past my window."

"That's not like you, Beth."

"Tim, she's here, isn't she?" Beth took a step forward, but Tim raised his arms, leaning both hands against the door frame to block her way.

"Yes," he admitted, "she's here."

"My God, Tim, are you losing your wits? You know she's engaged to Joe."

Until that moment Tim hadn't completely sold himself on the idea of taking Carmen with him. In broad daylight he could go riding out of the valley on the marked trail and leave Carmen behind. That would be the simplest and easiest thing to do. But now, confronted with Beth's discovery of their relationship, he turned stubborn. He would brazen it out.

"She may be engaged to Joe," he said, "but she doesn't love him. I was going to leave tomorrow night, Beth, but now I think we ought to go before daylight, before Mama Luz wakes up."

"We? You're not thinking of taking her with you! Dear God in Heaven!"

Carmen appeared suddenly at Tim's side.

"I am going with him, Beth," she said firmly.

"Leave us, Carmen," Beth commanded the girl.

"But—"

"I said, leave us alone—Now."

Carmen picked up her dressing robe. Tim and Beth stood aside to let her pass; she hurried silently toward the house and disappeared inside.

"You fool," Beth hissed at him. "Light a candle."

The room sprang into detail: the rumpled bed, Tim's clothes on the floor, Beth's grimly set features.

"You're irresponsible," Beth said. "I am deeply, bitterly disappointed in you, Tim. I kept having premonitions about this, but I kept telling myself it was only some absurd notion of mine. I can't believe you could do a thing like this. Haven't you even considered Joe's feelings?"

"Yes, of course. Many times."

"And you haven't guessed that he and Carmen might be lovers?"

"Lovers?"

"Just so, lovers."

"I knew she wasn't a virgin."

"Joe will come after you."

"Not a pleasant thought," Tim said. "But I've thought about it, and I don't want to leave without her."

Beth seemed suddenly to warm to him. She put a hand on his arm. "Tim, I'm sorry. I've no right to judge you. I know all too well what it is to be carried away by a passion. If you must leave with Carmen, and it seems your mind is made up, then you must leave here before dawn. Go immediately by the Western trail to San Diego, not through the Rancho Romero grant. Carmen knows the route, she'll guide you. In San Diego you'll be able to book passage on a ship for San Francisco. The harbor's always full of ships these days, I hear. If you come to realize, as I think you will, that Carmen is not the right woman for you, then take her to San Jose. She has a second cousin there, a widower. She's pretty and resourceful. She'll be all right."

Tim was aghast at Beth's impersonal disposition of Carmen's future. "Beth, I wouldn't leave with her if I planned to desert her. I'm surprised to hear you even suggest such a thing."

"Well, are you planning to marry her?" she asked.

"Not at present. I'm not ready to settle down."

"Good," she said. "I advise you not to. I think she's epileptic."

"I don't believe you, Beth."

"You must believe me. It's true."

"Does Joe know about it?"

"We've never discussed Carmen's life in detail. I have no idea of his feelings. Only Mama Luz's. She approves of Carmen, but then, she doesn't know they've been lovers. What else she knows about Carmen I can only guess. She keeps her own counsel and I respect that."

"Why didn't you say something to me about Carmen's epilepsy sooner?"

"I didn't know you were involved with her until tonight."

"You ought to leave this place, Beth," Tim said. "Come with us. It's not healthy for you to stay at Rancho Cielo."

"Leave? I couldn't leave. This is my home, Tim. Come, we must hurry. Time's precious."

"Please, Beth. You'll wither away up here. We'll go to San Francisco, start a new life there."

"That's impossible. Don't insist. I'll explain to Mama Luz that you're taking Carmen north to her cousin's. You decided on the spur of the moment to go north and Carmen wanted to go along, so you took her. I don't know if Mama Luz will accept it, but that's what I'll say."

"You know what my going means—?"

Beth nodded solemnly. "That we may not see each other again for a long time."

"If ever," Tim added.

"I love you, Tim," Beth said softly. "That won't ever change. But it's obvious that we're fated not to be together. Well, it's getting late. I'll go and see Carmen."

"You've changed, Beth, but I love you, too," he said, embracing his sister. "And I'm sorry . . ."

"It had to be," Beth said, "or it wouldn't have happened," and hurried off to Carmen's room.

Mama Luz was not so much shaken by the news of Carmen's departure as she was puzzled by it.

"How strange," she commented. "Why should your brother leave with Carmen if nothing is amiss?"

"Tim is impulsive," Beth said, "as Joselito is. We were talking last night after you retired, Tim and I," Beth felt obliged to embroider, "about what he would do in the future. He was grateful for your hospitality but didn't feel he should impose on you any longer. As I say, he's given to sudden flights of fancy."

"Well, he should have stayed to meet Joselito," Mama Luz said. "I regret that."

"It would have been nice," Beth agreed. "But anyway, we were talking when Carmen walked into the room. When she learned that Tim was planning to go immediately, she demanded to go along."

"Forgive me, but do you suppose there is something between them?" Mama Luz ventured.

"I don't think so," Beth lied, despising herself for dissembling. "But I do have a serious question about Carmen."

Beth told Mama Luz of the seizure. The older woman registered no surprise whatsoever.

"Ah yes," she answered calmly. "Many years ago I learned from Carmen's guardian that she was subject to these very occasional fits. It is not inherited epilepsy. The condition resulted from a childhood injury. When she was very small she was struck on the head with a rock thrown by another child in play. That's all there is to it, whatever you may think."

"You're absolutely sure of this?"

"Absolutely." Mama Luz crossed herself and said with a veiled glance at Beth, "I would not lie to you, my child, in the face of God."

"Of course not, Mama Luz," said Beth.

"I had hoped that Joselito would marry Carmen," Mama Luz said. "But sadly enough, in the past few months I have noticed his great indifference to the girl. He may have someone he likes better down in the lowlands; that could be the reason. I chose Carmen because, although she has no dowry, she comes from a good, God-fearing family. I thought she would gladly settle down here at Rancho Cielo, raise children, be a companion to me in my final years. I am to be denied that, I see." The old woman sighed. "Maybe it is all for the best. One must look on sudden change like that, otherwise . . ."

"I feel I should have done something to keep her from going," Beth said.

"No, you could do nothing."

"I hope that won't change your feeling toward me. After all, Tim is my brother, and he did take Carmen away. I hope I'm still welcome."

"My dear, you are like a daughter to me. Of course

you are welcome. I have only two worries now in life:
the safe return of Joselito and the coming of the rains.
They are extremely late, and after the period of drought
one worries and prays, and hopes . . ."

The rains came ten days later, in steady, rhythmic
waves of storms rolling up from the warm, humid southern
Pacific waters. The initial storm brought prodigious
thunder, lightning and hailstones the size of pigeon eggs.
After that, there was a steady downpour that lasted three
days and nights, much to the relief of everyone at
Rancho Cielo.

The reservoir and the terraces by the lake received the
welcome downfall, surviving it perfectly. The success of
Beth's project was a heady confirmation of her careful
planning. As the rain drummed steadily on the tile roofs
of the hacienda, it was falling in torrents on the parched
soil of the surrounding sierra's few flat areas. It coursed
between the boulders, bubbled through rocky courses,
much of it disappearing eventually into the natural underground reservoirs. Eventually enough water would be
stored in Nature's cisterns to assure a steady flow from
the springs all through the next torrid summer.

The rains continued to fall in a continuing series of
storms, bringing inches of rain in a matter of weeks, more,
in fact, than had fallen in the last several years altogether.
As the weeks passed and the weather turned toward
winter, the storms changed direction and began to drift
in from the north. Flurries of snow fell on the peaks surrounding Antelope Valley, although the snowfall was light.
It soon melted and joined the fresh water supplies growing underground. The marshy lake rose to flood level,
forcing the Pai Pais with their few small children out of
the Indian dwellings along the lakeshore and into the
drier abodes behind the hacienda where they would remain for the winter. No one complained about the cold
and dampness, however. The rain was an answer to all
their prayers.

*   *   *

One day after the rains had let up and the valley was experiencing warmer, sunnier weather, two riders came up to Rancho Cielo from the Romero estate. The men were accompanied by a mule caravan laden with supplies of all sorts. They were sent by Joe, accompanied by a letter for Mama Luz.

In the letter Joe sent his greetings to all the valley inhabitants and promised that he would be home in time to celebrate La Natividad. There were presents for all, and enough dry food staples to last the remainder of the fall and into the winter season. Joe asked to be remembered to Beth, to Creek and to the Pai Pais. He had heard, he said, that Carmen had returned to the north where she was born, and that Beth's brother had chaperoned her on the journey. This was not upsetting news, he said. In fact, it was perhaps as it should be, Carmen's going. He told his mother he did not regret the change of heart that took her away. This last news was a definite relief to Beth.

Joe returned much sooner than Christmas, however, and not jauntily on horseback. He was carried up the steep, torturous mountain trail by sturdy Indian bearers on a litter, and in great agony, for the trip was rough at best.

"A hunting accident," Joe explained at Mama Luz's tearful reception—she was normally calm in the face of emergencies. "Raul and I were out in the hills and some fool boy, the son of a cousin from Los Angeles, dropped a hunting rifle he was carrying. It exploded and caught me in the calf and just missed breaking my lower leg."

Beth was able to rise cheerfully and efficiently to meet any calamity head-on.

"Mama Luz and I will get you well in no time," she said. "Hunting accidents will happen," she added, making it easy for Mama Luz to accept Joe's explanation as the truth.

Beth didn't believe Joe's tale for a moment. He was

probably shot while galloping away from the scene of some crime, although she wished she didn't feel obliged to think that way. And she would never really know, since Joe would never tell her particulars. Robbing stagecoaches, rustling cattle, or whatever it was he was doing, would expose him to the constant possibility of injury, or even death. He was lucky, she thought, to get off so easily. But he was in considerable pain; he was paying for whatever it was he had done.

When Mama Luz retired that night after sitting at Joe's bedside until she could keep her eyes open no longer, Beth went to sit with him. Joe was restless and uncomfortable.

"I'll be glad to read something to you, if it will help you relax," Beth said. "You ought to try to sleep. How about some hot tea?"

"No tea, and no books, please," Joe said. "Talk to me, Beth. It's good to see you." He reached out for her hand and held it, his smile a grimace through the pain.

"It's good to see you, too, Joe, even under these circumstances."

"Tell me, what really happened between your brother and Carmen?"

Beth hesitated a moment. "I am not absolutely sure what went on," she said. "I *think* Carmen fell in love with Tim. You know how impressionable she is. Tim is the same age, and even though he's travelled some and city-bred—"

"Oh yes," Joe said, making it easy for her, "I know all about little Carmen. She's a sweet enough child, but not very wise. She falls in love with every eligible man who comes along. Before me there was Esteban Gonzales from San Diego. That was a ripe passion. Carmen stayed with the Gonzales family for a while until Esteban discovered that there'd been someone else before him, and a child—farmed out to a cousin—was the result of that one."

"Dear God!" Beth exclaimed. "I had no idea."

"Well, now you have, and you can relieve yourself of the doleful look of responsibility that clouds your face," Joe said.

"I didn't know," Beth said.

"My mother doesn't know, either," Joe told her. "Or if she does, her pride wouldn't let her admit it. She is always preparing the way for me, poor dear soul. She hasn't much else to do in life, and she can't accept that these are not the times of her girlhood. The world's changed place; it's fallen apart. The old standards are gone, and you have to make your own rules to survive." Joe winced suddenly in pain.

Beth leaned forward. "Let me look at the wound," she said. "I'm a very good nurse."

"It's not pretty."

"I'm not squeamish."

"I'm all right, I tell you," Joe insisted. "I'll be just fine. Creek will come tomorrow. He knows what to do. I'll be back on a horse in no time, and off to the wars. Wait and see . . ."

"I'm not talking about the future," Beth said. "I'm talking about now. I want to look at your leg."

"Mother and Creek will do it tomorrow. It's fine, I tell you."

"What must I do, throttle you with a pillow to see it?" She was surprised at her brusqueness but knew it was necessary in order to persuade him.

"You really think you know something about such things?"

"I do indeed. I've had some experience on the trail. Besides, as I said, I'm not the timid soul you've always considered me."

"Have I?"

"Yes, you have. Now, may I look at that wound?"

"All right, go ahead," he said.

Beth rose quickly before he could change his mind.

Delicately she unwrapped the layers of cotton bandages that covered his calf and ankle, trying not to gag at the stench.

The wound was parallel to the bone, a long, running gash that pierced the fleshy portion of the calf. It was a suppurating yellow crater surrounded by swollen, magenta-colored flesh. It lay close to the bone which seemed undamaged, and it certainly did not look good. No wonder he was in such pain, Beth thought.

"Well, what do you see, doctor?" Joe asked through clenched teeth, his head turned away from his leg.

"It shouldn't have been bound," Beth said. "It ought to be open now to get the air."

"The physician said otherwise."

"Well, he was probably thinking that you would be riding and exposing it to chafing and various disaffections such as dirt."

"He knew I'd come home with it."

"Didn't he give you any medication for disinfecting it?"

"None."

"That's curious." Beth scrutinized his face. "Joe, are you sure you saw a doctor?"

"Not a real one," he confessed. "One of the Romero mestizos at the hacienda has studied medicine. He bound it up for me."

Beth suppressed an exclamation of outrage before saying coolly, "Well, there's nothing I can do for you now. We'll cover it with a support so that you can sleep under a sheet and not cause further irritation. That long trip up the mountain was the worst thing you could possibly have done for it."

"You think the support will work?" Joe asked.

"It will help. Tomorrow we'll see what can be done."

"Creek will know what to do."

"Between us," Beth said, "we'll think of something." Anything Creek might suggest would have to be cleared with her, she swore to herself. She went out to the bin where kindling was kept and selected several foot-long sticks. She bound these together so they would support the sheet. She set it up over Joe's leg and pulled up the sheet. Exhausted, Joe was asleep even before she was finished. She put the back of her hand to his cheek, aware of a high fever. His condition did not please her, and she went to bed in a state of apprehension.

Beth arose at dawn. She walked to the Indian huts behind the hacienda to confer with Creek, already up and smoking his first pipe of the day, huddled dreamily in a coarse blanket by the small fieldstone fireplace in his hut. Beth explained that Joe's leg did not look right to her and she was extremely worried about him.

"I don't want him to lose the leg, or his life. We have no proper facilities here to take care of a serious case. Perhaps you can get some Indian medicine that will heal the wound?" she asked the old man.

"There is a strong herb that grows in the highest rocks of the sierra that we leave up there to cure. We do not store it in the valley because its strength is better preserved up high. We bring it down only as we need it. That is our way. Come," he said, "let us go and look."

They took horses and rode up into the bright crystalline air of the high peaks. Creek guided Beth to a spot not far from the location of the cave drawings. In a dry sheltered pocket of granite, Creek located a cache of dried herb blossoms, stuffed into the folds of a rough jute sack loosely stitched up. The burlap had kept the blossoms from being scattered about by the winds from the big storms, and in their sheltered location they had fared well. They were slightly damp from the weather, but they could be easily dried out, Creek advised, which would not damage their medicinal potency.

Creek opened the burlap sack, scooped out an ample supply of the herb blossoms and put them into his saddle bag. They carried these down to the hacienda, and dried them thoroughly in front of the open hearth.

"You must now make a powder of them, sprinkle it on

a steaming hot poultice and apply that to the wound. It will draw out the evil humors left by the bullet and allow quick healing," Creek advised.

"Are you sure this will work?" Beth asked anxiously.

"It works both as a tea or as a poultice. The Pai Pais do not have any strong medicines like the Americanos. But this works for us. If not, we can try other things."

Beth prepared clean cloths, ground up the dried herb blossoms until they were powdery and sprinkled them on the poultice. She then applied the poultice to Joe's calf. The heat made him wince with pain. Beth felt doubtful, on seeing the increased swelling and suppuration, that a mere poultice would heal the wound.

Joe became feverish during the morning. In the afternoon his discomfort increased. He complained of a sharp, throbbing ache in his calf that grew steadily worse.

Beth changed the poultice every hour, as Creek advised, but by evening she could see no marked change in the wound's condition. In fact, it appeared to have grown slightly worse.

Creek came at her bidding; they conferred in the kitchen.

"Continue with the dressings," Creek instructed, not overly concerned with her report. "In the morning we will see."

"But he's in such pain," Beth said, deeply worried. "I fear that moist gangrene may set in. I used to see it on the trail coming West." She knew that surgery might well have to be the end result if Joe's leg turned gangrenous. She didn't even want to dwell on the point that amputation could make a cripple out of Joe. She didn't think Joe, as restless as he was, could live like that.

Mama Luz was beside herself. Whether or not she accepted the story of the hunting accident, she was deeply agitated, knowing what might happen. She sat quietly in the room with her son, monitoring his slow breathing and dabbing his forehead with a damp cloth.

In the morning Joe's temperature was apparent in his scarlet cheeks and feverish body. He refused liquids and began to drift in and out of wakefulness. Beth stopped using the poultices, feeling that the hot compresses might be spreading the infection. She called for Creek again.

"There is one more thing," Creek said. "We will begin it soon."

Creek called together Red Deer and several other Pai Pai men. They went in a group to the communal house by the lake for a pow-pow. Pipes were passed around, and when the men were sufficiently mellow, incantations were made and slow dancing was begun. The men chanted in endless monotones while they shuffled back and forth in suppliant motions to the gods until dawn.

Shortly thereafter, red-eyed and unsteady on his feet, Creek appeared at the hacienda kitchen door, asking for Beth, who came at once.

"How is he now?" Creek asked.

"No better," Beth told him, "after your attention," referring obliquely to the pow-pow. "The fever still rages; it hasn't broken."

Creek shrugged. "Sometimes when a man is outside the tribe but understanding of it, our prayers will work for him. Joselito is like one of us. *If* he believes, then he can be healed."

"But what if he doesn't improve?" Beth asked. "What will we do?"

"I would like to try something else, something I believe in but not the same thing as our magic. It borrows from two worlds."

Mama Luz appeared in the doorway from the inner house, catching only the tail end of Creek's speech.

"What's that?" she demanded suspiciously. "What are you planning to do, Creek? I will not allow you to harm my boy."

"Señora," Creek assured the old woman gently, "I would not harm Joselito for anything. He is like a son to me. I have known him since he was a baby in your arms."

"But still you might hurt him, even without meaning to," Mama Luz said in a querulous voice.

Creek sent Mama Luz a kindly, patient look.

"We must do something, señora, since our magic has no effect and we don't have Americano medicine."

Sensing a radical action, Mama Luz began to sob. "Oh no, no," she protested. "You will hurt my boy."

"You must give me your permission, señora, to try something else."

Beth intervened. "You're saying that we have no choice but to follow your next suggestion?" she said bluntly.

"That is right." Creek turned to Mama Luz. "Will you give me your permission, señora?"

Mama Luz was crying into her hands by this time and could not answer. But as Beth led her from the kitchen she looked up and nodded sorrowfully to Creek.

Minutes later Creek and Beth met behind the closed door to Joe's room. Joe was momentarily conscious, though weak, seeming to surrender unaccountably to the infection rather than fight it. It was as if he'd lost the will to live, Beth thought, which sent a frisson of alarm through her.

Creek approached Joe, bending over him.

"Joselito, it's me, Creek," the old Indian said. "I am going to make you well. You must give me your will."

Joe moaned softly, his eyes fluttering, but said nothing.

"I will try not to hurt you, but if there is some pain, you must understand it is for your life. Bear with me for a while. Do you hear and understand?"

Joe's eyes blinked open briefly, he nodded at Creek, then his lids dropped shut again.

Creek turned to Beth. "I do not like it, this weakness. Please, you will stand at the foot of the bed and hold his ankles. With all your strength."

Beth did as Creek ordered. "Now, you must not let loose if he struggles. And while you are holding him, you must see in your mind's eye a cross."

"A cross, like the one I'm wearing?" Beth asked.

"Like that, if it is easiest. A square cross will do. But more than a cross, you must see it in the figure of a man clad in dark robes. His arms outstretched, fingers pointed out, toes pointed downwards, eyes like holes staring straight at you from a dark face."

"What does it mean?" Beth whispered.

"It is not for us to understand, only to accept."

Creek withdrew from its belt sheath the hunting knife he always carried. Its blade shone in the candlelight.

Beth could not stifle her sharp gasp of fear.

"Don't worry," Creek assured her calmly, "it will only hurt him for a short time. But you must hold him firmly."

He removed the poultice from Joe's wound, grimacing slightly at the rank odor. Then he bent forward over the infection, eyes closed, lips moving soundlessly, but only for a few seconds, moving the knife toward the wound. Starting just below the knee, he etched two vertical lines in the flesh down the shin bone with the knife's point, quickly and deftly. Joe moved but did not cry out. Next he made two more incisions across the shin and halfway around the calf. Joe convulsed slightly at the horizontal cuts, emitting a stifled groan of pain; but he did not open his eyes or cry out in distress.

Next, Creek made a circular cut to represent the figure's head, and five small cuts symbolizing each foot. Then a five-line horizontal right hand cut, and another for the left hand. All cuts were made in the same sequence in which he might have performed the Christian blessing, had he been making the sign of the cross with himself facing in reverse.

When he had finished he made a square cross signature in the air between Joe and himself with his right hand moving clockwise around the four points. Then he wiped his knife's point clean on a piece of cloth and put it back into the sheath.

"There," he turned to Beth, "Joselito is now protected.

He will be all right now. That was our strongest medicine," he said, and departed.

Beth sat in the chair beside Joe's bed, dozing for several hours after she made sure that Mama Luz was asleep. Shortly before midnight, Joe sat up in bed, blinked his eyes in surprise and asked a startled Beth in a strong voice for water. She gave him a drink, he thanked her and lay back on his pillow, eyes wide open and staring at the beamed ceiling.

"Are you feeling all right?" Beth ventured to ask.

Joe nodded slowly. "Comfortable," he murmured.

Beth touched his forehead and his cheek. The fever was gone; his flesh was cool. She pulled back the sheet and removed the wickiup framework that she had replaced after Creek finished his ritual. The yellow crater of the wound had ceased to suppurate, to her astonishment. The inflammation had all but disappeared in the few hours since she had last seen the wound.

Beth was stunned by the dramatic improvement; she would not have believed such a change were possible had she not seen the evidence herself. She hesitated to call the healing process miraculous, but no other word was quite as well suited.

"You're a lot better, Joe," she told him.

Joe acknowledged her words with a sleepy, relaxed yawn, turned his head on the pillow and drifted off immediately into a gentle sleep, snoring lightly. Gone were the ominous, attenuated whistling breaths of only a few hours earlier.

Beth continued to sit by Joe's bed in case he needed something. It was close to dawn when she awakened again. She checked Joe and found him still sleeping peacefully. She inspected the wound again; it was almost closed, the swelling nearly gone. The suppuration had stopped and the area was drying up nicely and would probably soon scab over.

Elated, Beth decided that she could lie down now and get some real sleep. She dragged her weary body to her room and lay down fully clothed across the bed. As she drifted off to sleep she wondered why one ritual worked in Joe's case and another did not. It seemed that what was ultimately needed was a human symbol of some sort impressed upon the flesh, as well as the square cross of a primitive pre-Christian theology. In combination these two forces were apparently formidable foes of illness—unless, of course, Joe's rapid recovery was no more than coincidental to the rituals and would have happened without them. But she somehow wanted to believe in miracles. The pure Indian ritual of chanting and invocations at the communal house had done nothing, while Creek's simple ceremony combining the two crosses had worked.

She decided to ask Creek about this puzzle, and Mama Luz too, but supposed that neither could tell her very much—nor probably could Joe when he got well. Faith would have been involved, and where faith was concerned, logic and reason weren't important, she'd learned. You leaped the chasm of illness from logic to faith and found abundant life on the other side, a miracle.

In two days Joe was up and outside; in three he was riding his horse again, and before the week was out he was talking about going away again. He began, however, to pay more attention to Beth than he had before, partly, Beth guessed, because Carmen wasn't around. She wasn't going to read too much into it, knowing it might lead to frustration.

18

ONE fine day while Joe and Beth sat on the portico extension in a pocket of warm winter sunshine, Beth decided to ask Joe about his recovery.

"What do you think happened when Creek performed his ritual on you?" she enquired.

"I knew what he was doing," Joe replied, "and I responded."

"I know, but how? Why?"

"Well, the wound was getting worse. I knew that, even in my delirium. But I was past caring. Concern, obligations, they weren't clear to me."

"What do you mean?"

"I was sorting out reasons for living as my spirit waited. When Creek made the pow-wow, I could actually hear the voices in the hacienda, recognize each one of them. As you know, I understand Pai Pai almost as well as English or Spanish. But the Indians were praying and dancing only for my pagan spirit to be at rest. The change came with the use of the cross; that was the crisis."

"I don't quite understand."

"Well, when I was very small there was a man named Tree among the Pai Pais, an uncle of Creek's. I once saw him perform the same ritual to cure a Pai Pai who'd been bitten by a red rattler. He cut a square cross in the bitten arm and then sucked out the poison. The Pai Pais say this goes way back to the mission fathers, a long time ago. It was unknown to them before then. They put great faith in the cross, though maybe not in the same sense that we do."

"There were two crosses carved into your shin," Beth said.

"Yes, I know. That's the Pai Pai way of recognizing the Christian cross along with the Indian cross," Joe said.

"And the mission fathers were acknowledging the pagan one by giving it equal prominence, is that it?"

"A priest probably wouldn't admit to it, but yes, I think that's quite accurate."

Joe stretched out his arms and legs in the crystal-clear sunshine. Both he and Beth were enjoying the brief respite of clear weather, for the rains had let up during the past few days, making Joe's convalescence outdoors possible.

"God, it's wonderful to be alive," Joe declared happily. "Sometimes I haven't thought so—Miguelito's death, our poor fortune at Rancho Cielo—but right now things are going well. We have the rains at last, we'll have crops this coming spring and summer. I have to thank you, Beth, for being such a Rock of Gibraltar."

"I only did what I had to do," Beth said without affectation. "One sees a need and fills it."

"You went far beyond any call of mere duty. I hope you know what I mean."

"I'm not sure," she said guardedly.

"Don't you know what I'm saying?"

"Of course. We're a family at Rancho Cielo, a mixed but congenial group—Mama Luz, you, myself, little Nate, the Pai Pais. There is really no division between us. We are all blessed by the place we live in, Antelope Valley."

She was surprised at her statement; the words simply poured forth automatically, beyond her control.

"Miguelito is dead," Joe went on. "I loved him as you did, I respected your bereavement. But there's just so much the living can do for the dead in that respect. He is now a memory, and the mourning is over and done with. We have to get on with life."

"Yes, we do," Beth agreed. "Speaking of getting on with life, I still feel terrible about what happened with Tim and Carmen. He was a guest, it should have been different."

"Forget about it, Beth. I never loved Carmen really, and she didn't love me, whatever she might have told you. It was my mother's fiction that kept things going, not mine. Anyway, we've been through all this before. I'm only concerned with you now, not other people."

"What are you trying to say?"

Joe rose from his chair. He turned to her with an expression so filled with strangled emotion that she knew at once what he wanted to confess.

"Dammit, Beth, listen to me," he cried out. "I'm in love with you! I've been in love with you ever since the first day I saw you coming in to Santa Fe."

"Joe, that's not true," she protested.

She remembered how impressed she'd been by his dashing good looks, so different from Michael's clean-cut manliness, and his informal nonchalance to most everything that she took seriously. She had always responded to him with spirit, never with indifference, she recalled. Perhaps with a shade more intimacy, when Michael was alive, than was necessary for a brother-in-law. But she hadn't entertained licentious thoughts, yet why had her heart felt heavy when he left her at Rancho Cielo and went away? Even though the emotion may have translated itself into burning resentment that he could walk out so casually and desert his obligations, she knew there had been more to it.

She did care for him, far more now, she realized, since he had passed through the valley of death and emerged so vibrantly alive. She could recognize the signs with reluctance, and knew that she had simply swept them aside until this moment, refusing to accept them. Yet even now she resisted the private admission. It was neither right nor comfortable, a leap off one of the valley's high cliffs, a fall from grace.

Joe didn't want a family, he didn't intend to ever settle down. Without doubt most women would find him very attractive in an extremely physical way, Beth was convinced. This would make it relatively easy for him to pick and choose lovers. Surely he wouldn't want the sober responsibility of settling down in Antelope Valley, help it to stay alive and thriving, a devotion the remnant band of Pai Pais expected of their chief as much as Mama Luz did. And while he would make a charming older companion for little Nate, teaching him to ride, to hunt, he wouldn't meet the challenge of being a parent; she hardly judged him as suited for that role. Though he was a man she would never get to know well, she felt sure, Joe still drew her magnetically, made her want to overcome her natural reluctance to respond to his words.

"Why should I lie about loving you, Beth?" Joe demanded.

"Well, why not?" she replied defiantly. "You lie about other matters, important ones."

"*I* lie to you? When have I ever done that?"

"Maybe you don't exactly lie," she conceded, "but there are large portions of your life that you share with no one."

Joe grinned boyishly. "What you're saying is, I share some of my days with Rancho Cielo and the rest with others?"

"Yes, I suppose that's what I'm saying—approximately."

"And you don't think it's fair of me?"

"Since you brought it up," Beth said with spirit, "no, I don't."

"Beth, I'm the kind of man who nurtures himself on privacy, putting my life into various pockets where it's never seen totally by anyone. Oh, I might drink away many nights with the Romeros, swap yarns with the vaqueros, so to speak, brawl with them, make intrigue with them in a kind of guerrilla warfare," he said slyly.

"But no single person knows me entirely. It's not in my nature to permit such a thing—that's my character."

"Yet I am entirely open with you, as open as the azure sky over us," Beth declared. "You know the details of my life from the day I was born in New York. You know about my happy times with Michael, and my sorrow. And my days here at Rancho Cielo. I've concealed nothing from you."

She knew this wasn't quite true, although wearing blinders was not exactly deliberate deception, she decided. No history of love could exist without facts, and in her case there were none.

Joe sighed deeply. "Dear Beth, you are a woman," he pointed out, "and I am a man. And too, you came from a world of money and privilege, where every advantage was yours. I come from hard, sun-baked earth and stone, from struggle, from mixed blood. A *coyote* like me has to protect himself in every way he can. My way is to be wily, to give just so much of myself in a flash here, so much there. You will have all my love, and it will be pure. That is all that I can promise. So, will you marry me?"

Beth was stunned, although she told herself she shouldn't be. After the initial surprise she experienced a rising resentment at his gall, taking for granted that she would acquiesce to his wishes.

"Marry you?" she said. "You're asking me just like that?"

"I told you," Joe said, "I love you. Isn't that reason enough to marry?"

"In the singular situation here at Rancho Cielo it may not be enough," Beth replied. "My role has always been that of favored guest. No one is more aware of this than I am. And I've tried to help in the valley as much as I could to make up for being brought here by you and taken in so warmly by Mama Luz. I wasn't her widowed daughter-in-law, Nate isn't her grandson."

"My mother and I are aware of your situation, as you put it."

"Have you told her how you feel about me?" Beth asked.

"No. I saw no need to. Although her strict sense of propriety wouldn't allow her to utter a word, she was conscious from the beginning of my feelings for you."

Beth gripped the arms of her chair. "I see. Everyone knew of your interest but me."

"Carmen didn't."

It was on the tip of Beth's tongue to say what she knew of Carmen's relationship with Joe, but she held back; there was nothing to be gained by such a revelation. It wasn't relevant to Joe's declaration, and Carmen was gone out of their lives, a void that needed no filling.

"Well," she said, "when would you want me to marry you?"

"As soon as possible."

"Would you expect me to become a Catholic?"

"It might simplify matters. My mother would prefer it, I'm sure. We can go to San Diego whenever you're ready."

"Oh no, I'm not riding to San Diego," Beth said firmly.

"Well then, we'll go to one of the border towns, find a priest there who'll marry us. We can stay at the Romeros and send for one from there."

"I don't think you heard me correctly, Joe. I am not leaving Rancho Cielo. There are considerations other than my own. For one, I can't leave little Nate as Mama Luz's responsibility. She's not well. I see signs."

"She is frail," Joe agreed.

"Besides, I won't subject my child to the hardships of a winter journey down and back. It was bad enough to bring him up in the drought. He might have died."

"Then you leave me no choice," Joe said. "I'll have to ride down and see if I can find a priest who will marry us here in a proper ceremony that will please my mother. She'll want a chapel wedding with all the Pai Pais present.

You'll probably want to become a Catholic. And it might be wise to baptize Nate in the faith, too."

Beth was mellowed by Joe's statement, but she wasn't ready to give him her answer.

"You have it all figured out, don't you?" she said, amused by his smiling self-confidence. It was obvious that he had given the prospect of marriage much thought from all angles, and was certain that he would be able to persuade her to accept him. How like him to be so certain of his success.

"I can see that you aren't persuaded yet," he said, "so consider another aspect of the matter. I know how much you love this place. I'd never have thought it possible with your background, but you've proven you do, all the same. Rancho Cielo is a passion with you. You've risen to all challenges, even made some for yourself. But if you want to keep your place in Antelope Valley, you can only secure it by marrying me."

"I'm not a calculating woman, Joe," Beth said with a faint smile. "I'm not expecting prizes, if I marry you."

"No, you're not calculating, I'll agree. Still, you wouldn't mind becoming grand mistress of the manor in case the bullets get closer to target in the future than they already have. Any fool can see that."

Beth was already contemplating the logic of his proposal as he spoke. It was so true, in fact, that she could no longer maintain a facade of deliberation.

"In any case," she replied, "I shan't give you my answer yet. I need time."

She might as well start with firmness, she thought, or she'd lose his respect. She didn't intend to be easy or unyielding, *if* she married him, but wanted to strike a happy balance between the two extremes. Since coming to Rancho Cielo she had fine-honed her sense of duty. This meant setting limits beyond which she'd never yield. She would not withhold herself, she'd be generous. But neither would she allow the weight of marriage to incline more toward Joe than to herself. And being a woman, a foreigner, she would need all the advantages she could gain. But she vowed to be fair always.

"Time," she reiterated, "to consider your suggestion."

Joe laughed. "You would call it a suggestion. All right, Beth. You may have until six o'clock tomorrow morning. At six I intend to ride off to the Romeros. But if your answer is no, I'll be gone for a month or two. On the other hand, if your answer is yes, I'll return in a week to ten days with a priest, even if I have to kidnap one at gunpoint. He can spend a fortnight or so here doing his professional business at the chapel for all the community. He'll reconsecrate the chapel, baptize little Nate, and marry us."

"That's reasonable enough. I'll give you my decision in the morning," Beth said. "What will you say to Mama Luz—or shall I speak?"

"I intend to do it, before I leave. She'll be pleased."

"I wonder."

"Oh yes, she will. She won't mind me going away this time—if you say yes. And I know you will."

"You'll know in the morning," Beth said, rising. "It's time to think about the evening meal."

"And time for me to see Creek and prepare for the journey."

They parted without touching, Beth going directly into the house as Joe paused to watch her go, his heart thumping away jubilantly under his shirt, his mouth cotton-dry. He had nearly brought it off, by God, and he felt like jumping up and down and shouting wildly. Best to remain calm, he cautioned himself as he went to find Creek. He hadn't won yet; she could always say no. Best to do no more than hope for the best. Prayers he couldn't recite, he never had been able to, but hope, he could hold onto hope; it was something he understood. One day he'd make an enormous haul, hit it rich, and he'd come home in triumph. Meanwhile, he would have her here, waiting for him, blessing the valley.

*   *   *

Next morning Beth gave Joe her answer in the presence of Mama Luz. She accepted Joe formally as her fiancé. Mama Luz burst into delighted tears. Overwhelmed by emotion, she clasped Beth in her arms and kissed her.

Joe embraced Beth carefully, with infinite respect, thinking how much he had wanted to have her come to his cabin, as Carmen had, and how he was even tempted to try to sneak into the house to her room after all lights were out. He didn't know it, but had he tried to make a late rendezvous with her, he would have been frustrated in his attempt. Beth had wedged a wooden chest against the door, in lieu of a lock. She did not intend to continue such evasive defenses once they were married—only until.

"A safe journey," Beth told Joe. "May God go with you. Come home soon. We need you."

"As soon as I can," he promised, thinking that the women talked as if he were going off to war.

"And all in one piece," Mama Luz said, reinforcing his thought, voicing the more hopeful aspect of a concern that had kept Beth awake long into the night, wondering if her acceptance of Joe was simply inviting tragedy.

Wrapped in heavy shawls the Indian women had woven from wool recently brought up to Rancho Cielo, Mama Luz and Beth stood outside in the cold, clear mountain air to watch Joe and Red Deer climb the trail that led them out of the valley. Mama Luz clutched Beth's arm as the two mounted figures disappeared over the summit of the ridge on their way down to the lowlands.

The women waited impatiently for Joe's return, spending much of their time planning for the wedding. Mama Luz was so quietly content with the engagement that she barely discussed the matter with Beth, only the practical details of the wedding.

"You will be a Porter for the second time," she pointed out once. "But now you will be more Delgado than Porter."

"What do you mean?"

"More Spanish than American," the old woman explained. "You have accepted our ways at Rancho Cielo, assuming the mantle of our blood. I love you like my own for that."

It was twelve days before Joe returned from the low-lands with Red Deer and a third party, a short man with close-cropped black hair and a café-au-lait complexion who appeared to Beth to be in his middle thirties. Though this visitor was small compared to Joe, he was extremely lithe and muscular, with an athlete's body. He wore a black shirt and jacket, tight black riding boots and held a flat black Stetson. An expression of warmth and alert compassion dwelt in his limpid, gold-flecked brown eyes, and his smile, revealing perfect white teeth, instantly il-luminated the moment of his meeting with Mama Luz and Beth.

He was Father Amos Conn, but it was not until dinner that night that the women learned more about him. He had come West from Louisiana via Santa Fe only six months before, he explained, spending some time in and around Los Angeles, mostly as the guest of various wealthy ranches, all Californios. He had gone north for a while but had returned almost immediately, preferring the south.

Father Conn said Mass at private chapels for his keep, christening babies, Spanish and Indian, and preparing potential converts for the acceptance of the Catholic faith. He had officiated at many weddings, and with his genial personality he must have been liked by all who met him, Beth imagined.

Joe had not heard of Father Amos Conn until he began asking around for a priest who might be available to officiate at his Rancho Cielo wedding. When he talked to people, they all evinced friendliness toward Conn, but there seemed to be a cloud surrounding both his back-ground and his origin. Joe heard someone say that Father Conn was part Indian. Others said he was an escaped Negro slave from the South. None of this made any differ-ence to Joe, and since the padre was free to come to An-telope Valley on a moment's notice, for a modest gratuity,

Joe brought him along. No priest had graced the Rancho Cielo chapel for a long time, and Joe felt himself lucky to be able to persuade Conn to perform the wedding ceremony and supervise the attendant rituals.

The dinner conversation at the hacienda that night centered around the rapid change and development of California with the United States presence, its statehood and its population growth. Father Conn was enthusiastic about its future and intended to remain in the West.

"It will one day earn its name of El Dorado," Father Conn prophesied. "I've travelled up and down its length, seeing most of it. Not only is it a place of fabulous wealth still untapped, it is rich in metals other than gold. The gilded land, yes, for its resources, and aptly named."

"You will settle then in Baja California?" Mama Luz asked expectantly.

"I'm not sure yet," Conn replied.

"There is a great need for priests here. The missions haven't provided us with enough of God's advocates in the past. Not since the Jesuits were driven out in the last century."

"I haven't yet become attached to a diocese," the priest explained. "For the time being I prefer to continue travelling, doing service wherever I am needed."

Beth's firsthand experience with priests was sketchy at best. She had been to Mass in New York a few times with a girl friend, but her parents had not encouraged attendance. She had a thousand questions to ask this most fascinating man who spoke several languages, including French, fluently. His conspicuous reticence about his past and Beth's natural reluctance to trespass unwanted in anyone's life restrained her curiosity. One day before Father Conn departed Rancho Cielo she would undoubtedly have a private opportunity to talk with him on a more specific level than during meals, and she would pour forth the questions that nagged at her.

After dinner, Joe took Father Conn to his cabin where the two men sat for a long time over a bottle of Romero brandy. The priest talked more than he drank, but the brandy that Joe consumed made him extremely garrulous.

"We've something in common, Father, that interests me greatly," Joe said at one point. "Like myself, you are of mixed blood, are you not?"

"That's right," Amos Conn responded. "You've probably heard the tale about my being a runaway slave, with a price on my head for anyone who can spirit me out of California and back into the South."

"Something like that, which is nonsense and wouldn't interest me. I'm a *coyote* myself. Ever heard the term?"

"Yes, it's almost as derogatory as 'nigger' is, I understand."

Joe stared in wonderment at the priest. "Good Lord, you don't even flinch at a word like that?"

Father Conn grinned engagingly. "Not at all. I'm not a nigger, I'm a mulatto, a mixture of Caucasian and Negro ancestry. My grandfather was a pure black Louisiana slave, his son—my father—was a freedman."

"I've never heard the word mulatto before," Joe observed.

"It's not widely used. My grandfather was born a slave. His son was set free by my grandfather's master because he saved the life of his master's daughter in a fire. Eventually in New Orleans my father met my mother, an educated Frenchwoman who came to America to be the governess to a plantation owner's children. They fell in love and were secretly married by an understanding priest, both being Catholics. My father died in a smallpox epidemic before I was born. My mother then went into private tutoring and centered her whole life around me.

"My early education was entirely my mother's doing, and it was heavily religious. When she heard of the work of archbishop John Carroll, the pioneering Catholic prelate in the United States until his death in 1815, she was determined that I should meet his successors. Carroll had always been sympathetic to the training of priests of color, including mulattos. •Mother took me to Baltimore as an exhibit, free in a slave state. A bright, cheerful boy with a profound interest in Church ritual, I caught the approving eye of officials and somehow convinced the governing members of the Sulpician seminary that I was prime material for the priesthood. I was accepted by the seminary in early adolescence. Thereafter came profound changes in my life."

"You remained in the United States after you became a priest?"

"I was sent to a seminary in the north," Father Conn explained, "where I taught for a while. A reasonable distance from the slave states, as you can imagine, for I am neither fish nor fowl where pro-slavers are concerned. A target to shoot at, perhaps, but little else of value."

"I know so well what you mean," Joe said.

"But make no mistake. I'm a free agent. I've been a full-fledged priest for a long time now. I am, however, an outcast in one important sense."

"And what is that?" Joe asked, fascinated by Father Conn's story. On the trail their talk had not been this personal.

"Among Spanish priests, I am considered a pariah," Conn continued, "among the Caucasians a mongrel. Belonging nowhere to a specific category, I was unable to find a place outside the seminary where I would be received without controversy and censure. That is, until I went to the West Indies, to an island that shall be nameless for personal reasons. There I established a parish among the poorest class of Negroes, no more than indentured servants really. Leprosy, the pox, congenital blindness, tuberculosis—all were rampant. I remained with the parish for several years, pleading with the wealthy to help the poor, doing what good I could in my limited way. But the wealthy were indifferent to the poor, except for one person."

"And you gave it all up to come back to America and travel to the West?" Joe asked.

Father Conn shook his head. "I was driven out," he confessed bluntly.

"Driven out?"

"A tale for a stormy night," Conn said. "I went to Santa Fe and met Father Garcia there, a moving force. He sent me to California. Through him I met many people, including the Romeros."

"Then you like Alta California?"

"I find it unique."

"And what about Baja?" Joe asked.

"Ah well, it's wild, almost savage, virtually untouched and liable to remain so. I am staggered by what you've done here—a pocket of civilization in the midst of the wilderness."

"Would you consider settling here?"

"Oh, I would have to have strong reasons for doing that."

"Baja needs priests like you, Father. There aren't any on the peninsula who would have readily agreed to come here, as you have."

"There aren't many as free to do God's bidding as I am," Conn replied. "I needn't remind you that Baja was once ruled by New Spain, now Mexico. California is probably the answer for me. But I am still wandering, surveying, deciding. And so here I am at your most pleasing hacienda, enjoying your hospitality, admiring your ladies of the house, yet with serious work to do tomorrow."

"I'm sorry," Joe said quickly, "I've kept you up much too long."

"Not at all, Joe. But tell me, what do you know of the Pai Pais' Christian leanings? I should know what I'm up against here. Although I'm pleased to join you and Beth Porter in holy matrimony, I cannot waste an opportunity to do God's work elsewhere among your people at Rancho Cielo."

During the next hour Joe told Father Conn what he knew about the Pai Pais' Christian background. At the close of the session, Father Conn said, "I'd like to see the chapel before I retire. Is that all right?"

Joe thought it a curious request since it was nearly midnight, but all the same he escorted Father Conn to the small building at once, lighting candles inside, to augment the light shed by several faintly flickering votive candles in red glass containers.

The chapel's interior had been meticulously whitewashed in Joe's absence, he noted, and the crude wooden benches freshly sanded down. The floor was brushed and immaculate. Above the altar the medallioned cross glittered in the candlelight.

Father Conn turned to Joe with a pleased smile, his gold-flecked eyes gleaming with enthusiasm.

"I wonder," he said gently, "if you'd leave me to a moment of contemplation?"

"Of course. Can you find your way back to your room at the hacienda?" Joe asked.

"God has brought me here to Antelope Valley safely," the priest replied without affectation. "I am sure He'll guide me to my bed when the time comes. . . . Goodnight, Joe. Thank you for bringing me to Rancho Cielo. I shall enjoy my sojourn here."

Joe left the priest kneeling before the rough altar, already lost in some dreamy ritual of religious contemplation. He was glad he'd found Amos Conn at the Romeros' and that he'd been agreeable to visit the high country on a mission of goodwill, to officiate at a mountain wedding.

And yet, Joe reflected, walking to his cabin under a bright half-moon, there was something undefined about the priest. Incomplete was a better word, perhaps. Joe was practiced at reading people's characters. He had no doubt that Conn was what he claimed to be, a bona fide priest. But the real story remained to be told, the events that had propelled him toward the West. Whatever the facts were, Conn's intelligence, his affability and quiet self-assurance, made him a man Joe could respect. A far cry from the dry-as-dust, one-dimensional Spanish padres he had known all his life whose behavior he held in mild contempt, dullards who clung to the dry monotony of ancient Latin ritual muttered interminably at their indifferent congregations, who had made a fine art of removing themselves from the people.

It pleased Joe that Amos Conn would be the one to join him in marriage to Beth. That the priest was a mulatto, one genetic step beyond the abused Negro, gave him a solid satisfaction he didn't need to analyze. He and Father Conn were members of the same society, with a strong common bond; they were both half-breeds.

The next morning Father Conn began in his brisk fashion to organize his parish. Through Mama Luz and Beth, the Pai Pai women were all assembled at the chapel an hour earlier than they would normally have met to perform their craft work and to exchange mild gossip. Conn went through a complete list of all Indians residing in Antelope Valley, making sure that he had the names of everyone who hadn't been christened. It would be up to the women to get the unchristened to the chapel.

In the afternoon a mass christening took place, with parents and children miraculously subdued and quietly willing—awed, in fact, by the decorative, black-clothed presence of Father Conn who, beyond a large gold cross on a chain, wore no garment or clerical collar to indicate his calling. Father Conn's innate sense of Church drama and his considerable timing and mellow musical voice made the event an impressive group ceremony, a splendid opening for his official residence at Rancho Cielo.

Included in the list of children who were baptized was little Nate Porter. Like the others, he cried when the sacramental water was dribbled on his head, and struggled to be put down. But Beth held him firmly until the ceremony was concluded, then took him out of the chapel and back to the hacienda, well aware of what her own direction would shortly be. There was no question now but what she absolutely must convert to Catholicism, and of course the priest would give her instruction.

Beth's initiation into the mysteries of Catholicism began the following day and lasted for almost three weeks, far longer than she had imagined it would. She had some vague idea that she would be asked a few simple questions and then invited to join the worshippers, but the actuality was far different. First, the significance of the seven sacraments was explained to her in great detail by Father Conn, whose eloquence impressed her almost as much as the contents of his indoctrination.

She learned that baptism was the first sacrament, without which the others could not be effected. Confirmation was next, then the anatomy of penance, or the act of confession. After that came the Eucharist, or the Communion. The fifth sacrament was the litany of marriage, the sixth an essay on servants of God, the priests, and their responsibility. The seventh sacrament dealt with Extreme Unction, or last rites.

Father Conn's articulate instruction where Beth was concerned bore certain points and explanations he would ordinarily have bypassed in the intricate process of preparing most subjects for Catholicism. He did not usually get such ripe, intelligent candidates for the religion, however, and so he spent infinite time illuminating Beth in ways that her serious mind could absorb. He knew he was walking on fertile ground from the questions she asked, aware too that she had never been really interested in any religion before, although she had a childhood Presbyterian background.

Beth was made aware of the Four Marks of the Church: One, or the unification of all Catholics under a single head of state, the Pope. She was advised that the Church was Holy, a fountain of holiness that had produced all the saints; that Catholic meant everyone in the world, a universality of belief and being that excluded no one. Finally, she learned that the Church was Apostolic, a lineage of succession from the Apostles of Christ down to the present hierarchy. And she understood at last the meaning of the Rosary, the chain of fifteen beads, five to each of the three sacred divisions: Joy, Sorrow, Glory.

Father Conn gave Beth her first Rosary. At one point in her instruction when she could follow the Mass properly, she told Father Conn how one of the Pai Pais, with the best of intent, had jumbled the tenets of holy service.

The priest was unruffled. "I'm not surprised. It's to be expected in such an isolated community. An Indian layman could only lead the Rosary, recite the Stations of the Cross, conduct a Novena service. He can't consecrate the sacrament. He'd have to be a priest for that."

"You've given us so much," Beth said. "It's a pity that we won't have you to continue saying Mass."

"Which brings me to a question," Father Conn said, circumventing her remark. "Will you and Joe continue to live at Rancho Cielo? I should think you'd want to take your young son and go live in the lowlands. What about the pueblo of Los Angeles, or North?"

"We still have an association with a store down there, Joe may have told you," said Beth. What Joe would not have told Father Conn, she assumed, was of his status as an outlaw for the murder of George Hearn, nor of his desperado days. Joe would not go easily to the confessional, unless it involved a girl, perhaps.

"No, Father," Beth continued, "I'm quite content to stay here indefinitely. My only problem is Joe's frequent absences. He has a wandering, restless nature. I don't know if anything will contain it."

"Not even your marriage?" The priest stared at her with his wide-open, gold-gleaming eyes. "You are a lovely person," he murmured. "Anyone can see that." Then abruptly Conn changed tone. "Where does Joe go when he rides to the lowlands?"

Even though Beth appreciated Father Conn's concern for Joe, she would not offer any information. Let Joe do that, if he wished.

"Oh, here and there," she said lightly, "to various places to pick up odd jobs. He's very good with breaking horses, as you know. And there's no better vaquero in all of northern Baja than Joe."

"He's not always in Baja, I gather," Conn said, which could only have come from keeping his eyes open at the Romeros' estate. "I'll speak to him. After your marriage he should stay here. The valley needs his authority."

"Thank you, Father," Beth said with relief. "I'll appreciate your making a thoughtful observation to Joe on the subject. I'm not sure that he will."

"I'll do what I can," Conn promised, and hoped that the priest's sagely chosen words would have some beneficial effect.

Finally the wedding day arrived, dawning clear and cold. The ceremony took place outdoors in the afternoon, only a few days before Christmas. It was quite windy and almost too chilly for the nuptials, but since every man, woman and child wanted to attend, the chapel could not contain all the guests. Joe and Beth were married in front of the chapel. She wore a simple, dark dress that she had made especially for the occasion, and wore her silver cross. For a wedding ring, Mama Luz gave Joe the thin, worn gold band that had been her mother's wedding ring.

Beth tried hard not to think about her shipboard marriage to Michael, although she could not entirely banish it from her thoughts. She experienced a moment of desperate second thoughts just before Father Conn pronounced them man and wife, but this brief panic was soon effaced by the somber passion with which Joe kissed her for the first time, and the respect he brought to the gesture.

A feast was laid on improvised tables behind the hacienda, kept to basic dishes by Mama Luz and Beth. Huge hams, roast fowl, a cold saffron rice dish, round black bread, preserves, pickled peppers and early greens from the terrace gardens adorned the table. Besides dried dates, apricots, figs and plums, there was a large flat wedding cake with thick homemade egg icing, large enough to give everyone a token slice.

The Pai Pais picked curiously at the unfamiliar dishes, trying to be polite, and there was a great deal of food left over. Only Father Conn, Joe, and the women partook of the Romero wine that was opened for the occasion. Joe had given Creek a bottle of brandy for his private consumption, so the old man left when the feast began to break up to retire to his hut and drink with his cronies.

Hardly a wedding to go down in the annals of high society, Beth thought later that day. Little Nate was confused by the comings and goings, and Beth tried to explain, knowing that he would understand very little, or remember it.

"You have a new father, darling," she told him. "Uncle Joe is now your father."

"My father Joe?" the boy said.

"Yes, my dearest, Joe."

He would have no memory of Michael, and since Michael had been replaced, perhaps this was as it should be. He would never be able to make comparisons.

Beth had misgivings once again when she donned her nightgown and waited for Joe to come to her. She had no misgivings when he made love to her. He was tender, considerate, and thoroughly expert, as she expected him to be. But she was totally unprepared for the devotion he brought her. Once again, she was forced to banish comparisons from her mind as unsuitable.

Afterwards as she lay next to Joe musing in silence, she realized that Michael had become a wraith in her past; she would no longer mourn for him; Joe was the living, dominant reality. She wasn't entirely sure yet if she loved Joe, for she was no longer the impetuous young maiden who ran off to marry Michael in the main salon of the *Indiana* as it sailed away from New York. She was more experienced at this point and slightly reluctant to give herself completely to Joe until she could count on his response to their marriage. Her own responses were now complicated by the passage of time and a mature wariness that would probably never leave her where Joe was concerned. She was prepared to live with this, if it didn't alter. However, she was now in a firmer position at Rancho Cielo than ever before; she would never lose sight of this advantage. No longer a guest, she was now a bona fide family member. If she had a child by Joe, the direct line to Rancho Cielo would be secure. She thought she would enjoy having a girl, but the choice was not hers to make. She thought of Tim, wishing he could have been present at the ceremony, wondering where he was now, missing his presence. She thought of Carmen, of Carmen's probable reaction to the news of her marriage to Joe, and this in turn blurred her attitude toward Joe. She turned her back on him in bed.

"Are you awake?" he whispered, throwing an arm over her, pulling her against him.

"You know I am," she replied.

"What's on your mind?"

"Our future," she said.

"It will be good because our love will make it good," he promised.

"I'm hoping it will be. When do you go away again?"

"The day after Christmas I'll take Father Amos down to the Romeros. He'll celebrate High Mass for us here, a real concession on his part, for Mother."

"You're just telling me this now?" she said. "Well, he's kind to stay that long. Mama Luz will be happy."

"He says we deserve it. We've given him you as a new convert, and a few of the Pai Pais, Red Deer among them. Creek has renewed his vows to the Church. Look, Beth, why don't you leave Nate with Mother and come down to the lowlands with us?" Joe urged her.

"No, that wouldn't work." For some unaccountable reason she didn't want a honeymoon below. Was she afraid that something would happen to Joe while she was along?

"Why not?"

"Nate's much too active for her to handle. She's simply not up to it."

"That's no excuse—we can bring him along."

"You know how I feel about taking Nate away from here now. No, Joe, I'll wait here for your quick, safe return."

"Well, one day soon Nate will be old enough to travel."

"Two or three more years. They'll go fast enough, with the new projects I have in mind."

"I really thought you'd want to get away, Beth."

"Staying at the Romeros' wouldn't be a honeymoon. Let's just leave the discussion where it is."

"And make love again?" he said, kissing the back of her neck.

"That, of course," she murmured, turning around to face him, to kiss him and draw him into her.

19

JOE and Father Conn left Antelope Valley the day after Christmas for the lowlands. Beth's farewell to Joe was impassioned. She suddenly did not want him to go; she was missing him even before he rode out of the valley.

Mama Luz wept when Joe left, and once the men had gone the light seemed to go out of life at the hacienda. During the next few days, Beth spent a great deal of time planning some new drying sheds for charqui, to be built near the lake and operated in summer when the Pai Pais would be in residence there.

Beth's mind lingered continuously on Joe; she also missed Father Conn. The priest had ingratiated himself

with the people of Antelope Valley; without its daily
Morning Mass, its hearing of confession, its quotidian religious routines, the chapel seemed empty, even though
the Indian women had begun assembling there again to
renew their craft work.

The day after Joe left the valley Mama Luz had a
dizzy spell and Beth put her to bed against her protesta-
tions that she was all right. Beth brought her hot soup in
the evening, sat and read to her until she drifted off into
an easy sleep. Mama Luz's condition worried Beth. For a
long time now the old lady had been gradually declining
in strength. The activities of the past weeks had taken
their toll, for Mama Luz was accustomed to leisured tran-
quility as a way of life. She was aging rapidly, but this
did not dim her spirits.

She said before she went to sleep, "I thank God each
day, Beth, for your presence. Without you, Rancho Cielo
would be a dull place. I wouldn't care much about living."

"Hush, Mama Luz. You'd get along just fine without
me," Beth replied, but she wasn't sure that this was true,
hoping that tomorrow would find Mama Luz improved.
Which was the case. Two days later she was up and about
again, as bright as ever, but careful to conserve her energy.

By the end of the week Joe hadn't returned from the
Romeros' rancho, and Beth began to wonder about his
prolonged absence. After depositing Father Conn at the
Romeros' he should have stayed on for no more than a
couple of days before returning to the high country.

Several days later a messenger arrived from the lowlands, a Romero ranchhand bearing a letter from Father
Conn. Mama Luz was lying down taking an unusually long
siesta when the letter came. Beth took it into her own
room to read so as not to disturb the old lady.

Dear Beth—the letter read—*Joe is dead.*
He went out with Raul Romero on what I have

since learned was a cattle raid. Both men were killed by Americanos, apparently by a posse of men who had worked for one George Hearn. The men have been waiting to ambush Joe, I understand. There are tales that Joe murdered Hearn a while back, but these are unconfirmed pieces of gossip and possibly untrue.

We buried Joe in the Romero cemetery. For reasons that you will understand, we could not send his body up to Rancho Cielo.

I shall leave to you the onerous duty of breaking the sad news to Mama Luz. I shall pray that your personal sorrow turns to strength at God's disposition. A proper Christian burial service took place at graveside, for both Raul and Joe. Masses were also said for the repose of the souls of Joe Porter and Raul Romero.

If I thought my presence would be of vital consolation to you and Mama Luz I would have made the journey up to Rancho Cielo myself instead of sending this message. Should you need to see me, however, and wish to make the journey to the lowlands, I shall remain here at Rancho Romero for another week, then I journey to San Diego. From there I shall sail north to San Francisco to see if I am acceptable to that Catholic diocese and can find a niche there. I may or may not remain in the North, as you can see.

Meanwhile, I shall pray for you in your extreme sorrow. Joe was a good man just coming into his own in marriage to you. Words cannot express my profound sadness over his death. May you find comfort in your newly-accepted religious credo.

I am

Your friend in Christ,
Fr. Amos Conn

For the next two hours Beth lived with the shock of Joe's sudden death and tried not to succumb to panic or grief. In a way, she had been prepared for Joe's death long before they had agreed to marry. She had come slowly to love Joe, knowing that the love, if properly tended, might grow and blossom into the happiest, most fulfilling time of her life.

While she could accept Joe's death, she didn't feel that Mama Luz would do so as well. And yet, she could not in all good conscience postpone telling her the news. Mama Luz would learn that a messenger had arrived from below, and even if Beth gave her some story about Joe sending a message that he would be home shortly, the truth would soon enough come out. Already the messenger had probably told Creek and the word would spread rapidly among the Pai Pais.

When Mama Luz awakened from her long siesta, Beth went to her, the letter in her apron pocket, her hand clutching it.

"How are you feeling?" Beth asked her mother-in-law.

"Good enough," the old lady replied. "Why? Is something the matter? You seem tense."

"A messenger came up from the Romeros'," Beth said, seeing no way but to get on with it.

"From down below?" Mama Luz sat upright, her features eager. "From Joe—?"

"No. From Father Conn."

"Bless the man . . ." Mama Luz crossed herself. "What does it say?"

"I'll read it."

Wondering if she were doing the right thing, Beth extracted the letter from her apron pocket, unfolded it, stared at it for a moment, then took a deep breath and began to read. She got to the point where Conn put the responsibility of telling Mama Luz the tragic news in Beth's hands, and paused to glance up. Mama Luz had fainted dead away.

Shouting for Maria, the old Indian housekeeper, to

come and help her, she and Maria brought the old lady back to consciousness by rubbing her wrists, giving her smelling salts and applying cold compresses to her forehead.

Later, as Beth sat with Mama Luz, she realized that her mother-in-law's fainting spell must have been a slight stroke. There was a measured stiffness to her entire left side, a slackness in the set of her jaw and a slurring of speech. When Mama Luz insisted finally on getting up, there was a pronounced inability to walk as quickly and surely as she had always done; she would lose her balance easily.

For the next fortnight, Beth spent most of her waking time in attendance on Mama Luz. Beth helped her walk outside for brief periods on fair days, and when it rained, she sat indoors with the old lady, listening to her recount the past, reading when Mama Luz requested it. She would bring little Nate in to play happily at their feet, for he was a joyful, energetic child who seemed to spread light wherever he went.

The weather turned colder, there were flurries of snow, lightly frosting the highest peaks that ringed the valley. Snug in the thick-walled hacienda, the two women talked about their lives. Beth lost herself in long, involved tales about her early life in New York, about how busy she was in school, with her girlhood social life, and yet how restricted it all seemed in retrospect compared with the simple freedom of Rancho Cielo.

"I find it difficult to explain," she told Mama Luz, "that I have never missed being in a city. First it was because of Michael, and later, even when I wasn't aware of it, because of Joe."

"It doesn't seem possible that they are both gone," Mama Luz said. "Miguelito I never knew really well. I suppose since he was not my baby I could not give him the warmth he required. In Joselito's case I was too motherly, I must have suffocated him, driven him away from Rancho Cielo."

"You did what you had to do as a mother," Beth reminded Mama Luz. "I shall make lots of mistakes with Nate, I imagine, but I shan't worry about them."

"You're stronger than I ever was," Mama Luz said. "I should have gone out into the world and met another man after Nathan's death, but I could not."

"We are of different generations, different worlds," Beth pointed out. "We come from different cultures."

"Sometimes that is hard to believe, you are so much like a daughter to me. It would be wonderful if you and Joselito could have experienced some years together, had a family of your own, settle down here, truly."

"Well," said Beth, "I am settled here. You can rest assured of that."

"I am glad. It is all I have to look forward to," Mama Luz said, drawing her shawl tighter around her thin shoulders. "Put some more wood on the fire, Beth. It's getting chilly in here, or is it the brush of the blackbird's wings? I shall be glad when summer comes and fires on the hearth are unnecessary. These old bones long for the heat that summer brings."

When Beth discovered that she was pregnant, she went immediately to Mama Luz to break the news first.

"I'm *pregñada*," she announced, expecting Mama Luz to react with excited surprise.

The old lady's reaction was quite the opposite; she took the news calmly, nodding her head slowly up and down in placid satisfaction.

"I expected it," Mama Luz said, "I knew it would happen."

"What made you so sure?" Beth asked.

"Because I have prayed and prayed that God would grant me this one last request in life before I go to Him. Now the Delgado bloodline will be secure. You must go at once to the chapel and offer up a prayer of thanksgiving for the Divine blessing of new life."

"I've already done that."

"Bless you again! It will be a boy. I prayed for that too. And he will be my heir, after you, Beth."

Beth refrained from voicing her private view that little Nate was outside the Spanish-Indian-American bloodline mix, thus disqualifying him as an heir. He was an American Porter-Lowell, not a Mexican Porter-Delgado, a coyote as Joe had been, with half of him Spanish-Indian. While Nate couldn't inherit Antelope Valley, any child of Joe's would have a strong legal claim, even if the mother were American, as Beth was. Anyway, it was much too complicated to worry about now. Time would take care of the details.

"Whether the child is a boy or a girl makes no great difference to me," Beth replied. "It will be loved and cherished because it is Joe's child and mine, his legacy to me. Porter and Delgado blood will be mixed with Lowell blood, and some Indian, of course. I think the inheritance that Joe's child receives will mark the beginning of a rich new existence for Antelope Valley. When the child is born we'll celebrate by starting a road over the summit and following the canyon trails down to the lowlands. It's time we opened up the valley to the outer world. We've been inaccessible except to a very few for much too long."

"How well you put it," Mama Luz agreed. "I wish I could do more than ponder the idea. Sadly, I am too useless to do much else. The strength of vision and achievement can be yours, Beth, but not mine."

Beth ignored Mama Luz's last remark. "I'm glad you see the potential," she said. "Rancho Cielo has a good future; it will thrive into the next century and beyond. The valley will produce for its people—Spanish, Indian, all who dedicate themselves to it for life. It is theirs, but also a part of Baja, of Mexico and the world. Whoever tends it can claim it."

Mama Luz smiled beatifically, clasping her bony hands together in her lap. It seemed to Beth that the old lady had rallied slightly during the last few weeks, her mind crystal clear, but she was still quite frail, Beth decided.

"You have spoken a vital truth, my dear girl," Mama Luz said approvingly. "Now, run along to the chapel and pray again, this time for me, so that God will know through your new faith of my hopes joined to yours."

Beth went dutifully off to the chapel, thinking that prayers couldn't possibly make a boy; she wasn't steeped enough in Old World superstition to believe that. But praying might help her give birth to a healthy child of whatever sex. A boy would be named Jaime Delgado Porter, after Luz's father, the boy's great-grandfather. And if the child were a girl, she would be named Luz Delgado Porter.

Although pleased with her pregnancy, Beth had not yet by any means reconciled herself to Joe's death. She couldn't help but wonder, were the deaths of the Porter brothers, both her husbands in succession, some grim curse she may have brought upon herself for running away from her responsibilities in New York? Unlikely, her pragmatic side told her, still, retribution figured strongly in her new belief. But then, she knew she couldn't continue to think like this. Her only hope of survival was to point herself toward the future, eschewing the melancholy past.

As Mama Luz slowly seemed to improve and the child grew and stirred within her, Beth decided to write to Tim; she hadn't even told him of her marriage. The pique she had felt when he ran off with Carmen was dissipated. Tim had given her a banking address in San Francisco where he said he would be calling for mail from time to time, but she had never used it. Now she wrote to Tim to tell him of her marriage to Joe and his tragically sudden death on the range. She expressed no illusions about Joe's nefarious goings on. She had hoped, she explained, that after escaping death by a bullet that very nearly cost Joe his leg, his luck would change, or at least his point of view. She had depended too heavily on chance, the law of averages, and not enough on God. In her new-found faith she hadn't expected God to offer his power and make her life perfect, but she would humbly pray for moral support. She'd ask Tim to return to Antelope Valley, to come and live with her until the child was born. At least if he weren't still with Carmen, and she didn't think he was. She didn't want to be alone with just Mama Luz at her side. The old lady was exceedingly delicate, too much so to assume the responsibility of a child's birth. The Pai Pai midwife would be present, but she wanted Tim there in the house to greet his niece or nephew when the child arrived.

It was almost three months before an answer to her letter came from Tim. He would be on his way shortly, he explained, having already been north to the gold fields, seeing nothing there to attract him permanently. Sacramento was a frontier town, too far inland for his taste. Carmen, he said, had refused to live with her second cousin in San Jose, preferring a livelier life.

"She found it," Tim said in his letter, "by running off with a Sacramento riverboat gambler." Tim didn't sound too dismayed, Beth noted. "A rather uncertain future but perhaps what she was originally created for, a vessel of pleasure. After all," Tim added cynically, "with her passionate nature she could easily apply herself to the job of getting a man wherever she went. As for holding him, that is another consideration altogether. I mourn with you, dear sister, the loss of Joe. On the brighter side, I shall look forward eagerly to seeing you again soon. The news that you will have Joe Porter's child, a man I never met, makes the journey up to the high country again an event to anticipate . . ."

It was a beautifully green and fertile spring in Antelope Valley at the time of Tim's arrival. Wildflowers were blooming on the sunny eastern flanks of the lowland hills. In the high country the Pai Pais had already planted summer vegetables.

Without a cash crop to sell below, Beth was beginning

to worry already about the following winter, but she was determined to put that thought aside until Tim's arrival. At that time she would discuss her problem in detail, and it would be wonderfully comforting to have him around. It wasn't practical, of course, to imagine that Tim would stay on at Antelope Valley indefinitely. The spot seemed ill-made by Nature to contain its menfolk for very long. Even Nathan Porter had only been content to remain for reasonable periods at Rancho Cielo. His sons were no different from him in this respect, preferring the openness of the outer world to the sealed-in life of the valley. The lure to keep them grounded here would be wealth, Beth realized. But even if there was enough money to buy cattle and sheep, what would they do during drought times for animal feed?

Maybe she ought to go back to Nathan's papers, Beth decided. Perhaps she had missed some vital clue laid out by Nathan as to how Rancho Cielo could best survive, for he had taken Mama Luz's devotion to the place seriously.

It was while Beth was engrossed in rummaging through Nathan's possessions in the study one morning that Maria came running to her in hysterics.

"Quick, señora, Mama Luz has fallen!"

Beth went at once to her mother-in-law. It seemed that she had risen from her bed—where she'd spent most of the winter—and taken a few steps, then fainted in a heap on the adobe brick floor of her room.

Together the two women lifted the limp, wasted body into bed. Taking Mama Luz's pulse, Beth knew immediately that the old lady had sustained another crisis, possibly another stroke. There was nothing they could do except tend her. She remained unconscious and breathing shallowly all the rest of the day. Beth sat with her into the night, falling asleep in a chair, finally creeping off to her bed as the corridor clock struck 2 A.M. She was miserable and depressed, already feeling the loss of Mama Luz. The anticipated emptiness was almost keener than she had felt over the deaths of Michael and Joe.

At dawn she rose and went to look in on Mama Luz. The old lady wasn't in her bed. Alarmed, she hurried through the house, saw the study door ajar—it was usually locked, these days, with the key in the door. She poked her head inside and Mama Luz was there. She lay on the adobe floor beside the heavy desk that had been carried up the mountain piecemeal on muleback and assembled at the hacienda many years earlier. Mama Luz was sprawled on her stomach, her right cheek turned upwards, a bloody gash on the temple. Apparently she had fainted, striking her head against a sharp corner of the desk as she crumpled.

Beth dropped to her knees with a cry of anguish. She felt for a pulse; there was none. Mama Luz was already cold. She must have died, Beth surmised, from a massive brain hemorrhage caused by the severe blow to her temple.

In the old lady's right hand was clutched a document. Beth pried it from Mama Luz's icy fingers and examined it: A last will and testament, to supersede all other existing documents, written only hours earlier in Mama Luz's faltering but careful script. In it she left Antelope Valley and all the accoutrements of Rancho Cielo to Beth, in trust for her child by Joe when it came of age. If the child died before Beth, then she became sole heir. She could leave the estate to her brother, but only if he were married with children. If not, then the estate must go to Creek, head Pai Pai, or to his nearest of kin, Red Deer. There were no Delgados fit to tend the grant, Mama Luz made quite clear, in both Spanish and English text.

Mama Luz had probably risen in the middle of the night after Beth had gone to her own bed. The idea was logical. With great effort she had walked through the darkened house, lit a candle in Nathan's study, sat down at his desk and taken pen in hand to write a new will. It was her last act in life, but it left Rancho Cielo in the hands of the person most dedicated to preserving it, Beth reflected with satisfaction. The only question was, how did she manage the sleight-of-hand tricks the estate would require in order to survive?

She thrust this complex question aside, incapable of dwelling on it now, too engrossed with her own inestimable loss. Mama Luz had been her mainstay at Rancho Cielo, although the old lady had always claimed just the reverse. She had been Beth's reason for stubbornly going on. "You, my dear, are *my* light in life," Mama Luz had often insisted, but the opposite was true.

With Mama Luz gone, a flame had been extinguished. Even though she would soon have Joe's child, her whole world had collapsed in on itself. But if she grieved over Mama Luz's death, the Pai Pai community was inconsolable. The women beat their breasts and tore out chunks of their coarse black hair in a frenzy. The men sat in a circle in Creek's hut, smoked their pipes, told stories about the old lady, and chanted. All were secretly terrified over what would now happen to them with their precious guardian dead and the gringa becoming head woman.

Mama Luz had been their sole symbol of leadership, their talisman, for they had no real tribal force to guide them, being a remnant group. They had given their trust to the señora. With her dead they were demoralized.

In death, the Pai Pais insisted on sending off Mama Luz to her eternal rest in their own way. Recognizing their passionate need, Beth made no obejction.

To satisfy Creek and Maria and the other Pai Pais, Beth allowed the men to make a pallet of poles and hide thatching on which they carried the body of Mama Luz to a high flat ceremonial rock behind the hacienda on a rise of ground. There, above the Indian huts and with a view of the valley looking toward the lake, the pallet was encircled by the adult Indians, lighted all night by four torches, while the men chanted and danced out their special ritual designed for the repose of Mama Luz's soul on its journey to the Hereafter.

Compared with the brief and moving Catholic cere-

mony for the dead that Beth herself read next day in the
chapel, the Pai Pais' devotion was the more fervent and
touching. Everyone in the community, including babies,
attended the burial service in the valley cemetery.

Only once during Beth's reading did her voice falter.
This was when the thought suddenly crossed her mind
that Mama Luz had not lived to see the child she was
carrying, and would never know, in life at least, the joy
that it could bring her. As her voice broke, however, her
fingers touched the Rosary in her dress pocket given her
by Father Conn. She felt renewed by fresh strength.
Thinking of him and how he had brought her into the
bosom of the Church, she cleared her throat and continued reading the service to the end.

The bleak weeks of waiting for Tim's arrival Beth spent
mainly in Nathan Porter's study. If she had felt a strong
sense of dedication to Rancho Cielo before, that loyalty
was now doubled. She was desperate to find a way to
support the valley and its inhabitants, and this despera-
tion finally gave way to obsession, then near-panic.

She knew such single-mindedness wasn't good for her
in her advanced state of pregnancy, so she prayed a great
deal to calm her nerves, spending many hours on her
knees in the chapel, or in her room at the hacienda. Her
one bright hope was the anticipation of Tim's arrival. His
imminent appearance never failed to cheer her whenever
she felt down.

Brother Tim was on his way at the peak of the hot
summer weather. He was bringing all sorts of needed
supplies—coffee, tea, dried fruits and meats, flour, salt.
There were gifts suitable for an unseen niece or nephew,
whichever, and some toys for little Nate, with a surprise
for Beth, which Tim hoped would lift her spirits.

One morning in late August Creek came to Beth to
alert her that Tim's party was arriving. He had been
sighted on the summit ridge.

Beth ran immediately to the lookout mound where she

had observed Tim on his first visit to the valley. Telescope in hand, she recognized Tim at once but was unable to identify his companion, who appeared to be an adolescent boy, fair enough to be a gringo, as nearly as she could make out.

Damn! she thought. Why in thunder was Tim bringing a boy along with him? She wanted him to herself. Besides, it didn't make sense. Tim hadn't mentioned that he'd be traveling with anyone in his letter. Unless of course this was someone he'd picked up at Rancho Romero, a guest who'd remain in the valley only for a brief visit. But she resented having company. She wanted all of Tim's time and attention for herself. She certainly wouldn't let him go gallivanting off in the hills with some child while she languished at the hacienda, sulking away in his absence, feeling deprived. With some irritation, she already saw her pleasure over Tim's arrival considerably curtailed.

She waited impatiently for Tim, his companion and their train of pack mules to descend from the summit ridge to the valley floor. Then Tim galloped toward her, jumped from his horse and ran to her. She still hadn't gotten a good look at Tim's companion as he swept her up in his arms.

"By God, you're a sight for sore eyes!" Tim exulted, embracing her. "Fat with child but still beautiful. It's so good to see you!"

Glancing past his shoulder Beth declared, "I see you brought a guest with you this time."

"I sure did." Tim's eyes twinkled, and he turned toward the figure on the horse. "Maggie, come here . . ."

The individual whom Beth had mistaken for a young male because of the boy's travel costume of buckskin breeches, jacket and cap, slipped down from the saddle and walked toward her. The boy had turned into a young woman.

"Maggie McKenna," Tim announced to Beth. "At least,

she was Maggie McKenna last week. Now she's Mrs. Timothy Lowell. We were married in San Diego."

Tim caught Maggie's hand. "Maggie, meet my big sis, Beth."

The two women shook hands formally, Beth smiling so vigorously she thought her cheeks would crack.

"You're married," she muttered in a dazed voice. "You didn't say anything in your letter about a surprise."

Maggie laughed, and her laughter was gaily musical, infectious.

"He didn't know me then, Beth. We only met five weeks ago."

Beth studied her new sister-in-law. Clear violet eyes, wide serene forehead, soft wavy ginger hair, Beth saw now, with the cap swept off, and that warm, impish grin. Maggie stood only to Tim's shoulder, slim and gamine-like. No wonder Beth had mistaken her for a boy at a distance.

"It was love at first sight," Tim said proudly, slipping an arm around Maggie. "In San Francisco."

"It may have been love at first sight for Tim," said Maggie, "but it was love at second sight for me. I'd already seen him the day before at the bank, but he hadn't seen me yet. He was too busy withdrawing money."

"Well, so," Beth said, "congratulations to you both!"

"I'm about to die of thirst," Tim announced. "We made a record trip up the mountain from the Romeros and missed the last spring. We're just about out of water."

"Then let's not stand here in this heat," Beth said. "We'll go to the hacienda."

Creek and Red Deer took the horses and mules to the corral to water and unload them.

"I thought from what Tim said you'd be much older than you are," Maggie told Beth, walking between her and Tim. "But you aren't. You're young and beautiful."

Beth smiled. "I'm not used to such nice compliments, and I thank you. Most of these days I feel a million years old."

"That's usual when you're pregnant," Maggie observed in a practical tone of voice. "This is your second, isn't it?"

"Yes. But it's not the coming child that's made me feel old." She turned to Tim. "Mama Luz just died, suddenly, from a stroke."

"Oh Beth, I'm so sorry," Tim said.

"It's all right, I'll live with it."

Seeing the tension in Beth's face, Maggie said brightly, "You should have an easier birth with a second child."

"I'm worried about being so far from civilization, as we Americans term it," Beth said. "I was in the lowlands the first time, but there are no doctors here. I know how to deliver a baby myself, but I can't do it for myself."

"I can do it for you," Maggie said.

"Everything's going to be just fine," Tim said as they entered the hacienda. "Maggie's a nurse. I only married her to bring her here to you!" He grinned, squeezing Maggie's shoulder.

"A nurse?" Beth exclaimed. "How marvelous!" She was thinking of the villagers and their complaints. Maggie would be a visiting angel for them.

"Oh, not quite a full-fledged graduate," Maggie said. "I left my Philadelphia nursing school in the last term to come West. I had some foolish idea that I could dance, and I'd make my name as a singing actress. It was all because I'd seen Lola Montez on the stage and was convinced I could do more, and better. I'm not bad, but I'm not that good either. Besides, I didn't bring my guitar."

"There's one in Nathan Porter's study," Beth said. "I don't know if it's any good."

"You know, I was about to give up when I met Tim."

"I showed up in the nick of time to rescue her from a life of sin and shame," Tim quipped.

"Oh Tim," Beth scolded. "Don't say things like that. It's not respectful."

"Why not?" Tim replied. "Maggie's a woman of the world. And she knows I'm a terrible tease."

"He takes some getting used to," Maggie admitted with

a twinkle as Beth seated them in the hacienda living room, cool and comfortable after the intense dry heat outside.

"She's been around enough to put up with me," Tim said.

"In nursing school we worked with all kinds of people, and all sorts of diseases. Sometimes it wasn't very pretty, but it was vital and necessary duty. I don't regret a moment of it. I just didn't want to make it my life's vocation."

"She's switched to me," Tim declared, "and I couldn't be happier."

Beth wondered if Tim had told Maggie anything about Carmen. If he had, she rather imagined that Maggie's bubbly sense of humor and the practical would allow her to look upon his life before their marriage as very much his own business, so long as he didn't resume his casual ways. There didn't appear to be much chance of that, from Tim's enthusiasm. And Maggie looked entirely capable of handling Tim, Beth decided, as she withdrew to get a pitcher of sun-brewed tea to quench the thirst of the weary pair.

How joyous, Beth thought, as she poured the tea from an earthenware crock into a china pitcher, to have some youth and vivacity about for a change. She'd really had enough of death and dying, of melodrama. She wanted her life to change, but it would have to change here at Rancho Cielo, for this was where she belonged.

For the next few weeks Beth was the happiest she'd been in a long time. The sorrow of Joe's murder, and then his mother's death—these had receded to the bearable point where she could view them in perspective and without shedding private tears.

She began to do the chores she'd put off doing for too long. Among these was sending the original of Mama Luz's holographic will by sealed-pouch courier through the Romeros' system to Mexico City, to be filed there

with the government's Land Division. Beth retained a
copy, of course, and was vastly relieved when she got
word back from the Division that the will was on file in
their archives. It would in due time be officially processed,
once the sex and name of the child were established, she
was advised.

Beth was also informed that if she needed any legal
advice she could contact the Honorable Hector Delgado,
a lawyer, a representative of the Mexican government and
a relative of the late Luz Delgado Porter. The attorney
resided on his estate near the border in a town called
Tecate.

Beth recalled Mama Luz speaking of Hector Delgado
with some disdain, certainly not with anything approaching affection. This was shortly after Beth arrived at Antelope Valley. Delgado, she recalled, was a second cousin
of Mama Luz's—their fathers were first cousins. He had
a large family of his own, and the two spurs of the Delgado clan hadn't been too friendly, according to Mama
Luz.

Why Delgado's name should come up in connection
with the filing of Mama Luz's will puzzled Beth but didn't
worry her in any way. Duly a document would come
through by courier from the capital making her legal
guardian of the Delgado estate for her child, she was
confident. She would deal with any problems about
Rancho Cielo if and when the time came to discuss such
matters with the lawyer from Tecate, which she hoped
would never happen.

Beth and Maggie became fast friends, with a clear and
open understanding of the limits of their friendship. Beth
was overjoyed to see Tim so happy with Maggie, and Tim
was delighted that his wife and sister got on so well.

Maggie and Beth made a jolly lottery game out of the
exact date the baby would be born, with an amused Tim
standing by, watching them enjoy one another's company.

"You remind me of Grace Morley," Beth said one day to Maggie, as they sat drinking tea by the hacienda kitchen stove.

"Who is she?" Maggie asked.

"Oh, a childhood friend of mine with a grand sense of humor. She married the man I jilted in New York," Beth explained.

"Did you have any regrets about leaving?"

"No, I'd do the same thing again. Michael was a wonderful partner. I would never have tired of him, I'm sure. Joe was an extension of Michael, in a way. And both of them are tied up with Rancho Cielo."

"You love it here," Maggie said, "you really do."

"Of course. I think you might stay at Rancho Cielo, too. What are your ideas?"

Maggie hesitated, not knowing quite what to say. She knew that Tim wished he could get Beth to agree to clear out, leave the estate to the Indians, quit the valley entirely. They could always make a decent living elsewhere, was Tim's argument. It wasn't as if Beth had been born at Rancho Cielo, related by blood to the Delgados, he had told Maggie. "We're not staying here for the birth of our first one, I can tell you that right now, Nurse Maggie," Tim had said firmly, which closed the subject for the moment. It could always be opened again, if need be, Maggie had decided.

"My ideas about this place?" Maggie mused. "Well, it's beautiful, for one thing. It's wild and rugged, exciting and a bit frightening, as you say it is. But it's also very lonely. You can't stay here forever without a man, Beth."

Beth shrugged indifferently at this statement, her unwavering gaze fixed on Maggie's features.

"I can do almost anything a man can do, I've had to learn how. I oversee the valley, plan improvements. And for stronger arms than mine I have the Pai Pais. They're loyal and dependable. I'm quite secure and content here."

"But you can't build a real town here," Maggie pointed

out reasonably. "You don't want it to be any more than a family enterprise. With two young children you're going to be thinking about change."

"We'll manage just as we are," Beth said, almost sternly, Maggie thought.

"You'll continue to exist, yes," Maggie conceded. "But you won't be living in any sense of the word. It's a live burial, Beth. You're wasting your youth and beauty here on this barren place. You're only a few years older than I am, and I say it's an awful waste. Besides, you don't want to raise two children here, do you? Tell me honestly. You know and I know it isn't fair to them. They need a broader life."

"I've come to think that the outside world offers very little that can't be learned here."

"Oh come now, Beth, it offers *life*. This is mere existence."

"Father Conn said something when he was here about Antelope Valley being the world in miniature," Beth stated. "He said there was no sin here because this place is under God's eye. I believe it, and I like the idea of living in a state of blessedness."

Maggie said, "I was born into the religion that you converted to. But sin's everywhere, we learn to live with it for the associated joys. You mustn't lock yourself away because of the tragedy you've already experienced, Beth dear. We're new friends and I value you highly. But I'm more in the world than you are, and I don't want to see you recede from it, from reality. I—"

Beth stood up suddenly, clutching her extended stomach urgently.

"Dear God," she breathed, "the child's coming."

"It can't be," said Maggie, "not until next week. I'll lose my wager." She bounded across the room to Beth. "Here, take my arm. I want you to go lie down."

"I'm sorry." Beth had turned pale, a film of sweat beaded her brow. "Yes, I must die down. Right away . . ."

* * *

The baby came the following morning after an exceptionally long and difficult labor.

Maggie remained in constant attendance; she could not have done more. Maria stood by, ready to do Maggie's bidding, scurrying back and forth with hot water, towels, and whatever else Maggie needed.

Tim hovered in the background, tense and silent, almost as though he were the father and practicing a form of couvade, Maggie decided. But since he was only the brother it would have to be called something else. A rehearsal for their first child's arrival? He stood anxiously in the doorway several times until finally Maggie banished him with a little push, sending him out into the corridor looking for Creek, who would offer him a drink.

Jaime Delgado Porter was a healthy, nine-pound boy, delivered by Maggie and cooed over by his Uncle Tim almost as soon as he was brought bawling into the world. Little Nate showed exceptional curiosity about his new brother. As soon as Beth was up and about he followed her whenever she was holding Jimmy. He would drape himself over the crib that had been his not long before and stare endlessly at the little boy. Jimmy was fair-haired and blue-eyed, while Nate was dark-haired and dark-eyed. The two brothers' prime distinction lay in their oppositeness of coloring. Otherwise, they had the Porter serenity of brow and looked more like the picture of Nathan than like their respective fathers. Nursed by Beth, little Jimmy grew larger and healthier each day. For the time being, no issue at Rancho Cielo was more important than little Jimmy.

20

DURING the fall and winter, talk reached the valley from down below that attempts were being made to reinstate Antonio Santa Anna as head of state; he would be brought out of exile and made president of Mexico once again. The complex and violent political history then being made in Mexico City had little effect on Antelope Valley. Lost in time and the winter mists that brought a wet but exceptionally warm season without snow, the valley dreamed on. Its tiny group of white and Pai Pais were wrapped in a state of suspended being.

As the length of Tim's and Maggie's visit at Rancho Cielo stretched into months, Beth came to appreciate Maggie's company more and more. She no longer placed parameters on their relationship as sisters-in-law. Maggie was a gem; not only amusing and lively and optimistic, breathing life constantly, but also valuable to have around. She was filled with new recipes which she taught Beth and Maria, fresh concepts for dealing with household problems, and was becoming much admired by the Pai Pais for her tireless nursing efforts on their behalf. No ache or pain was too small for her to consider and to suggest treatment with some simple home remedy. What Beth had at first mistakenly thought was boldness in Maggie she now began to appreciate as forthrightness and an unselfish devotion to life, marks of strong character.

She herself, admitting this privately, had escaped into religion, in a sense, while Maggie had escaped from Catholicism into the world, as Maggie herself had pointed out.

Tim had changed a lot with his marriage to Maggie. He was less self-concerned, more interested in the world around him as a challenge rather than as a handy vehicle for the expression of his whims. On his first visit to Rancho Cielo he had shown an elaborate indifference to Beth's seriously-conceived plans for developing the valley into a self-sufficient agricultural system. Now he appeared to find interests everywhere and was eager to plan changes with Beth. He would never be a direct heir to the estate, at least as long as Jimmy was alive, but apparently he had decided, largely through Maggie's influence, to stay around for a while and make himself useful.

With help from Creek and Red Deer and a carefully chosen group of Pai Pai men, the terraces were tended and planted during the late winter in a new variety of vegetables. Cornfields were laid out in areas where the Pai Pai had never planted before. From the Romeros' estate Tim ordered seeds hitherto unknown in the valley— apple, peach, summer melon, apricot. He established a small nursery for the care and raising of seedling trees to be set out in strategic areas to replace those mature trees that the Pai Pais cut each year. No one had ever thought about reforestation before in the valley's history. Several Indians were sent down to the lowlands with Creek, commissioned to purchase a small herd of goats. These were soon multiplying and giving milk for the boys and the Pai Pai babies, with enough left over to make a supply of hard, sharp mountain cheese.

All sorts of vital repairs were made throughout the valley to whatever buildings required them, which was the majority. A wood-burning, updraft adobe kiln of round design and impressive size was built, so that terra-cotta tiles could be produced for roofs and need no longer be brought up from below. The tiles were also particularly welcome for floors, replacing the crude adobe bricking that wore down quickly into dust.

Beth and Tim put their heads together on plans for a trail wide enough for a wagon right-of-way. It was planned to reach from the valley floor to the summit ridge and down to the lowlands, connecting with a wagon trail already marked out that led toward the Romeros' property and the border. The trail would cut the trip from Rancho Cielo to the lowlands by two whole days, it was estimated, and would make the shipment of goods much easier. Needed items could be brought up to the high country far easier and in greater quantity than ever before.

All of this took money, and Tim was generous with what he could afford. Sometimes, however, he and Beth locked wills on his choice of projects, and in this case no money was required.

Tim had found that the Pai Pais had no recreational drink and decided on a solution.

"I shall make my own *pulque* for the Indians," he announced to the women at dinner one night. The spiritous Mexican liquor was made from the sap of the maguey, or century plant, that grew down on the flatlands below the valley. This brought about a spirited discussion between Tim and Beth.

"You can't do it," Beth declared firmly.

"And why not?" Tim retorted. "These poor indigents need a little joy in their lives once in a while. Life's a bitter pill for them, it seems to me."

"And you're going to be the Good Samaritan who sugar-coats it. You know the Indians aren't supposed to drink."

Tim grunted. "It's not a law. And that's pure hogwash about firewater and the Indians' demoralization. The Pai Pais are a gentle, civilized people. Come on, sis, let me go ahead with my plan."

"We get little enough work out of the Indians as it is," Beth replied.

"Even indentured servants need some incentive to work hard."

"And you think furnishing them with pulque will help? It'll just give them a ready-made excuse to lie around inebriated."

"Sis," Tim said patiently, "I don't intend to *keep* them drunk, just portion a little cactus nectar out to them now and then, as a reward for jobs well-done. Come on, let's make a supply of pulque, crock it, ration it out judiciously."

"We're already feeding everyone in the valley," Beth pointed out. "We don't have to give them libations too."

"My dear sister, they need an incentive to work beyond a pat on the back now and then," Tim declared. "They don't own any property and precious few possessions. You're lucky they're here. Sometimes you stand so close to the forest you don't see the trees. Why not give them a little fun occasionally?"

Beth was tired that night, and perhaps her weariness made her vulnerable to Tim's enthusiasm. Maybe she did expect too much of the Indians, she thought, just as she had always expected too much of herself. It did seem a very un-Christian attitude, and one Father Conn would probably frown on, she was fairly certain.

"All right," she relented, "you can do this on your own. I wash my hands of it, just in case it's a fiasco. I don't really like the idea, but I have to allow that your idea will please the Indian men a lot."

Tim grinned and turned to Maggie. "Beth is sounding more and more like her father all the time. The domineering parent."

"I'm only thinking of the consequences."

"Well, don't worry," Tim said. "And thanks for the release. I know everyone will be pleased."

So, with old Creek, Tim descended to the flanks of the sierra that faced east toward the Colorado River basin. There, with Creek's enthusiastic help, for the old man was jubilant that the long-absent pulque would once more make its appearance in the valley, the two men removed the barely formed buds from the flower stalks of the century plant that grew plentiful by Nature's blessing. Then they scooped out hollows in the plants' hearts and marked each tree.

Into the hollow was collected the sweet sap of the plant, the aguamiel. After returning later with pack mules to retrieve the sap in large wineskins, fermentation was begun at Rancho Cielo. A highly intoxicating milky liquid was the final result, a type of alcoholic drink that dated back to the pre-Columbian Indians, and not savored by the valley-bound Pai Pais in decades. Pulque made Saturday nights a lot jollier for the Indian males. It also made them more repentant at Sunday morning chapel service, Tim pointed out wryly to Beth.

However, there was no comparable reward for the Pai Pai women, who scorned the pulque. Beth solved this by issuing all mothers an extra ration of raw sugar and flour, so they could make simple cookies for themselves and their children. Everyone was happy.

When the weather grew warm and balmy again, Maggie's daily tempo seemed to change, Beth noticed. One morning over breakfast she told Beth that she was pregnant.

"I think it's God's sign that we ought to move on," Maggie said reluctantly. "I hate to, but we must."

"Leave Rancho Cielo?" Beth was unprepared for such a sudden decision. "Why be hasty? Aren't you happy here?" Then, as an afterthought: "Is it something I've done?"

"Oh Beth, it's nothing like that," Maggie assured her. "Tim and I have been talking about going for some time."

"And said nothing to me until now about it."

"There wasn't any firm talk. But we did plan before we came here to have our baby in California, on American soil."

"You're probably right," Beth conceded. "I shouldn't

interfere. I keep forgetting that Baja isn't the United States of America. I suppose I've got a foot on each side of the border having one Mexican son and one American."

"We want to make sure that our child is born in California. I've a cousin in Sacramento. We might go there for a spell. Tim can work in Ed's store until he decides what he wants to do."

"Well, I suppose I can't persuade you to stay," said Beth.

"I don't think so."

Beth smiled. "If Tim had told me it would have started an argument, but I can't argue with you, Maggie. I shall miss you terribly."

"Oh, it's not like we're going away forever. We'll be back. The place has a definite enchantment. It's wonderful when the weather's right, high and healthy. But then, the enchantment is mainly you," Maggie said warmly. "I'm very fond of you, Beth."

"And you're like a sister to me," Beth said. "When will you go?"

"That will be Tim's decision, but it will be fairly soon."

Later the same day, Tim talked with Beth.

"We'll go in April, before the really hot weather comes on," he said. "I know you want us to stay, and it's been a difficult decision to make, but we must go. We're really primarily thinking of the child."

"I understand," Beth said.

"I was hoping you would. By the way, when I was riding up by the peaks the other day I was reminded of something and wondered if you knew about it."

"What's that?"

"You've seen the cave drawings?"

"Oh yes, that's where the Pai Pai women got their designs when we were thinking about doing some commercial weaving."

"Have you ever seen the mysterious figure nearby?" Tim asked her.

"I don't know what you mean."

"Well, Carmen took me up there once. I want you to see it. Will you go there with me now?"

"Yes, Tim. If it's important to you."

They rode up to the cave shelter and Tim led her to the drawing. She was awed by the religious mood of the crude human form, which seemed naggingly familiar.

"It must be very old," Beth observed. "What do you think it means."

"Probably a key to some mystery of the valley," Tim said. "Who knows?"

"Yes, but what? It has a priestly form. When Father Conn comes up again I must bring him here. I've been in Antelope Valley all this time and never known about this. Why didn't you say something to me before?"

"I left rather suddenly, with other things on my mind."

"And now you're happy," Beth said as they walked to their horses. "Your life's working out beautifully."

"It seems to be," Tim agreed. "It was good that I ran off with Carmen."

"I didn't think so at the time."

"Otherwise I'd never have met Maggie."

"It was fated."

"You're always talking about fate. I wish I could be so certain of the predestined course of life."

"God has things worked out for us."

"If I believed your theory life would be a lot easier to take."

"It isn't a theory, it's a religion," Beth said. "It's what makes life bearable."

Before Tim and Maggie had packed their few possessions preparatory to leaving Rancho Cielo, a visitor arrived. It was Mama Luz's second cousin, Hector Delgado, the short, stout, baldheaded lawyer from Tecate.

Even after a body wash and a change of clothes and a few glasses of the Spanish brandy he'd brought with him as a gift, Delgado was still not relaxed. After dinner he sat in the living room with Tim and the ladies. Delgado hadn't had a pleasant trip up the mountain to Rancho Cielo. Terrified of red rattlers, of pumas, wolves, even coyotes and non-existent bears, he had slept holding his rifle. With his Indian guide he shared guard duty, so that one of them was always sitting upright with his back to the campfire, peering into the surrounding darkness, ready to fend off an attack of wild beasts, or bandits, which he feared as much as rattlesnakes.

Delgado had a lot to say about conditions in and around the border in his heavily-accented but excellent American English, carefully skirting the fact that the Porter brothers had both been murdered under questionable circumstances. After all, Beth observed with a trace of cynicism, Delgado was a lawyer, with a lawyer's canny sensibility and tact.

"I must say," Delgado opined, "the sierra country is every bit as wild and formidable as I was told, never having been here before. Not exactly a congenial place to live. I'm amazed at the comfortable community that exists here."

"But you live in Baja," Beth stated, "and this shouldn't surprise you." She hoped fervently that Delgado wouldn't stay longer than just overnight, but knew that she had to extend him whatever hospitality he required. "Let it be no longer than three days, for guests, like fish, can stink after that time," Mama Luz used to tell her. It was, however, a hidebound tradition at Rancho Cielo never to refuse a passing visitor food and refuge. After all, the area was even wilder than the plains the pioneers had crossed.

"Nothing about the countryside surprises me, señora," Delgado replied. "What surprises me is that you, such a young and exceptionally beautiful woman of grace and charm, should choose to continue living up here in this isolated wilderness. More or less by yourself."

"A great deal holds me at Rancho Cielo, señor." Beth countered in her measured Spanish. If Delgado intended to intimidate her with his good English, she could certainly show off her Spanish in the same way. "First of all, many memories. My first husband, Michael Porter, often visited here with his father when he was a boy, and Joe Porter, my second husband, was almost entirely raised here. Besides, during my time in Antelope Valley I became deeply attached to Mama Luz, as much as I ever was to my own mother. I still grieve over her loss, even if I don't wear somber black always." This was a thought, Beth realized, that she had never consciously allowed herself to entertain until that moment.

"Ah yes, sentiment is noble, loyalty to the dead commendable." Delgado crossed himself with solemn quickness. "But there are practical considerations. You have two small boys, señora. They should have all the opportunities that civilization can offer them—friends, fine schools, a chance to enter a rewarding profession. In brief, a worthy life. Here they'll be little better off than savages, like those miserable creatures who exist in the valley with you."

"I don't look upon the Pai Pais as primitives, Señor Delgado," Beth said, bridling. "They are my friends. They protect me and we all work together as one group to maintain ourselves. I find life anything but dull or isolated here. There are numerous challenges. In fact, I don't feel that I'll ever live anywhere else."

Delgado chewed on her remark for a moment, leaving the conversation floating in the air as the cheery blaze in the fireplace crackled.

"Well," he observed at length, "facts might intervene so that you would have to make a choice." His smile was deprecatory.

Tim sat up, suddenly attentive. "How so, Señora Delgado?"

"I will explain," Delgado said briskly, opening the leather pouch he had been carrying with him since his arrival.

He extracted a document and unfolded it. He said to the trio, "Here is a document that may interest you. A will that Luz Delgado made four years ago when she needed money and traveled down to Tecate to negotiate with me for it. The Rancho Cielo property in Antelope Valley was deeded to me by this document upon Luz Delgado's death. That is, unless she paid back the loan before that time, which she did not."

With a flourish Delgado handed the document to Beth as Tim and Maggie looked on in stunned silence. Beth inspected it with trembling hands. The will appeared to be executed in Mama Luz's florid handwriting. It bore a date four years back.

"Sir," Tim said, "wouldn't a more recent will cancel out your claim to the estate?"

"Under regular circumstances, yes—*if* there were no lien on the estate," Delgado said. "But in Luz's case there was a question of debt. If you'll read the document carefully you'll see that unless the loan was repaid by the time of her death, the property is either mine automatically or may be sold for the settlements of her debts, whichever I prefer. As lien holder, the courts will allow me to make the decision."

"I can hardly believe it," Beth murmured in a daze, her whole world threatened in a manner that she simply could not have foreseen.

"Your late mother-in-law was not versed in the refinements of the law," Delgado pointed out unnecessarily. "Either because of the delirium of her final illness, or out of sheer innocence, she completely ignored her debt to me. Or possibly she assumed that a new will would abrogate the previous one, which was naive of her, to say the least."

"What was the amount that she owed to you?" Beth asked, almost afraid to hear Delgado's answer.

The lawyer produced another document. "Four thousand dollars in United States Federal currency," he said, handing Beth the paper.

"I don't have four thousand dollars in any kind of money," Beth told Delgado. "I don't even have a thou-

sand dollars to my name. And there is absolutely no way
that I can raise it." She didn't even dare glance at Tim.
Even if he had that much money, she couldn't ask him for
a loan, for there was no way of paying him back. Rancho
Cielo was hardly a money-making enterprise, nor would
it probably ever be. The most that could be hoped for
was self-sufficiency on a modest scale. Maybe her destiny
was to leave with Tim and Maggie when they departed.

"So, Señor Delgado," she said with a sinking heart,
"where does that leave me?"

"As a debtor, señora," was Delgado's swift reply. "I
am not a hard man, nor a greedy one. I could easily refuse
to make claim on the estate if you could see your way
clear to make me four semi-annual payments of one
thousand dollars each over the next two years, cancelling
the entire debt."

"But I told you," Beth said, "I don't have the money."

"Perhaps there is money in your United States family?" Delgado suggested.

"Sir, we've already received our inheritance from our
father's estate," Tim told the lawyer bluntly. "We don't
expect more, and we're not too solvent at the moment."

"Well, I could reduce the cash payments if you had
some other form of reinbursement—jewelry, gold ingots,
property in the United States," Delgado explained. "But
I must have some regular return on the loan. After all,
señora, I support a large family with many demands upon
my resources. I'm not trying to be mean, nor gouge you,
God knows, but I am always needful of money. The loan
has already gone a long time without repayment."

"Señor Delgado, the Land Division has never sent me
any notice whatsover that you were the original heir to the
estate," said Beth. "In fact, I haven't heard anything at
all from them since they acknowledged receipt of the
will I filed."

"That's because they had the previous will on file and
contacted me instead to notify me of your claim. You see,
your son by Joselito wasn't even born then, so the Mexi-

can government was under no obligation to inform you as guardian of the estate's status."

"But doesn't the closer relationship of my son as Mama Luz's grandson supersede your claim?"

"Not when there is a lien against the estate. Believe me, señora. I am not falsifying procedure. I don't have to do that, since all the details are officially documented and recorded. All I want is the return of my loan, then the property is yours, free and clear. I wrote frequently to Luz, reminding her of the obligation. She ignored my letters."

"She never mentioned receiving letters from you, señor," Beth declared.

"All the same, they were sent. Copies are here, in this pouch, if you wish to see them. Finally I ceased to press her. I'd made an excellent short-term investment that was paying off handsomely for a while, but has since dissolved itself, I'm sorry to say. A silver mine in the mountains south of Tecate. The ore has run out."

"Then what you really want is the forfeit of this property to you so you can exploit it for minerals," Tim said. "Isn't that right, sir?"

Delgado shrugged his shoulders, but beneath the studied nonchalance his composure had obviously been shaken.

"I can't deny that the thought has entered my mind, yes. But this spot is so remote from wagon trails and shipping routes of any kind. No one has studied its potential. Specialists would have to be brought in from the United States to make geological surveys and assess the area. This is a very costly procedure; it takes a great deal of money to initiate such a project."

The statement lay unspoken between them that Delgado would know exactly how to involve interested parties. In fact, he probably had made a complete study not only of Beth's background and finances but of Antelope Valley. He was moving within safe bounds, determined by legal means to wrest the property from Beth's hands.

She immediately envisioned her valley being overrun with American mineralogists, its pristine remoteness violated, never again to be the same, its people either made slaves to progress or driven out entirely.

"All right, Señor Delgado, I'll think about it," she murmured faintly. "We can talk again in the morning."

"As you wish." Delgado nodded toward the documents Beth had spread out on the table. "You may study these further tonight, if you like. I shall plan on leaving tomorrow morning after breakfast for Tecate. Keep the documents for your records. There are other copies in my safe at home. The originals are in Mexico City, of course." Delgado rose to his feet, bowed to the ladies, and nodded to Tim. "Well, I shall say goodnight. An exhausting day lies ahead on the trail for me."

After Delgado had gone out to Joe's cabin where he was spending the night, Tim exploded in uncharacteristic fury.

"The son of a bitch," he muttered. "He's a grub, a leech! Somebody ought to stamp him out!"

"Don't talk like that, Tim," Beth said.

"I'm sorry, sis," Tim apologized. "I got carried away." But he slapped his right fist into the palm of his left hand.

"What can we do?" Beth asked sadly. "Hector Delgado has a clear lien on the property according to the papers."

"It would seem so. But what if he's lying? Suppose the documents are forged?" Tim speculated.

"We don't know that. The fact is that Mama Luz may easily have borrowed money from him, if he offered it to her, not thinking of the consequences. The money would have been for sustaining life in the valley, or for Joe, possibly even for Michael. Come to think of it, the biggest part of that money—if it actually were borrowed—may have gone to Michael and Joe to buy the goods Michael purchased from Father in New York. Mama Luz was an extremely generous woman. If he's on the level, how can we blame Delgado for wanting his money back?"

"He's a monster," said Maggie. "What he really wants is Antelope Valley, and he knows it's your home."

"Sis, I could lend you a thousand," Tim offered. "It's about all we have but that would keep him quiet for a while and give you some time."

"No, Tim, I can't accept your money. Something will happen, I know it. God simply won't let us down."

Maggie sent Beth a look of incredulity. "You're not going to stay on, you can't. You're coming with us, you and the boys."

"No," Beth said firmly, "I won't even consider leaving. Something will happen before Delgado can return to try and drive me out. I know it will. I've been through hellfire and brimstone in the past few years, trials enough to test Job's mettle. But I have my sons and I have my faith. And my rights." Beth rose, tears in her eyes; Maggie stood up and went to embrace her.

"God smiles on this valley," Beth declared, "and on its people. Nothing can change that, not all the Delgados in the world."

"There, there," Maggie soothed, holding her tight.

"I am going to kill Delgado," Tim vowed.

"Tim, shut up!" Maggie rasped over Beth's shoulder, and Tim subsided with a frustrated groan.

A few minutes later the three of them went to bed deeply troubled.

"She could at least come along with us," Maggie whispered in Tim's arms. "There's no point in staying on. She'll just be dragging out her departure. I wish she'd accept your money. We'll get along somehow."

"You don't know Beth like I do," Tim replied. "She'll do what she thinks is morally right even if it means walking into a firing squad. Stubborn's a mild word for her. You should know that by now."

"I do know it. Say, maybe the Romeros could lend her the money," Maggie suggested.

"On the basis of what? The Romeros have an opulent

life on the surface," Tim said, "but no money. I wish I
had a solution, but I don't see one on the horizon. All I
can say is, if there's a just God he'll smile on Beth. If
running off with Michael was a sin, she's more than atoned
for it, or so it seems in my ignorance of such matters."

"We'll pray that things will work out for her," Maggie
said, kissing Tim's cheek.

"You pray for both of us," Tim told her. "I'm sleepy.
We're leaving in a couple of days and there's a lot that
has to be done around here before we do. Goodnight,
love . . ."

Tim rolled over and was asleep at once, as Maggie remained awake, postulating a silent prayer for Beth's welfare and future.

21

BETH's parting with Maggie and Tim was tearful with
promises to meet again very soon. San Francisco was even
mentioned as a rendezvous point, although all three of
them knew that this was an unlikely choice. Unspoken
between them was the realization that Beth would remain at Rancho Cielo with the boys on borrowed time,
and that it was a probable certainty that in six months or
less she would join Tim and Maggie somewhere in Northern California—perhaps in Sacramento, if they remained
there.

Beth would in any case stay on through the summer
season, see that the Pai Pai harvests were in, that things
were going reasonably well. This would carry her up to
the deadline for payment of the first thousand dollar in-

crement to Hector Delgado. Beyond that moment she refused to speculate on what might happen.

In the chapel each morning and evening she would repeat her fervent prayers to a listening God, beseeching Him to hear her, to make her continuing life possible at Rancho Cielo, her beloved valley. Her prayers included the Pai Pais, of course, but they were mainly concentrated on Nate and little Jimmy, the two strongest forces in her world. She saw no reason why, with a little management and some Divine intervention, she couldn't raise the boys right here in Antelope Valley, tutoring them herself with imported books. She was an excellent teacher; it wouldn't be difficult for her to give them their basic instruction. Later on she could think about sending them off to schools, to further their education.

About a week after Tim and Maggie had left, Father Conn came over the summit ridge trail to Antelope Valley. His visit was unexpected but most welcome; Beth was overjoyed to see him. After dinner, with the boys put to bed, they talked of Joe's death, for they had not met since that event.

"As a priest I'm supposed to give solace where the need exists," Father Conn told Beth. "But what can I say to you about Joe Porter that you don't already know? I found him to be sympathetic, sensitive to people's needs. He was a man of admirable qualities. You loved him, so you know what I'm saying."

"Yes, Father. I did love him—perhaps not quite in the sense that some husbands and wives are affiliated," Beth found herself saying, wondering whether she shouldn't keep this data for the confessional, or simply eschew altogether the luxury of intimate conversation. Although a priest as confidante rather than confessor was appealing, there was a kind of magnetism about Father Conn that made her hesitate to say all that she wished to say.

"You loved Joe," Father Conn said. "The quality and size of love aren't as important as the declaration."

"I didn't marry him for prestige," Beth said, "or to escape from a restricted but formal life into an adventurous, open one, as I did with Michael. I married Joe because this was the one sure way to bind me to Rancho Cielo, to make me a part of it in a way I never could be otherwise. Michael had no real attachment here. Being his widow did not give me the security I sought, so I had to find a purchase-hold, and I did. Was that wrong?"

"No, because you loved Joe. It wasn't an immoral act."

"Yes, I loved him. I didn't know him as I knew Michael, but my loyalty was his."

"You could marry again, Beth," Father Conn suggested.

"What are you saying?"

"I know how you feel about Antelope Valley," Amos Conn said, "how it's become your sacred trust, your whole life. But all the same, I don't think you'll want to continue living here indefinitely, all alone. It isn't healthy for a young woman like yourself."

"At present I see no other life," Beth said, slightly ruffled that the priest should suggest that she abandon Rancho Cielo. Why didn't he just say she was obsessed unreasonably, and let her deal with that? She had told him very little; now she would have to go into detail about Hector Delgado.

"There is an obstacle," she explained, "a very large and serious one. It might block my path and send me down the mountain in defeat."

Father Conn's expression became alert, curious.

"What kind of obstacle?" he asked. "Some unexpected problem left you by Mama Luz, or Joe?" Conn's question was a mere guess, but intuitively he had come close to the truth, Beth observed.

"There is a man named Hector Delgado, a second cousin of Mama Luz," Beth began, and went on to explain about the meeting with Delgado and the documents he brought with him.

Father Conn said quietly when she was through, "We

shall have to find a way to solicit God's intervention, Beth." He crossed himself thoughtfully. "There is a way. In faith there is always a way. I have had many good reasons to become a cynic, but I'm not one. In some situations I find myself looking on the dark and dismal side of doubt, instead of turning my thoughts toward the sunlight of hope. It might seem impossible to you at the moment, even with your faith, that the future of Rancho Cielo can be controlled by you. I have seen and learned enough to know that all things are possible. Small and large miracles are wrought daily; we shall have to move forward on that premise. Prayer does indeed move mountains and change the shape of valleys. There are even less exalted ways of dealing with your dilemma."

"How so?"

"One thing that can be done is to offer you an alternative to the eventual loss of Antelope Valley."

"And what is that?" Beth asked eagerly.

"As you know, I've recently come from San Francisco. The city is beginning to pass from a lusty boom town into a remarkably interesting and substantial community."

"I've never been there," said Beth.

"You would find it quite a challenge, I am sure," the priest told her. "It takes no great wisdom to suggest that it will grow rapidly into a significant California landmark, the Western capital of the United States. Cultural interests will meet and meld at its crossroads. Artists will gravitate there, as they do to New York, and patrons of the art will proliferate. For instance, I am lucky to be good friends with a man who appreciates the finer things in life. His name is Evan Patrick. He has a wife named Claudia, an accomplished pianist, and two children, a boy and a girl, who are both quite musical. Evan is a remarkable man, what I might call an instant millionaire. His schooners ply the Pacific silk route between San Francisco and Shanghai, sailing to other remote places as well, taking hides and lumber from California to the Orient, returning with the kinds of cargo that Michael and Joe Porter sometimes dealt with in the past. Silks, cotton goods, jewels, jade, ivory, many spices."

Beth nodded silently not wishing to interrupt Conn's flow of conversation, curious as to how the priest intended to fit her into the world up North.

"Evan is Catholic, as are the members of his family. He is a man with immense sophistication, broad understanding, enormous compassion. He beseeched me to remain in San Francisco and settle there. And while I would not be able to follow my devotion to God officially, he wished me to instruct his children. I feel that my value lies in mobility, however, at least in the West. Very politely and with considerable reluctance I refused Evan's generous offer to become tutor to his children, and religious counselor for him and Claudia. I think Evan was disappointed with me for passing up his offer, though I know he understood my reservations."

"If the position would have given you security," Beth said, "perhaps you should have considered further before making such a decision. Nothing like that could happen in Southern California, or in Baja."

"My reasons were broader than just the job," Father Conn said. "I wanted to come back here."

"To Antelope Valley and Rancho Cielo? Why?" Beth asked.

The priest smiled engagingly. "Because I feel a curious peace in this valley. The moment I ride over that ridge and begin to descend to the valley floor I feel it. It is a powerful experience, Beth, and it happened the first time I came here."

"As it did with me the first time I came."

"And you have never left it for a day since. But now there are clouds on your horizon, which is why I mentioned the Patricks and the fortuitous coincidence that has taken place. I told Evan and Claudia about you. They thought you remarkable for remaining here. Should you go North, Evan said, you should contact them. If you wished, you could take the position that I refused."

"But I'm not qualified," Beth protested.

"You will be warmly welcomed and amply compensated, have no doubts. And you are more than qualified. Yes, there'll be a place for your boys, and a place for you as tutor to the Patrick children."

"I'm grateful to you, Father, for thinking to plead my case. But I shan't leave the valley until I am driven out."

"Well, you will have time to think about it. Don't close the door yet. Evan said he would consider no other applicants until I had talked to you and sent him your answer."

"I'm overwhelmed," Beth said. "Why not take the job yourself, Father? It would be ideal, especially since you say you aren't hopeful of ever becoming a part of the San Francisco diocese."

The priest shifted his position, studied his hands. At length he said, "Perhaps I ought to explain something to you. It's been on my mind to tell you this when I saw you again."

Sensing an important issue whose nature she could only surmise, Beth said, "Don't explain anything if it will give you pain later on, Father. There is no need to. I have always accepted you as I found you. That's quite enough for me."

"My dear Beth, I admire your clear-mindedness. You are a finely sensitive person. Thank you for making it easier than it would be otherwise. I must, of course, tell you everything. Probably I should have done so long ago. It was only my fear of losing your respect and faith in me that made me hesitate. But since you'll possibly be going out into the world one of these days soon, and you may hear stories about me, I thought you ought to know the truth."

"Tell it if you must," Beth said quietly, pouring the priest a brandy before settling back with her coffee. His features were strained and tense in the candlelight, she

noted, and immediately wondered if she shouldn't restrain
him, and let unspoken matters remain unspoken. She
might regret his candor.

"Here it is calm and beautiful outside," said the priest,
"and what I have to tell you is a tale for a stormy night.
But it can wait no longer." The priest sighed, took a sip
of his brandy. "I believe I've mentioned to you that I
lived and worked on an island in the West Indies?"

"Yes, of course. You had a parish there among the poor,
you told me."

"On the Isle of St. John, which is ruled by a small but
powerful band of whites, though my work was with the
Negroes. What I didn't tell you was that among the white
aristocrats on St. John was a marvelous white woman of
quality whose husband was the wealthiest plantation owner of them all. A volatile man . . ." Father Conn paused,
sipping at his brandy again. "To make a painful story less
harrowing is to make it brief. Very well. The white lady
of quality was engaged in many good works, among them
certain assistance to my parish. We met many times,
spending hours together on matters concerning the parish-
ioners. Then one winter's afternoon, when a tropical storm
had closed in and it was dusk, we discovered that we
were in love. Appalled by the idea, we hurriedly separated. But the passion was stronger than we were. We
came together again, the two of us alone, and we made
love . . ."

Beth gripped the arms of her rocker. Should she stop
the priest before he regretted his confidence? But from
the haunted, driven look on his face she knew that he
must be allowed to relive the anguish of his confession.
In a most peculiar way their roles were reversed. She
might be sitting behind the confessional screen, she the
priest, Father Conn the penitent.

"My lady implored me to go away with her, to leave
the parish and the island. We would flee to New York, she
said, then lose ourselves somewhere in the North, where

her husband would never find us. I would have to give up the priesthood entirely. I had already violated my vows. A spoiled priest and an unfaithful wife. A sorry future for us both. No, I told her, we had already made a grave and sinful error. We could not compound it by flouting our mistake before God. I said I would leave St. John, and that our love must die. I begged her to leave, and she did. Seen coming from my rectory by her spying, jealous husband, she was shot in my garden. She bled to death among the flowers. I heard the shot, escaped and made my way to the port. I stowed away on a steamer that was sailing for America that night. I survived, my lady died. I am directly responsible for her death, for my bed in Hell . . . Now you can understand why I can never again be a priest in formal circumstances. Yes, I can say roving Mass throughout the Southern outposts of California. I am perfectly safe and at home in the remote and lawless wilderness of Baja. This is my exile. I felt when I first came here that I had found a place of mission. I still feel that strongly, deeply . . ."

Father Conn paused and did not look at Beth, knowing what would be in her glance. A turgid silence fell between them. He took another sip of his brandy, his features more relaxed, as if his tale for a stormy night had finally exorcised his agony.

In a daze, Beth's first reaction was mute response, then wonderment, then slow growing anger as the enormity of his crime began to reveal itself to her. She stood up slowly, pale, the cords in her neck like ropes, her hands fluttering to her bosom. She glared at him and said in a rasping voice, "You made a mockery of my marriage to Joe! Everything you've done here is a sacrilege!"

"No, Beth—" Father Conn was also on his feet—"that's not true. I may have been banished from the Church in that I may never have another parish. But I am still an agent of God, my faith is as powerful as ever. God has not rejected me; my penance is to rove, to bring solace where it is needed. I am unofficially blessed by the Bishop of Baja California."

"But my marriage to Joe isn't legal," Beth protested. "My son is illegitimate in the eyes of the Church!"

"Your marriage and the birth of Jaime Porter are legal in the eyes of God and man. I am human, Beth, but I am not devious or a monster."

"But you've sinned!" Beth said.

"My dear Beth, we have all sinned countless times, as the Church teaches."

"How could you ever pay for such an enormous sin as the one you committed on St. John? That poor woman lost her life because of you."

"I shall pay for it in thought and recompense the rest of my life on earth."

"That doesn't alter the fact of your guilt."

"Nothing mitigates it. But I can't change what has happened."

Beth sat down, her hands clasped on her knees.

"You will have to go. You have betrayed me. If Hector Delgado gets wind of the news that you are not what most people think you are, he will know that my marriage to Joe is not blessed by the Church. My son Jimmy will cease to be heir to Rancho Cielo."

"Listen to me, Beth. Your marriage is perfectly legal. You have nothing to worry about. What concerns me is your singlemindedness. If you refuse to accept the Evan Patrick offer, if you won't leave this place before you are sent away, you will bring misery upon yourself and your children. I told you my story for several reasons. All of them will now have to remain unstated."

"Please, Father, no more tonight," Beth begged in a shaken voice. "I've heard enough."

"I would like to stay on a few days," he said "so that I might attend to the needs of the Pai Pais, and to talk further with you."

"You may do as you wish," Beth told him indifferently,

and saw him out the door, which she bolted after him as
he walked to Joe's cabin.

If only Tim were here, she thought, he would know
how to deal with Father Conn. Why was she even calling
him Father any longer? He was a mere culpable man,
caught in the coils of mortal sin. He had lost the right to
her veneration.

In the middle of the night she was prodded wide awake
by a strange dream. As she lay brooding in the dark she
began to put the dream together. It had concerned a
priest, although this one did not in any way resemble
Father Conn. He wasn't handsome, as the mulatto priest
was. He had looked thin, rather ill, a brown-robed padre
with a face carved from the anxieties of another age.

The priest had spoken to her she began to recall. But
only one word: Wait! And then he had spread out his
arms, stretching his fingertips, his sandaled feet, as if he
were floating in the air. Before she could determine where
she had seen the familiar pose before, she slipped off to
sleep again.

In the morning the dream's image of the priest had receded to a vague blur, almost erased from her mind, although she clung in troubled apprehension to the mood of
the dream, reluctant to explore it further, to relate it to
Father Conn or herself.

Beth's strongest thoughts of the morning centered
around the priest. She felt a deep loss where he was concerned. She walked around for the first hour of her day
with the burden of this. A sense of grief gnawed at her
until at last, rationally, she had to admit to herself that
she had no business exploiting her emotions in this care-
less self-indulgent manner.

Pulling herself up sharply, she realized that she'd lost
nothing but her own blind faith in the purity of one human being—a remarkable man who had brought her into
the intricate web of Catholicism, given her understanding
and ultimate enlightenment, a focus and a purpose. And,
she lectured herself, she really had no right to assume that

Father Conn was a perfect vessel of God, holy in every way, above and beyond sin. The Church's teaching had embraced forgiveness and tolerance; she must never forget this. One could have faith without strict adherence to principle, even if one became a pariah. In fact, she might well be guilty herself of the sin of censure and ostracism, cruel and unreasonable judgments, by placing the unfortunate priest in the category of the damned.

How easy it was to judge others, she thought over her morning coffee. She had certainly made an excess of selfish stubbornness by her adamant refusal to leave Rancho Cielo. She had flailed herself with this resolve and in doing so had placed a heavy burden of empathy upon others, and set the stage for future sorrows.

Also, she knew she hadn't been fair with the Pai Pais she knew best—Creek, Red Deer, Maria. She had neglected to advise them of her dire predicament, of her insolvency, the core of all her troubles: money. She would not be without blame when they found that she was no longer to be depended upon for guidance, that she was deserting them without telling them the truth about their future in the hands of Hector Delgado. Or perhaps someone even worse to whom Delgado would soon enough sell the estate for exploitation at a substantial price. The poor Indians would either be driven off the land or would become slaves to the whims of whoever managed them.

While Beth was having her dark morning thoughts, Father Conn went to see Creek. The priest considered Creek the spokesman for the Pai Pais and felt that perhaps he could shed some light on Beth's refusal to give up on Rancho Cielo. It was obvious to Conn after his talk with Beth the night before that she'd been alone at Rancho Cielo for too long a time. The raising of her sons, the welfare of the Pai Pais and the frustration of not being able to raise the money to satisfy Hector Delgado had all taken their toll of her nerves and sensibilities. He didn't blame her for her austere, highly personalized interpretation of the Church's teachings. In isolation from practicing Catholics, she had simply assumed protective coloring, adapting what he had taught her to the stark landscape of her mountain world. If this made her judgment of others exceptionally harsh, it was because she had accepted the mantle of asceticism as her life role.

Father Conn understood that it was impossible for Beth to see his Isle of St. John tragedy as an event to be absorbed into life, relegated to historical significance, thus allowing for the present and the future where he could be of some practical use in the world of men and women. He had given Beth solace when nothing else would have satisfied; he had brought her soul to God, where it would always remain, no matter what she thought her transgressions might be. His duty now was to persuade her to leave Rancho Cielo, to sail to San Francisco and become part of the Evan Patrick family where she would be nurtured, protected and loved. Once she had made the transition, the obsession with Rancho Cielo would diminish, and in time disappear completely.

Creek greeted Father Conn with surprise and deep pleasure. The priest had never come to him before; this was an honor and he knew that if Father Conn asked a favor, or his advice, he would be inclined to do all he could. As he seated Father Conn on a pallet on the adobe brick floor, his wife bustled about to make hot tea and broke out several of their cherished sugar cookies which the priest refused politely, with gratitude.

"Father," Creek said when the men had their mugs of tea and the amenities had been exhausted, "to what do I owe your treasured presence in my house this morning?"

"Thank you for allowing me to get to the point," Conn said. "My visit concerns Señora Porter. I'm worried about her. As you know, she is a woman alone now, and her future here is not the brightest."

Creek mulled this over for a moment, took a sip of his tea. "Ah well, we will always care for her here in Antelope Valley," he said, his leathery features wrinkled in a

a prideful smile. "She is what Joselito used to call her—
a mascot, our priceless jewel. If I may say it, granting
your permission, Father, she is our own angelic presence."

"You have my permission to say that," Father Conn assured Creek. "There's no heresy involved. She is a Madonna, as Mama Luz was. But I am worried about the
señora."

"Worried?" Creek frowned. "How so, Father? Is something wrong I don't know about?"

Father Conn didn't know quite where to begin. He
might be telling tales out of school, he thought, nosing
where he had no business. But somebody had to shake
Beth Porter loose from her cocoon of idealized dreams.
If Creek knew of Beth's financial problems, maybe he
would deal with Beth herself in a manner that would make
her see the dead-end reality of her situation. It might spark
a crisis, but then, Conn was used to critical happenings.
His life as a parish priest had been filled with them, they
were in his blood. No need to shy away from one more,
he thought.

"How much do you know about the lawyer, this Hector
Delgado, and his recent visit to Antelope Valley?" the
priest asked bluntly.

"He came unannounced by letter," Creek explained.
"to discuss the details of Mama Luz's will with Señora
Beth. That is what we all know. The lawyer Delgado is
a representative of the Mexican government's Land Division office and resides in Tecate. We know that these matters must be settled when someone dies; it's not easy as
our life is, where we pass on possessions before we die
by word of mouth. In my case I have no children living
here. My old woman and I have only our pots and pans
and a few clothes to leave to others in the village."

"I see," said Conn. "Well, what you heard was only
part of Delgado's story. We all keep something secret. As
a padre I hear many confessions and give many penances.
The sin of omission is one I can spot instantly. We are
all guilty of it, myself as much as you, Creek, or anyone

else. What I'm saying is, you were not told that the lawyer Delgado was here to make a hard deal with Señora Beth."

Creek's eyes narrowed suspiciously. He'd had enough to do with the outside world to be immediately alerted by such a statement. "What kind of a deal?" he asked softly.

"A money deal of course. He holds a legal lien on the Antelope Valley property. In other words, he is entitled by law to collect a certain sum of money over a given period of time. If this money isn't paid, the land and everything on it—" Conn reinforced this by spreading out his hand—"all becomes the property of Hector Delgado."

"No," Creek breathed quietly. "No."

"It seems that Mama Luz made a will several years ago when she was hard-pressed for money. In her need the estate was virtually signed away. The money has not been repaid."

Creek wagged his head in despairing astonishment. "This cannot be, Father. We saw no money at Rancho Cielo."

"I imagine not. The money went outside," Conn said, "to help with a business."

"Ah yes," Creek said, understanding immediately, "it went to Joselito and Miguelito."

"That's correct. And now more money is needed, a sizable sum. Señora Beth must now find that money if she is to repay the loan to Delgado and stay on at Rancho Cielo."

Creek stared at the flickering flames in the small stone fireplace. "What must we do, Father? Kill this Delgado?"

To Father Conn, the old Pai Pai sounded quite sincere.

"Not that, of course, but what else I don't know. I came to you, Creek, without saying anything to Señora Beth that we would confer. I thought you might have some solution, since I have none. I spent most of the night trying to figure ways. There aren't any that I could find."

Again, Creek wagged his head. Cross-legged, his hands trailing on the dusty brick floor, he sat dully for a moment, then almost automatically he leaned forward and began to trace a pattern with his index finger. It quickly grew into the same figure he had carved on Joe's leg when Joe was ill with the infected bullet wound. When he was done he sat back to regard his design.

"I can't say it will work, Father. We have a place of Pai Pai prayer that is very powerful medicine. It has nothing to do with the Church."

"I understand," Conn said, thinking that the voodoo rituals he encountered in connection with his St. John parish had augmented his Catholic rituals. Dreary and protracted Indian rites would be less exciting, but if one believed, strange things could happen. He nodded soberly in response to Creek's words. "Where is this place?" he asked.

"Come . . ." Creek rose to his feet. "We will saddle horses and ride there now."

"Is it far?"

Creek grinned. "Only in time," he declared.

Beth didn't see the two men riding off down the valley toward the marshy lake and the jumble of grey peaks that rose above it to the West. Had she done so, she might have gone out to the corral, taken her horse and followed out of curiosity.

Creek and the priest dismounted at the top of the trail close to the cave shelter. Conn was led to the flying figure of the padre on the rock wall. Recognizing a Christian image, however crude, he crossed himself quickly.

"Since this figure came into being, people have come here to see it, not knowing what it was," Creek explained. "Joselito and Miguelito, and then the Spanish girl, Carmen Aguilar and Señora Beth's brother, Tim, and the señora too and Mama Luz once, I think. But no one has truly seen it, this shrine of ours, as we see it. It goes back a long way to the time when the Jesuits were here. Follow me, I'll show you. But watch out for *zingales*, the red rattlers. They are plentiful here. They guard the shrine, it is said."

Following Creek, Father Conn was amazed at the laby-
rinthine trail they took, turning first to the right, then to
the left. Finally, after several minutes of strenuous climbing they reached a wide sandy aperture between the boulders.

Creek paused. "This is it," he said, echoing a conversation that had taken place on the same spot almost a hundred years earlier.

"What is it?" Father Conn asked, thinking that perhaps
the old Pai Pai was getting senile and had brought him to
this spot whimsically, on a wild goose chase with no real
end purpose to it. "Come, come, Creek," he said urgently,
"you're leaving me in the dark. Please explain."

"I will do my best to bring you into the light," Creek
said solemnly, seeing the priest's doubt. "Listen to me . . .
When the Jesuits were in Baja, one Padre Miguel came
up for a visit from Mission Santo Tomas over on the Pacific Coast. He made only one visit, but he left his blessings on Antelope Valley. He healed the sick, saved lives,
and leaving his glories behind he departed, never to
return."

"Go on."

"I am the only Pai Pai who knows what lies inside that
cave, Father. No one else will venture up here because
it is taboo. The cave was entrusted to my safekeeping upon
my father's death."

"I don't understand the purpose of our journey."

"If you weren't a priest this could never be. But we
know you well, as a good man with love in your heart for
all, like Padre Miguel of the past. The time has come that
my father told me about, a time when something has to
be done with the object. It was left here, we were told, to
set us free. And someone would come to do this. You are
the man . . . Now are you ready to enter with me?"

"I am ready," Father Conn said, quietly impressed with
Creek's sincerity.

The old Indian led the way into a rocky defile, too narrow to traverse on horseback, so that they were forced to

jump back and forth from one sloping rock face to another until they reached the defile's summit where Creek stopped abruptly.

"It is down there, concealed in the rocks," said Creek.

"Where?" Father Conn could see nothing that looked like a cave opening.

Creek pointed to a dark slit of an aperture between two grey boulder slabs.

"Ever since the cave was shut by an earthquake after the Spanish soldiers drove the Jesuits from Baja, no one could enter it. Then, ten years or so ago we had another powerful earthquake in the valley. It opened up the rock again. I don't know why, but that is what happened. I came here one year and it was miraculously opened. Come, I'll show you."

They descended with care to the narrow aperture between the rock slabs. It was just wide enough to squeeze through. Inside the opening the passage grew wider. Creek stopped to light a candle he had brought along. After an abrupt ascent passageway, the cave floor leveled out. Its ceiling was a natural dome rising toward a ledge that formed a crude, natural altar, Father Conn observed. Dry and clean, the cave bore no evidence of red rattlers. The priest's eyes were drawn to the altar as he approached it behind Creek.

Creek stopped some feet from the ledge and stepped aside. Father Conn could not restrain a cry of surprise and crossed himself again.

On the ledge of rock sat a chest, perhaps a yard long and eight inches deep, and about the same width. Because of its ornate Spanish design, Conn was fairly certain it was a relic from the time of the Jesuits.

"Come, look at it," said Creek.

The priest stepped forward to inspect the chest. Its brass bindings were dull from decades of neglect, its once-oiled wood grimy with layers of dust. As Creek held the candle, Conn stepped up closer to examine the chest. The dark wood—mahogany, Conn thought—had not dried out or cracked, probably due to the even temperature of the cave, protected deep in this solid rock chapel from the extremes of heat and cold that seasonally plagued the valley.

Conn reached out and touched the chest, running his hands over the convex bulge of its lid. His excitement was so great that his normally steady hands trembled visibly. His breath agitated, he tried to pry open the lid of the chest with his bare fingers. It was locked and would not yield to the pressure. He turned to Creek, who was smiling oddly at him.

"I'll need your hunting knife to open this," he said.

"No need . . ." Creek reached under his tunic and slipped from his neck a rawhide cord from which dangled a large, crude brass key.

"This will open it," he said. "My father gave it to me on his death bed."

Conn stared at him. "And you've never even had the idle curiosity to look inside, not even once?"

"The temptation was there, yes, ten years ago when I discovered the cave was open again. But I was already beyond curiosity, I respected the taboo, just as you cross yourself in respect to your God. I had no right to violate the taboo, not at that time. I would have brought down illness and famine on my people in the valley. How could I do that? My grandfather, Mateo, handed down what must be done. After the earthquake in 1767 he said it would be a long time before the shrine could be entered. That turned out to be true. Even my father thought so in his lifetime. We cannot build a great cathedral here to house the treasure, of course. But we can make a small shrine to honor your God and mine, a practical idea. What is in that chest will preserve the valley for all of us. That is how the story comes to me."

"What's in the box?" Father Conn asked.

"Here. Look for yourself." Creek handed the key to Father Conn.

The priest bent over the chest and inserted the key in

the lock, applying gentle but steady pressure to the key handle. At first the lock refused to yield, then slowly it began to turn under the pressure, at last clicking free.

Father Conn dropped his hands to his sides for a moment and took a deep breath. Whatever excitement he felt over this unorthodox ritual, its mystery had something to do with the Church. He was almost afraid to look into the box, not knowing what to expect: artifacts, jewels, antique gold coins, whatever. He crossed himself once again, then reached forward and opened the chest while Creek held the candle high so he could see easily what was inside.

Within lay a thick roll of aged canvas. Father Conn's heartbeat decelerated. This could only mean that the roll contained paintings, he thought, depressed. But dutifully he reached down into the chest and lifted out the roll with extreme care. He wondered why the padre would seek this remote cave in which to cache the paintings.

"You may look at them," Creek said.

"This isn't the place to make an examination," Conn replied.

He replaced the roll in the chest, locked the chest lid and lifted the chest in his arms. Between the two of them, the chest was transported from the cave to the spot where they had left their horses.

There, in the bright sunlight, Father Conn could wait no longer. He unlocked the chest, opened it again and lifted out the cylinder of paintings, with Creek's assistance.

He stared at the top picture in virtual shock.

"God in Heaven!" he muttered. "We'd better take these down to the señora right away. I don't want the responsibility of damaging any of them."

"Are they very valuable?" Creek asked eagerly.

"I don't know," was the priest's honest reply. But in his heart he knew, he knew. How could a painting that bore the signature of Bartolomé Esteban Murillo not be extremely valuable—perhaps priceless.

22

"WHAT on earth is that?" Beth asked, as Father Conn carried the brassbound chest into the hacienda living room and set it down on the table with great care.

"It's a relic from the cave of the flying padre figure," he told her.

"You were there this morning?"

"Yes. I went to talk with Creek early," Conn explained. "I was deeply troubled about your predicament and took the liberty, forgive me, of telling him about Hector Delgado and the plight of Rancho Cielo."

"You had no right to do that without my permission, Father," Beth said quietly.

The priest emitted a weary sigh. "My dear Beth," he murmured with gentle patience, "somebody has to do something for you, and I'm the closest at hand. You can't stand alone on a mountain top expecting God to do it all. Even He needs help on earth."

"That's blasphemous!"

"Hardly that. Merely practical. Creek was quite shocked by the fact that you might lose title to the estate. I thought he would burst into tears, but then, a subtle change came over his features, a kind of peace. He stared at me with the brightest gaze I've ever seen on his face. He told me a story," Conn said, and went on to explain in detail about the cave shrine and the antique chest. "For almost a hundred years this treasure has been waiting for Antelope

Lee Davis Willoughby

Valley to need it enough to seize it for the common good of the community. By leading us to it, Creek has performed the noblest act of his life. He has brought his moribund culture and the living Church together in a gesture that may save your world here at Rancho Cielo."

"I don't follow you."

"You will in a moment," the priest assured her. "I think we've found the solution to your dilemma, Beth. It may be a way for you to remain at Rancho Cielo forever, if you choose, to raise your sons here, administer to the Pai Pais—whatever pleases you."

Father Conn produced the brass chest key.

"This is the tool that will change the future." He tapped the lid of the chest. "It's all contained in here."

He inserted the key into the wooden chest and turned the lock. Then he raised the chest lid and gently lifted out the roll of canvases.

With Beth's help, he slowly spread out the roll of paintings. There were three.

The top canvas, as Conn had already seen, bore the signature of Murillo. The subject—The Birth of the Virgin—was painted with exquisite delicacy. Both of them stared at the picture in transfixed silence for a full minute. By some miracle, the painted surface of the canvas had remained supple, virtually untouched by age.

The second canvas was signed by Diego Velásquez, its subject The Madonna and Child. Father Conn had read a great deal about classical religious painting while at his seminary. He wondered if perhaps this canvas might have been painted by Mazo, the artist's son-in-law, who copied many of the master's original works to meet a commercial demand and using the Velasquez signature. In any case, the color values were extraordinarily subtle and yet vibrant.

The third canvas elicited an exclamation of joy from Father Conn. It was unmistakably the work of El Greco, the master of Toledo, and the signature verified this. It was a magnificent, glowing study of the Repentant Peter, probably painted around the beginning of the seventeenth century, making it the oldest of the three canvases. Its colors were as distinct and fresh as though they were applied only recently. Overshadowed by the more popular masters with more accessible styles, such as Murillo and Velásquez, El Greco had fallen out of favor after his death, Conn knew, but the priest was certain that El Greco would return to full and rightful glory in the latter part of the nineteenth century or in the next, as one of the most visionary of all artists.

When they had thoroughly studied the paintings, Father Conn said, "The treasure is breathtaking," and there were tears in his eyes. He rolled up the trio of paintings that were no larger than 30″ x 40″ and replaced them in the chest.

"God has granted your wish," he said, closing the lid.

"They are holy objects," Beth said, still in awe of the treasure. "But what must we do with them? The proper thing would be to keep them in the valley, to build a special shrine for them."

"Then you'll lose Rancho Cielo," Conn cited practically. "I think you should dispose of them. I know paintings. These are immensely valuable. We have to find the right buyer for them."

"I don't want to sell them," Beth protested. "It would be a sacrilege."

"You have no choice but to sell," Conn told her. "They aren't yours to sequester. They belong to the Pai Pais, to Nate and Jimmy, to the whole world actually. Look at it this way. You're doing an incalculable service to art, to beauty and to religious celebration by offering these pictures to the world. Many millions will find inspiration in them until they collapse into dust. Which, from the look of them, will be hundreds of years from now. Do you understand?"

"Yes, Father. I suppose we'll have to sell them," Beth said, her voice melancholy, regretful.

"You must," Father Conn agreed. "And I know just the market for them: my friend Evan Patrick."

"The shipping magnate in San Francisco?"

"The same. Evan has unlimited funds. He knows a good investment when he sees one, but more than that, he's a connoisseur of fine art. He'll go mad with joy when he sees the canvases. I'll take them to him, but you must come along with me."

"How can I go with the boys? It's not possible."

Father Conn shrugged his shoulders, refusing to argue with her. "It's your decision," he said tranquilly.

"I'll have to stay," Beth said, "and you must go alone."

"To San Francisco by ship, with the paintings? What's to prevent me from running off to New York or to Europe with the paintings and selling them to the highest bidder for a small fortune, never to return?"

"My trust in you," Beth said without hesitation. "You would never put yourself in that position. I wasn't so confident about you last night, Father Amos. But I am now. You'll go, you'll return as soon as possible with enough money to pay off the Rancho Cielo debt to Delgado, and the rest of the money banked, apart from your expenses."

"That's what I had in mind."

"When you've returned, where will you go then?"

"I'll have to give that some serious thought while I'm away, Beth. One thing I do know for sure. I shan't practice the role of a roving priest in perfect favor any longer."

"How do you mean?"

"Well, for one thing, I pondered long and hard last night about your reaction to my story of St. John. What happened was unsupportable."

"Although I reacted honestly, I had no right to judge you so severely," Beth said. "I know you're a good person, Father Amos. I've admired you so much in the past."

She had qualified him, the priest knew, because she refused to look into her own heart at this point and recognize what was there. In time she might change; he would have to see.

"I'm glad there's some admiration left," he said ruefully. "I know I can never atone for the St. John tragedy. But I won't let the enormity of that guilt plague me any longer, as it has these past years. I can make a strong, new life out here in the West, I'm certain. I take you as a good example. I can be of great service to people as a layman, divested of the bogus role of priest. Believe me, I'm not looking for an easy way out, Beth," Conn added. "I'll take the rough times with the glad ones but I intend to make my life a model of good works, wherever I am."

"Well then," Beth said, "let's get you ready for the journey to San Diego. Will you want to leave in the morning?"

"That's good enough for me," he said. "And you're still willing to trust me with the paintings?"

She nodded. "Creek will accompany you to San Diego, and perhaps Red Deer as well. You'll have to go on from there by yourself."

"So, you do indeed trust me."

"You're the one who'll have to live with your life, just as I live with mine. Our paths were fated to cross in this way. That seems evident from what has happened."

"By the grace of God, may they continue to cross," Conn declared.

"We shall see," Beth murmured. "I'm going to the chapel now. I want to give thanks to God for the blessing He has bestowed upon us."

"I shall pray too," Conn said, and walked with her to the hacienda door, watching her move across the sunlit earth toward the chapel.

At last, he reflected, he was to have a second chance at sacred trust, an opportunity to prove himself. He must sell the pictures, return to plant this valley and make it a paradise, build a road from the valley to the lowlands. The Church wasn't everything; it was filled with frail figures. So in a sense it was still his, even if he were no longer acceptable to it. Only a weak man accepts the role of outcast. He would never be weak again.

Beth knew that Amos Conn was watching her as she walked to the chapel, but she did not turn around. There was no need to confirm his presence, just as she would not worry about his new commission. He would travel to San Francisco with the paintings and she would pray for his safe return. And in his absence she would reflect on many matters besides the vast improvements she would make at Rancho Cielo.

When he came back, if her prayers were heard, then she might begin to implement the decision about him that was forming in her mind. One thing was certain— whatever happened, she would never surrender the valley. Delgado and his minions would have to carry her out in chains. She was the custodian, and if Amos Conn returned in glory he might wish to join her in that sacred duty.

EPILOGUE

Amos Conn was gone from Rancho Cielo for six weeks on his mission. Each week of his absence was a tense and nervous time for Beth Porter, but she survived by dint of planning for the future and faith through constant prayer. Beth believed that Conn would come back to her when his commission had been fulfilled.

When Conn returned he had accomplished a great deal: He had sold the old masters' paintings to Evan Patrick for the sum of $50,000 in gold. Amos knew that Patrick would use the pictures for altar pieces to enoble and enrich a small, quite beautiful chapel he was having built for the San Francisco Catholic community as a memorial to his son, who had been killed in the Mexican-American War.

Next, Conn had opened bank accounts in the name of Beth Lowell Porter in both San Francisco and San Diego banks. He had also stopped in the town of Tecate on his return and paid off Hector Delgado the full $4,000 lien against the Delgado estate, much to the scheming lawyer's complete surprise and ill-concealed chagrin; he'd fully expected to develop Rancho Cielo as his own property. And while in Tecate, Conn established another bank account there for Beth, so that she would have proximity to ready cash accounts both in the United States' California and Mexico's Baja California.

Amos Conn did not leave Rancho Cielo again soon after his triumphant return. With money at hand for the development of Antelope Valley, he entered wholeheartedly into the work alongside Beth. The first project to be completed was the road to connect Rancho Cielo with the lowlands trail, thus making it possible for wagons to negotiate the still-arduous trek up the mountain canyons to Antelope Valley. With the completion of this much-needed thoroughfare, fruit trees were imported, building materials brought up, and large amounts of staple supplies. Rancho Cielo began to expand in a most gratifying way, awakening from the inertia of its past.

Beth built a large chapel which also served as a community meeting house. The small chapel became a schoolhouse, over which Beth presided and where she offered basic education to Nate and Jimmy and to the resident Pai Pai children.

In due time, Amos Conn dropped his priestly trappings of collar and ritual and dressed as a simple layman whenever he traveled on business abroad. Although he continued to conduct services at Antelope Valley, the inhabitants understood his role as their unofficial but beloved spokesman for the Catholic Church and accepted it comfortably.

Mineral strikes were recorded in nearby areas of Baja

some years before Lee surrendered to Grant at the Appomattox Courthouse in April of 1865. Rancho Cielo was a sufficiently developed community by 1863, however, to afford to explore its mineral potential privately for silver, gold, lead and copper ore. After tentative probes, a modest silver deposit was discovered within the valley. The big strike came several years later, in the late 1870's. This immensely rich deposit was found only a few hundred yards from the rock shelter where Padre Miguel had sequestered his precious masterpieces. This find was made by Nate Porter, then fresh from his geological studies at a Jesuit college in San Francisco.

Gold, copper and lead were subsequently found in sufficient quantities to warrant limited mining at various points in the valley; but it was the silver ore that made Rancho Cielo rich.

The standard of living that Beth had sought for the Pai Pais and for her own family in the valley was realized as the years passed. She was able to send her sons to higher schools outside the valley. All Pai Pai children were privileged to attend mission school in San Diego at Amos Conn's suggestion, thus giving them a taste of the outside world, and ways to meet it.

Nate, as already indicated, showed an aptitude for minerals. Jimmy, however, eschewed higher education in the 1870's in favor of life as an ordinary seaman. At first he worked among the fishing fleets that were netting such rich bounty from the Sea of Cortéz's Western shores. Later he became the captain of various fishing vessels that plied the Pacific waters of Baja. Ensenada's environs were his home port during the 1880's by which time he owned several small fishing craft and was thinking of founding the first fish cannery in Baja territory. He did not ever again settle permanently in Antelope Valley, the place of his birth. He did, however, visit his mother often in her late years taking his children, a boy and a girl born of his marriage to Raul Romero's daughter, Conchita.

Nate's residence in Antelope Valley was broken several

times to do surveys for various Baja estates such as Rancho Romero. While on one of these assignments he met, courted, married and brought home as his bride the very young grand-daughter of lawyer Hector Delgado from Tecate, Dolores Delgado. Dolores bore Nate three children, thus bringing Spanish blood to mingle with the bloodlines of Michael, his father, and Beth, his mother.

Beth fell deeply in love with Amos Conn about six months after his return from San Francisco, a natural solution to a sympathetic situation. They were married by an imported priest who diplomatically overlooked the fact that Amos was a spoiled priest, treating him as the layman he now preferred to be. In 1860 they produced one child, a girl, whom they named Luz.

Tim and Maggie settled down on a ranch on the San Francisco Peninsula. The Lowells made several trips to Rancho Cielo to visit Beth and Amos, each of these times imploring Beth to come and visit them. Beth thanked them warmly and that was the end of it.

Amos Conn died of a heart attack in 1885. A dignified white-haired, quiet-voiced gentlemen in his late years, he was greatly mourned at Rancho Cielo.

With her small corps of Indian servants, her splendid hacienda, her grandchildren who all visited her from time to time Beth lived on until 1902, at which time she died quietly in her sleep.

Well-loved by the Pai Pais and her family, Beth led a full life, a rich one. Without actually being aware of it, she was the first of the pioneer women at half-century to set down permanent roots in Baja California. She had decided early in her life that once she had entered Antelope Valley, she would never leave it. And she never did.

Today Antelope Valley and Rancho Cielo compose a year-round resort area, operated by descendants of the Porter clan.

Where the Delgado hacienda once stood is an air-conditioned Spanish-style main lodge with forty deluxe guest suites. On the site where the Pai Pais' huts were originally located, there now exist several attractive bungalows set among trees and flowerbeds, available for guests who want the ultimate privacy with kitchen facilities. There are two swimming pools, tennis courts, an exercise course. Guided hiking and horseback tours are available to visit the Indian rock drawings, and the padre figure, as well as the now-abandoned silver mine diggings. So that the world may be brought even closer than the aforementioned amenities there is 24-hour radio contact with San Diego and all other points, but not TV, only video-taped movies.

Backpackers who disdain such refinements may hike up the old Indian trail into Antelope Valley, camping out at their own risk beside springs, pausing at the summit ridge for a breathtaking view of this isolated paradise. Winter snowfall is never heavy enough to afford skiing, and torrid summer discourages all but the hardiest lovers of high country trekking to whom hot weather is no deterrent.

Rancho Cielo, however, still dreams on in spirit. Once so remote that few knew of its existence, a place bypassed in the turbulent historical growth of America and Mexico, and the rest of the world. Today the valley is still a relatively unknown pocket of Baja California's majestic sierra wilderness. The mountain lions still prowl for prey at night, the bighorn sheep leap among the high country boulders, and the red rattlers still strike with deadly effect. The spirit of the lovely, single-minded Beth Lowell Porter Conn still wanders through the peaceful valley, safeguarding its destiny for all time.

THE YUKON BREED

Lee Davis Willoughby

In Dawson, the lusty, newborn tent city at the mouth of the ice-choked Klondike where it emptied into the big Yukon River, gold fever coursed through the veins of every man, woman and child. It drove some to cheat, to steal, to ravish and to kill.

It drove lanky young Matt Monroe to risk his life on a last-chance gold strike—and it sent him in pursuit of breathtakingly beautiful Lolly Fedderson, who belonged to his bitterest enemy.

The gold fever raged in the mysterious Henry Boise, in his nubile, almond-eyed daughter, Laura Lee, and in the suave, handsome Calvin Ramsey—all of whom had secrets to hide.

The fever reached its boiling point when the cry went up in the streets of Dawson that one of the "Yukon Breed" had struck it rich beyond his wildest dreams. In the frenzied aftermath of that strike, a bad man would die violently, a good woman would lose her mate and find a lover—and a man with a shady past would begin an astonishing new life.